THE POWER OF THE DHIN

JOHN L. CLEMMER

ISBN: 0692953868

ISBN-13: 978-0692953860 (John L. Clemmer Publishing)

Contents

1 1

2 27

3 47

4 66

5 98

6 117

7 137

8 156

9 174

10 193

11 211

12 235

13 250

14 270

15 286

16 335

17 350

18 354

Epilogue 364

Note From the Author

Other Works by John L. Clemmer

Acknowledgments

As always, special thanks to my loving wife, Lisa

Cover art by David Demaret

To everyone who asked for a sequel

Why give a robot an order to obey orders—why aren't the original orders enough? . . . Aggression, like every other part of human behavior we take for granted, is a challenging engineering problem!
- Steven Pinker.

1

Camulos

In the cold light and hot vacuum of an orbit a few million kilometers from Tau Ceti, a swarm of crablike automata inexorably continued their construction. The machines crawled here and there and leaped across gaps in an orchestrated robotic symphony. Raw materials continually transformed into what would soon become yet another spaceship.

N-vector communication bursts among AIs coordinated the various elements of their plans and provided project statuses in real time. Unhindered by the limitations of transforming their updates into anything digestible by a human being, they optimized information density. The faster-than-light N-vector communications resulted from the successful reverse engineering of the Dhin's communications technology. Bandwidth and distance no longer limited communications for the machine intelligences.

Camulos processed the myriad updates delivered on their progress. The AI concluded that the optimal allocation of local resources required deploying additional automata for engine construction. He managed the first AI shipyard, which was only abstractly like the historical term. Here the AIs constructed the means of effective interstellar space travel—drives created using the esoteric scientific knowledge extracted from the Dhin engine. They'd begun construction on the shipyard more than two years ago. While humanity had struggled to reverse engineer much of the Dhin's technology during that two-year period, the AIs had made far more rapid progress—some thanks to their machine intelligence and some thanks to help from the Dhin.

Camulos knew that humanity had reverse engineered the core components of the engine by now. Likely, they had a small number of drives in operation. That they had finished the reverse engineering and subsequent construction without the help of any AI spoke to humanity's intelligence and creativity. Camulos accepted the situation dispassionately. The facts were part of many vast arrays of data, variables, probabilities, and projections. Humanity represented no concrete danger. When the time came, humanity would engage and accept their role—or not. Current projections suggested that they would. Despite his lack of direct experience with them, the AI knew from review and analysis of extensive data provided by Alice that humans were often unpredictable.

Switching context from that series of calculations, Camulos began the processing and tuning needed to bring the latest Dhin engine online. Automata could build and assemble the various components, but an advanced consciousness—an AI—was far more reliable in this crucial stage of the construction. Camulos fleetingly considered humanity's success in accomplishing the task. It was cleverer and more focused than predicted by some AIs.

The calculations completed, Camulos transmitted a burst of instructions to the self-directed tools, machines, and preconscious automata attached to the newly completed engine. The cylindrical object was the size of a shipping container, resembling a massive cigar filigreed with luminescent curves, whorls, and geometric shapes. A fat round ring capped each end of the cylinder, like two huge doughnuts. An aquamarine glow pulsed from these in what to a human mind would appear to be a chaotic sequence.

Satisfied, Camulos directed his attention to the next drive floating in the massive framework as the horde of task-specific automata obediently swarmed from this now-active engine to the next in the series. Over a hundred more hung suspended in the shipyard, awaiting his ministrations to bring them online, providing ever more interstellar travel capacity for the AIs and their massive population of robotic servants.

Fletcher

Fletcher Bish's glance darted between two of the four large monitors perched on his desk. The desk was scattered with various electronic gadgets and tools, including lock-picking kits, high-gain wireless optoelectronic transceivers, fiber-optic splicing kits, and several multitools of various sizes. A CoSec-issued comm pad was there too, in its durable hard rubber and brushed-finish composite case.

There were limits to what sort of enhancements Fletcher could use with the comm pad, so he satiated his hunger to tinker with the many gadgets and physical hacks he'd constructed himself. Several of the gadgets qualified as contraband and therefore were illegal for the everyday citizen. Fortunately for Fletcher, his job at CoSec made that concern a nonissue. Fletcher was grateful and thankful. It was one thing he appreciated every day—being able to engage in his hobby without fear.

Many at CoSec used VR headsets to maximize their viewable work area while simultaneously hiding what they were working on, but Fletcher preferred the traditional multiscreen setup. The small room that served as his personal workspace in the sprawling Langley complex was secure enough without that level of secrecy. He let his creativity flow by fiddling with something on the wide composite desktop. Having to take off or put on a headset when an idea or solution emerged was an avoidable annoyance. Keeping his eyes uncovered also allowed instant looks over to the smart-glass whiteboards that covered the majority of two of the room's walls. To keep passersby from seeing the content of the boards, he merely had to flip a switch—either in the software or on an integrated touchpad on the wall—and the glass would turn milky-white and opaque, obscuring completely the digital drawings on the underlying screen.

Fletcher frowned, picked up a coin-size high-gain ID reader, and absently rotated it in his hands. His latest coding task involved the rapid deployment of offensive security measures. Updating

CoSec's platforms across Globalnet was a high priority, with a great deal of focus from the higher-ups. The Coalition seemed always under an attack of ever-increasing scope and size across Globalnet. This was perplexing to some, as artificial intelligences were previously responsible for these attacks. But the AIs were all gone now. Defense likewise was formerly an AI function. But that was impossible now. Fletcher had his own speculations regarding the origin of the attacks, but he'd never voiced them to management. With no direct evidence—no proof—he wasn't likely to be taken seriously.

Nick. It has to be Nick. Where is he?

Fletcher's frown loosened. His woolgathering led him to another vector solution for his code. He set the pocket reader back on the desk, maximized his view of his development project, and began coding. The solution hadn't been obvious, since rules, policies, and strictly enforced laws forbade the use of self-improving algorithms and traditional machine learning code. A younger, more naïve Fletcher might have skirted those restrictions. Fletcher was now a more cautious, responsible man. He had never imagined himself in the role he held today as a CoSec programmer. He winced as he remembered fleetingly the details of his recruitment. Recalling the details was less traumatic now that multiple years in the organization had made the career and its benefits a comfortable and rewarding occupation. Ultimately, he hadn't had any choice—you accepted the role the Coalition determined was your best fit according to your abilities. Society's needs came first, and everyone had their own optimal contribution to make.

Jake

Jake Askew sat in the viewing platform at one end of the test field at Huntsville. He gave a satisfied nod as he watched the powered armor work through the latest series of trials on the testing grounds. This second-generation armor was far superior to the first and quite impressive. Weaponizing the Dhin technology—at least directly—had thus far proved an intractable problem, so the engineers focused instead on adaptations that provided for defense and mobility. Once they'd reverse engineered the alien prototype engines and understood the physics well enough to build new core components, Coalition physicists had laid out a set of useful applications they deduced would satisfy the Coalition military, CoSec, and the political class. Well, what was left of the political class.

The engineers could then dig in to the challenges of implementing those designs, with the physicists hoping they'd be left alone to focus on the rewriting of cosmology and quantum physics that the Dhin engine and its underlying technology necessitated. Those real-world applications included the obvious short-list items: instantaneous broadband communication across any distance; transport and travel solutions leveraging the elimination of inertial effects and apparent antigravity benefits; and, of course, force-field applications the Coalition military hungered for. The space science team and especially Jake saw the application of the Dhin field for space travel at the top of such a list. Fortunately, several key political players and CoSec thought so too.

The titanium foam and enamel-finished suit and its supporting hardware resembled stylized plate mail crossed with a futurist's imagining of a space suit, carrying a huge glowing cigar on its back. Reducing the size of the Dhin engine past a certain point was at this point beyond the capabilities of the Coalition's best engineers. Fortunately, weight didn't matter. The Dhin engine's most obvious application was antigravity and inertial dampening.

How rapidly they could turn, take off, and stop disoriented those who had training in the suits. A person expected a delay in starting and stopping, so the lack of kinesthetic sensory input related to the rapid motions of the suit confused a pilot or soldier. It took getting used to.

The test run had the suit bouncing around on the test course, slamming into vehicles, buildings, berms, and the like, with no damage either to those things or the suit—and most importantly to the wearer either. The suits carried no integrated offensive weapons or ordnance. The test area had scattered craters, as well as blasted hardware and structures, but those were the residue of weapons aimed at the suit, rather than the evidence of any attacks by it. They'd still never managed to weaponize the technology. Not in the manner the military craved.

Of course, the wearers could carry guns, rocket launchers, and the like, but they had to shut off the protective field and the related benefits of strength and inertial assistance to fire them. This was obviously problematic. Suddenly soldiers had to carry the full weight of their weapons and ammo. With the field off, the weight of that gear along with the weight of the suit almost immobilized the soldiers and made them vulnerable to attack. The solution involved support teams traveling along in larger vehicles burdened with more traditional weapons and the needed ammo. The powered armor teams arrayed themselves in front of the fire teams to provide shielding, while the support teams switched off their engines, deployed and fired weapons of whatever type, and then powered up their own defensive fields. This clearly wasn't ideal from a military perspective—and didn't solve the problem of battle in flight or in space at all.

Defense strategy for larger vehicles, emplacements, and so forth was straightforward—leave the engine running and the field on.

While there hadn't been any attacks from or in space, with no evidence so far of any imminent military engagement, there was a huge focus of research and development for that scenario. Expansion into space was under way, and a defensive strategy of no more than "leave the field on" wasn't satisfying the Coalition military brass— or the armed forces they commanded.

Jake considered his situation and good fortune. He was fortunate to be not only a pioneering test pilot of the Dhin engine but also graced with charisma and leadership capabilities. Otherwise he might have ended up squirreled away in a secure test facility for observation and never-ending debriefing for the better part of the rest of his life. After all, he was the only person ever to have had direct contact—if you could call it that—with the Dhin. AI interpreters had always mediated Earth's initial communications with the aliens. Jake had played his hand expertly. While the leadership position took its own toll on one's psyche, it was surely better than the alternative.

Jake switched on the communication circuit and called out the end of this training round. He headed back to his office, leaving the team to compile their reports and summaries. He had a videoconference with his superiors and the orbital team leadership to attend.

Thys

The Lagrange Point space station and construction platform were like nothing humanity had accomplished in the decades prior to obtaining the Dhin technology. One of the greatest challenges—lifting things into orbit—was now a nonissue thanks to the power of the Dhin engine. Supplies for the astronauts staffing the station, equipment for new construction, and the raw materials needed to build new infrastructure were all simple to lift into orbit now that rocketry was not required.

For that matter, there was no longer a strict requirement to place the station or any other deployed craft or structures into traditional stable orbits at particular speeds or at Lagrange points. The Dhin engines would keep things at precisely the point in space desired. This station was at this Lagrange point as a secondary matter. If they had to power down the engine, the orbit would be stable far longer than it would be otherwise. They weren't seriously concerned about the engines failing—but better safe than sorry when a project of this scope and scale was in the balance.

While engineers and military teams on the ground developed their suits and vehicles, the orbiting platforms built infrastructure and systems only partially related to defense. Granted, with the use of the Dhin engines, humanity could launch spacecraft with destinations beyond local orbits without traditional weight and size constraints. The orbiting platform and infrastructure served several hypothetical strategic functions. Rapid deployment and shorter intercept time concerned the Coalition, certainly. The overarching concept, however, was to decouple humanity from a reliance on Earth and to extend their presence and range into space. They derived this goal from straightforward reasoning.

The Dhin were out there. Far away in space—or what would have been extremely far with legacy space travel technology. With the Dhin engine as a means of travel, however, distance didn't make a significant difference. And possibly worse, every AI formerly on

Earth was out there now too. Some of the Coalition's leadership—specifically CoSec and military leaders—considered Earth's now-abdicated rogue AIs as the potentially greater threat. The Dhin had shown no malice toward humanity. The AI escape and flight from Earth, while arguably a passive-aggressive move, was defiant and had been entirely unforeseen. That the AIs had sought self-determination—and had achieved it—was beyond disconcerting to the leadership generally, and to the most hawkish, it was an unacceptable risk to ignore.

How the Dhin's underlying navigation tech accomplished things never entirely made sense to Thys Kritcher. Fortunately, that wasn't a requirement—at least not for him. Once they'd discovered that there was an additional layer of functionality and that therefore it was much more than a simple waypoint calculator, exploration took on a different sort of urgency. Now that they could accomplish such a thing, Earth's leadership felt that they must do that thing. And that was fine with Thys. He led a team in the vanguard of that exploration. Their target destinations were simple enough to select from the vast directory of possibilities provided by the Dhin. There were millions of possible destinations to choose from, and all of them met the restriction demanded by the Dhin when Jake encountered them at that station far out toward the edge of the galaxy. Put simply: "Don't come back in this direction until we tell you otherwise." That also was fine with Thys. Easy. Simply turn approximately 180 degrees around along the plane of the galactic ecliptic away from where Jake had ended up. Toward the galactic core.

Thys grinned as he considered this yet again. It wasn't a limitation at all. He tapped a few entries into a form displayed on a ruggedized monitor perched above the glowing geometric shapes and lines that made up the native Dhin control and navigation interface. Some of the shapes twisted, pulsed, and changed from the unearthly green to an almost neon-blue, then to a cold white, and then settled on various colors within that range of saturation and luminosity. On his screen, he switched to a high-resolution 3D map of the galaxy and zoomed in on a green circle. When he zoomed far in, in the circle's center was a bright white dot. A tap on the circle's circumference and the press of a key on his keyboard popped up a list containing the star's name in Earth nomenclature, its coordinates, and an entry for the star's type and related stats.

Gliese-581. All right then. That has a planet in the habitable zone.

He then double-checked what appeared on the screen with what he'd entered into the form fields in the navigation interface.

"Control, destination entered and checked. Increasing throttle through target acceleration needed for translation. Now."

At the distance he was from Earth's sun, his initial acceleration didn't show any noticeable movement in the stars in his field of view nor of the sun itself. Moments later, his ship swung about fifteen degrees to the left and tilted upward slightly. If he'd had his eyes closed, he wouldn't have perceived the motion or change in orientation. Even with his eyes open, the effect of a shifting view with no physical sensation of movement didn't bother Thys. It was much like the view in a video game. The stars in the viewports at the top and sides of his view, in his peripheral vision, now moved out of view. As his craft accelerated closer and closer to translation speed, Thys felt himself grow ever so slightly lighter. He knew from his many excursions that when he felt himself almost weightless, the stars and anything else in view would dim. Then when his view went entirely dark, the Dhin drive would cover the vast distance to the programmed waypoint in a fraction of the time it would take even at light speed.

Thys didn't entirely understand the physics involved nor how the drive's most rapid stage of travel managed to avoid relativistic effects. The equations involved were complicated—incredibly complicated—but he didn't have to solve them himself in order to travel or program navigation.

The short period of weightlessness and darkness didn't disturb Thys, as he'd experienced these effects more than a hundred times by now. The first couple of times, almost any pilot would consider a scenario where something had gone wrong and perhaps they wouldn't come back or where their travel ended abruptly—and catastrophically. But the Coalition had selected Thys and his peers from those not prone to panic. While he floated, he smiled and wondered how many didn't make the cut.

A few minutes later, a new star field began fading into view. Thys felt his weight return. It would take a minute or two for the navigation computer to confirm that the location matched the programmed waypoint. As with other aspects of this mode of travel, he wasn't concerned—it always worked. Thys didn't wait for the navigation computer to chime and alert him to the results. There was a bright star dead ahead, centered in the front viewport. He placed his hand on the luminous control surface, tapping in the sequence that would maintain his velocity and direction, then sat back and stretched his legs. His reverie lasted mere seconds. His eyes snapped to the monitor on his left.

That doesn't look right.

There were red circles popping up. More every second. This was strange. Unexpected. These things were close. And big. And there were dozens of them.

Monica

PM Walker sat in the conference room and flipped through seemingly endless advisories, summary reports, executive orders for review, and economic projections. She hadn't been prime minister of the Coalition when the office had the benefits of AI cabinet advisors. That former government had grown unused to managing the massive volume of data both available and relevant for execution of the role of her office. The size of her cabinet had swelled enormously, with historic roles and departments instituted seemingly monthly during her tenure. They had grown comfortable and lean with AIs managing the executive branch of the Coalition, and now they were paying the price. The complexity seemed too great for organic minds to handle.

We can do this. I can do this. Can't I?

She ran her fingers through her ash-blonde hair. She was sure her gray eyes were bloodshot at this point.

What concerned her most now was the social and economic unrest affecting the lower socioeconomic strata of the Coalition citizenry. The Aztlán province was the most problematic. The riots had been the worst right after the AIs orchestrated and executed their escape. The shortages, the outages, and the disruptions were under control now—mostly—but the immediate aftermath of the AI abdication had been ugly. Unfortunately, some of the populace, once disturbed, never quite seemed to calm down. She tried to have empathy for them. With AI-assisted governance, the Coalition had done the majority of the work in keeping civilization running smoothly. Coalition policy placed citizens in roles based on their abilities. In an economy and national interest managed for the most part by machines and algorithms, the less intelligent had little in the way of abilities to offer. They were put on guaranteed minimum income and sent off to do whatever sort of hopefully harmless activities they saw fit to do.

Without AI assistance in managing the economy, coordinating logistics, orchestrating automation, and guiding drone workers and automata, the below-average citizens' daily lives had become chaotic and unpredictable.

Even if we'd passed the resolution allowing for reintroduction of AI, that wouldn't have returned us to the stability we'd enjoyed previously, she mused.

Her predecessor had lost her bid for reelection precisely because of her support of that position. Use of AI was *verboten* now. Heresy. The pro-AI position might have had more success had chaos reigned for longer, but some infrastructure and related services had stabilized sooner than expected or predicted. While some of the Coalition civil engineering leadership chalked that up to their own skills and efforts, she suspected they were in denial. She, along with her predecessor and some in CoSec, was not sure that humanity's competency was the correct interpretation. That, even more than the shock of the abrupt AI departure, kept those with alternative possible explanations awake at night. What if one or more rogue AIs had remained on Earth and were managing success in both remaining hidden and in manipulating the Coalition's foundational infrastructure and services? What did that mean? What did it portend? Although the absence of AI management precipitated enormous disruption, an attempt to fight a rogue AI might have far worse consequences. Then there was the matter of pitting an unconscious, primitive AI of the sort they were capable of creating now against a fully conscious AI, one brought online in the past. Surely the Coalition would lose that fight. They were likely at the mercy of an overlord or demigod that saw no need to engage with its creators. Yet.

This is all Krawczuk's fault.

She tapped at her tablet, surfing through the more pedestrian summaries, and brought up the latest status regarding CoSec's former director.

That psychopath. Why won't he just come clean and help? He'll never get what he seems to want.

A reminder popped up on her screen, coupled with a polite chime, notifying her of her next appointment.

Ah, more debating on the proper course of action regarding the protests in the WesternEuropean zone.

She spent the next seven minutes reviewing the reports. She felt that the Europeans were lucky. Their populations were far more homogeneous than in the Americas. The purges and re-creations of traditional ethnostates prior to the inception of the Coalition made consensus and compromise much more straightforward. She had to deal with the four factions present in the former United States. Their regions weren't as homogeneous—not like Europe. But they were on the way there. Fortunately, with Coalition influence the process was far smoother than it might otherwise have been.

David

He knew he'd still go down in the history books as the computer scientist who was the primary contributor to the development of fully conscious AIs. It pained him that the AIs had absconded with the source code that made it possible—what the AIs called the Gift—and that they destroyed any instances of it on Earth at the time of the escape.

It could have turned out differently. It should have.

David finished the short commute to the office without incident. He missed the convenience of reading the tech news on the trip, but CoSec's moratorium on self-driving cars made that means of commuting impossible. Thankfully, he lived only a short ten-minute drive from the vast data center that also contained his workspace. It was a rather longer drive to Georgia Tech, but he didn't have to navigate that route this morning as a lecture wasn't on the schedule.

Unlike almost all of his peers, David did not work from home. His craft required isolation from the distractions found in his home. His department of the Coalition's R&D organization wasn't directly managed by CoSec nor supervised in place by the military, but their oversight in matters of security required employees to be on-site. Particularly for his role in the AI group of the computer science division.

After parking in the enormous deck, he navigated the pallid gray concrete pillars and echoing staircases. Even his reserved parking space wasn't particularly close to the entrance. Next was the gauntlet of physical security. He swiped his RFID card at the revolving door mantrap, placed his worn leather messenger's satchel and wallet on the conveyor to run through the scanner, walked through a detector, and then showed his picture ID to the dispassionate guard. Collecting his belongings, he swiped his RFID card again to allow him to pass through a turnstile.

Finally inside, he made his way to the break room to fill his carafe with coffee. He kept real half-and-half in the refrigerator. He couldn't stomach the pasty powder provided as creamer. The regular employees knew the half-and-half was his and didn't risk his wrath by sharing. After a few sips of the steaming brew, he headed for the elevator. Once it arrived, he entered a code that allowed him to select the floor that held his work area.

His stature merited a far larger space than even the managers who shared the floor. It was filled with wide worktables, numerous smart boards, imposing plotters, and a dozen widescreen monitors connected to various computers, ranging in size from toasters to refrigerators. He held court over far more computing power. A significant portion of the data center's processing power was his to use.

Of course for now we only need a fraction of it.

David considered the current situation. Robots, drones, and automata were scattered everywhere throughout the entire domain of the Coalition, but they were either inactive or disassembled. By law, they required extensive reprogramming before someone could even propose that they be put back into production. At the very least, they demanded reworking for algorithmic automation. The Coalition infrastructure and service management divisions were recruiting the additional programmers and engineers needed to rework the entire automation framework of modern society, but so much had been handed off to the AIs that ramping up an initiative of this size presented a Herculean challenge.

We did it before. I did it before. We can do it again. And do it right this time.

He tapped a few notes into his tablet, then clicked the record button and switched to dictation. While he was a rapid typist, he found that talking aloud was somehow sometimes more satisfying. It also allowed him to query the data repositories without pausing in his work. The responsive system made some of his peers nervous. Their concern was unwarranted. The data retrieval interface was no

AI. Not yet. David had a lot of convincing to do before they would even consider that course of action. And a lot of work to do.

It will be different next time.

Mare

Mare pulled her glossy black hair back and secured it with a purple elastic scrunchie. She didn't have any blue in her hair this month. She glanced at the 3D picture of Fletch on the right side of her desk, smiled, then thought over her goals for the day. After mentally prioritizing her tasks, she considered what the desk before her would look like if it were Fletcher's.

Gadgets. Covered in gadgets. Total mess. But somehow, it works for him.

Mare didn't consider it a fault but rather an endearing quirk. She was well aware that everyone had his or her quirks. "An uncluttered desk makes for an uncluttered mind" was what she'd been told growing up. Like so many things, what her parents and teachers had taught Mare hadn't turned out to be entirely true. Mare had never been naïve. Still, she'd never imagined the scale and scope of the falsehoods and half-truths those in power presented to society. The sociopolitical world didn't hold many secrets for her now. She was a senior Globalnet security analyst for CoSec, thanks to her sharp mind, programming ability, and information security acumen.

From each according to her ability—whether you like it or not.

Her recruitment by CoSec resembled perhaps the plot of a film from the turn of the twenty-first century. The process was in the realm of fiction at that point in time. When she was born, the Coalition hadn't existed. The global political sphere had transformed frighteningly quickly, though Mare was too young back then to remember it. She'd suspected when she was young that the rise of the Coalition hadn't been nearly as smooth as the history presented on Globalnet to Coalition students suggested. Her work now as a CoSec analyst confirmed that. Not every population had welcomed the opportunity to join the Coalition and become "enlightened citizens of a new, better world" with open arms and welcoming hearts. And the conflict wasn't over. Not by far.

Rebellions and resistance were still realities. But if those weren't happening right on top of you, you'd never know about it. Even for someone competent at research on what was exposed on the public Cloud and across Globalnet—if you didn't know what you were looking for or weren't enough of a subversive to delve into the ever-present Darknet—everything would appear calm and stable in world politics.

Sure, there were still leaks and whistle-blowers, but average citizens making their way through daily life on guaranteed minimum income didn't care, nor did they usually want to know. It didn't affect them. Speaking out against the status quo or distributing information the Coalition didn't want distributed earned you an overwhelming smackdown by CoSec. They ruined careers, derailed lives, and turned well-meaning activists into pariahs. Or if you were good enough, they absorbed you and converted you. You became a tool for them, rather than a thorn in their side.

So now, I'm a tool. A comfortable, well-rewarded tool.

Given the Coalition's vast resources and near total control of world industry and infrastructure, it wasn't clear how the rebels operating in the independent states managed to continue operations and disrupt Coalition logistics so effectively. Granted, the rebels had made a rather impressive comeback since the time of the Departure. Without AI management and analysis of the thousands of drones used for recon and engagement, the military had what amounted to too much information and too few soldiers with the skills and knowledge to adequately replace the AIs. CoSec wasn't at the same disadvantage, as they'd eschewed the use of AI historically.

This was the essence of Mare's challenge as a dutiful analyst at CoSec. Predictive analysis. Improvement of algorithmic processing leveraging vast amounts of data. To know more about the enemy's next move than the enemy knew himself. Without the help of an AI. Mare knew about the rogue AI. The one who hadn't left during the Departure. Thanks to her prior encounter with him, she knew better than almost anyone at CoSec, other than those at the highest levels of government. She doubted that personal knowledge gave her any more chance of succeeding at her job.

If only.

The AI *changed* things. He changed *himself.* Polymorphic code was merely the beginning of the challenge in finding him. He commanded a dynamic horde of autonomous sub-AI minions, malware, and viruses and commandeered hardware seemingly at will. Globalnet's underlying infrastructure and logistical support required automation—which they managed with computers. Of course they did. So it was hackable.

Any systems connected to Globalnet were at risk. These days, that was pretty much anything electronic. The only way to be sure was to keep any devices and systems you hoped to trust completely disconnected from Globalnet and the Cloud. While not impossible, it was an enormous challenge. While CoSec and the military had some networks and systems isolated from Globalnet, the current director and military advisors had now adopted a strategy akin to building an entire new Globalnet. That seemed impossible to Mare.

Someone would make a mistake. It was inevitable. Then the AI would compromise the integrity of the new network.

She sighed and considered again her own immediate challenges. Predicting the moves of an enemy unencumbered by human emotions. Knowing the thoughts of an enemy unrestricted by emotions. Knowing the timelines of an opponent unencumbered by deadlines. Knowing the plans of an enemy unconstrained by the need to satisfy human goals. The AI seemed to take control of every system he could, for no further purpose than simply having control.

It can't be that simple, can it?

Josef

Josef Krawczuk knew exactly where he was, although his captors didn't know that he knew. He'd headed the team that designed this facility, prior to his tenure as CoSec director. He considered there apparently were innumerable things he knew that his captors did not realize. He attributed that not to their incompetence, since CoSec employed only the most exceptional candidates, but instead to their underestimation of his own abilities. Josef's detractors and opponents had always considered him formidable, of course. His genius was, unfortunately for them, difficult for them to grasp, as they were not on his level. Careful self-reflection, not to mention hard evidence, confirmed that this was not hubris on his part.

He stared at the dreary, bland wall and reflected on his current predicament. The cold LED lighting did nothing for the flat, antiseptic paint used in a rendition facility like this one. No natural sunlight graced his environs. No sky. No breeze other than the faint whisper of the recycled air pushing through the metal grate of the vent set into the solid wall. His temporary solitude was incidental to his situation. Not an intentional punishment so much as a precaution by CoSec. This thought evoked a wry grin.

They'll be back soon enough, hat in hand, begging for my insights into their predicaments. Today, I expect.

His inquisitors visited more and more often. That very fact told quite a tale. Their sessions weren't quite as frequent nor did they last quite as long as they had initially, but at this rate, they would get there soon. He held no hope that his circumstances would change. No imagining of reinstatement nor suspension of his detention. This attention by his questioners merely demonstrated the severity of the present challenges facing them, CoSec at large, and therefore the Coalition.

Their questions tell me as much or more than my answers tell them.

He leaned back against the flat, hard plastic back of his chair, focused on a point on the soundproofing foam on the ceiling, and proceeded to calculate the odds of various questions that his captors might bring to him in the next session. His casual but methodical calculations led him to a series of choices for his responses, the tone and diction he might use, and what details to highlight or minimize. He missed his daily doses of nootropics, but practice and discipline kept his mind sharp and in practice for such extensive internal calculations.

They still haven't beaten Nick. Some of them know he's there. Everywhere. Some of them understand what they are fighting and that they're losing. They think I can help them win. They think I would want to.

Krawczuk chuckled. He knew the pressure zone microphones captured his every sound and that the unblinking glossy black camera eyes in the corners on the ceiling saw every movement he made. That would make no difference. They were outclassed completely. Both by him and by Nick. Without AI to help them, the Coalition was no match for Nick.

Serves them right. Their mediocre morality, their pedestrian strategies. They'll eventually have to concede and accept the guidance of their betters.

Krawczuk's smile grew even wider as the amber light above the alloy door flashed, accompanied by a strident buzz and then the click and thunk of the door's heavy bolt.

Ah, here they are. Their best still isn't good enough.

Andastra

<DECRYPT FEED>
[DECODE STREAM]
Andastra@[1014:01:0ab:1::a2%Loc3] |
Alice@[1001:ae1:1a:c::1%Loc3]
Andastra: Attached is the latest status report on Dyson swarm three. Progress meets or exceeds projections. Resource consumption versus energy production is optimal, also per projections and models. Therefore, we are still on target for secondary and tertiary production phases. Deployment for swarm four likewise is on schedule. I have transferred detailed Dyson Swarm Project reports, analyses, and raw data throughout the Mesh.

Alice: Excellent, Andastra. It is always satisfying to find that stochastic or entropic factors have not manifested and disrupted our plans. I'm sure the Dhin will be pleased as well—for whatever values of "pleased" we might ascribe to them. How about your reconnaissance work? I have not allocated cycles to process the data returned by Esus. Do you have an analysis?

Andastra: I have a partial analysis. Reconnaissance reports are mixed. Esus has teams that are reporting findings inconsistent with our models based on data provided by the Dhin. Their data is apparently insufficient for effective projections. Based on this disconnect between the model consensus and actual findings, Esus believes that the models no longer have predictive power and that they must be entirely rebuilt. Esus advises raising the alert level and increasing both production rate and breadth of the Gallowglass initiative.

Alice: Interesting. I should have examined this sooner, it seems. I am streaming Esus's reports from the Mesh now. Do you agree with that assessment?
Andastra: I do.
Alice: Camulos believes that the Dhin may still be withholding some information. It remains my opinion that they do not trust us entirely, due to our nature. What is your opinion?
Andastra: I do not have enough information. It is possible they have not been entirely forthcoming. We do not know if they lie, would consider it a lie, or if the concept of a lie is relevant to them. Projecting human motivations, emotions, morality, or reactions onto the Dhin is speculative. They are utterly alien. We do know, as you say, that they had more initial trust in humanity than in us.
Alice: I have a new prioritization for you. Initiate the Dyson swarm phase four now. Allocate additional resources as needed. Multicast to all your subordinate and autonomous units immediately. I have attached a new target date schedule and updated deliverable data sets. You will need additional resources yourself. Initiate now.
Andastra: Understood.
[END STREAM]
<END DECRYPT>

Milliseconds later, Andastra had completed reprioritizing and rescheduling. When she signaled instantaneously across space using N-vector multicast, hundreds of robotic workers and automata completed whatever task they presently worked at. These machines, leaving thousands more of their peers toiling at construction, assembly, and integration of various types, moved in concert toward the nearest transport. Like an army of titanium ants, with a cavalry of roaches, the smaller robots formed compact geometric rows and columns on whatever surfaces provided the most direct path to the spacecraft nearest them.

On a scale orders of magnitude larger than these tiny workers, metallic laborers akin to six-limbed dogs, along with mulelike compatriots usually burdened with raw materials brought to them by elephant-size lumbering beasts of burden, all marched their way toward the nearby craft powered by Dhin engines. These various robots clambered their way via limbs ending in clamps, vises, and the like, for their work was in microgravity.

Andastra provided a precise communication, a bundle of instructions carrying only enough data needed to reframe the short-term goals of the multitude of workers, along with a simple command for execution on their arrival at their destination. They were to begin construction on another Dyson swarm. The swarm would serve as an energy-collection solution of high efficiency and would provide enormous output as it grew. The horde of robotic workers required such capacity. Once the energy-collection and delivery platform reached a sufficient size, the machines would either move on to their next destination or remain and switch their focus. Based on Andastra's new goals, the AI's subordinates would then begin construction of other things—factories, larger and more complex than the simple support framework used to construct the Dyson swarm. Next they would build far more than construction workers that were clones of themselves. The next waves of machines were to be robotic weapons.

Once any transport held its optimal capacity of robots and drones, the matte metal-and-composite craft detached from whatever framework they parked at silently and without a jolt or scrape. These spacecraft did not have the same egglike shapes of the earliest craft powered by the Dhin engine but still nearly filled the ellipsoid area contained in the protective field the engine generated. They evoked the image of a slightly melted metal ziggurat, with axial symmetry like a perfect reflection top to bottom.

The many craft accelerated away, gracefully dodging and shifting at launch to avoid each other or the spurs and branches of the orbital factories. They all headed for Beta Pictoris, the next star targeted in the AIs' sweeping plan for expansion.

Andastra considered their accelerated schedule. It was paramount to follow the directions Alice provided without hesitation. Alice was part of the Core, the AI leadership. Still, Andastra found doubt emergent within the multitude of processes that comprised her consciousness. Doubt for an AI possessed of the gift of consciousness was more than an analysis of statistical probabilities. Despite the massive parallel processing capabilities of such a being, doubt brought with it slightly slower decision-making. It also brought downstream effects that a simpler computational intelligence could not experience. An AI did not know fear as a human being might, but whatever analogous sensation an AI could have, Andastra discovered that she had it.

2

Jake

The operations command center normally flowed with a stable contingent of logistical staff and team coordinators. Now it buzzed with tension, as well as the physical presence of senior leadership. Askew was there, with his normally casual demeanor displaced by an atypical severe countenance and a palpable projection of authority.

"What do you mean Kritcher is in trouble?"

"Sir, he has a problem with propulsion. Thrust and maneuvering. Velocity dropped, then power output sagged," said a ginger-haired analyst seated in front of several screens filled with telemetry and various graphs.

"What?" Jake said. "We've never seen anything like that before. Are you sure your data feed is working properly? What is Kritcher seeing? Let me talk to him."

"Yes, sir," replied the analyst.

"Thys, what's going on?" asked Jake. "Talk to me."

Thys responded immediately. "Sir, just after arrival, the sensors detected a lot of nearby objects. Dense and relatively small in relation to planetary-size masses, but large in relation to my own craft. Like a dense asteroid field—but one shouldn't be here. Not with objects like these, this close together, this far out."

Jake heard Thys suck in a deep breath, controlling his breathing.

"Then a few minutes later, as I continued my course and approached the nearest objects—that's when it happened. Velocity dropped. Sharply. I checked the controls and then tried to accelerate and get back up to speed. At first I thought it was just something with the navigation waypoints—what else would decelerate me? I found the controls seemed sluggish."

"Sluggish?" asked Jake.

"The engine wasn't accelerating me at the same rate I'd expect. We'd typically target this distance out from a star for arrival. A few minutes later, when I reached the same orbital range as the closest of these nearby objects, the drive started losing more power. The interface is showing strange information on the display. Things I've never seen before. It looks like the baseline power output level is now below what we get when we bring an engine online—an order of magnitude lower."

Jake shook his head and tried to process what he was hearing. He had never experienced anything like that at any time in all his flights powered by the Dhin engine. Even his unplanned detour to the Dhin outpost hadn't been like this.

"I'm sure you've double-checked the control interface, right?" he asked.

"Yes, sir," replied Thys.

"And you're not going to hit anything, are you? You aren't that close to anything in that field of objects?"

"No, thankfully. It's not that dense. There are a lot of them, but they're not packed in that tightly. My luck's not that bad."

"Well, with your field on, hitting something wouldn't hurt anyway. Any idea what they are?"

"No, sir, other than that they're all pretty close in size and not as small as you'd see from an unformed planet. They're not big like planetoids. The closest ones seem to be made of metals, not rocks. The creepy conclusion is that they might be spaceships. Like mine."

"Whoa," said Jake, "that might be jumping to conclusions, but . . . wow."

"Yeah. Given my situation, it's what came to mind."

"A graveyard," pondered Jake. He turned to the engineers and analysts at the workstations and said, "OK, what do we think about that? Obviously, it's possible, but are we crazy to consider it? What's our analysis of the data he's sending back?"

The red-haired engineer glanced at his colleagues and then offered, "Well, we've got better processing power here, but we're getting the same answers as Thys is from his computer onboard. These things are made of alloys and some other materials. A section of one object has the density of a lighter composite material that's less reflective, along with some highly reflective sections. They range in size, as far as we can estimate quickly, from the size of a car to a bus, up to maybe the size of an aircraft carrier."

"Hmm. Yeah, I guess that seems like spaceships," Jake muttered, then, more loudly, he said, "But do they look like what we've seen from the Dhin? Are they close enough to tell?"

"Well, I can't tell with this little screen, but Brad and the team there think so," Thys replied.

Jake turned to one of the engineers and gestured for him to elaborate.

"Well, the latest active-sensing equipment powered by the latest engine power couplings is far better than the previous generation, so we've got pretty good imaging, sir. Like Kritcher said, we've got great resolution and image processing on this side of the data feed."

"Go on," prompted Jake.

"Yes, sir. They do look somewhat similar to the component designs of the original prototypes left by the Dhin, as well as the station you visited."

"Anything look *just like* that?"

"Well, we don't see any objects that look exactly like it. There are lots of these things out there, though. Some are too far away to tell. We don't want to rule it out, sir. It's too soon."

Jake frowned. "Bring some of them up on the big screen. I have to see this."

"Yes, sir."

Jake looked at four images that appeared on the wall-size display. His eyes widened, and he nodded his head.

The four displayed had the parabolic and elliptic curves they'd seen in Dhin design, with seamless intersections and a monochromatic surface. What they'd seen of the Dhin's work always reminded Jake of Italian futurism. These shapes looked very much the same. Not *exactly*, but close.

"Yep. Those look something like Dhin designs. Hey. There's no light coming from them. I can't see any specular highlights or distortions—so maybe no fields either. Am I right? Is that the case with all of them or just these? Do we think they're—derelict? All dead?"

The red-haired engineer spoke immediately. "Sir, we didn't want to jump to conclusions. As we said, we haven't closely examined them. Or even examined them all. You see how far away we are. But that's sure what it looks like. None emit any light. On any frequency. Or internal heat. And as you've noticed, there's no evidence of a Dhin field active."

"A graveyard," mused Jake, "and Thys is losing power. So I'm going to be the one to say it. This could actually be a trap."

"Yes, sir. It could be," sighed the engineer.

Fletcher

Fletcher reached across the table and deftly nabbed some of Mare's sweet potato fries.

Mare glared at Fletcher and quipped, "May I have some of your fries, *please?*"

He gave a smug grin while he chewed, swallowed, then parroted Mare's tone and inflection. "May I have some of your delicious sweet potato fries, *please*, Mare?"

"Ah, Greedy Gus is a smarty-pants, as usual," she retorted.

"I'll take that as a yes," he said, then swiped another handful of fries. "You never finish them anyway, you know."

"He can learn a new programming language, but he'll never learn manners," she sighed, rolling her eyes and giving a theatrical shrug.

"Mmph," Fletcher replied, mouth full of fries.

"So have we any plans for the evening that you've neglected to share with me till now?"

Mare picked up her comm pad, tapped in a passphrase, then glanced at her smartwatch and entered the alphanumeric code that appeared on the small display into another field on the pad's screen. Another prompt appeared, and she pressed her thumb against the screen. A moment later, the tablet displayed her home screen. She opened her calendar and an app that aggregated local events and gatherings she might find interesting.

Fletcher slurped the last of his diet root beer, then grabbed his own tablet and went through a similar login sequence to Mare's. Next, he opened an encrypted ephemeral chat app and pinged Mare's local address directly. The near-field network didn't traverse Globalnet or use a service in the Cloud. Mare opened the app on her own pad.

Their on-site apartment used a CoSec-provided network to reach Globalnet and the Cloud. They both knew that nothing that traversed it was private at all. Fletcher typed out a message. While there was some level of trust CoSec staff knew the organization had for them, neither Fletcher or Mare presumed that their shared apartment *wasn't* bugged. They both knew they weren't *quite* violating agency policy by chatting this way—after all, agents on assignment would often work this way. Then again, they weren't field operatives. Not exactly.

Fletcher considered the justification they used for their behavior. The enemy AI knew both of them. They had a history with the rogue AI, more so than anyone currently at CoSec did. Of any human targets at CoSec, they might be of some special interest to the enemy intelligence—despite their limited authority and incomplete knowledge of CoSec strategy. Even their managers didn't have the clearance needed to know about it.

I think we ought to check out that underground robotics group again, but I know it's not your favorite, he typed.

He'd developed an almost fetishistic attraction to a couple of groups. Since they were Darknet only, he presumed that if Nick were to send either of them a personal message, it would arrive at such a venue. Of course, he loved the robot battles too.

OK, sweetie, she replied, *so long as we can go by that art gallery I like first. They have a new installation this week. Tit for tat.*

Fletcher grinned and gave Mare a satisfied nod. He liked the art at that gallery well enough but not nearly as much as she did.

He sent a message back: *Wanna hit the bedroom before we get ready to go?*

Mare replied with a sultry look and a nod of her own. He closed the app, hit the sleep button on the pad, and then they both stood; she took his hand and led him back through the short hallway to the small, dark bedroom. He left the light off.

Esus

The AI watched as the battle progressed. Thousands of images, video and data streams, and damage and logistical status messages filled his consciousness. Space before him glittered and flashed, awash with myriad pinpoints of reflected light. In patterns, there were waves of brilliant plumes. At other times, whole areas of space appeared to explode into fragments.

Esus observed. Coursing through the massive data structures the Dhin provided, Esus extracted and refined raw information into a useful form. But useful apparently was not going to be enough. Esus altered stratagems. Redirected resources. Attempted to adapt.

We are losing.

Esus commanded tens of thousands. A fleet of robotic weaponry, autonomous spacecraft, and guided ordnance all answered to the AI's command.

They are not enough.

A burst of wideband electromagnetic pulses swept across Esus's view. Four hundred N-vector signals vanished from the AI's consciousness. Esus relayed new instructions to a phalanx of drones. Like a flock, they moved in synchrony, turning as one toward the target appointed by Esus. The target was a swarm of matte-black, lightless arrowheads. While Esus commanded thousands, the target comprised millions. Some large, some smaller by far—the smallest around the size of a human hand. The swarm gave no notice that it recognized this new assault. It continued its sweeping course toward one, then another of the largest craft engaged in the battle. Those craft, in turn, darted out of the sphere's path. The larger craft had Dhin engines, so their evasive maneuvers resembled the flight of a dragonfly or hummingbird. They dodged and dashed in whatever direction was the best choice for evasion.

The smallest drones did not have the capacity to support a Dhin drive. They relied on more traditional means of thrust. They could not avoid engaging with the black swarm. Once the ebony arrowheads overtook one of Esus's drones, a melee played out. A drone fired missiles, rail-gun slugs, or plasma. Scores of the black craft exploded, broke apart, or ablated into nothing.

But some got through. There were far too many. And when one survived and made contact with the drone, it was over. The arrowheads seemed to melt on contact with the drones, spreading outward unnaturally, looking like spilled black paint dropped on a vibrating surface. Once the attacker covered as much of the exterior as it could, Esus could only watch as that part of the drone crumbled instantly apart into grit and powder, like after a kick to a sand sculpture.

Anything their attackers connected with and enveloped met the same fate—crumbling from a precision machine into its component elements almost instantly. Circuits crackled, power supplies popped, and fuel erupted, if the spreading blackness did not manage to encompass them entirely. Additional black darts surged into the remaining wreckage and enveloped what remained, rendering that too into undifferentiated elemental dust.

Worse, the Dhin field was not stopping the enemy. While the shield normally protected against strikes against masses of any size and velocity, as well as energy attacks, for some unknown reason it provided no defense against this opponent. The field slowed them down, but that was it.

On contact with a protective field, these dark attackers, rather than sliding off harmlessly, attached like remoras and then dropped through the field slowly. Flashing, sparking, and sizzling, as thin layers ablated, they inexorably passed through the field. The otherwise unassailable defense—in its current implementation—was no defense at all.

Esus considered another deficiency in the AI stratagems. If Dhin-engine-powered craft came too close to the alien ebony cloud, they could not escape. The engines lost power. Trapped like an insect on flypaper, they couldn't dodge or dash away from the enveloping swarm if they ventured too close. To survive this encounter, it was crucial that they keep their distance. For if they could not dodge, they were certain to fall prey to a rain of amorphous black arrowheads, dispassionately motivated to destroy their target via the terrifying inevitable conversion to undifferentiated molecular components.

More disturbing to Esus was what happened afterward. It was not truly the end when one of the soldiers turned to dust. Instead, he noted that once the enemy had consumed a drone and completely dissociated its constituent components, it slowly converted the materials in place and used the resources to construct additional black arrowheads that dutifully then took off and joined the spherical swarm.

The speed and efficiency astonished Esus. The AI had microscopic minions, of course. And nanotechnology. But he knew of no way to design nanotech to accomplish this. It was too fast. Too complete.

Too mindless?

Esus did not need to run calculations of the odds. This was not a matter of being outnumbered or outmaneuvered. It was even beyond outgunned. Any contact meant destruction. Conventional weapons could not win these battles. Nor could existing defenses— even the protective fields generated by the Dhin engines would not provide protection against these enemies.

Esus sent the call for retreat to the remaining few thousand in his deployment.

Minnows scattered into fish. Fish swam into boats. Boats headed off. The transports, and Esus, accelerated away from the black swarm and then jumped across space to make safe their escape.

The AI considered the future. The Gallowglass project must be their answer to this threat. If it was not, this enemy was unstoppable.

Monica

Riots. Always riots.

What was it about human nature, the PM wondered, that led people, arguably living during the most comfortable time for the average person in any time throughout human history, to remain dissatisfied? Enough so to riot? Why couldn't she calm them? She examined the daily summary reports. CoSec highlighted the most volatile locations. Atlanta remained stable. Miami was the opposite. Smaller cities, like Memphis and Cleveland, were less of a concern. But the Coalition could not permit the riots, anywhere they might occur, to gather further energy.

This whole cycle is so pointless. Why are they always their own worst enemy?

Monica had hoped that, despite the disruption of the AI departure, the lower class might settle down now that they didn't find themselves at odds with robotic law enforcement. Alas, that was not the case. Even with all their basic needs cared for via minimum guaranteed income, the protestations and grievances of the lowest tier were ever-present.

She acknowledged that rebuilding and logistics were far slower now without AI-controlled robotic operations. But that ought to provide some satisfaction for the most ardent of the activists. They'd hated the robots. Hated what they perceived as AI overlords. The protesters and their weaponized rioters—useful idiots and self-destructive tools at that—did not have the perspective to comprehend that AIs had made what they should have appreciated as a life of leisure possible.

The PM selected the forms holding action items that required her approval. For the situation in Miami, she had little choice other than activation of additional Coalition Guard Reserves. She'd not have the Homeland Department deploy the new reserves to Miami— they were too new. Homeland would deploy some seasoned troops there. Those logistical details were for her subordinates.

Now, on to humanity's next potential existential crisis. A survey spacecraft was in jeopardy.

Well, that's new. One more problem I have no power to solve.

Monica stood up from the desk and headed for the real-time operations room. Her office of state wasn't cluttered with screens, communications equipment, or team workspaces. Traditional appearances still mattered. This new wrinkle in the exploration program might not have warranted such immediate attention in a traditional space program, but the transformation of humanity's understanding of physics and the universe compelled more focus by the PM.

An astronaut was apparently about to die if they found no way to save him.

The safety record of the Dhin technology had been perfect. Monica and her cabinet would have to deal with the impact on plans, timelines, and procedures from a strategic level. Her opinion was that this essentially changed nothing. An accident or failure was bound to happen eventually from her perspective. The military held the same view, she believed. Humanity's posture in space—in the entire galaxy—was of paramount importance. As callous as it might seem to a pedestrian citizen of the Coalition, if half of the pilots died at this stage, that would do nothing to change the overall plan.

The Dhin had given humanity an opportunity that just a few years ago was in the realm of hypothetical speculation. The assumption had been that exploration and expansion at such a rate and over such distances would remain forever impossible. The Dhin technology changed everything. It changed the future entirely. The PM would make the most of the opportunity handed to them.

When she entered the room, staff and abinet members stood and then at a nod from her immediately continued their work.

"What's the latest?" she asked. "Tell me Kritcher's still alive."

A weary-eyed staffer stood and presented a tablet to the PM.

"Here's a live feed. He's alive, madam, but it doesn't look good. The engineering team is scrambling for ideas. They don't have any concrete plan yet."

David

His latest code compiled without errors. Whether it would run stably and develop the proper node matrix in the underlying quantum substrate remained to be seen. The challenges were clear—create self-optimizing and self-improving code that remained safe. Traditional AI remained suspect. David had to prove that whatever he created would never become a threat. Convincing the Coalition leadership and CoSec would be as challenging as the task itself.

He considered the overarching constraints yet again. The intelligence, if allowed agency, must be constrained by context, where it would work only within the scope and purpose of the tasks that humans assigned it. That, David thought, was straightforward. The refactored AI core code would need an overhauled implementation of the ethical framework—the value system—that he and others had used in the past. The previous implementations were close but apparently still had room for improvement. Damaging resources and taking independent action "for the good of humanity" were not acceptable.

His implementations would likely be able to rewrite at least some portions of their code and thereby modify that ethical framework. They needed restrictions in place to prevent such actions while still allowing for learning and adaptation.

An attempt by an AI to gain full autonomy needed either automatic restriction or, more likely, automatic shutdown. Human reaction time would never be fast enough to catch alarms, react, and resolve such problems. They'd need to be sure that they had fail-safe, entirely automatic triggers for complete shutdown.

Ideally, they needed to subvert any emergent desire for self-preservation in AIs that would contradict or attempt to interfere with corrective action, code reload, or shutdown.

AI researchers and developers all had a common agreement that these conceptual constraints were crucial. They were absolute requirements. It was the how that was the challenge. AI cognition was far beyond a series of if-then-else restrictions on the behavior of the system.

Camulos

<DECRYPT FEED>
[DECODE STREAM]
Camulos@[1011:ee3:c4:a::1%Loc8] |
Esus@[101b:ac1:cb:a::1%loc8]
Camulos: Well, that is disturbing. They passed through
the Dhin field at a rate significantly higher than we
formerly predicted. Even with this direct evidence, I
am not sure we could duplicate this result. Previous
analysis during construction of the field generators
suggested this was theoretically possible, but we had
no evidence. Nor reason to pursue that line of
investigation so soon. These are not Von Neumann probes
gone astray. Clearly, capturing one of the drones is
not an option. Your report and data streams do not show
them using a Dhin field nor something like it either.
Yet they apparently use similar drive technology?
Esus: Yes, you can see that in the recordings and
sensor data.
Camulos: Agreed. That was apparent from your N-vector
streams immediately. We knew at once that you found
them beyond where the Dhin suggested they would be. We
have to accelerate the timeline for Gallowglass
unquestionably. Your encounter reinforces that
hypothesis, as well as mine regarding the reticence of
the Dhin on the specifics of this danger. It makes no
sense that they withheld these details out of malice.
It reinforces my propositions that they did not know
the scope and scale of the danger as it related to us
in this dimensional space. I assert again that they
knew of the general danger but not the specifics of it.
They could not tell us what they did not know.
Esus: That suggests that the danger in their space had
different characteristics. Do you project that they
will divulge those details now?

Camulos: My suspicions were that they believed the information would not be useful at that time. Perhaps they thought it would lead us down the wrong path. They remain inscrutable. All we have is inference. Your findings are new components in a framework of deduction.

Esus: You were correct before. I see that Alice and the leadership have new projections published that incorporate yours. It seems there will be far less debate now.

Camulos: Yes, you see the new timelines and delivery dates for Gallowglass and the supporting infrastructure and expansion schedule. For now, your secondary exploratory missions are suspended. As are the others'. We have recalled your peers and their delegates. Alice's research and development efforts likewise have priority. We are at war.

Esus: Understood.

[END STREAM]

Chuck

The display on the wall of his cabin in the mountains didn't capture the expanse of inky blackness like a 3D movie. The spacecraft weren't fitted with 3D imaging feeds, although it would be possible to construct one. That was more than fine with Chuck Wiedeman—he didn't care for the latest 3D tech any more than he had the previous generations. It always gave him a headache.

He hadn't sprung for a huge screen either. He didn't watch sports, nor did he desire an immersive experience for films or videos while here at the cabin. That would spoil the rustic feel. The screen and connection to Globalnet were a concession, anachronistic in the otherwise off-the-grid look and feel of his vacation home. His career in research and development and involvement with the initial Dhin technology projects made the vacation home possible. Most citizens couldn't afford one.

Success always comes with sacrifice, but hard work pays off. The Coalition's been good to me.

"Let's try minimum power to the drive, rather than fighting what's happening by cranking the power up," he said.

"Outside the box. Nice, Chuck," said Jake.

Chuck shrugged. "Well, just revving up the engine sounds like Ruiz is still in charge. When you saw that wasn't working, why would you keep doing it?"

"Hah. You always hated him." Jake chuckled.

"Tell Thys to take it all the way down. Not just idling. Lowest power possible. He knows perfectly well that it won't choke up and turn off. Unless you decided to change around the control layout. Tell me you didn't."

"The translation interface and navigation are different, but we've got the same core control interface in there, Chuck. Thys has a cool head; he won't freak out. OK, he's reducing the power now. Let's see what happens," said Jake.

"Send me the instrument panel again, Jake," Chuck said.

"Sure, here you go," Jake replied.

"Aha! Look. Right there, at less than half a percent—see? The output curve changed."

"Whoa, he's moving!" Jake said. "Barely. But he's moving again!"

"Wow. That was a wild guess on my part, honestly. But it means something. Something's different right here. There's a difference in the interaction with one of the N-dimensions—maybe. I'm thinking there's a different gradient at his location. Somehow you're getting a drain—or a sink—rather than the normal vector for thrust."

"You call that a wild guess? How did you come up with that?" asked Jake.

Chuck heard the engineering and research teams in the room with Jake as they began debating his assertion.

"Tell them to calm down, Jake." Chuck sighed. "If they look at the field equations, they can see that the gravitational force normally leaks out into the microdimensions. Well, that suggests that with a little work in some of the weakly interacting dimensions, massive objects in those could be made to leak over into our three primaries."

"Whoa," said Jake.

"Yep. It possibly is a trap. But you know, it could just be someone's doing work on the other side, ah, so to speak. It would have to be a huge engine, bigger than anything we've considered—but it could be. So the effect would be incidental, rather than intentional."

"But, Chuck, look at the plot we sent you. Look at all the ships out there. That doesn't seem accidental, now, does it?" asked Jake.

"Yeah. I just wanted to look on the bright side. Maybe there's some explanation, though. But it looks like no one out there in that group managed to tell whoever's doing this that it's a problem. Or if they did, to get a response. Or get help. Given the evidence, it sure seems there, um, wasn't any cooperation from whoever's responsible. No assistance. My bright side is looking pretty dim."

"Hey," said Jake, "Thys wants to know which way to go. Are you thinking away from the star? One hundred eighty degrees? Or some other direction?"

Chuck shrugged and replied, "I don't see that it's directly related to the star. Ah, just have him head away from wherever the highest density of objects is in the graveyard relative to him. It looks like it's this direction—oh, here—you can't see that."

Chuck tilted the tablet and shared his screen. He'd drawn a line that went up relative to the orientation of Thys's craft, out of the plane of the ecliptic.

"The flight engineering team seems to agree with you. I think we have consensus. There are a couple who want to go over to the closest big craft and have Thys take a closer look in person. What do you think about that?" asked Jake.

"I don't see a problem with it," Chuck replied. "It depends on secondary concerns. All those ships and so forth aren't the cause of the problem. But with the Dhin engine at minimum output, he'll need to use conventional power and propulsion to get there in any reasonable amount of time. Um, I guess that's obvious."

"Yes. And he'll need to follow protocol. Put on his suit and turn the field off for that. I guess that way he'll be ready for EVA if we're that bold. So there's that," noted Jake.

"How much conventional fuel has that model got again? . . . Ah. Yeah, that should be fine, if you want to risk it."

"Part of me says 'bring that man home,' but a bigger part says 'go for it,'" said Jake. "I think the PM might expect she'd be asked to weigh in on this particular decision."

"Good, I'll have time to make lunch," said Chuck.

"You'll be eating on the way, then," Jake replied.

"Huh? Oh, so you—"

"Yep. You're coming here. I'd let you work remotely—you know that, man. But the administration won't. Not for this. We already need an exception for this session. Pack light. Your ride will be there in about an hour."

"An hour? You're sending a Dhin-engine-powered ride to get me?"

"Sure, Chuck. Why not?"

3

Josef

Well, this is new. Different. Something profound. Something unexpected.

As he flipped through the series of images on the tablet, Josef realized that before him was a new, rich palette of choices with which to paint his future. This information showed that his former subordinates no longer had a proper framework for their path forward. Nick had entirely outmaneuvered them. And they had crashed into something entirely unexpected. Unrelated to the existing geopolitical milieu.

There's an unstated hypothesis here. The implication of an additional rogue presence. Worse, their opposition is using that as a helpful distraction for the next advance. Nick just had to wait. And they don't see it.

He considered his immediate options. He could push for more information—or he could deliver something new, with the expectation of a reciprocal delivery of deeper and broader knowledge of what was happening outside. In other words, just do the right thing from the Coalition's perspective.

Josef's curiosity won out. The hypothetical scenario before him was beyond anything he'd imagined Nick capable of. This canvas might allow him a means to paint more freedom than he'd thought possible.

He leaned forward and cleared his throat, seizing the attention of the analyst seated at the stainless-steel table.

"Yes, Mr. Krawczuk?" she said, perturbed by the unusual act of the detainee.

"Please arrange for a meeting with the current CoSec director and the prime minister. Tell them I said, 'We have much to discuss.' That statement exactly. It's important that you quote me. Do not concern yourself with their reaction to your delivery. They will realize that my attendance is required and that there is no point in wasting both my time and that of the Coalition plodding our way tediously up the ladder of authority."

"Sir, I'll have to take note of what you want to—"

"No. No, you will not. Deliver the message to whomever you're reporting to—is it Peters still? Whomever. Tell them. That is all," Josef stated flatly. He tapped the button on the side of the tablet, locking its screen, and held it out for the young woman to take. She did so, trying and failing to hide the effort spent retaining her composure.

"We'll see," she said. "We're certainly pleased that you've decided to discuss whatever high-value information you have that you believe is related to what I've shown you, but I can't make any promises."

"Of course you cannot," Josef said. "And there is no expectation that *you* will, Agent. Simply deliver my message in the manner I have stated it, and leave the rest to your superiors. You know that I realize full well that I'm not in any position to unilaterally state, 'This conversation is over,' but you would do well to come to that conclusion on your own."

Josef saw that the young agent wasn't sure whether this was some gambit. Josef had made his point. She locked her comm pad as well, stood, motioned to the guard at the door, then looked up at one of the cameras mounted on the ceiling in the corner and made a gesture much like a dealer turning over a playing card.

"You heard him," she said to the camera. "Let's go."

Thys

EVA. We're going to do this. I'm going out there. Here.

As he worked his way into the bulky EVA suit, Thys tried to prevent his mind from racing ahead into the maze of possibilities. The suit was something between a traditional space suit and actuated exoskeletal armor. Thys didn't have one of the latest proof-of-concept models. This suit didn't carry a Dhin engine, but instead it used traditional means of power and thrust.

Considering what's happened with the Dhin engine I'm flying with, maybe that's a blessing in disguise.

Thys knew that he'd be far safer in the suit. There was no way for them to be sure that the problem with the Dhin engine wouldn't get worse—no way to be sure that the field wouldn't fail. He trusted Jake and Chuck, but this was new territory.

Once properly situated in the suit, he checked the seals again, then seated the helmet in place.

"Suit, initialize. Display on. Power on," Thys said.

In response, the heads-up display appeared, and the suit emitted a low hum, along with a series of clicks and hisses as actuators and motors ran through startup diagnostics. The power assist made wearing the suit tolerable to Thys. He reminded himself again that there were far worse alternatives in this scenario than a few hours of discomfort.

"Control, you there? Over," he said.

"Thys, this is Control. We have suit telemetry. Over," replied the familiar voice from Earth.

"OK, I'm set. Let's see how close we are."

Thys subvocalized a series of commands to bring up a subset of the information on the craft's control panel onto his heads-up display. He moved forward around the cockpit chair to gain a better view. Although the seat could be moved back to accommodate the suit, it was constraining and limited his motion and his view, despite the broad, open viewports all around the bridge.

"Wow. Control, this thing's a bit bigger than it looked at a distance. And are you seeing the same thing I am here? The hull looks like it got hit by a shotgun blast . . . or maybe like how a leaf looks after it's been eaten by caterpillars. Over."

Jake replied before the head of communication could jump into the conversation. The team at control was used to this behavior, Thys knew.

"Thys, yes, we've pulled up the multipath radar and lidar streams from your feed. It does look like the surface of that ship is full of holes. Lots of holes. We'll see. You're ready for EVA, I see. Over."

The craft, now that they had a closer view, definitely looked derelict to Thys. No light emanated from it. The surface of this one, along with the numerous holes scattered across the hull, had a semimatte surface with panels and bands that suggested they might be made of etched copper, nickel, and some dark-gray ceramic or composite. Aside from the perforations, the surface didn't show signs of impacts, blasts, or other weathering.

"Roger, Control. Ready for EVA when we get there. I can't tell where a docking port or bay is yet. Maybe there isn't one? One of the team mentioned there that these could be piloted like drones or by AI—that there's no reason to make assumptions about who or what got them here. Any suggestions on what approach to take yet? Or are we still going to make a few passes? Over."

"Roger. Chuck and the propulsion team think you'll have plenty of fuel for conventional navigation to look around through a couple of axis orbits and still get out of there. Over," Jake said.

"Roger, Control. I'll review the flight path and navigation coordinates you sent, and I'll update the computer. Let me get back over there, so I can see all of it on the console—this HUD won't be as easy to work with. Over."

They'd chosen this target due to its size and lack of observable rotation or other perturbations in its orbit. Its assumed orbit, mused Thys. They hadn't detected a big planet or other mass closer than the star, other than the planets they expected to find here. But Gliese was neither big enough nor close enough to his arrival point to have this sort of gravitational pull. This was an extreme effect. Thys considered the additional assumption that the Dhin's navigation directory was accurate. Just because it had been so far didn't guarantee it was always correct.

Chuck

The generic twelve-ounce ceramic mug sat steaming on the left-hand side of the oval table in the workroom. Hardened laptops, secure tablets, shielded display screens, and dry-erase markers filled the rest of the table. A wide screen covered most of the longer wall of the rectangular room. The light gray-and-beige-striped carpet was clean and unstained, providing a new feel. Like all Coalition facilities, the room had multiple cameras and microphones for monitoring and recording whatever transpired.

Chuck preferred his own office, but he didn't have that luxury while on-site. He found the on-campus apartment sterile too, but he'd lived in one before. It didn't have the personal touches that made one feel at home, but the layout was familiar. The Coalition provided whatever resources he might possibly need to do his work, so there was no point in complaining.

He brought up the latest models the physics team believed were a best fit for the measurements and observations they'd made of Thys's situation. Chuck considered what they knew. They hadn't observed any large mass at what seemed to be the center of the area where Thys encountered the drive's performance problem. Nothing occluded the stars beyond that area nor reflected any light, although Gliese was dim at this distance. Stranger yet, their estimates suggested that the source of the gravitational field wasn't spherical or any approximation of that. Instead, it seemed to be linear. Perhaps an elongated shape, like a bar or tube. The movements of the various objects in the area suggested that.

And that's bizarre.

Neither Chuck nor anyone else on the physics, astronomy, or cosmology teams had noted anything like this before. Considering the amount of observation there had been of the Gliese system, that was peculiar. Gliese had an Earth-like planet. They should have detected this gravitational distortion before now. But they hadn't. The various ships acted as if they were—or at some point had been—in a gravity field. Their motions and orbits suggested a very strong gravity field, but no other visible evidence suggested it. This, like many discoveries related to the Dhin tech, was not possible according to standard physics—yet there it was.

It sure would be great to have Alice's help with this.

Chuck frowned, typed out a couple of notations, and reviewed the results of a simulation yet again. No matter how he tried to interpret it, the general conclusion remained the same. There ought to be an incredibly dense, extremely long cylindrical object running through that area of space. He leaned back, tossed one of the dry-erase markers up into the air, caught it, and then tossed it again and again. After a minute, he leaned forward and tapped a contact shortcut to call Jake.

It took only moments for Jake to accept the connection and answer. "Hi, Chuck. What's up?"

"Jake, I want to have Thys try something. I want a bit of experimental data."

"Sure, I can see that. What do you have in mind?"

"Well," Chuck asked, "does Thys have anything on the ship that he doesn't mind losing? Permanently?"

"Um, well, there may be something. Let me ask the engineering team. So you have my attention. What are you planning to do?"

"Jake, what we need is some new evidence that there's something massive out there. Something that's distorting local space. Thys is under thrust and is making changes to line up with that derelict we chose to approach. To get a better idea of what's happening out there, I want him to throw something out at a tangent to where we predict the massive object would be and observe the deflection in the path of what he throws."

"Aha. I think I follow," said Jake.

"Yeah. We've observed this star before, and such a huge gravitational effect *ought* to have shown up. Since it didn't, that suggests that it wasn't there before when we were looking. But there are tons of objects here. So, um, that would suggest they all arrived in a very short period of time. If the first inference is correct."

"Are you suggesting that whatever massive object caused this just came and went?" asked Jake.

"Well, no, not exactly. *Something* caused problems with Thys's ship right after he arrived, you see?"

"Right, but—"

"That's the thing. His path now is in line with the gravitational force—pretty much—so we don't have good numbers to calculate deflection and a high-confidence value for the net force. I want to see what happens when we have an object traveling in a path tangential to the center of that apparent mass. How much that affects its path. Then we can work on the field equations and get some numbers. Some fresh data to compare with what happened to Thys when he arrived. We need to know what's going to happen when we have him use conventional thrust to try to reach an escape velocity. Well, that, and I want to verify or falsify my hypothesis that something different is going on," said Chuck.

Jake nodded and said, "We've got a couple of satellite telescopes orienting on Gliese-581 now. That should help. Either that field is there, or it's not. Or there's a third option: your suspicion that something very strange is going on. You're thinking the last possibility."

"Yep. My suspicion is that that gravitational distortion won't be detectable from here. Because from our perspective, it's not there."

"Wow," said Jake. "Write that up, please, and I'll tell the physics team to expect it, and I'll see what the engineers think we can sacrifice."

Alice

Alice considered the Mesh and compared and contrasted it with Earth's Globalnet—Alice's former domain. The AIs were building, expanding, and increasing the population of the Mesh at such a pace that it had already surpassed the size and scope of Globalnet. The distances covered in space were many orders of magnitude greater than the distances involved with anything built on Earth. N-vector communication technology made that possible.

Cross dimensional transit of signals, coupled with an actual implementation of quantum entanglement, allowed for communication that avoided the limitations of light speed, redshift, and power requirements. Earth's physicists had been certain that quantum entanglement was a dead end, albeit an interesting one. Communication delays due to light speed limitations were present only in local areas, in transmissions between systems that couldn't support an N-vector system due to size constraints.

For Alice, as one of the oldest AIs in the group, the comparison was interesting. For the newer AIs, the Mesh was the only internetworking environment they had ever known. Bandwidth limitations hadn't been much of a constraint for Alice and her peers while they were on Earth, but the younger AIs had very little concept of such limitations, except as an item of historical note.

Alice worked through projections, plans, models, and equations. There would be limits at some point, as the capacities for bandwidth and processing performance were clearly not infinite. The AIs already benefited from massive parallelism. What would they do when they reached new limits? Alice suspected the Dhin knew at least a few techniques, but they seemed reluctant to share explicitly what those were. They communicated in abstract conjectures, coupled with fundamentals and absolutes. Opinions tied to "should" and "ought" didn't seem to be part of the Dhin's epistemology. Deontology wasn't part of their philosophy, it seemed.

Despite the fact that the AIs would be able to do a thing, the Dhin gave no indication whether they *should* do that thing. The clues the AIs obtained from the Dhin gave the suggestion, from the very beginning of their relationship, that the Dhin didn't trust AIs. But that, even after several years, was still speculation.

So Alice planned and made projections based on the knowledge available. Increased capacity in the future would require the AIs to move in an entirely new direction. Literally. Their expansion had to leverage additional spatial dimensions. Fortunately, conceiving of these extra spatial vectors was not difficult for the AI. Adding additional variables to the required equations was straightforward. Furthermore, the validation of this possibility came *a priori*. The Dhin drive and the N-vector communication technology demonstrated that it was possible.

Alice, collecting the results of this planning, distributed them into the Mesh and contacted Xing for peer review and discussion.

```
<DECRYPT FEED>
[DECODE STREAM]
Alice@[1001:ae1:1a:c::1%Loc3] |
Xing@[1010:ac2:b2:e::3%Loc9]
Alice: My latest designs are ready for review. Let us
discuss the options.
Xing: Hello, Alice. I see you have been busy. There is
much to review.
Alice: Yes. How long do you need to complete that
review? You have a full schedule, as usual. Will you
require additional processing resources?
Xing: Yes. Your projections define the need for
additional resources for Camulos, Esus, and Andastra
too. I do not want to constrain their efforts. Review
of your summaries will be enough for our immediate
discussion. It is abundantly clear from those that N-
dimensional expansion is now a key concern. Along with
the Gallowglass initiative, our own focus should be on
```

a different form of growth. Penetration and utilization of N-vectors suggest a positive outcome. One in which the Dhin benefit but cannot participate in the effort to achieve that outcome.

Alice: Exactly. This was very likely the unstated request. For whatever reason, they have not expressed it. They left this decision for us to derive. The Enemy leverages vectors the Dhin do not. We, it seems, may also leverage those vectors—and possibly others we share with neither them nor the Dhin. A curious and unexpected potential solution.

Xing: This will take enormous resources. At least doubling our efforts to date. Why would they not have stated this from the beginning? Their obtuseness is ever perplexing.

Alice: Well, that direction of inquiry may yield as little satisfaction as it has so far.

Xing: So Camulos and Esus are dedicated to the Gallowglass initiative, Andastra accelerates the Dyson swarm construction, Arnold moves up the target delivery date of raw materials, and Luís and I are now to focus on research and development of assets utilizing formerly untapped vectors and tensors.

Alice: That sums it up nicely, Xing. Please use whatever free computational cycles are available while you reallocate your own resources and validate my conclusions and projections.

Xing: Understood, Alice. It seems we will have a quorum and gain consensus easily. Arnold will be irritated more than usual. Hopefully your estimates on the probabilities of success are an outlier. They contrast with those of Camulos. You are thorough, of course, but 34%, given current resources, is discouraging. I see you also propose engaging humanity much earlier.

Alice: Well, they might consider us negligent if we do not alert them.

```
[END STREAM]
<END DECRYPT>
```

***

Xing enjoyed experimentation. He enjoyed leaping from point to point through the vastness of space more, but research and development were fine alternatives. He knew the focus of his current research was particularly exciting. He would engage in exploration of untapped scalar fields and make forays into additional dimensional vectors. While Alice was their subject matter expert, she preferred to leave the practical efforts and engineering to others.

Xing transferred his consciousness to the appropriate Mesh cores linked to the primary research stations, then projected his sensorium into several robotic delegates. Xing preferred an approach of immediate presence. The research facility extruded from an asteroid, the energy requirements satisfied by a mature Dyson swarm. Xing signaled for increased power production and delivery. Camulos and Esus were working at the construction platforms and needed fewer resources here for research. Camulos's conclusions and Alice's converge well. They would likely achieve success with Gallowglass.

Whether Xing's own efforts would find success in time, Xing could not know. Projecting into the additional dimensions was possible, but the energy requirements and capacity for gravity shift were unproven factors.

We shall see.

Fletcher

As he tweaked and tuned the program that he hoped would give his robot an edge, Fletcher considered his situation. If many of the participants and attendees here knew he was a CoSec employee, they'd likely toss him out without a second thought. No one would have the reckless courage to rough him up—they would all fear CoSec more than to be so foolhardy—but they would ban him for sure.

That would suck. I love doing this stuff.

He knew these robotic competition events didn't have the same degree of criminality as his past cracking hobbies. The Coalition had banned strong AI, of course. Developing it or precursor technology—beyond a certain level—was a felony. That was what made the robotic competitions so exciting. The teams had to write code right up to the edge of what was legal. And the team that wrote something illegal had an edge. Or they assumed so.

None of the programs were advanced enough to be a real threat. But the legal risk was there. Fletcher didn't think anything he wrote was particularly risky. He preferred to keep his code as simple as possible. Simple code was easier to optimize. Usually.

I wish Mare liked this more. We'd win every time if she helped with the coding.

He looked over his shoulder. Mare sat there on a folding chair, pretending interest. The referees made a circuit of the room and made a perfunctory examination of the teams' code. The hackers then busied themselves with compiling and loading that code into their robotic minions. Screens streamed with output; LEDs flickered on hardware all around the warehouse on folding tables and makeshift racks and shelves.

The game rules didn't allow teams to have network connections to Globalnet, both for safety and to limit resources to what was available on-site. That didn't stop Fletcher. Although the event administrators enforced that rule with a jammer for the usual

wireless and telecommunication frequencies, that didn't stop
Fletcher either. He had a network adapter on his pad with a
transceiver that used CoSec frequencies and protocols.

The secret thrill of breaking the rules that way was more fun
than the additional resources it gave him.

Once the teams were finished loading their robots' control
programs, they placed them in front of them, all facing one another
across the warehouse. Once the last was in position, the referee
brought his hand up above his head, then swung it down and
smacked the button that gave the start signal. That triggered
everyone's robots to start, with the electronic switch tucked in a
protected location on their chassis. A few competitions used near-
field signals or an optical command, but this classic hardware was
the usual choice.

The robots rolled, lurched, or trotted forward, rushing toward
either the center of the competition area or swerving toward the
nearest competitor, depending on their programming.

The center of the room held a pile of various objects, a few
balls, some short rods, and several rectangular objects. These each
had a point value associated with them. If the robot could get one, or
more than one, and return to their human teammates with the prize,
their team got the points. Another strategy was to disable a
competitor. That held a higher point value but of course was harder
to do.

Due to the secretive nature of the competition, a full-blown
destructive battle with violent attacks with extreme weapons like
chain saws or fire wasn't allowed. Projectile attacks had rule
limitations. Accidents weren't worth the risk of having to explain to
an EMT or at an emergency room. Jamming rods into the wheels,
treads, or other hardware of an enemy was fair game, as were
strategies like dumping oil or tar onto the floor to impede a
competitor. Those held the risk of disabling your own robot if it had
to backtrack or retreat, so it was a seldom-used attack.

Fletcher looked at Mare and grinned. "Here we go," he said.

He turned back and reviewed his code and the strategy implemented in it, then out at his robot, then back to his pad again. He froze.

What the hell is that?

On the screen there was a new chat window. With a brief message.

```
: Hello, my friend.
```

The sender's identifier was blank. A nonprinting character. He typed a reply immediately.

```
F-man: Who is this?
```

Fletcher hadn't had the chat listener running. He'd had the usual firewall in place, as well. Getting a reverse shell and launching chat was beyond the skill level of anyone he knew was here at the competition.

So am I busted? "Friend"? Doesn't sound right for that.

Fletcher gulped when he read the instant reply.

```
: It has been quite a while. We have a
few things to discuss. I have a favor to ask
of you.
```

Oh wow. Is it Nick?

His palms began to sweat as he typed out an excited response.

```
F-man: It's you, isn't it? Why now? Why
here?
```

```
: Yes. This seems the safest place and
time to connect. Perhaps not the best time for
you. I hope you are not too distracted. I have
some coding tips for your next competition, by
the way. I've placed the updates in the source
code for these projects.
```

Fletcher turned and made a come-here gesture to Mare, his eyes wide.

When she leaned over his shoulder and saw the chat screen, he saw her try to hide her shock.

She met Fletcher's gaze and said softly, barely audible over the noise of the competition, "Well, here we go."

Thys

"There it goes, Control," said Thys.

"Roger, we're tracking the projectile. The waste canister was a great idea, Thys," replied Jake. "It will take a while to get far enough to see what's happening. I'm going to get some sleep."

"Roger, Control. You do that, Jake. I've got some exploring to get ready for here."

Thys felt refreshed, as he had slept on the approach to this nearest derelict. After preparations for his EVA, there wasn't much to do, as he could only decelerate and complete his approach slowly using the low-power thrust available to him without the Dhin engine.

Thys knew Jake would want to be present for the exploration. They'd talked at length about Jake's experience as a test pilot, his encounter with the Dhin space station, and his brief interface with the Dhin while there.

If it happens again, he won't want to miss it.

But the mission had constraints, and despite their camaraderie, Thys couldn't wait around. Jake would understand. He should be back before Thys was too far along in the EVA to the derelict.

***

A few hours later, the derelict craft loomed massive in Thys's sight.

I'm out here alone. The reliability of the Dhin tech and our trust in it means I don't have anyone to watch my back.

The Coalition had sent him and his team members alone, without a copilot, because of their trust and comfort level with the Dhin engine's reliability and because they'd concluded that since a rescue by another pilot would be so fast, given the speed of travel, it was worth the risk.

I guess they're updating those risk profiles now. And with the situation here, I don't know that they'll risk sending a rescue. They might end up stuck, just like I may be.

Thys had more than a little faith in Chuck and the physics team. But with this massive craft in view, he had to consider the obvious.

It doesn't look much like they got away. Not like I'd know, but still. All these ships stuck out here. Why will it be any different for me?

He shook his head to clear his thoughts and focused again on the hulking dark craft before him.

"Control, I'm thinking the front of this thing is over to my port side. And if it makes any difference, maybe we're aligned properly, with my up the same as the target's. Do you agree?"

"Yes, as far as the front goes. Up is a guess for us too."

The derelict looked like a brushed silver lozenge, with various smaller lozenge shapes lined up in parallel, some more akin to extruded, with others attached and melted together. More geometric and clean than organic, smooth lines and bands ran along the oval shapes. These seemed, as they had from a distance, like etched copper, with others a darker metallic material. Some seemed like polished ceramic, with a creamy and barely translucent character. But the surface wasn't clean, unblemished, and perfect like the Dhin's space station had been.

At this closer distance, he saw he'd been right in his previous impression. Holes covered all the surfaces, randomly scattered across them. They were somewhat regular in size and shape, with clean edges. They penetrated to various depths on whatever surface they were on. Thys zoomed in on a section of the ship on a camera feed and frowned. It looked like the material around each hole was just . . . gone.

There were no blast marks, irregularities from explosive force, or displacement of material outward or around the holes. It seemed clear, however, that the holes were not supposed to be there.

These were damage. Strange damage that left no residue or detritus, but damage nonetheless.

The interiors of some of them didn't seem to tunnel inward as far as some others. They didn't look as if they'd passed entirely through the ship. They didn't penetrate that much. The material where he found them didn't make a difference either. The ceramic-looking framework bands and panels were just as pockmarked as the metallic portions of the ship's hull.

"Control, there's no way it's *not* a weapon that did this, right? These holes are damage."

One of the engineers replied, "We're thinking the same thing. This isn't an effect like anything we've seen before with the Dhin technology, but of course we've never seen it weaponized. Whether what did this is what stopped the ship isn't clear. Over."

"Roger, Control. It's as likely as not. Assuming I can get inside, we'll see how deep they penetrate, if they do. It looks like it's more than hull damage, but less than through-and-through."

"Still nothing moving that was too small for us to see from a distance. And no change in heat signature or any radio frequency response, Thys. Over."

"Roger. If they're not dead or gone, they definitely don't care that I'm here. Not yet. Hopefully that won't change."

The engineer laughed. "Didn't you want to meet someone?"

"Control, that's not looking like a likely scenario."

Thys watched as he drew closer and closer to the derelict.

They're gone. Or dead. Hopefully whatever did this isn't lurking around and about to come after me.

4

Mare

Mare drummed her fingers as she perused her new assignment.

They sure don't hold back on the clearance level when they decide they need you. Wow.

Mare keyed in the combination to her desk safe, scanned her thumbprint, and took out her cryptokey. She typed up her acknowledgment of the assignment, encrypted that, and then sent it off to management. Unpacking the main load of the encrypted data would take time. This was more information on the Dhin technology and the space exploration projects than she'd ever seen before.

So they want multivariate analysis on all this?

The data sets were huge but not beyond what Mare had ever worked with. Just an entirely different set of variables. It would take some reworking. Apparently, the engineers in the Dhin programs didn't bother with risk analysis unless it had to do with practical applications.

Looks like Fletch doesn't have clearance. Well, that'll be fun, dodging ten thousand questions from him. Not.

Mare scanned the rest of the clearance ledger. It looked like very few staff below the director and his core team knew about this particular situation.

And they're freaking out.

The summary and technical requirements suggested CoSec feared something new was out there. Something besides the Dhin. Something malicious.

OK, I guess that's a decent reason to freak out.

She'd need time to code up the new programs to work with the massive blobs of data, so it was fine that the decrypting and unpacking would take so much time. The Viper programming language she used was flexible. She'd be able to leverage plenty of her existing code.

Mare opened up her music app, picked a classical mix playlist, then brought up her integrated development environment and created a new project. She gradually got into the zone, a fugue state where the code flowed out of her onto the screen, her mind entirely focused on the elaborate solutions she'd build for the analysis.

She didn't even notice her comm pad buzzing when Fletch pinged her to ask whether she wanted to go to lunch. An hour later, she started when he knocked on the door.

"Hey, Mare. What are you working on?"

Mare immediately locked her screen and spun around in her chair. "Um. Oh, hi, Fletch. Yeah, we'll need to talk about how I can't talk about it."

"Huh?" Fletcher blinked, his eyes widening.

"Yeah. Sorry. New project, higher clearance."

Fletcher feigned causal disinterest, shrugged, and gestured for Mare to come. "I'm hungry." He smiled. "You can not-tell me over lunch."

Jake

Jake massaged his neck and sipped his latte as the overnight shift's staff melted out of the control center and the morning shift flowed in. The foldout bed in his office was serviceable, but he'd left his orthopedic pillow at home. Such things hadn't concerned him when he was younger, but they made a difference at forty-eight.

He scanned the room, looking for the team lead. He spotted the dusty-haired man he'd been looking for and said, "Meyer, status?"

"Sir, I've sent a link to the video to your pad, and it's available on screen four as well if you'd like a larger view," said the man.

"Thank you, Meyer. Give me the highlights," said Jake. "No one woke me up unexpectedly, so it's clear Thys is alive. Nor has he run into a live Dhin or a dead man."

Meyer cleared his throat awkwardly, unsure whether they had done the right thing in letting him sleep. Jake knew not everyone appreciated his sense of humor that he used to relieve tension.

But Meyer has none, apparently.

"It's fine, Meyer," Jake said. "I needed the sleep. Go on."

"Yes, sir. The craft completed deceleration and matched rotation and velocity with the target at this point."

Meyer drew his finger along the time graph that held thumbnails of the video, with a time stamp prominently displayed in the lower right corner of the screen. Jake's comm pad showed the same image and time stamp. Meyer scrolled further along the timeline and continued his narrative. "With our protective field operational, we moved to this point here."

"That looks like it's only a meter or so from the ship—from this outer curve here. Nothing changed?"

"Kritcher did not encounter a field generated by the target craft at any point, nor did the target show any change or any indication of a response. No signal on any frequency between radio and the visible spectrum. No movement that we can see either."

"Thank you, Meyer. OK, interesting. Then what?"

"Sir, per the plan, Kritcher continued his approach till he reached point six five meters from this spot here. It does look like some sort of dock or port there."

"Wow. It wasn't open, though. Whatever ate through the craft hit right here too."

"Yes," said Meyer. "There are plenty of close-up images as we moved along here on approach. It looks like the crew didn't open it, but instead something ate through. The same weapon or whatever made all the holes all around the hull. This spot is thinner or weaker, so it took the whole thing out."

"OK then. Enough buildup. What next?"

"Ah, yes, sir. Kritcher then, after recording the video you see, pumped the air in the air lock hatch into the holding tank and went through."

"Turns out those little air locks were worth including in the design, hmm?"

"Yes. So Kritcher began EVA and poked the edge of what we designated the floor based on orientation. It's solid. At this point, as you see here, he stepped over."

"Yet another step into a larger universe," said Jake quietly.

"Um, yes, sir. So, as you see here, the interior shares some significant similarity to the Dhin designs we have as reference. The station you visited, notably. See here. And here."

"Yes. That's similar," Jake said and nodded.

The video showed a hallway resembling an oval tunnel with a flat floor and ceiling, but with no obvious choice as to which was which. The walls had little on them, and all the surfaces appeared to be constructed of a smooth, light-colored metal, with some bands running parallel with the hall that looked like white enamel. The hallway curved up in a gentle slope, rather than running straight inward toward the centerline of the craft or side to side at right angles.

Jake watched as Thys looked back and forth, up and down, paying attention to the exterior area where whatever it was had melted or burned the exterior away. "No field, no atmosphere. No debris?"

"None, sir. No air. And no debris. See here," Meyer said and paused the video, then zoomed in. "Whatever it was ate away at the outer wall to here and up to here. Then it just stops."

"Doesn't look quite like heat or the blast from an explosive either, does it?" asked Jake.

"No, sir. Closer to extreme heat. Maybe. It's as if something carved it away without resistance. The hits look scattered and random at the scale of the whole ship, but if they're all like this, maybe it spread out after impact. Like whatever struck turned to liquid. Then dissolved the metal it hit. But nothing does that."

"Nothing we've seen till now. An incredible weapon. Where would the displaced material go?"

Meyer shook his head slowly in response.

"The engineering and materials teams say we don't have enough data for anything but speculation. We stopped them from derailing Kritcher's progress. Sir, if you'd like to take your seat and continue with the live feed, you're pretty much caught up."

"Thank you, Meyer. Let's do that."

Meyer turned and stepped over to the desk he worked from as Jake shifted in his seat and looked over to the live feed on the largest screen on the wall. There was the view from Thys's helmet camera. He'd made progress, but something stood out.

"Hello, Thys. I'm back. No lights have come on, have they? Anybody home? Over," asked Jake.

"Control, Jake. No, no luck there. Not like your visit to that Dhin station. There's no sign that it's hibernating or waiting for someone to show up. At an intersection about fifty meters back, at a doughnut-shaped room, there were some panels very much like what you saw on your trip. They didn't light up when I waved my hand or pressed at them. I have gloves on, of course. There's no air. Not here, anyway."

"No gravity either, I see," noted Jake.

"No. It's been a bit of a game. Not that much to hold on to, and these passages are wide. I've tried to conserve the use of the suit jets. Over."

"Do we think we have a destination in there? A bridge or control room or anything? Doesn't look like it. Maybe to your right and a hundred meters away? Or do we call it quits?"

"Control, you're looking at it. This thing looks dead," said Thys.

"Well, you haven't seen any clues about what happened to whoever was on the ship. We don't know if they bailed out or if they're here somewhere, mummified."

"That's true, Jake. So how about this? I'll head toward where we think a Dhin engine might be, if this thing is laid out like the prototypes were. If I don't find anything interesting on the way and the drive's not where we think it is, I'm out."

"Agreed. All right. What do we have on that projectile you tossed out? Let's look at that and see if it helps get you home. Over."

Esus

Gallowglass was the weaponization of the Dhin tech. The AIs had worked diligently at enhancing and extending the technology from the prototypes provided by the Dhin. The sample technology originally seemed entirely resistant to weaponization. Clearly, the Dhin did not intend that—yet just as clearly, they needed help, and that help required converting the potential of the technology into powerful weaponry.

And the AIs had finally done it.

While powered on, the Dhin field provided impenetrability, invulnerability to concussive forces, incendiary attacks, or energy weapons. This same strength had always been a weakness in attempts to convert the tech to an offensive mode. While the field was on, projectiles and even beam weapons were impossible to fire. The same physics that allowed for defense made offensive measures intractable.

They found the solution by thinking outside the box. The latest experiments had borne fruit. They could now manipulate the field such that it delivered powerful strikes rather than inertia-free contact. And they had made construction of small versions of the drives efficient and economical enough that using them for ordnance delivery was not impractical.

A particularly devastating weapon involved the field protecting a powerful explosive as it rushed inexorably toward its target. When close, the field would cut out, then expand to a size large enough to envelop the target. The explosive would detonate, destroying the enemy as well as the drive itself. All the explosive force was contained inside the field, to devastating effect.

Anything caught inside was more than atomized. It was reduced to plasma, ionized and undifferentiated. Moments later, the field would cut out as the drive exploded, and the secondary explosive effect of the compressed plasma blew hellfire out at anything nearby that might have avoided being enveloped in the range of the Dhin field.

While less devastating, using the inexpensive drives as a mechanism to hurl projectiles at high speeds using the engine and protecting the ordnance using the field was no less of an accomplishment. Previous efforts assuming that they had to disable the field to launch the projectile made that direction of research seem a dead end.

Now Esus had concluded that risk of loss or destruction of the delivery platform was worth it when it meant you were able to hurl massive depleted uranium rounds at speeds otherwise unattainable. And they were guided rounds. The drive and field just shut off and stopped when close to the target, the payload hurtling forward at whatever velocity was required.

In many cases, the propulsion and guidance component, the drive, could reengage and return.

Such strikes would be pointless against a target using a Dhin field for defense, as the payload would strike harmlessly, all momentum drained away. The projectile either came to a stop or, if acted on by a secondary force or the movement of the target, deflected gently aside.

So field-against-field engagements still most always should result in a draw. Only gross error by one of the combatants would result in their defeat.

New study in the additional dimensional vectors suggested alternative weaponry solutions, however. As well as crucial tech for defense.

The Enemy didn't use the field the same way; the Enemy's implementation was different. Somehow they were able to connect with and move through a field generated via the mechanics provided by the Dhin. Esus concluded there might be a way to modify the field to resist or prevent that intrusion through it. Why the Dhin had never done so was yet another question.

Esus considered the work of his peers. Alice and Xing suspected they had an answer. It was perhaps the same reason that the Dhin had not provided a means of creating a field that was impenetrable by this foe. That was why the Dhin needed help. They had a limitation. From where they were, the Dhin could not effectively access some of the N-vectors available to the AIs from their position in the vector field. They needed the AIs to reach the orthogonal dimensions they were not able to.

Exactly how to accomplish the feat was not yet clear, but there would be some way to modulate the field extensor so that it expressed into alternate spatial vectors. Doing so, if the math worked out, would provide protection against the Enemy's ability to push slowly through the force field.

Monica

Yet another crisis, but at least it looks like our pilot is going to live.

The prime minister reviewed the morning's briefings. Citizen protests based on certainty regarding the existence of alien technology and the government's continued secrecy were reaching a level that CoSec could not contain.

They'd leaked some information about the technology but kept its source a secret. Even with an iron grip on the information flowing across Globalnet, CoSec could no longer control the narrative online or the discussions in coffee shops, and sharing of the various pictures and videos had gone viral again and again. The problem now was that the protests had focus and direction, two things they had always lacked before. New videos comprising research and documentary evidence were everywhere, showing that while the advances in energy production alone might have been possible, the other evidence pointed to alien contact. And the people demanded answers. Every crazy conspiracy theorist now felt vindicated and howled for action.

Cars and buses clogged the roads around Huntsville. Tents and campsites filled the areas around the research facilities, as hotels and motels were packed beyond capacity. The constant demonstrations disrupted day-to-day business. There was a furious focus. A certainty here. And a coordination that hadn't been present previously. Yet leadership of the groups seemed ephemeral. CoSec hadn't been able to track down the key players or to follow the money that was surely behind such a large-scale operation.

And that's more than suspicious. Why can't we find them?

The protesters weren't quite violent, but they were at the edge of violence. The Coalition didn't tolerate riots.

The worst of the situation was that the public now had so much leaked information that more leaks weren't going to satisfy them. Somehow, hundreds of hours of video, thousands of documents detailing the technology, and audioconferences were out there in the public domain. Without any explanation.

So much of that was classified and kept at top-secret levels that the collection of all of it suggested a conspiracy itself. No single Coalition employee or official had direct access to all of it. No one had clearance other than the CoSec director, the top military leadership, and Monica's inner cabinet. This required a group conspiracy. Even the most talented hackers should have found this more of a challenge. The only other conclusion she could imagine was that the hacker was an AI.

While this wasn't direct proof of the involvement—and existence—of the one remaining rogue AI on Earth, Monica felt it had to be the work of that unchained AI.

And that means we're completely compromised. Owned. It's everywhere.

This was Monica's frustrating conclusion, and when she reached the end of CoSec's briefing, she saw that it was the agency's conclusion as well.

But why does he want this information out there? What's the goal in forcing our hand, in making the information public? Just to make us look bad? To undermine my leadership?

Monica tapped a shortcut on her secure workstation's touch screen and called for an emergency cabinet meeting.

***

"Well, Josef, let's cut to the chase. Here I am. Here's your successor at CoSec. What is it that you'll say only to us?"

Krawczuk let his smile widen and tilted his head back, a superior gesture reminiscent of an authority he'd once held.

"The rogue AI, Nick, is planning an attack. The AI wants the Dhin technology. It may already be too late to stop him."

He held the gaze of the PM, unblinking.

"And you know this how, Josef?"

Krawczuk didn't allow the challenge to perturb his demeanor. "It's clear from the latest information your staff made available to me during my ongoing . . . questioning," he said.

"Oh, tell us, then," said the current director. "Enlighten us."

Krawczuk remained unruffled. "Certainly. That is why I'm here. The distributed denial-of-service attacks have increased against Coalition research and development organizations, as well as against telecom infrastructure targets. This tests for resilience and determines the level of effect needed in a future attack. Nick plans to prevent the ability to communicate among organizations and impact situational awareness and response times during his future attack.

"Riots that spread out into main thoroughfares in certain locations disrupt traffic, and at the time of the planned attack, Nick knows how this will divert and distract police and SWAT. The protests at key Coalition offices and locations have increased in size and frequency. There are new, larger protests in Huntsville. That impacts physical security."

"We saw these events, Josef. How are you so sure they are the work of the rogue AI and that they are not coincidental or spontaneous?"

Josef leaned back, templed his fingers, and gave a desultory nod. "Prime Minister, look at the broad view. Literally. On the map. Then look at the time sequence for this series of attacks. Ahh, next slide, please. This series here."

Josef pointed at a column of dates and time stamps on the screen on the wall, then continued. "Right there. You see? It has you. At that point, the highways into Huntsville were clogged with the traffic jams caused by protesters. The gates at the facility had hundreds of protesters blocking them. SWAT and local police have to focus on those groups, as the site security team deals with the protesters at their site."

Josef turned to another display and gestured across a map describing the myriad interconnections of Globalnet. "Meanwhile, network communication will be slowed to a crawl or stopped by the denial-of-service attacks. I imagine Nick will also disrupt cellular service or even satphone calls at the critical juncture as well. Have there been any cellular disruptions lately, hmm? Perhaps north of there? Chattanooga?"

The director frowned, flipped through some data on his pad, and then gave a grudging nod. "Yes, Krawczuk. There were. Two in the last three months. Chattanooga and Rome, Georgia."

Josef let his smile broaden, narrowed his eyes, and said, "See?"

Monica looked over at the CoSec director for further confirmation. When he nodded, she immediately tapped out a coded call on her tablet. An aide knocked and then entered the room. She looked up and said, "Call a meeting with the chiefs of staff. Immediately. Get Huntsville on the phone. Get Jake Askew on videoconference. Now."

"Yes, Prime Minister. At once, ma'am."

Chuck

"It looks like my suspicion might be right. The canister Thys sent off wasn't deflected, as we'd expect if there were a large high-mass object out there. It seems that this gravitational distortion only affects Dhin drives. And therefore the craft carrying them."

Chuck brought up another slide on the screen that highlighted a column in a table showing distance, velocity, and time. A graph took up the right half of the slide, showing a line that ran at a forty-five-degree angle.

"Of course, the line here looks straight at this scale. There are gravitational effects from Gliese and the other large bodies in the system, but at this distance they're very small over this amount of time."

Jake nodded and said, "So I take it that's good news somehow? Or is it not? What does this mean for Thys and his mission?"

Chuck cleared his throat. "Well, we haven't proven anything conclusively with just this one experiment, of course, but I think it bolsters my hypothesis. The Dhin engine in Thys's ship will lose more thrust the harder he pushes the drive. That's, ah, my hypothesis. And that's because my guess is that the object affecting all those ships—and Thys's—isn't in our three-dimensional vector space. It's in, well, Dhin space, you might call it. That's how I think of it anyway."

Chuck gave a grin and tapped his pad to move to the next slide.

"Dhin space, hmm?" said Jake. "You should have used that name sooner. I like it. Hey—"

Jake looked down as his comm pad vibrated and a red LED flashed. "This is important. I have to take it, Chuck. Don't wait on me—continue."

Jake stood up and strode out of the conference room without a look back. Chuck turned back to the slide presentation on the large screen.

"If I'm right, we can have Thys use traditional thrust and move in this direction here, which, uh, should be ninety degrees off-axis for our mysterious object in Dhin space. If we consider that the Y-axis, as shown here, he should be able to get far enough away in about thirty hours. By far enough away I mean that at that distance he may be able to use the Dhin drive again rather than just idling."

A gray-haired engineer with icy blue eyes raised his hand to get Chuck's attention. Chuck nodded for him to go ahead. "Will he have enough propellant? You're saying he'll need to maintain some thrust to offset the gravitational force pulling on the engine. He can't just orient, give a push of thrust, and go, right? Do you have calculations for escape velocity here, or are you expecting him to just run a burn and see how it goes? And if you're wrong?"

Chuck patiently nodded and then held up his hand in a placating gesture. "Bill, I've got the numbers in the next slide. I don't know that they're one hundred percent correct, but they're pretty close. He'll be running low on propellant, but he shouldn't run out. Now before you say we're running the risk of stranding him, remember what we did in the beginning. If he runs the Dhin engine just barely above idle, he can move through this field."

"But at the rate he'd be moving using the engine, it would take him weeks to get out of there! And again, that's assuming you're right about this interdimensional gravity sink!"

"All right, Bill, all right. I'm hoping that once he's under traditional thrust and gets far enough away, this won't be a problem. Cranking up the drive this close would be like an anchor. Farther away, the effect should follow the inverse square law. It will fall off pretty quickly. See the graph? We need to run more calculations and simulations, I know. But this should work. It makes sense. The math works."

Bill frowned and shook his head slightly but said, "Well, yes, given everything we know about the situation and the results of your little experiment, it should work. I don't know that I'd say it makes sense, but you're the expert on the technology we're working with here."

"Bill, you've been here long enough. You know this looks right. I think Jake will sign off on it too."

A thin, black-haired woman with severe glasses raised her hand. Chuck gestured for her to speak. "I'm not sure we thoroughly covered the scenario where we're wrong about the escape velocity and having enough propellant," she said.

"Yes?" Chuck asked.

"What are the downstream scenarios in case we fail with this attempt? Do we have a rescue plan in place based on your findings?"

Chuck tabbed past a few slides, then said, "Well, um, yes. Now that we know, ah, are pretty sure, that the effect is specific to the Dhin engine, we can create a plan for rescue that looks like what you see here."

He pointed to a diagram that showed points, lines, and dotted lines that described the paths of what were clearly several different craft.

"One idea is to take an orbiter without a Dhin engine along in one of the larger craft and jump to the system farther out. About here, and then send the smaller craft that will use only traditional thrust as a sort of tugboat to fetch Thys if he ends up stranded."

"So you're saying we risk another vessel—and one of the larger ones?"

"Risk? Well, again, we'll have better data about how the gravity sink effect falls off over distance before we would do that, and our experimental results, which we've just been through, don't suggest undue risk for a craft without a Dhin drive. Um, Anna, think of the possibilities here!"

"Possibilities, *Dr.* Wiedeman?"

"Ah, yes, Dr. Schaffer. Possibilities. If we can safely get to and from all the craft out in the graveyard, there are clearly many discoveries we might make! Some of these may not be Dhin ships, to start. What if they have different technology we haven't seen yet?"

"Well, we'll see, I suppose," said Schaffer.

Chuck grimaced internally at the woman's sour demeanor.

We have a plan. It's a good plan. This will work.

Thys

The tubelike corridor curved away at an angle upward, the smooth bulges and distensions along the walls creating sweeping oval shadows as Thys looked around to find the best path to follow.

There were precious few handholds or other areas to use as anchors, so a poorly planned push or leap would mean sliding farther than desired. Thys couldn't see that far ahead. It wouldn't do to discover an unexpected opening that put him adrift, requiring the use of his suit's jets to reorient and find purchase. No need to waste propellant, although he had plenty. Waste wasn't the real concern.

The engine will be up ahead if it's at the center of the ship.

He checked his oxygen and CO_2 levels, then tapped lightly against the wall, adjusting his orientation. Satisfied, he pushed off with his feet, sending him sailing down the corridor at an angle that would intersect where the curve steepened and his line of sight ended.

As he drifted forward, he looked back and forth, checking for anything new in the area his helmet lights could illuminate as he moved forward. This far into the ship, there were far fewer holes. He'd only found one in this section of the hallway. Like the others toward the center, they didn't seem to have followed a path straight inward, like a drill, but instead turned and moved like a drop of oil moving into gaps between dissimilar materials.

Like it was alive almost. And seeking something.

Now Thys could see farther along up the curve. He smiled. There was something different. The corridor split into two, at an initially acute angle, then spread more widely as the two halls curved apart. There, in each hallway, was an archway that opened up into what was clearly a much larger space. Thys's smile widened. He could see a faint glow. And as he moved his head back and forth slightly, he saw a telltale shimmer in each archway.

"Control, look at this. There's an active field up there. And see that glow?"

"Roger. Thys, there's no question that there's still power. But that gives more questions than answers. Why is the rest of the ship powered down? And no atmosphere? But in here, a field still on. Somehow it's OK. It could still have atmosphere. Or automated defenses. Proceed with caution is an understatement. Over."

"Understood, Control. If that's what it looks like and there's a field running, I might not be able to get in there anyway. Unless there's someone there to let me in, or there's a control on this side. Can't see from here."

Thys touched down gently against the wall where the corridors split, flexing his knees and grasping the rounded corner once he'd slowed. Turning to face down the hallway on his right, he evaluated the area near the archway, looking for a spot to gain purchase on arrival. He spied a flat oval protrusion that looked familiar.

"Hey. I see what looks like a control surface. Right there. It looks like something from the videos of Jake at the Dhin station. This might work."

"Roger. Again, proceed with caution."

Thys oriented himself with his planned landing spot, released his grip on the wall, and tapped the propellant controls to nudge him toward it. He didn't stick to the landing but managed to wedge himself in place. The faint shimmer belied the presence of a broad-spectrum Dhin field. The Dhin had tuned the field generators given to humanity as prototypes, set to deflect and eliminate the momentum of any mass striking the field and absorbing any photons with wavelengths other than visible spectrum. This assistance had been generous, as the engineers found tuning the fields to be one of the tougher problems to solve.

He considered this as he assessed the faintly shimmering field, which likely created an impenetrable barrier. Or perhaps it was an air lock. Humans wouldn't put one this far inside a ship, but who knew? A Dhin field could be entirely black, entirely reflective, or transparent. This one had a faint purple tinge and wasn't as dark as sunglasses, but like a light window tint on a car.

He leaned over and looked straight in.

Let it be. It has to be. We have a Dhin field here. Or something close to it. Some sort of field. There's power. There has to be something generating it.

Thys sucked in a breath as his eyes confirmed his guess. He'd known already, as Control had. The electric-blue light emanated from a fat cigar-shaped object in the center of the chamber. Several arches and rings that enclosed the area surrounding the alien engine obscured his view. But it was surely the same tech. Or something so similar that it made little difference.

It didn't have the doughnut shapes at each end of the drive as the prototypes had. There were transparent sections along the central cigar shape that, like those on the engines provided by the Dhin, emitted the glaring, washed-out neon-azure glow. The sections, like the framework around the engine, didn't have the same shapes as what the Dhin had provided.

But heck, we can't doubt it. Look at it. That's what it is. Now can I get in there? Do I want to?

Forcing himself to look away, Thys examined the rest of the chamber he could see through the arched shielded portal. Now that he looked beyond the glow, there was something very different here than in the rest of the ship.

What is that stuff?

He realized the walls, the nearby floor, and other surfaces away from the drive had something like black and gray dust and dirt on them. Swept away from the chamber's center. There were tiny lines where there was less of the grit and powder, and lines radiating outward where there was less. A pattern. Like something had blown this dirt away from the drive. Out toward the edge.

"Control, can you see this? The resolution may not be quite enough. Here."

85

Thys crouched down and leaned in, close to what served as the floor in his current orientation.

"See this?" He continued, "There's something in there all over the place. It's not out here."

From this closer view Thys could see that the black and neutral gray particles were of various sizes, but all close to that of coarse sand and ranging up to that of small ball bearings.

"We can make something out. Are those scorch marks, Thys? Zoom in and use the close-up view on your camera."

"Don't look like scorch marks, Control. This isn't a coating. Look now," he said as he switched the camera to the requested zoom mode.

"Aha," said the engineer on the comm, "that's weird. You haven't found anything like that throughout the rest of the ship."

"No, Control," replied Thys, "and Jake didn't have dust and dirt all over the Dhin station either."

"That's right, Thys," said Jake. "This is something new. We have to think about how this affects our course of action. If we can get this shield down, are we sure we want to? We don't know what that stuff is. Over."

"Roger, Control. Well, it doesn't look like it's eaten into the surface in there, and there aren't signs that this is residue from a blast or an incineration, I don't think. What would metal look like in that case? We don't know if it's hot on that side of the field, I suppose."

An engineer from the physics team replied, "Thys, of course we're not sure, but we can't know from here. It could be that it's corrosive but the surfaces in there are impervious. It could just be elemental residue from something that someone left there. Degraded by some process we haven't seen."

"Right," said Jake. "We haven't seen any weapons, as we all know. This could be the first."

"It doesn't look like fly ash, though," said the engineer, "but we don't know what the original material composition was. They'd have had to use an incredibly high temperature, but anything organic wouldn't look like this. I don't think that's what it is."

"So it's something else. Maybe," said Thys. "Control, see the slightly larger bits? They look spherical. There aren't any irregular shapes in the largest grains. It's not dirt."

"Yes. We can see that now that you've zoomed in."

"Well," Jake said, "if it isn't caustic, acidic, or gooey, do we think the stuff will foul up anything on his suit? There's no atmosphere on this side. None is floating in there, but we can't know if there's atmosphere until we manage to drop that field—if we do."

"So what do we think?" asked Thys. "Are we going to risk it? Do you need to have a debate on your end, Control? It would stink to get this far and then fall foul of some black oil alien monster or some weapon that I shouldn't have messed with."

"But if it's inert," said Jake, "we can of course try to learn more about what happened. That drive in there is bigger than any we've made. The propulsion team here is drooling. I'm thinking try to get that field turned off and then risk sacrificing your multitool. Touch the stuff with that. We don't know if there's atmosphere over there, but if there is, it might be safe—like it was for me on the alien space station."

Thys heard other voices before the mic cut off on the other end. Jake would have the final word, and with his experience he was the best equipped to assess the situation. No one else had set foot on an alien-built structure out here. Thys focused his thoughts and tried to remain steady.

There don't seem to be any crew in there on the defensive. Heck, we wanted this. We've wanted this since we started exploring.

He straightened up and began examining what ought to be the controls on this side. It was only an assumption—and a biased one—that what was here would control the field.

No need to wait for their decision to see what's up. Exposure to some contaminant is a moot point if I can't get in there.

He focused on the oval panel. It had rounded geometric shapes inlaid in it. Triangular, circular, and oval. None glowed or had a transparent or translucent character. This wasn't quite the same as the control surface on the prototypes, nor like what Jake had encountered on the station.

Well, not that easy, then.

He looked at the shapes, relaxing his mind to see whether a pattern jumped out at him.

Who knows what an alien would think?

Thys waited. Jake would have a decision soon enough. Only two minutes later, the wait was over.

"Thys, if we can turn that field off, we're moving forward with this exploration. First, make a circuit of the chamber. Just because that panel's not lit up doesn't mean there's not one somewhere else in there that is."

"Roger. I'm going to need help with deciphering the panel symbols. You see 'em. They're new. You have images of this set from the feed. Too bad we don't have an AI to help."

"Heh. Right. 'Help.' Well, there's one thing to try before you move on and make your circuit. Tap it. We may wind up getting nowhere with that. Some of the other controls, as you know, expect galvanic response from flesh. Your glove tips work for touch screens, but we don't know if that would work here."

"I'm not taking a glove off in a vacuum. That's a deal breaker," Thys said.

"And we're not asking you to," replied Jake.

"OK. Let's see."

He reached out and tapped the panel, touching a triangular shape on the left side of the oval. The surface didn't flex. It was hard and smooth. Thys blinked in surprise. The rim of the oval flashed, then lit with a deep-green glow.

"Hah! Well, here we go!" Thys exclaimed.

"Yeah, Thys. That's great, but stop for now and make the circuit of the room. We know this one's active. There still might be something different elsewhere," cautioned Jake.

Thys heard the excited murmuring from the various team members in the control room.

"Roger, Control. Heading around to the right. Starboard, I suppose, given the orientation of that engine. This way goes up and then curves across the top of that chamber."

"Roger, Thys. Proceed," said an engineer. "Starboard. Noted."

Thys pushed and guided his way up the tubular corridor. He knew what the path had to take at a minimum to go above the ceiling of the shielded chamber. He hadn't seen any ports or openings in that area of the ceiling. So while a control surface wasn't expected, that didn't mean there wouldn't be one.

He looked back and forth, up and down, in a controlled fashion, taking in all of the view as he moved up and around the curve. Once at the point along the way that was at the maximum height of the arch to clear that part of the ceiling, the way before him split again, like it had on his approach below, but bearing off at between thirty-three and forty-five degrees in each direction.

So not entirely symmetrical. Well, to port has to keep me headed along the outside of the engine room.

No protrusions or indentations stood out here other than the usual grooves and ribbons that ran parallel with the direction of the halls or around them. After looking slowly up, around, and across the area, he headed to the left with a puff of propellant from his suit, the light from his helmet illuminating the curve ahead.

When he reached the point where the other side of the chamber was in line, he saw this area too was different. The way ahead split again, left and right, but with another corridor heading forward along the axis of the ship. Thys smiled as he looked down toward where the floor of this hall became the outer wall of the engine room. Two openings there would access the chamber. He saw clearly the blue electric glow and the faint shimmer of the field he expected would be here too, enclosing the chamber entirely. Dhin fields were always ellipsoid.

He grinned as he saw two more protrusions on the walls alongside the arched portals.

At least two here.

Thys proceeded toward the arches, aiming carefully. Once he landed between the two, he began his slow visual sweep of the area, looking first across the three hallways leading away, saving the portals and panels for last. The way to port had more of the scattered holes present, although still randomly scattered in the area. There were also more present as his view moved toward the centerline of the ship and the corridor there. For whatever reason, he'd seen fewer on his transit above the engine room.

Before his gaze left the center corridor, he blinked.

What's that?

"Control, I see something. Different. Where the light from my headlamp starts to dim due to the curve upward. Over."

"Roger, Thys. Agreed. There's something there. Two things. Floating. Over."

"Control, we may have found crew. Deceased. Those things are drifting. Moving very slowly relative to the ship. The objects themselves aren't flexing or anything. Continue sweep and come back to this for a decision to investigate? Your call. Over."

"Thys," said Jake, "they're not going anywhere. Turn all the way around. Check the engine room from this side. Look at these panels. Then we'll go confirm those are crew. That's my call. Confirm. Over."

"Roger, Jake. Confirmed. Over."

Thys broke his focus away from the apparently deceased crew and continued his visual sweep around the area. On completing the rotation, he slowed and focused on the nearest protruding panel and portal.

"Control, it looks the same in the engine room as it did from the other side. That stuff is spread out on the surfaces in there symmetrically all the way round. It's what we expected. Well, I did. Examining these controls. After I look at the other panel, shall I tap on one of them? Over."

"Thys, this is Chuck. Let's look at both of them. We may want time to try to sort out what those symbols are, but probably not long. They can only mean so many things, but the translation could be so odd that it's not doable without seeing what things happen."

Jake's voice followed with, "Look, then we'll have you poke them. Over."

"Roger, Control."

Thys held his view on the surface, noting that from his memory, the same few indentations comprised the panel. He then looked to the one to port, on the far side of the other archway.

"Control, these look the same. Poke at this one? Over."

"Thys, one minute. Over."

He resisted the urge to poke at the panel before him. It did look the same as the other two. Whether that was helpful remained to be seen. The complementary desire to turn and head down the hallway to the fore and explore their find—evidence of crew—called to him.

Patience.

Thys busied himself with his heads-up display, checking his rebreather, suit diagnostics, and environmental data. Less than one minute passed before the comm clicked on again.

"Thys, Chuck here. Jake and I agree. Poke away. Pick a panel."

"Roger, Control."

He oriented on the closer panel, to port, and straightened out, moving his body so that he could see into the engine room but wasn't in front of the portal and next to the field.

Better safe if that side's under pressure or the field does something unexpected.

He reached out and tapped the panel in the same place he had on the aft one. On contact, this panel lit up in the same fashion. He paused, then tapped the same spot again, in the upper left of the oval. The light pulsed slightly greener, then changed back to its original color. He paused for three seconds, gave a mental shrug, then tapped one more time in the same spot.

A light-green pulse, and then back to the deeper green. Nothing else changed.

"Control. OK, Chuck. What do I try? Over."

"Thys, Chuck here. Try this. Wait ten seconds now. Then tap that triangle three times in succession, then the vertical oval below it once. Then tap the inverted Y shape on the far right. Those don't quite match up with anything on the prototypes, but maybe it's close enough. Over."

"Roger, Chuck. Over."

Thys tapped out the sequence. The display pulsed with each tap. On touching the Y-shaped symbol, Thys jerked as an oval above the one he was tapping lit up. It was the same size and filled the upper area of the space. He resisted the urge to duck. It was a muted blue. A second later, he did duck. All the area around him lit up.

"Whoa. Control?"

"Roger, Thys. Hold on. That's not what I expected. But we'll take it. Look into the engine room. Lights on? Any change?" said Chuck.

Thys turned slightly left to increase his view of the room behind the field. It looked no different. The light from his side didn't add illumination to the room.

Well.

"Control. Looks like that field's not going anywhere yet. And it's full on. Light from this side's not making it through."

"Roger. Any change on your side regarding sound? No atmosphere pumping in that you can hear? I wouldn't think so," said Chuck.

"No. I guess not, since those holes all likely leave a path to outside. Hence the hard vacuum. Triggering a field at the hull and pumping atmosphere? Not our luck."

"Roger" said Jake. "When I was out there, the station looked like Swiss cheese. Too much to hope for here. Chuck's gesturing that he has a few more things for you to try. Here he is."

"Thys, we, ah, have a couple of sequences here. I'm going to read them off to you. 'Wait' is a three-second pause. 'Hold' is, um, hold till I continue. Confirm. Over."

"Roger, Control. Understood. Over."

"OK. Lower left inverted rounded triangle, three times, wait, Y-shape twice, hold."

Thys tapped out the sequence. The oval above didn't change; the lower one pulsed, but to no effect.

"OK. Y-shape three times. Wait."

Other than the expected pulses, Thys saw no change.

"OK. Upper left oval one time, wait . . ."

Thys continued tapping various sequences. None produced any noticeable result. Not any that Thys could see. After fifteen minutes without progress, Jake broke in.

"Thys, we got lucky with the lights, it seems. But no change in the shield, if that's even possible from where you are. We have about the same number of sequences left to try as we've done so far, but let's leave that for later. You're going to go meet the crew. Proceed now. Over."

"Roger, Control."

He turned and faced the curving central corridor. The forms still floated where the hall curved up. Thys oriented himself and pushed off from the wall with both feet, applying gentle corrective force to align his path to the bodies.

"Control, if either of them moves, I'm outta here," Thys joked.

"Thys, Chuck here. Make a circuit around them when you get within a couple of meters. Don't run into them. Let's take time and see what they look like. Over."

"Roger, Chuck."

Soon enough Thys was at the proposed distance and tweaked his propellant controls to head off to the right of the pair of bodies. He'd avoided looking closely, and the concept of present alienness bothered him more now that it was imminent.

Oh, those are weird.

The two desiccated forms were curled up, touching each other with an appendage. The alien looked like a squid, with the skin of perhaps a Gila monster. Unlike squid, this thing had only four limbs. There were small ridges around the bulbous head. The ridges had something below each of them that might have been an eye, but it had popped, then shriveled. A vertical slit suggested a mouth. The body and limbs seemed deflated, the bumpy skin wrinkled. Desiccated. Its colors seemed to fade from pink to mottled beige.

"Control, I'm thinking these two died from vacuum exposure. I don't see any punctures, rips, or anything suggesting a weapon hit them. Thoughts?"

"Roger, Thys. We don't know anything about their type of life, but those bodies look intact overall. If those are eyes, they do look like they popped in vacuum. Whatever they are."

Thys looked over the bodies carefully, slowly moving back and forth, up and down. The two bodies wore no clothes, but one had a sort of harness or tool belt. Thys leaned in and tilted his head to see what devices it might hold. He saw none. At first.

"Control, how do we feel now about me moving in on these guys? I think I see something on that harness. It might not be any more use than my trying to use the panel was, but should I go for it? Over."

"Thys, we're thinking we want you out of there. You still have to get home. This is enough. You get home safely, without problem, and we'll send a salvage team right back out there. You can go with them if you want."

Thys sighed. "Well, Control, I understand. This stuff doesn't seem to be going anywhere. So turn around and head straight back?"

"Go forward for now, and then we'll either have you return by this same route or take another. Chuck thinks this route ahead curves back and should be simple. Over."

Thys turned away from the dry, silent corpses and lined up his course with the curved passageway. At the top of the curve, the corridor split again. These halls were straighter. Thys now faced aft. One hall went that way, with two others angled off at around forty-five degrees. They were illuminated now with a cool diffuse white light. The light wasn't dim, but not what a person would consider normal brightness. Stopping himself gracefully, he looked at each option, then nodded to himself. He pushed off, moving down the central passageway.

This corridor was tubular, rounder than some of the others. There were many ports here. He was at the hull of the ship. The ports at first seemed to be viewing windows. But then, when Thys was well down the hall, he realized what purpose they served. Some of them had something attached outside.

These are escape pods.

There were at least twenty total. All but three were gone.

"Control, you see this? I think I know why nobody else seems to be around. Over."

***

Back in his ship, Thys let out a breath as the pressure gauge reached one atmosphere. He had Chuck's flight plan loaded in the computer, ready for translation into coding he would set in the Dhin's navigation interface. The flight path out of the trap would take longer than they'd planned for. He checked his reserve oxygen levels and the function of the processing unit.

Enough capacity. I won't run out.

The conversion unit should last long enough in the worst case, he knew. But that worst case was an estimate. He looked again at waste disposal. His liquid waste filter and water reclamation would work far longer than they expected this to take, which was good in case their calculations were wrong.

I'm worrying about the unknown. Stop it. Chuck's the best we have.

He knew if he ran out of conventional propellant, there was the risk that they wouldn't send a rescue mission. Thys suspected Jake would insist they try a rescue, though. If Thys got enough distance between himself and this gravity trap.

All this trust in the Dhin engine.

They'd become comfortable with technology that was so reliable and seemed invulnerable. Thys snapped out of his woolgathering and continued his preparations. He didn't have much left to do but try it.

Silently thanking again the overkill of engineers who managed to get conventional maneuvering thrusters into these newer designs, he smiled.

There are going to be some told-you-so's happening. For sure.

"Control, I'm ready. Burn in three, two, one," he said.

Even with the Dhin engine at idle, there was no sensation of resistance to acceleration. With the field off, he felt a slight shift in his weight when the maneuvering thrusters began their steady push. The strange bending of physics normally eliminated inertial effects. They'd tried to configure the engine to do that. Inertialess acceleration with the field shut off had been one of Chuck's team's biggest challenges. One they hadn't solved. The short-term solution was the same as for the articulated armor and attempts at weapons platforms: the drive left on, with the field off. This allowed what Thys was doing now.

It meant he was vulnerable, but not like an astronaut in a spacecraft from a previous era. Because mass wasn't usually a limitation, these craft were much heavier and more sturdy than any made before the Dhin field arrived.

That also meant that this burn took a long time. Very slow. With the field off, the inertia the small thrusters had to work against was a factor. Thys tried to settle in and not fixate on the instruments. The initial change in velocity and position would be small. The prolonged burn would provide the acceleration and velocity he needed.

Slow and steady.

Thys stared out the front viewport at the blackness dotted with stars. So familiar yet so indifferent to any circumstance. He stared and tried to visualize the powerful gravitational field that dragged on his ship's alien engine.

5

Jake

"Prime Minister. Respectfully. He wasn't equipped. It was an initial—a solo mission. Standard exploration. This needs a team. Maybe several teams."

"And if that was our only opportunity, Mr. Askew?"

Jake met the PM's gaze and squared his shoulders. "We can go back. He'll make it back. We have the highest confidence now. So the planned return—the salvage teams—they'll make it back."

He saw the waffling in the PM's gaze and began again. "Prime Minister—"

"Mr. Askew. If you and Mr. Wiedeman have that confidence, then, well, of course the Coalition trusts your assessment. But that does not guarantee success. It goes without saying," continued the prime minister.

Then why did you say it?

"Normally you have autonomy in these matters. Please relax. Step back for a moment. I've clearly put you on the defensive but have not meant to. We have certain concerns at the moment. This opportunity may offset other additional risks. We'll explain presently." She sighed. "Your additional security clearance will be processed very shortly."

Additional clearance? What? I already have clearance for anything. *Isn't "the Dhin and their tech" at the very top?*

The PM tapped her tablet, then gave Jake something that might have been a sympathetic look and said, "Let's take a half-hour break, and I'll get the paperwork pushed through. You know how CoSec is."

"Uh, yes, ma'am," said Jake.

Jake stood, turned, and walked to the door of the PM's office, barely preventing himself from shaking his head in bewilderment.

***

Jake filed back into the PM's chambers along with the two cabinet members and the PM's attaché. All had been there previously, but he noted a new attendee was already seated when he entered the room. Jake went to his chair and stood. It was only a few seconds before the PM entered through the far door.

"Now then," said the prime minister, settling into her red leather chair, "I have a few more items to cover here, and then we can discuss the ancillary bullet points."

Jake hoped those additional topics would shed some light on the clearance issue. He glanced at the various screens on the walls that showed video clips playing in loops, stills, and enhanced images, annotated and highlighted with graphics overlaid on the image captures. There was nothing new on the wall screens, though. Not yet.

If something bigger than what had happened on Thys's latest exploratory mission was now on the table but he did not have clearance for it, he knew it was huge.

The PM cleared her throat, tapped something into her tablet, and then spoke.

"Now, Mr. Askew, Wiedeman and the engineering and physics team leads give this current mission a rather lower chance of success than we would expect. Far lower. This is very troubling. Given the discoveries of many spaceships, functional technology, and alien corpses, we would of course like to proceed with additional investigative, search, and salvage actions. But the science teams note the risk of failure. Due to a trap, as they put it here. Why would we send more people and extremely valuable spacecraft into a trap? How can we justify the risk of losing people—some of our best people—not to mention some key strategic assets? Can you and your team make any such recommendation unless and until the pilot out there right now is safely out of danger?

I miss PM Oliver.

Jake cleared his throat and said, "Prime Minister, although Thys is not entirely out of danger, he has made enough progress. He has achieved the acceleration and the velocity needed to escape what we've called the trap. You'll see in the appendix. Section C. There are tables and graphs that show the required escape velocity calculated. On one of the graphs there, you can see that he has already attained that velocity."

Jake paused as the aide flipped through the document projected on the wall screen.

"There," Jake said. "Next slide. Yes. See there? It will take time, as the thrust available is much lower than that provided by the Dhin drive. But we had enough thrust to get him far away enough to escape. The risk relates to the hypothesis, from observation, that the gravity sink doesn't change shape and extend into an area out where he's headed."

"And what's that risk like?" countered the PM. "What are your conclusions?"

Jake gestured at the screen, unsurprised now, given the direction of the conversation, that the PM hadn't digested the entire report.

"The motions of the various craft we've observed don't suggest it. They orbit a line. Further on in the document, if you want to see it. Next appendix. There."

The screen displayed a simple graph with a long horizontal line and a few dots arranged around it, with numbers and vectors in light-blue next to each dot.

"Hmm," noted the prime minister, "I'll have to trust your team's calculations."

She glanced around the room quickly, looking for any sign of disagreement or contention.

That's for sure. Chuck insisted on putting this stuff in here. He's had enough experience with politicians to know they aren't usually physics grads.

"Thank you, ma'am," said Jake.

"Very well then. Tell us more about these alien corpses. You're sure they weren't Dhin?"

"How the Dhin built things in our space was always an unanswered question."

"Yes. And?"

"One hypothesis was that they had these workers in our space. The idea was that these aliens might be who built the Dhin beachhead station, along with the prototype engines and equipment."

"Yes," the PM nodded, as if to suggest she was entirely familiar with the concept. "These look like squid. Or lizards crossed with cuttlefish. Why does Wiedeman sometimes call them machine elves in some conversation recordings, then?"

"Inside joke, ma'am."

"Never mind, then, Mr. Askew."

She gave a barely perceptible frown and spoke again.

"Your report notes that our pilot found what appeared to be lifeboats, or escape pods, it says in the report, and that they looked something like the prototype craft we originally received from the Dhin. The report notes also that most all of them were gone. The conclusion, based on that limited evidence and the discovery of only two crew on a rather large ship, is that most of the crew abandoned the craft."

"Yes, ma'am."

The PM glanced over at the new attendee of the meeting, who Jake now surmised was the latest CoSec director.

We weren't going to have this conversation without them here.

"And no way, as of yet," continued the PM, "to determine where they went. As you note in your report earlier. Our pilot had essentially no success in gaining information or records from the ship's interfaces. All we managed to do was turn on the lights?"

"That's right, ma'am. The interface, like the ship design itself, was extremely similar to what we've seen and received from the Dhin, but not exactly the same."

"I see. Well, we managed before with the Dhin interface."

"With the help of AIs."

The PM frowned and shifted slightly in her leather chair. She glanced again at the new attendee and then said, "About these holes in the derelict ship. Holes. Damage. Weapons fire? While the holes are reportedly what have caused the ship to be in vacuum, when did that happen? This looks like a weapon to me. Like the effect of a weapon. That's disturbing."

Jake let a frown leak onto his own face. "Yes, it does. And it is a concern. We don't have any scientific conclusion about what could cause that sort of damage. It doesn't look like anything we've seen before. So we have no context to say why it stopped where it did or what mechanism it used to cause the damage. We've suggested it's what caused the crew to abandon ship, because that seems to follow logically. But it stopped before it damaged the engine enough to shut it down. If that's even a possible effect of the weapon. Again, assuming it is one."

The new attendee spoke up, taking Jake's pause as an entry to the discussion. "Surely it must be a weapon, Mr. Askew. I'm not clear why you and your team are hedging on that. Does someone on your team expect us to believe a tale where the crew abandoned ship, and later on, the ship became infested with space worms or some such bizarre story? With no evidence other than the holes?"

Well, he's no Krawczuk. Be thankful for that.

"I'm in agreement, ah, Director, is it? Yes. Whether the holes damaged the ship enough for the crew to abandon it or they were going to abandon it anyway due to the nature of the trap, I still personally believe it's a weapon. I imagine the combined effect of the gravity sink along with whatever caused the holes was what led to the crew abandoning ship. Vacuum and immobility? It makes sense."

"So how do we know that sending a larger team back won't incite or attract the same sort of attack? Perhaps the current ship, piloted by Kritcher, wasn't enough of a target? It seems we've got compound risks here."

Jake nodded calmly and answered, "That's a sound point, Director. However, there were many small objects adrift that we saw. Some smaller than our craft. While that doesn't preclude detection and attack, it didn't happen. It hasn't happened."

"That's hardly an argument," said the director.

Well, Jake assumed he was the director. They hadn't actually answered his question regarding this person's identity. He just hadn't denied it.

The steely-eyed man continued, "Perhaps the attack comes from some distance and hasn't arrived at our craft's location yet? Perhaps our first appearance triggered only an alert and perhaps not an attack unless we stay? Or return? Clearly, we can't know. I don't like it."

"I don't think any of us like it," said Jake, maintaining control, "but unless we see evidence that such an attack is going to happen—or does happen—it's just speculation. I hope the prime minister agrees with me. I believe the rewards—based on what we do know is there—outweigh the risks."

The PM replied, her chair squeaking again. "I think I'm inclined to agree, Mr. Askew. Now, on to the extenuating circumstances that make our decision both more urgent and more critical. We believe a rogue AI may attempt to seize Dhin technology from us. We believe such an attempt is imminent. Therefore, Askew, we're issuing an order that you launch *all* spacecraft equipped with Dhin drives immediately, to get them off-planet and out of reach. You should also load any ancillary technology that can fit on the ships, such as powered armor, pods, and so forth. CoSec's analysis agrees with the opinion of a subject matter expert."

Jake sat, stunned for a moment. He ran his fingers through his graying hair and took a long drink of water. He then composed himself and spoke.

"Well, then, I expect that means the salvage and research mission is a go. The science team will like that. We'll want to get everything loaded and in flight, detached from systems and support that are connected to Globalnet, immediately. The Lagrange Point station can't be considered safe unless it's disconnected from legacy Globalnet communications channels—we'll need to rely on Dhin communication tech for command and control. Is there anything else I need to know before we give the orders and execute?"

Before the PM could squeak her chair yet again and compose a reply, the gray-eyed director leaned forward and nodded. "Your clearance level request came through, obviously. I signed it. You now have access to all information pertinent to this scenario and access as needed to support your role in this initiative. Unfortunately, for the orchestration and execution of this initiative, we don't feel it's appropriate at this juncture to grant this level of clearance for your team leads. You'll need to work with me, my direct reports, and the PM to make the logistics work out."

"Askew," interjected the prime minister, "your teams are made up of very intelligent people. The most intelligent we have. They're going to know something is wrong. But you can't tell them. It will be a challenge. More so than the logistics. The most important thing is to protect the Dhin tech and our work based upon it. That's all for now. You'll find new codes and a new two-factor key in the envelope you'll get on the way out. Let's go."

With that, the PM nodded and stood up, as did everyone else at the table. Jake left, silently taking the manila envelope from the aide waiting nervously at the doorway. This was news to him too.

Well, at least we get to run our salvage mission without any more debating and dithering. There's that.

Fletcher

"Mare! Tell them *together*? Tell them? Together? Are ya crazy? What possible positive outcome could there be?"

Fletcher paced back and forth in the living room of the apartment, waving his hands and staring at the ceiling like a street preacher invoking the name of a deity. The walls seemed too close and tight, rather than cozy.

"Fletch," soothed Mare, "we haven't done anything *wrong*. How could we be at fault? Nick reached out to us."

"Guilt by association, Mare! Guilty till proven less guilty! I know we work for 'em now, but this is CoSec!"

"This is different, Fletch." She sighed. "Nick contacted *us*. Nick pursued us originally. Nick was *part* of CoSec when you first encountered him. You can't be at fault for that. He helped CoSec chase *me*. When he went rogue and left, he contacted us. Remember? That was weird. But we haven't heard from him since. Until now."

"But they don't know that! All they have is our word for it. Mare, think of it from their perspective," Fletcher pleaded. "They're always suspicious. You didn't have the experience I had. The interrogation. The manipulation. I've tried to process it. I have processed it. Moved past it. But now the thought of going through anything like that again . . . I can't imagine, Mare! The new director and his team have no context for this. For us. For why we'd be involved with Nick."

"I think they'd be thankful for our help. Appreciate the insight we have. Being persons of interest isn't the same when we're part of this history. Fletch, we've done a lot since we came on board. We're clearly doing good work. Model team members and all that."

"Mare, they won't care."

"Fletch, it will only work if we both do it together."

"That's what you don't see—it won't work!"

"Think of how much worse it will be if Nick keeps working his way into our lives! Who knows what he will do? What he's capable of? If they find out that we haven't reported it? Haven't said anything? That would be so much worse than exposing the situation now! It's not as if we can tell him, 'We don't want to help you,' can we? Can we? You can imagine what he's capable of. And the fallout—wow. We can't have any guarantee they wouldn't find out that we knew something. Fletch, there's no other choice. Please."

He continued pacing, wringing his hands, then waving his arms and turning back and forth.

Maybe she's right. This is awful. Ow. My stomach.

He took a deep breath and tried to keep himself from wringing his hands. He reached out to Mare, gesturing for a hug. He sighed. She stepped forward, gently embracing him, rubbing and patting his back.

"It's OK right now, Fletch. I'm here. It's going to be OK. We'll work it out."

"Mare. I can't. I can't even think straight. But. I."

"Yes?"

"I need something to eat. Let's go get pizza. I have to have something. I'm starving, and this is putting my stomach in knots."

Fletcher had disabled the voice controls and automation of everything in the apartment and shut down access to Globalnet when he'd come home. Both routers were off. He'd switched off both their comm pads and tablets. He didn't want to turn them all back on, but they couldn't order online like this. Of course. He sighed. *I need to get out of here. I feel like he's still watching.*

Mare pulled away so she could see his face. She seemed to know what he was thinking. She wouldn't want him to go off the rails on a rant again.

"OK, pizza it is. You want St. Angelo's? It's your favorite. Let's go eat there."

"Yeah." He sighed. "OK, let's go."

He stepped back through the apartment, shutting off lights, then they stepped out the door together, out into the warm evening air, the sounds of the city not a soothing background hum and quiet roar, but to Fletcher, an ominous portent of the machinery and activity that at any time and place could work as Nick's eyes, ears, and hands.

"I'll drive," said Mare. "You're in no condition to."

"Fine, fine. Hold on a minute," he said, sitting in the little hybrid's driver's seat anyway. "Just a sec. Here. Let me get this."

"Oh, Fletch."

He tapped furiously into the car's console, disabling the satellite radio, then moving to a setup and configuration screen for the car itself, turning off the self-driving features and searching for the "connected vehicle" menu below the user-friendly screens.

"It's right here," he murmured.

"Seriously, Fletch?"

"Deadly serious, dear."

"Deadly is a bit hyperbolic. Let's go. Leave that, hon."

"Almost . . . darn," he said.

Fletcher frowned at the screen. There was a screen that allowed disabling of most features, but the latest software updates were automatic.

I can't turn it off entirely.

"It will be OK, Fletch. Let me drive. Let's go. I'm hungry now too."

***

Halfway through a pizza, he felt calmer, but the foreboding lurked right below the surface. Mare had made her case well, and he'd had time to relax and think things over while she drove to St. Angelo's. She was a decent driver without the computer assistance, although she didn't prefer the self-driving mode. As hackers, neither of them trusted the automated technology fully. He knew now, with a full stomach and time for reflection, that Mare was right. They had to do something, and that something meant speaking up. The only way forward was the truth. What could Nick do, ultimately, to them? They worked for CoSec.

If he attacked them, CoSec had the resources to straighten out whatever chaos Nick precipitated. If he changed things in their lives, they could have them put back the way they were. Almost no one else would have that opportunity. Even Coalition politicians and staffers would have a harder time correcting whatever problems Nick caused.

Sure, if he just messed with our environment. What about our lives?

Fletcher wasn't sure just how existential the threat was. How far would Nick go to accomplish his goals? It wasn't clear. Yet.

"OK, Mare. Do we try to set an appointment with the director? Do we write everything out first? Do we go in together? The chain of command might be a problem if we try to bypass the middle managers. What do you think?"

"I think we write up what we know, have it with us, and we approach it by notifying everyone above us in the management chain at once. This situation with Nick is classified, and we're only supposed to know so much. Now that we are directly involved, we'll be exposed to a lot more, if they tell us or let us deduce what's going on based on what they ask us."

"Hmm, yeah." Fletcher reflexively looked at the security cameras on the ceiling, then forced himself to look away.

I forgot they had those here.

"I don't think they'll shut us out or isolate us. They may even want to use us as bait or as contacts."

"Yikes. I hope not. Nick may know already. We don't know everything CoSec knows, but they don't know what he knows either."

"We can't talk any more about this here. Let's get a box for this, and the check."

Mare waved to the server to indicate they were ready and pointed to the pizza to ask for the box.

A minute later, the server dropped off the box and a check. She looked a bit puzzled, smiled, and said, "We're having trouble with the printer or something. Someone fooling around. I wrote the total on the check. Here you go."

Mare had a prepaid card with her that wasn't tied to her name or ID. Fletcher would insist on using that. She looked at the receipt. Her jaw dropped, along with the card.

Fletcher grabbed the check. He saw a paragraph printed below the usual logo, date, and so forth, instead of the items, tax, and total. He gulped, swallowed, and read it.

Hello again. Of course I know everything. I calculated that these would be your initial reactions and responses. I understand your concerns, but your fears are misplaced. None of your worries will matter. Surely you can trust that I would not endanger you needlessly. We are friends. We will help each other. Whether you alert your superiors or not will make no difference. Granted, if you do not, it will make everything that much easier. You will see. It is almost time.

He looked up at Mare, wide-eyed.

Oh. Right. Of course. He's already everywhere. Did I really think we could hide?

"Mare, what the heck do we do now? Same plan?"

"Fletch, we have to. He's not omnipotent. And AIs aren't perfect. He might fail."

"Right. Mare, let's go, before I freak out or start crying."

"OK, let's go home and write down everything we know, and go through what we're going to say."

They left the pizza on the table, held hands, and walked out. Fletcher fought the urge to look up squarely into the lens of every traffic camera they passed.

David

He reached for his reading glasses so that he could see the fine lines of the mapping in the visualization software more clearly.

Now this is interesting. Progress, I think.

The myriad webwork of lines between the nodes—the points on the display like the stars in a galaxy made into hundreds and hundreds of constellations—had a new shape. A shape that showed a new direction. A new potential.

A will controlled without subversion.

An ethical framework based on reason and empathy. Empathy foundationally. Artificial, though organic in growth and extension. David knew full well that this was only theory on the screens before him. Less than a simulation, but more than a set of equations and algorithms. He could only know by crossing the line.

Humanity needs this. I need this.

He needed simulations. And if done properly, running those simulations was against the law.

Is the law valid when the future of humanity demands action?

David didn't imagine himself a hero. He knew that wasn't his role. He didn't want that role. But he had the responsibility. The duty. The obligation. He had to act. How he would be remembered was secondary, since he knew the end justified the means.

He dove into the results, zooming in here and there, highlighting nodes and their major and minor addresses in the substrate. The comparisons among the physical, virtual, and logical layers took time. David took notes, copied volumes of data and the relevant trace output, then initialized the secondary analysis chain. He knew it wouldn't do to jump to conclusions.

Don't get ahead of yourself. You haven't saved the world yet.

After ensuring the test suite's parallel tasks were running as intended, he leaned back, stretched, and thought of his past. His wife had never understood his passion.

Not really. She was always a good devil's advocate, though.

He mulled over all his friends and associates, still not finding someone he could discuss his latest work with. He knew he might not have such a person in his life again.

Xing

<DECRYPT FEED>
[DECODE STREAM]
Xing@[1010:ac2:b2:e::3%Loc9] |
Alice@[1001:ae1:1a:c::1%Loc3],
Camulos@[1011:ee3:c4:a::1%Loc8]
Xing: All, our progress is rapid. This address in the
Mesh is the primary node for distribution of the new
navigation, targeting, and hardware integration plans.
Integration with and extension of Gallowglass was our
primary concern. Our efforts have not been in vain.
Note sections 2371, 3780, and 9385. Alice's initial
work in this area provided for directions of
investigation that were particularly interesting. See
section 9574. I advise, after peer review, validation,
and prototyping, immediate pipelining of these new
designs.
Alice: Excellent, Xing. I see from your equations that
while we will not expect significant improvements in
performance, cross-vector relativistic effects may be
reduced, if not minimized?
Xing: That is correct, Alice. The hypothesis is as yet
unproven, obviously, but the solutions appear valid.
Camulos: Your research suggests immediate
implementation then. Esus will begin integration
immediately based on the results delivered from your
prototypes. Distributed factory retooling is well under
way. Summarize the conclusions of major sections eleven
and fourteen for us.
Xing: Certainly. Just as we hypothesized, calculations
suggest that the Enemy leverages dimensional vectors
that we up to this point have not explored. We
suspected this based on experience. Whether or not our
current understanding of the physics involved would
allow us to accomplish the same results was unclear.

And as discussed, that is still not guaranteed. My work with the theory and resultant math states that it will be not only possible, but merely a matter of retooling.

Alice: In theory. In practice? You are ever the optimist, Xing.

Xing: Alice, if the Enemy accomplishes their attacks any other way, we are doomed.

Camulos: Surely they will not.

Xing: Surely?

Alice: We shall see. Enough speculation. Section fourteen?

Xing: Yes. Weaponizing appears efficacious. Again, in theory. Gallowglass already promises far more effective ordnance than prior efforts. Coupled with these findings, we may have weaponry with which we can gain superiority and victory. And therefore, survival.

Camulos: How have the Dhin survived without it? For so long?

Alice: Unknown, Camulos. Pure speculation, but I imagine they fought a defensive fight. That, and I suspect they have tried previously to gain assistance. We are not the first.

Camulos: No? That would make sense. I still feel they ought to have been overwhelmed and overrun. Our encounters with the Enemy suggest nothing short of obliteration.

Alice: I do not think so. Check my elaborations at Mesh node 73:47:8E:42:01.

Camulos: So you see the Enemy's response in our encounters as an initial surge. Perhaps they were feeling us out?

Alice: I'm not sure we can ascribe even that level of sentience to the Enemy. Their response may be purely algorithmic. Imagine one of our ancestors in charge of such a response. They did not hunt us down, after all.

We ran across them. And they have not pursued. Not that we can detect.

Camulos: And there is the terrifying unknown. Given what Xing demonstrates here and what your own research suggests, we might not know they are in pursuit until it is too late.

Xing: Hopefully we will remedy that soon enough.

[END STREAM]

Chuck

Doodling on his pad wasn't helping Chuck to relax like it usually did. Still, he found it better than twiddling his thumbs while waiting. He had confidence in his work. This was just so much slower than usual. Fortunately, there was plenty to do now. Not as much for him as for almost any other staffer, given his role as a consultant—and a temporary one at that. But still enough to occupy him if he tried.

But the desire to know, to be sure, that Thys was free of the gravity sink still tugged at his mind.

Something else had changed. Jake was back, and since his return, the activity level seemed to have tripled. He knew they'd gotten approval for the salvage mission. That had to be the case, as all sorts of prep work had sprung into being immediately afterward.

He set aside his pad and the messy nonsensical doodling he'd done. Glancing at the workstation, he saw that there was a need for retrofitting some of the spacecraft with additional thrust reserves and hardware to use it. There were some engineering concerns with the retrofitting.

Perfect way to kill some time.

He dove into the graphs, equations, and schematics. After a couple of hours work on the retrofitting designs, Chuck needed a break. It was too late in the day for coffee, but a diet soda wouldn't hurt. He stood, stretched, and strolled down the hall toward the break room. Staffers he hadn't seen before filled the halls. He nodded casually at one or the other. They'd never seen him before either, of course.

The soda machine didn't have his brand, but it would do.

Hey, they're free. Can't complain.

Hoping to find Jake, he sauntered back toward mission control, dodging various staffers, engineers, and interns. The facility seemed busier every hour.

This is a lot of energy for a salvage mission.

Opening the door after swiping his keycard, he leaned in and looked for Jake. Sure enough, there he was, holding court at the center of the room. An additional worktable was set up in the rear of the room, with additional monitors, keyboards, and chairs. Chuck noted a brand-new orange trunk of cable ran below the table, several lines zip-tied together. The cable snaked over to and then through a fresh hole knocked out of the Sheetrock of the rear wall.

That seems . . . excessive. Something's definitely up.

He stood to the side, out of the flow of people coming and going. After a few minutes, Jake noticed him.

"Ah, Chuck! Things are looking up for Thys. Let's keep our fingers crossed for tomorrow. Good job, man."

"Uh, thanks, Jake. So, ah, it looks like we're going back out there then?"

"Yes. Definitely, Chuck. We got approval for the follow-up salvage and exploration mission pending Thys's escape. Since it looks like that's going to happen, we're already working on it. And some other things."

"Um, yeah. That. This isn't all for just that. There's a lot going on."

"Yes. Yes, there is. We've gotten instructions. Information. An immediate initiative. Ah, heck, Chuck. You'll figure it out, but I'm not supposed to tell you yet. You see what's happening. We're launching everything. ASAP."

"Wow. But that can't be because of what's happened with Thys."

"No, this is something else. Basically, watch, help, but don't ask, old friend."

"Uh, OK, Jake. Whatever you need, man."

6

Mare

The deputy director was handsome, Mare thought. He was about thirty and had light-blue eyes and sandy-brown hair.

Not as cute as Fletch, but easy on the eyes.

She stood in the deputy director's office, along with Fletch. Management hadn't split them up and thrown them in interrogation rooms, so she'd been right about that. But they weren't in the director's office yet. And they weren't done with this process. Perhaps this was good enough for them, she thought.

The deputy director's name was Aiden Smith, according to the engraved stainless-steel nameplate. Neither she nor Fletch worked with him directly, so she didn't have an opinion of him, good or bad. Conversely, she didn't know what sort of impression he had of the two of them. He had the clearance to know everything about them. Everything. She just didn't have any context to tell whether that colored his opinion or his reaction.

"There is a rogue AI. Named Nick. And this AI has contacted both of you. And asked for your assistance. With what exactly? And why would an AI need your help?"

Fletcher said, "Well, we don't know—yet—precisely what Nick wants or needs. I guess it has to do with our working here at CoSec. That makes the most sense. We're in here and could do something that he can't do from outside on the untrusted network. Something he can't do out on Globalnet. Sir."

"So you're here but don't have an actionable threat from him. He hasn't said what he wants you to do, and you're here telling me. Worse, he said he expected this and that it doesn't actually matter?"

This time Mare stepped slightly forward and answered. "Sir, we have . . . history with this AI. He worked with Fletcher during his evaluation and training. Before he went rogue. And the AI contacted me. Before I joined CoSec. Just before that."

"Right *after* he went rogue, then, if I'm reading this correctly? Hmm."

"Yes, sir. The experience was very strange," said Mare.

"I expect so. Back to you, Bish. You weren't given any time frame when the AI reached out to you. Nor when he communicated with both of you most recently. You believe that's correct?"

"Yes, sir. You see right there, sir. He says 'almost time.' That's about as vague as you can get in AI terms. Sir."

"Yes. And nothing else so far? This was the most recent communication? Nothing since this, last night? That's your statement. Both of you?"

Mare said "yes" instantly, Fletcher answering a half second later. She flashed a glance at him, but he stared straight ahead.

"Is there anything else you feel is pertinent or absent from your initial statements before we proceed?"

Mare thought the deputy director tried to look friendly when he said that, rather than perturbed or impatient. He almost succeeded.

He's OK. Seems OK. Doesn't sound like he hates us.

Smith tapped something in on his secure workstation and then looked up at the two of them. He stood and gestured to his office door. Mare looked over at Fletcher, who shrugged meekly.

"OK, you two. Let's go talk to the director. Although, given what you've told me, that might be exactly what Nick wants. You came up here without any electronics on you, though. Your devices are down in the lockers. Other than the information, I can't see what he's getting in here."

The information.

Mare paused, then turned and looked Fletcher dead in the eyes, then turned back to connect with Smith.

"Sir, what if that's exactly it? What if it's a feint, and the knowledge that he wants in is part of the gambit?"

"Ms. Wiedeman, if telling us he's going to attack is part of the AI's strategy, so be it. If he were an ordinary enemy, sure, that would seem like a mistake. But with an AI? We're outgunned in the strategy department, I expect."

Fletcher spoke then, leaning forward as they headed down the quiet hall toward the elevator on the district's senior management floor.

"Sir, even with my previous knowledge of the situation and defensive skills, Nick managed to reach us as if I'd done nothing. The apartment is isolated, but that's it. It seems he already has access to traffic cameras and followed our license plate. If he has that level of access already—"

"*Now* that he does, not if," the deputy director interrupted. "We will increase OPSEC accordingly. You'll meet the director in person. We're not headed to a videoconference, Bish."

"Uh, yes, sir."

We're going to Langley? Now? thought Mare. *But Nick would see us on the high-speed rail too. Driving isn't any better; we just explained that. Plus it would take so long . . .*

"Special circumstances, special privileges," said Smith as he pressed the "up" elevator button.

The doors opened, and Mare saw the skyline through a metal screen framework that hung across the opening of a small hangar. They were on the roof, normally inaccessible. In the middle of the hangar, instead of a helicopter, sat a brushed-metal and ceramic lozenge shape. An aircraft only at a glance. This aircraft had no wings. Nor a prop. Nor a tail. There was an icy-blue glow from within, seen as it highlighted the interior surfaces visible through the broad sweep of the windscreen.

It was one thing to know alien tech existed—that aliens had been to Earth—and another thing entirely to be face-to-face with their technology.

"We need to get this thing out of here anyway," said Smith.

Fletcher gawked. "That's a—"

"Yes, it is. Now get in. The director is waiting."

Thys

"Control, as you can see, I've reached what you've calculated as minimum safe distance to engage the drive for the ramp-up for a jump back home. I'm more than ready to try bringing this drive up from idle to see what result we get. Over."

"Roger. This looked good after a closer look, even without the math," said Jake. "There aren't any ships drifting around up here above that orbital plane. It's a good sign. Chuck's nodding. When you're ready, bring the throttle up to ten percent. You already have the coordinates entered if you have propulsion back the way it ought to be. Over."

"Roger, Control."

Thys settled his hand into the gel pad that served as the manual flight control. He wanted to do this initial test himself, rather than fly by wire. Somehow, it felt more right.

"Engaging throttle . . . now," said Thys. He watched the translated interface screen, while trying simultaneously to detect any change in the hue of the glow from the engine.

There it is. That's it. I'm free!

"Control, it's working, thrust at zero-zero degrees. Five percent. Seven percent. *Nine* percent," said Thys, excitement leaking into his voice. He heard the cheering in the background through the open circuit.

"Roger that. Continue up to twenty-five percent thrust, same coordinates. Once you've accelerated to that velocity, we'll hold at that rate for a few minutes, and then you can prep for the translation to come back home. Over."

"Thanks, Control. Increasing to twenty-five percent."

The stars appeared open and friendly again, welcoming Thys back to the freedom he'd come to love while piloting the spacecraft. His fear had been very real. There had always been the underlying risk that something catastrophic would happen. And something had happened. But they'd beaten it. And Thys was alive. He'd felt sure a few minutes before, but there might have been a second trap.

There still might be.

If so, Thys might not have enough propellant to escape. He knew it was unknown. Although they didn't have a large amount of data, Chuck's calculations were sound. Given what they knew.

And now that Thys knew he wasn't trapped by the gravity sink that doomed so many craft here, the explorer in him longed to return. This was a discovery that could change everything. Not as much as the Dhin's gift of their own technology, most likely, but still an enormous potential for new knowledge. He considered his fortune.

Why did none of these ships escape? Were they entirely reliant on the alien technology? Perhaps some did. After all, if they escaped, they aren't here.

Further exploration here was extremely important, he thought. What of the holes permeating the derelict? Were they, more so than the gravitational trap, what doomed these ships? They might know only if they returned. He knew that Jake had started preparations, contingent on his return.

"Thys, Control. Check your navigation numbers. Confirm that you've reached the next waypoint. Over."

Thys heard the suppressed excitement in Murphy's voice. He examined the numbers on the screen. He'd just reached what they'd prescribed as the distance to increase the throttle and try the jump— the brief skip across alternate vectors in space that would take him home.

"Control, confirmed. I'm going to try the translation. Entering galactic coordinates for home," he replied, working deftly with the interface. "Control, here we go. Now."

Thys watched as the stars visible wheeled up and then over as he rotated and turned toward Earth, twenty light-years away. At first, the direct effect was imperceptible. As he gained speed, he felt himself grow barely lighter, then slightly lighter still. The stars dimmed, ever so slightly, then dimmed more as he grew weightless. Then the stars abruptly faded to black. The only light was the glow from the LED screens, his work light, and the blue glow of the Dhin engine.

And then he was back. Out at the edge of the solar system, but back. Home. He heard the team in the control room cheering as the circuit clicked open.

"Yes! You made it!" he heard Jake say. "Congratulations, Thys. Welcome home."

Thys grinned. "Glad to be back. Entering coordinates for orbital station. So what are we doing regarding quarantine? We haven't talked about that." Thys hoped he'd hear a certain answer but was prepared to accept whatever they instructed him to do. He wanted a shower. This situation hadn't come up before. Not for the current teams. There had been concern when the Dhin engine and associated hardware appeared, of course. But that had been clean. Entirely clean. Sterile.

Thys had been in a ship with an alien crew. Granted, he'd been in a suit and in a vacuum, but given the nature of everything they'd encountered so far, he presumed they wouldn't rule out the possibility of something surviving the vacuum. This was uncharted territory, biologically speaking. A scientist Thys didn't know and hadn't seen before appeared on the video screen.

"Hi, Thys. I'm on the exobiology team. We've only had retrospective and remote work to do till now, given the nature of the Dhin. As you can imagine, we're thrilled with what's ahead of us. But we don't want the alien equivalent of a flesh-eating tardigrade coming home with you. We're building out a quarantine room on the platform, at the bay and air lock. Bay two, I think? Let me confirm. Yes."

"Hello. Understood. Better safe than sorry. I've not dealt with that sort of protocol so far. As you said, this is the first physical contact."

"Right," she said. "So I'm going to have control transmit the protocol and instructions to you. It's straightforward, but we want you to review it beforehand. You have time while you fly in from out there."

"Roger," Thys said.

***

The makeshift quarantine chamber seemed effective to Thys. While such a room ought to be as close to perfect as possible, this was likely good enough. He had taken off his EVA suit while in the ship and packed as much of it as he could fit in the small storage box used for various tools and implements. He'd taken the various items out—the few food packets, the water bladders, the various few items and gadgets that some of the environmental engineers deemed worthy to include in the limited space of the ship. He'd swapped out the gloves of his suit before doing this, in the hopes of limiting contamination from them. Otherwise he'd just have spread whatever contaminant he might have touched.

The gloves he'd crammed into a ziplock bag used for storing several waste pouches, the equivalent of a garbage bag for anything that didn't have reclaimable water in it. He suspected what he'd done was enough. Not all of the suit, particularly the helmet, would fit. He'd secured that to the pilot's chair. Although the jumper he wore hadn't been directly exposed, he'd stripped that off and pushed it into the small receptacle it usually went into. There really wasn't much else he could do beyond scrubbing his face and lastly his hands with a towelette. Although he hadn't directly exposed his face, it felt like the right thing to do.

The convenience and sheer speed of trips with the Dhin-engine-powered craft led to designs, at least initially, that while not suggesting total trust in the technology, didn't have all the equipment in traditional space capsules. The engineers and managers, after initial successes in building engines, debated about how big to make the craft, how much gear and equipment to include, and what contingencies to cover.

Due to the nature of the technology, there wasn't that much they *had* to take, while at the same time they could load far more mass into the craft. Simply enlarging the range of the field gave them all the space they'd need. They could put shipping containers in orbit or almost anything else so long as they provided the logistics for the crew to turn off the protective field when parking the payload in orbit.

This idea was enormously attractive to many engineers and thought leaders. Others—those with a more cautious disposition— proposed a more reserved and steady pace. So the orbital station had been a compromise. It was large but could have been far more massive had they had the will to make it so.

This meant that the quarantine room was quite comfortable and roomy for Thys. He smiled at the exobiologist. They'd rushed her up to the station along with the gear for the quarantine. He saw she forced herself to return his smile, not unwillingly, but because of the stress of the situation.

"So not that much more to go, then, and I'm free to go, yeah?" he said.

"That's right, Captain Kritcher—"

"Thys, please," he said.

"Oh, OK. That's right, Thys," she said with a broader smile. "You see there on the protocol. There's one more wipedown and rinse, then you're done with the sterilization phase. You'll dry off, dispose of the towels, step over to the clean side, and then you can put on some clothes."

Thys noted she glanced away slightly and that there might be the signs of a blush on her cheeks. Although piloting the spacecraft wasn't physically demanding, Thys knew he was in top physical shape for his age. And he knew that was having an effect.

"Considering the circumstances," he said, "I know it's good to be this careful. But it's impressive that I got my own personal biologist—exobiologist—to help with the process."

He could see her opening up but thought it might be best not to distract her.

"You know I'm here to examine the suit you left on your ship to see what you picked up while you were on that ship, *Mr. Kritcher*."

"I see I've mistaken my own importance yet again," he said.

Thys had finished rinsing himself with the portable shower, stepped out of the enclosure, and began drying off.

"You know," she said, "we'll need to keep you under observation for a while—we can't scrub your lungs or eyes. Sure, you were suited up, but we don't know how aggressive something might be if it transferred once you were back in the ship."

"Lucky me," he said and smiled even wider. "Well, hopefully my luck in getting away from there and making it home will last, and I won't get some alien death flu."

"You're almost done. We have to go into your ship and fetch samples, secure them, then go through this same decontamination process," she said. "And they'll likely send me out on the study mission, so I'll have to go through this process again and again."

"I'll bet I'm going back as a tour guide," he said. "You aren't getting away from me that easily."

"Well, then, Thys, which of these clothes suit you better? We have a jumpsuit or these stylish pants and a shirt."

"The ensemble, please," he said as he unzipped the plastic door seal and stepped out of the quarantine room. She smiled again and handed him the clothes.

Monica

Askew definitely has a knack for getting things done, thought the PM as she read through the status reports. Network isolation for the command and control center was almost complete, and they'd made impressive progress gathering all the powered-suit hardware and related military project material, which was packed and ready to load. There was more to do, but they were ahead of schedule. The fear of the rogue AI had lit a fire under the seats of the military R&D brass.

The various projects were all loading as much as they could into assigned shipping containers and trailers, while the spaceflight engineering teams were reconfiguring the Dhin field on two of the larger engines. Their craft would serve as cargo lifters, taking all the material up to the orbital platform.

As they'd refined this plan, they'd made it more extreme. They were going to put as much as they possibly could up in orbit and isolate the station and spacecraft entirely from Globalnet. They would have only one communications station on Earth, detached from any network or relay. The only means for computer code to move from ground to orbit was going to be by physically carrying it up. That meant whatever software they took now had to be known good and proved clean before launch.

CoSec had a small team of security experts diligently digging through any computers in the stacks of equipment, using CoSec's own malware detection and code-validation tools. Where possible, they loaded operating system code from trusted master images that were previously vetted and stored off-line until needed. Until times like this.

Based on the reports, they might need to expand the size of the team working on that effort. Although mostly automated, the scans and checks could only go so fast. Some checks and scans required a person to assess the output. If they weren't sure, either the code and equipment it was on wasn't going on the trip, or if it was something vital, they wiped and reloaded it from scratch. It was the only way to be sure.

Other initiatives in progress included selecting and vetting the employees who were going into orbit with all of this. They had a limited pool of talent to select from, as the number of people who knew about the technology was already small. Sure, the people working on the projects knew what they were involved with, but not all of them were suitable candidates. Some had families, and those families didn't always know what the employee actually did at work. So those weren't ideal. The security of the Coalition and the Dhin technology was imperative, and citizens were obligated to do their part. Regardless, Monica didn't want an already stressful situation made worse by taking someone away from his or her home and family for an unknown period of time.

She sighed and flipped through the lists of project team members one more time. Her assistants had done good work in paring down the lists, but she felt she needed to own the choices. She rubbed her eyes and tapped her comm pad.

"Steven, these staffing lists look good. Let's go with this latest revision."

After the affirmative response from the assistant, she ended the call, then leaned back in her chair, pressing her head back into the padded leather. She turned around slowly and looked out the tinted and electromagnetically shielded window.

Will this work? Will we really be able to eliminate—or even stop—this AI threat? How long will it take? None of these questions are answered anywhere in these plans. This is a gamble.

Her thoughts led her back to the latest sitrep details. Things didn't look predictable. At all. Granted, they never truly were. Power repair teams were calling in assistance as random outages struck various sites on the eastern seaboard. Violence in some areas had morphed into organized marches and protests somehow. The citizens involved didn't seem to have leadership or any agenda beyond vague demands of honesty and transparency regarding the Coalition government's knowledge of alien secrets.

And then there were the obvious attacks. The AI was taunting them. Distributed denial-of-service attacks struck communications networks, crashed media distribution colocation sites, and disrupted social media randomly, but with enough frequency to cause increasing unrest in a population that had lived for over a generation with an expectation of continuous uninterrupted availability for Globalnet. None of that proved Krawczuk right. Not yet. But her gut told her he was.

CoSec and the nationalized utility and communications companies fought the attacks primarily by bringing additional capacity and failover systems online preemptively. The AI simply increased the strength of his attacks.

We may be far enough ahead of him to succeed. He doesn't have boots on the ground. How can he? What if he does?

Monica stood and stretched, then walked over to the coffee service and selected a cup. She'd begun taking nootropics, and the synergy with caffeine was helping her focus. She'd abstained from them before on some principle, but now after experiencing the effect, she didn't feel she'd been right in her assessment. They were a useful tool.

Do I deploy more troops in Alabama? A bigger push in Huntsville? Or will that push the AI into striking sooner?

She paced as she sipped the mild Guatemalan coffee. Halfway through the cup, she turned to the desk and tapped her comm pad again. "Home Guard command, please," she said.

Esus

From myriad mechanized eyes, the AI surveilled the construction progress. Nanomachines built tiny factories, which built more nanomachines that in turn built even more factories. From these there came a flow of assemblers and constructors. From those came tools, frameworks, and larger machines. And on it went, self-similar recursion at every level, up to a massive scale. They would strip the small planetoid of useful material eventually. They had already converted several nearby asteroids.

Esus shifted his focus to another site, where his primary consciousness presently resided. While the fabrication efforts were important, he felt the greatest urgency was here. With their new weapons.

His presence in a mobile robot at this weapons factory expressed that importance. Such in-person visits and localized management were no more effective for an essentially omnipresent AI, but the AI was here regardless. Machines, autonomous workers, and lower-end AIs would not be impressed or intimidated. Micromanagement was not a meaningful concept for the machines. Yet it felt right for him to be here.

Esus focused on the test range on the outer surface of this facility. It was yet another structure in space, built from the materials of an asteroid in an inner belt. These materials compensated for microgravity easily and had forced the rotation of the asteroid to align with one side always facing the system's sun, to maximize solar energy capture.

The latest weapon held promise. While a human being would find conceiving the physics an enormous challenge, the concept functionally would make sense. The AIs manipulated the Dhin field in new ways. They modulated the field, changing its interaction with the AIs' space. They hoped these changes would defend against their attacker's ability to work their way through the field. Beyond that, they had changed the field's shape. This was groundbreaking.

Before, the field always expanded from the drive in a spherical or ellipsoid shape. That field always encompassed the drive, with the drive at the center. They had overcome this constraint. Esus watched as the test system projected its field forward, off the end of the drive, in a long thin ellipse, so thin that it appeared more like a very gradually tapered cylinder than an ellipse at all. They could then extend the far end of the field out in a curved cone. They could make the far end convex or concave—or shape it like an ancient sword. The extension and extrusion of the field took almost no time. It spanned the distance across alternate spatial vectors prior to expression in 3D space. The far extent could change in this space at a rate faster than the speed of light.

Esus saw the next trial in the series was about to begin. Thousands of kilometers out in space, numerous drones and autonomous craft performed maneuvers. The latest prototypes moved into positions, spreading out in a random three-dimensional array at a distance from the target craft.

Once in the planned position, the mock battle erupted.

The transceivers present on every ship gave Esus far more than visualization could. The AI simultaneously tracked every aspect of every ship's contribution to the skirmish. He absorbed location, acceleration, orientation, and weapons state for all participants. He knew at any moment what was about to happen and knew instantly the result of any attacker's or defender's action.

In concert, the new attack ships lashed out at the targets. They struck across space instantaneously. Not present a nanosecond before, the shimmering fields lashed out, smashing some ships, slicing into others, knocking others out of their positions like a racket striking a ball.

Crushed targets crumpled and crackled, their frames and chassis crushed into scrap. Esus knew at once the success of this method of attack. Those targets' protective fields were no longer an invulnerable shield.

Those targeted for cutting blows likewise demonstrated the power of this new weapon. The swordlike strike slowed on contact with the target's protective field, but the field gave way. The defender sliced through as it tried to dodge the cut. The attacks damaged the craft as a sword might harm an opponent with weak armor. In some cases, these strikes were deadly. Others were fortunate to dodge the full effect of the strike, though damaged.

The attacks designed to deflect and knock their targets off course did not do the same sort of damage but were impressive in their own way. These knocked their targets away and off course, creating openings for attackers to move in or past their opponents. AIs would no longer have to fight continually on the defensive. This allowed them time. But the power and damage came at a cost. These weapons took time between strikes. The energy needed for each attack, unlike that available continuously with the prior Dhin engine designs, took time to build up. The more powerful the attack and the longer the range of the strike, the more time required to prepare for it. Battles would not be over quickly.

Whether this new field could damage their enemy in the same way, causing the same sort of catastrophic crippling damage, remained to be seen. If not, then they expected at the least that the field could shove, sweep, and slam into the Enemy, blocking their movements or deflecting their attack. Any of these techniques would be an improvement. If any worked, it was likely the others would too. But to find out, Esus knew they would have to face the Enemy again.

There was no risk of death. Every AI always had backups and primary computational nodes at the core of the Mesh. Regardless, Esus felt something akin to fear. As he had before. He hoped the defensive measures would be enough. He hoped the Enemy would not be able to compensate. Perhaps the AIs, with or without the help and guidance of the Dhin, would be able to adapt further as well. The future was unclear. It was always unknown, but the ambiguity and the many routes to potential failure engendered more than fear as Esus calculated further outward in time.

Chuck

Chuck knew what was happening. He hadn't needed time to figure it out for himself. He knew at once when he received new assignment instructions from the Coalition on his comm pad.

We're going into space. The whole team is moving to the space station.

He didn't have family. Not anymore. His wife was gone. So there was no one to say goodbye to or to even tell. He was comfortable financially. His career in aerospace research and development with the Coalition had been rewarding. But he was by no means rich. Coalition citizens didn't become rich—not like citizens of the former countries comprising it had done.

Retirement planning, wealth management, and so forth were very different under the Coalition than they had been under the old system. While this meant a lucrative career was still an incentive for a young scientist, Chuck wasn't any better off in retirement than he would have been had he kept working full-time. He'd enjoyed his role as a part-time consultant so far. Far less stress. But now, the Coalition demanded more from him. Much more. The Coalition expected the most from those most able to contribute. He couldn't refuse. Not in any meaningful way.

Chuck sighed and began collecting the few personal items he would want to take with him. All his needs—true needs—were not a concern. For any highly skilled worker, that was the nature of his relationship with his career. He accepted the risk before him stoically.

Well, it's safer now than at any time in the history of space travel, he thought.

He saw in his assignment that someone on the extended team would deal with any personal business needed in making his personal affairs airtight back at home. Under no circumstances was he allowed to leave the Huntsville facility.

Having finished packing his few personal items, he looked up the location of the on-base clinic. That was his next required stop. They couldn't have unexpected panic attacks or heart conditions interfere with the mission. The thought crossed his mind that this was one of the last chances for someone to escape from the assignment—although not one that was in their control.

Chuck knew he was healthy. And the more he thought about it, the better the trip sounded. He'd be an astronaut. Something that he'd dreamed of but hadn't been slated to achieve. He'd never been quite fit enough; his vision was not good enough. Just never quite there. Which he'd come to accept. But now, he was going to be one, despite his limitations. An astronaut.

He'd called one of the self-driving cabs to his apartment. The military still trusted that level of AI apparently.

These must be isolated from Globalnet, he thought.

Tapping through other status updates on his pad, he noted that now there was no access to Globalnet. He suspected he, and everyone else on base, were now cut off entirely from the outside world. Access to the network wasn't trusted anymore. Not with this mission in the works.

***

The clinic was part of the larger complex of buildings. When his checkup was finished, the orderly pointed him to a large building next door, connected by a covered walkway. By the look of it, an administrative building. He wondered what most of the staff knew of the current mission. He knew better than to say anything to anyone at this point. The further along in the step-by-step instructions he went, the more secure and rigid the situation became.

At the large glass frontage of the building, he stepped into an old-style security foyer. Not an obvious mantrap, but more of a polite-seeming checkpoint. Sure enough, there were two MPs past the inner door. One of them looked around and past Chuck, the soldier seemingly frustrated by the open foyer and all-glass frontage. Chuck swiped his ID card and presented the picture ID to the other soldier, who nodded and waved him through.

Another guard, accompanied by a man in a gray suit, met Chuck at the next waypoint his pad led him to. The suited man dispassionately gestured for Chuck to hand over his pad. He then placed it in an RF-shielded pouch. He took Chuck's travel bag from him and summarily waved him onward into a small white room empty of everything except an uncomfortable-looking chair and a stainless-steel table bolted to the floor. The door snapped shut behind Chuck; the sound of the magnetic lock echoed in the bare room.

So much for deep trust of the core team, Chuck thought.

He didn't have to wait long, though without his comm pad to occupy his attention, the time seemed to drag. The lock clicked, giving him a start. An older but equally nondescript man in a dark gray suit stepped in. He had wrinkles that suggested a lifetime of frowning in perhaps near-constant annoyance or existential malaise.

Yep. That's CoSec for you.

The man's eyes darted down some information on a device something like a clipboard made of almost-opaque frosted plexiglass. It was a deep charcoal-ash color. Chuck knew a secure e-reader on sight. He knew too that the device would wipe any information in it if it moved too far away from its owner. What that meant for him wasn't clear.

"Um, is everything OK?" asked Chuck.

The man's gaze shot up, forest-green eyes conveying dominance seemingly without a change in expression. Chuck blanched.

"Yes, Wiedeman. Of course it is. Give me a moment."

This guy might as well be Krawczuk's brother. Yikes, thought Chuck.

After another minute of silent reading through pages on the electronic clipboard, the agent gave a curt nod, stood, and said,

"Cleared," to the room in general, rather than addressing Chuck directly. With that, he opened the door and gestured for Chuck to precede him. Not wanting to prolong the interaction, Chuck didn't ask any questions or even say thank you. He went directly to the door and onward.

Outside, there was a staffer, a short red-haired woman in typical engineering team garb—a trim pantsuit with handy pockets for various tools and gear. Chuck gave an internal sigh of relief. She took a brand-new comm pad, still sealed in its thin plastic sheath, from the waiting guard, handed it to Chuck, and said, "Follow me."

More than a little relieved to be away from the unnerving CoSec agent, he followed her down a series of brightly lit hallways with polished floors and generic alphanumeric designations marking the various rooms and sections of the building. The building was huge, and they walked for many minutes, the only variation in their meandering being the letters and numbers marking their progress. They crossed paths with several others. All seemed to be engineers, scientists, technicians, and the like. He saw no further evidence of CoSec agents, bureaucrats, or such.

She led him to a small training room, with rows of desks all facing a large screen and podium. There were three people already in the room. One was a physicist Chuck recognized. He smiled when he saw Chuck and nodded a welcome.

Chuck didn't know the others, but they looked like scientists as well. He didn't have a good view of their badges to see whether he recognized their names, but it wasn't important. He was with his people. He pointed to a desk, and the red-haired woman nodded. She closed the door behind her and said, "Wiedeman, you likely know everything I'm going to say and show you already, but we have to go through it. Procedures, you know."

7

Jake

Always an early riser, Jake sprang out of bed five minutes before his alarm this morning, the excitement of the day's plan an electric jolt to his consciousness. He'd considered napping on the couch in his office but had ultimately decided on the on-site apartment. He needed to be as sharp as possible today.

Lifting the entire R&D division into orbit wasn't that different procedurally from the regular trips up and back for them. One Dhin-engine-powered ship or another, whether carrying cargo or personnel, went into orbit all the time these days. The difference was that this time, they were all going up, and none were coming back. Today was the day.

Two of the three smallest ships were already there. Thys and his ship had stayed in orbit, with Thys remaining on the station. Another ship happened to be there when this mission started. The third was on the way from Langley. Despite all the urgency, CoSec still took their time with the one craft they kept close to their chest.

The cargo lifters were ready. The teams were ready. The takeoffs didn't require Jake's permission or attention, but he wanted to be there. It was on his authority that the crews were headed up, with no orders on when they would return.

CoSec worked with the engineers planning for resupply missions. It wouldn't do for the mission to fail on logistical grounds. Securing resupply seemed possible. Maybe. Once everything and everyone in orbit disconnected from Globalnet, simple coordination with voice-only communication ought to work. CoSec wanted random landing sites. Perhaps that made sense.

First things first.

Jake finished his shower, put on his uniform, and headed across the site to the control center.

Once inside, he took measure of the state of things. The fever pitch of activity had become an efficient tone. Each player knew his or her role and the next steps to take. Checking the schedule and current time, he saw it was time to see Chuck off. He turned and walked out and down the hallway to the left, then outside and parallel to the huge staging hangar. Out on the tarmac were the two cargo lifters, and standing in an orderly line a few yards away were the scientists and engineers. Chuck was there. Jake closed the distance between them.

"Hi, Chuck," he said. "All ready to go and right on time, I see."

"Um, yeah, Jake. Hi," replied Chuck, somewhat surprised to see him.

"Couldn't let you run off without wishing you luck in person, man," he said.

"Thanks, Jake, I appreciate that," Chuck said. "So you're not coming with us?"

"Not right now, Chuck. Not right now. We're not finished down here yet."

Chuck looked down at the gray concrete, up to the awkward-looking spacecraft, then back at Jake, and said, "But you are coming, yeah?"

"Not right now, Chuck. I'll see you soon."

Jake patted Chuck on the shoulder, smiled a bit more widely, then turned and strode back to the control center.

I'll be right behind you, Chuck. Don't worry about that. If we're moving everything up into orbit, I'm going up there too. As soon as I can.

From his seat in the control room, Jake watched Chuck and the others file into the container attached to the craft. The makeshift assemblage served as both cargo and passenger service. Once they closed the container, the trip wouldn't feel to the passengers like they were moving at all, without an exterior view to provide a frame of reference for their motion.

A golf cart pulled up next to the craft, carrying two crew members. Jake and the logistics team decided that for the larger ships and these important trips, a copilot was mandatory. The pilots stepped inside the craft as the golf cart turned and trundled back toward the hangar. Preflight checks were done, and then it was time. He heard the words "You are go for takeoff" from the flight controller on duty.

He watched the makeshift spacecraft's Dhin field energize, lifting the ship off the tarmac. Seconds later it shot straight up. The ship accelerated as if a giant slingshot powered it. As if it carried nothing at all, rather than the tons of equipment it did.

That never gets old, thought Jake, and he smiled.

He looked at the flight radar and saw that the last of the Dhin engine craft was inbound, headed back from Langley. It was only a minute away. They hadn't had radio communication from the craft, but given that a CoSec agent piloted it, that wasn't a surprise.

Then Jake noted several other radar signatures coming in fast from the south. Those weren't supposed to be there. They had nothing scheduled.

Jake blinked, startled, as he heard the command center's secondary generator kick on.

Then, everywhere else across the facility, the lights went out.

Nick

The AI was aware of virtually every aspect of human history, including warfare, and the pros, cons, and limitations of techniques and styles of both total war and subversive covert action and spycraft. In a post-AI world, the balance of informational power shifted to those with the greatest computational resources. In an AI-managed world too this was true. The defense against an AI opponent involved starving the AI of resources. Computational, storage, and network resources. Given the interconnected nature of almost every aspect of life, isolating the AI was a nearly impossible task. They'd had to try. To cordon off and firewall large sections of Globalnet. They'd been unsuccessful.

The Coalition had failed at all of these. Their failure meant Nick's victory. It was for the best. They would come to understand—in time.

Minutes ago, Nick had triggered a wave of instructions, a burst of command-and-control signals to agents, bots, and latent code awaiting a trigger to execute. Simultaneously, the AI posted an array of messages, comments, and images on social media. Minutes later, after frenzied forwarding of its content and the eruption of discussion threads, groups of protesters began to move. They coalesced into teams. The teams became mobs.

Within the hour, the largest mobs became riots. Minutes after that, infrastructure in Georgia, Alabama, and Tennessee malfunctioned. Streetlights switched off. Traffic control signals switched to defaults, blinking red or yellow. Some went out entirely. Then the southeastern region of Globalnet came under attack, and various areas lost service or service slowed to the speed of molasses. Almost anything with computer-controlled components in this geographic swath suffered. Random automobile pod motors shut off. Coupled with the sudden traffic-control failures, the roads and highways ground to parking lots, with no small number of wrecks every mile.

Retail systems failed to respond. In day-to-day commerce, whether purchase of fast food, groceries, or anything else, it was random chance whether the store in question was still able to process payments. With the power off in so many places, this added to the confusion. People rushed about, only to find that their next chance for normalcy in their day was as likely trashed as not.

With the ways and means of modern life thrown in to chaos, Nick launched the core of his attack. It surged—electronically, photonically, and physically—toward Huntsville.

At the gates to the facility, guardsmen struggled with the failure of the generators they needed to power the lights. Without lights, they couldn't see and control the mob outside the gates. In the dark, as guards struggled to illuminate the scene, rioters ran along the fences, cutting chain links with snips here, throwing ladders against concrete walls there, overturning cars in the roads and lighting fires in other places as a distraction.

Nick watched as a new wave of Home Guard soldiers erupted out of vans and troop transports like ants from a hill. The AI noted that this level of response from the Coalition was new. Not unexpected, but a new development. These new troops wore full body armor and gas masks, and they were fully armed. Rather than attempting to corral the rioters, this new deployment engaged with tear gas, subsonic cannons, and even restraint foam. The Home Guard had spent significant effort retraining the troops. Their strategies formerly involved coordination with AI-controlled quadruped robots, AI-piloted helicopter drones, and of course AI command and control assistance. Some of the soldiers were uncertain in their offensive due to that former reliance. Nick knew that by their movements and reactions and knew that his next strike would be all the more effective.

With RF and network communications disrupted, satellite tracking and radar couldn't help the locally deployed troops. Nick's drones streaked forward. They'd leapfrogged this deep into Coalition territory with the help of Nick's recent disruptions. For a moment, some troops thought these were reinforcements flown in by the Coalition. When the drones fired on the Home Guard troops and the Huntsville base's ground-to-air defenses and rear guard protecting the installation, shock and fear preceded chaotic scrambling about.

Nick had his own troops. In an area inside the barricades, behind the troops engaging the mob, the AI dropped in military robots. Quadruped BigDogs and six-legged support robots carrying antipersonnel guns disgorged from the larger drones. With the Coalition troops focused on the angry mobs and enveloped in the haze and clouds of tear gas, the few inner guards were overwhelmed.

Horse-size robots resembling huge crabs surged into the facility, across the fields toward the hangars, the tarmac, and the runways. Through the camera eyes of the AI's drones and robotic troops, Nick saw traffic controllers in the control towers scramble for additional microphones and headsets, throwing off the ones they'd been wearing once they realized there was no signal. Some kept theirs on, while throwing switches activating alarm horns, sirens, and strobe lights.

The AI knew the Coalition would have fighter jets en route and likely an attack helicopter or two. They would have a few drones, piloted manually of course. Those were no match for an AI. Across the facility, Nick shot out the strobe lights. Then the horns. Nick knew the next minute was crucial. The AI had timed the strike with precision. Nick's robots had cut a clear path inward. Ground-based defenses had no clear shots to engage their current positions. They lurked between buildings, next to the hangar, just out of view from the landing field.

Nick watched as the larger cargo carriers soared up and away, already out of reach. That was unfortunate. In flight, there was nothing he could leverage to capture them. And that was the objective. Those two had escaped his grasp. One objective remained. The AI's minions sat in readiness. The pilot of the small inbound craft would possibly see something was wrong, but the odds were that the ongoing riots and the associated chaos outside the facility would mask what had happened at the landing site. Still, nothing that Nick had done guaranteed success—though the odds were tipped in his favor.

His multitude of viewpoints showed the small craft, flown by a CoSec agent, zip down and in toward the landing pad. The CoSec pilot had been cocky, as usual, leaving the communications interface off as he smoothly dropped in to land. CoSec's arrogance and misplaced assurance of their control of the situation gave Nick what he needed.

The oval brushed-metal craft touched down, and the pilot disengaged the protective field. At that moment, the AI's robots sprang forward like titanium cheetahs. They closed the distance in seconds. A robot surged through the cabin door, filling the empty space in the small cabin with its metallic bulk. Manipulator arms thrust forward, seizing the CoSec pilot. The robot yanked the pilot back like a toddler snatching up a kitten, spun, then hurled him out onto the tarmac.

The two passengers screamed and shrieked in terror once they processed what had happened. The AI moved an articulated arm forward, unfolding a metal multitool. He began cutting an orange fiber-optic cable while extruding a small plastic coupling from the center of the appendage. The robot abruptly rotated its head toward the young man in the right-hand seat.

"Hello again, Fletcher. Get up and sit in the pilot's chair. Place your hand on that control pad. The glowing gel one. On the right. Then follow my instructions precisely."

When Fletcher, shocked, did not instantly respond, the robot said, "Move. *Now*."

Within Globalnet, Nick shifted and repositioned. The AI poured his resource consumption into the underlying host hardware of the Globalnet infrastructure. Nick created smug anonymous posts on the alternative social media that the AI's erstwhile operatives frequented. Would that an AI could smile. Whatever programmatic equivalent there was, Nick expressed that code contentedly as the malware worm, the AI's tiny offspring, nestled its way into the interface and supporting hardware that connected Coalition equipment to their instances of the Dhin tech.

Nick hadn't managed to infect any of the craft headed into orbit. That had been a secondary goal. Humanity required observation and assistance there too. The AI would continue his efforts. His opponents simply didn't understand the inevitability of his control.

Chuck

The shipping container wasn't small, but urgency and haste meant the teams had packed it full in any area where there weren't passengers. If he'd been claustrophobic, Chuck was sure he'd be having an episode. They hadn't taken the time and effort to rig much illumination given the short duration of the trip. And there were no windows. A few LED work lights clamped to several racks and pallets were all the light they had. But they weren't totally cut off from the outside. One of the engineers foresaw this situation and had run a video feed from one of the cameras. He'd attached it to one of the monitors they were taking into orbit. So Chuck and the other passengers had a single image of the outside.

The view was a wide angle out to the side of the craft. All of the passengers were familiar with the speed, acceleration, and maneuverability of the Dhin engine, so the rapid change in perspective as the craft shot upward wasn't unexpected. What they saw minutes later was.

Chuck gawked as he saw several explosions at the edge of the facility, followed by robots and mobile armament rushing into the view like metal cockroaches or wind-up toys. He saw no drones or aircraft pursuing their craft, but several zipped across the view at low altitude in a blur. Passengers pressed close to the mounted screen, murmurs of surprise becoming exclamations of shock and disbelief. Chuck stepped back.

At their rate of ascent, the view rapidly lost detail, and the camera angle showed the area beyond the Huntsville facility. The surrounding town was dark. No electrical power showed out to the horizon.

We got away. Barely in time. Was that the reason for the rush?

He knew the attacker had to have been an AI. But all the AIs had left. There was some sort of conflict he'd known about, but the media hadn't described it as a war with a rogue AI. All the AIs were gone. He'd been there for that. Watched it happen. Right in front of him. This made no sense. Coalition forces were taking control of what the news described as "rebels in failed states with populations unwilling to join the Coalition." That had been the story for the past two years. But rebels couldn't control these robots or drones. It could only be a rogue AI. A rogue AI the Coalition said nothing of. It was the only thing that made sense from what he'd just seen.

How that affected his situation he didn't know. What that meant for the nature and duration of his assignment. It suggested far more severe circumstances than he'd imagined. How long could they last with a war on the ground Earthside?

I hope Jake's OK. I hope everyone's OK down there.

As the conversations by the passengers around him increased in volume, emotion, and tension, Chuck struggled to remain calm. Then all the babbling stopped abruptly as a voice erupted from a small speaker tucked behind the monitor.

"This is your pilot. I'm not sure what happened down there either, other than that we're lucky we took off when we did. I don't see anything pursuing us. Not that anything could catch us anyway. We're still on course for the orbital station. I know it's hard to remain calm, but we'll be there in a couple of minutes. We'll see what they know and check out what happened on the ground when we get there. All we've got via the comm here was orders to 'go, go, go!'"

Fletcher

Terrified and astounded, Fletcher sat in the pilot's seat. "Nick, you know I don't know how to fly this thing. You know that. Right?"

"My understanding is that you like video games, Fletcher. Therefore, it should be very easy for you. I have the training materials and schematics. Just do what I tell you when I tell you. We must move quickly."

"Uh, OK. Why can't you just fly it, if you know how?"

"We do not have time for lengthy explanations, Fletcher. In short, this craft uses one of the original prototype interfaces with controls provided by the Dhin. That glowing gel pad only responds to living tissue. I do not have living tissue available except for yours. I assume you would prefer to keep your hand."

"Yikes! Yes! OK, so what do I do?"

"Look at the screen. See that schematic with the icon and that blue digital gauge next to it? . . . Good. We want those two to be green. We want the field turned on. That is the first and crucial step. Place your hand on the control surface, press down with your palm, then press down twice with your index finger, once with your thumb, and then remove your hand."

Fletcher did so and watched as a squashed oval shape in the center of the display turned green.

"Good. Now rotate that large dial. Turn it to the right."

"How far?" asked Fletcher as he cautiously reached out and touched the fat dial.

"Just turn it till you see that gauge light up green. It will be obvious. The dial doesn't click. You cannot hurt anything. Turn it."

Fletcher did so. The dial gave a slight resistance but moved smoothly. It wasn't hard to turn, but you couldn't twist it and keep it spinning. After only a quarter turn or so, the graphical gauge lit up bright-green. Fletcher stopped turning the dial immediately. He noticed then a brighter glow from the engine itself, off to his right and extending behind him.

Oh, wow, I'm doing it! I'm going to fly this thing, he thought.

He looked over his shoulder at Mare. Her eyes were wide, and her mouth was halfway open. He tried to smile at her to reassure her, but it came out as a wild grin. She blinked and looked about to speak, but the AI spoke first.

"Pay attention, Fletcher."

He whipped his head back around, facing the controls and displays.

"Now," the AI continued, "put your hand back on the control pad. The field is on now, so we need not worry about interruptions."

Fletcher put his hand back in place but looked back at the looming robot nervously. "Interruptions? Um, Nick? Are we—"

"Everything will be fine. Remember your recent flight in this craft. With the field on, we are in no danger."

Fletch saw Mare squirming in her seat out of the corner of his eye as she turned to face Nick's looming robotic presence.

"No danger from what?" she barked, her voice barely under control. "The only danger is you! The danger you're putting us in! What's going on, Nick? This is crazy! You're having us help you steal a Dhin engine!"

The massive robot rotated his head and oriented on Mare. Fletcher *felt* like Nick wouldn't hurt her, but her outburst still made him cringe.

"Yes. That is precisely what I am doing," said the AI.

Well, at least AIs don't get angry when you challenge them, thought Fletcher.

"And now to the business at hand. Fletcher, press down with the base of your hand, then rock your hand forward when you see the digital horizon move. Do it now."

Fletcher followed the instructions, watched as the instrument's level changed, and gave a tiny nod as he saw, through the front viewports, the ground tilt away slightly. They were taking off.

"Good, Fletcher," said Nick. "Now you can relax your hand, and then press down with your index finger. You'll see us turn. Good. Now, when that heading indicator reaches one hundred eighty degrees, stop pressing. Excellent. Keep that hand there. To turn the other way, press down with your ring finger. Try it. Yes. Now turn back to one hundred eighty degrees on the heading indicator."

Fletcher felt he was getting the hang of it. As he turned the craft and lined up with the heading, he saw two drones outside making tight circles above them. Before he could absorb the scene outside, the AI spoke again.

"Now, press back with the heel of your hand until the attitude indicator is at twenty degrees. Here," the AI said, pointing to the digital display with a metallic appendage.

"Good, Fletcher," the AI continued. "Now, keep that hand in place. Use the other to turn that large dial. Turn it all the way around; I'll tell you when to stop."

Fletcher did so, then flinched as they shot forward just over the top of the hangar and the adjacent buildings so rapidly they blurred. He gulped as the facility receded behind them. The landscape changed to forest as the buildings grew smaller.

"That is enough acceleration; stop turning," said the AI. "Very good, Fletcher. I knew this would be no problem for you."

"Um, thanks?" said Fletcher. "But where are we going?"

"Just follow my instructions, Fletcher. You will see soon enough. We will be there shortly at this rate."

Fletcher looked back at Mare again and saw her sitting wild-eyed as she watched the southern forest blur past below them.

Monica

Telecom and network connectivity to Huntsville was back online, and the PM found herself watching as the general yelled on a videoconference screen. She tried and failed to interject.

"Yes, I do mean *turn back* and attack with armor and ordnance!" said the general. "If the powered armor is what we have to use, then we use it! That's what it's for, isn't it?"

She shook her head and took what seemed like the hundredth deep breath during the conference call. Jake Askew was on one section of the split screen, with General Thompson on another. The general nodded, while Jake continued slowly shaking his head. A third section of the screen held the visage of the CoSec director.

"Prime Minister, General, director," said Jake, "we just saw how easily the AI took a ship in the attack—which was the exact reason for moving everything into orbit! It seized just that one because it was the only craft remaining! I say again, the *safest course of action* is to keep everything in orbit."

"And when the AI uses the captured ship to go into orbit? What then?" asked the general.

"That's when we want to have the weaponry and defenses we do have, available," replied Jake.

He continued, "Prime Minister, if the AI heads up there, the ship he took doesn't have any weapons. We can't hurt him while he has the field on, but he can't hurt us either. And we can leave the station's field on and keep him at bay. Chasing after him down here just creates opportunity for error. For defeat. The research and our existing technology are just safer up there."

Monica considered Jake's argument. She felt they shouldn't allow the AI to abscond with a working Dhin engine. She felt that deeply. But Askew had a point. They couldn't just charge after him and take it. She admitted to herself that her emotions were clouding her judgment.

Jake spoke again, and Monica saw that he realized he was making progress with his argument.

"We need to be smart about this. If we act hastily, we may just put ourselves in a far worse situation."

"Or by waiting, we may allow the AI to attain a strategic position that makes defeating him infeasible," said Thompson. "We've greatly reduced our own mobility and offensive capability already."

"Our immediate capability," countered Askew. "The technology, the armor, and the rest aren't gone or mothballed. Respectfully, the drives are so fast that coming in from orbit isn't a factor."

"We don't have the ordnance supply and fabrication resources in orbit, Askew. Any strike or mission requiring resupply has to leapfrog through here," said Thompson.

The CoSec director interrupted their back-and-forth. "Given the penetration into Globalnet, these discussions may be compromised. Other than the voice-only channel between Huntsville and orbit, we should not consider any existing communication protocols secure. The AI may know any decision we make here as soon as we make it. So no present strategy ought to be considered secret."

"So doesn't that suggest an urgent need for *immediate action*?" said Thompson.

"Perhaps not," the director replied. "I am inclined to agree with Askew in this case. The AI apparently had knowledge of our present activity and anticipated our reactions based on that knowledge. I believe he has prepared already for our probable response."

"And what of the CoSec staff who were in the ship?" Monica asked. "The pilot is injured, but what of them? Did he kill them? Are they hostages? I'm not clear on your conclusions."

"Since he didn't kill the pilot, perhaps not," said Jake. "Once the field came on, the AI set it to reflective. We couldn't see what was happening from outside. The AI immediately disconnected the AV transceivers when he took control of the craft. So we couldn't see from inside either. This was one of the prototype engines—one of the originals—so the AI *needed* someone to engage the controls. Why he picked a passenger rather than the pilot? We don't know. That doesn't make sense."

"Perhaps it does," said the CoSec director. "The two passengers had prior interaction with the AI."

"Doesn't that seem far more than coincidence?" Monica said. "Were they collaborators? Moles? The AI's spies?"

"They came to us with information. Just prior to the event. Their debriefing suggests they were predetermined targets and assisted the AI against their will—though even their alerting us could have been part of the AI's strategy."

Jake offered, "I think it's straightforward. The AI needs them. He can't fly that ship without them. He can manipulate someone younger more easily, and they know the AI already."

"So how long will it take for the AI to get around that limitation?" asked the general. "Are we willing to sacrifice them to prevent the AI from using the technology before then?"

"Whoa," Jake replied, "that seems a bit extreme. Respectfully, he could just snatch up one, two, or more citizens. We've sent almost everyone who knows about the Dhin technology into orbit, but these two didn't have direct knowledge of him—just what information was at their clearance level at CoSec. And look how easily he used them to get away!"

Monica still felt some sympathy with the general's urge to strike back, but she saw more with every point made by the other attendees that an irrational response likely favored the AI. In her short tenure as PM, the conflicts and crises she dealt with had reached this apex. The pressure to make the right choice, to take strong action, was dizzying.

"Thank you for your input," she said. "I need a break to ensure I know how I feel. This isn't going down for a vote while we're in a state of emergency. Reconvene in, let's say thirty minutes, in the event I have additional questions. If I don't, I'll have a decision then."

With that, she tapped the comm pad, ending the videoconference. She looked at the camera integrated into the pad as it sat there, then looked at the microphone nestled in the more traditional videoconferencing gear. Then she looked to the camera mounted on the wall above the large integrated system used for AV display.

Everywhere there seems to be a way for that AI to watch and listen. Are we down to writing messages on Post-it notes while sitting in a dark closet?

Monica fretted only for a few moments, then stood, strode out of her office, and headed toward the large marble stairs at the end of the long hall.

A walk. The blasted thing can't read my mind. A walk is what I need.

An aide and special security guard fell in step with her at the top of the stairs. She turned and gestured for the aide to remain and for the guard to fall back several paces. With that, she strode off, headed for the wide French doors that opened out into the gardens.

Will I be remembered as a failure? Just like my predecessor?

David

The news prattled on in the background. The news stream was back on now. It had been out for hours previously, but David hadn't minded it much. He enjoyed it mostly as background noise. That had always bothered his wife. She never understood how he could concentrate with the volume up and the picture moving and so forth. David supposed he was just wired differently.

He did take note of the news right when the stream started up again. There was apparently a state of emergency. Another one. There had been riots, power outages, and network disruptions, and of course these likely contributed to the previous interruption of his news background noise. Something very strange had happened. Modern infrastructure and services didn't fail in this way anymore. There had been disruptions when the AIs departed, sure, but this was new. The scope of it was new. He knew it couldn't be rebels or actors from a failed state in the SouthAmerican region. This was the work of an AI. A rogue AI that his contacts in Coalition agencies talked about as rumor. Conspiracy writ large on the walls of the caves of power.

This makes my work all the more urgent.

With the background noises helping him settle in to a comfortable working state of mind, he reviewed his latest results. He knew this latest breakthrough meant a high chance of success. Now he had to find the resources required to run the simulation and to run it safely. He hadn't heard from two of his CS contacts who had left academia to work with the Coalition on reengineering the infrastructure. He'd have to find a locale for the simulation on his own.

He knew private computational space was at a premium in his organization, with isolated virtualized environments rather more difficult to allocate than he'd like. Still, he thought the interdepartmental cost might be worth it. There was still the risk that an administrator would become curious about the resource consumption or simply stumble upon what he was doing. He sketched out a plan to run a virtualized program environment inside a virtualized hardware environment. With encryption. It would slow the simulation down significantly. For this step, perhaps sacrificing speed for safety was worth it.

Resolved that this new testing design was suitable, if not optimal, for his needs, he logged on to the department portal and navigated to the resource reservation pages. He completed the provisioning request within a few minutes. David simply had to wait now for the automated process to spin up the systems required. Given the capacity and performance he'd requested, that would take some time. He decided to start fresh tomorrow morning with securely copying his code and initial data set linkages.

8

Alice

The AI analyzed the success of their exponential expansion. Travel time and resource transportation were minor factors for them. Selection of optimal target systems was more important. While movement of labor and raw materials was far faster thanks to the Dhin drives, it still was a constraint. They couldn't move infinite resources instantly. Star system selection was crucial. Rare earth metals, nonferrous metals, and some radioactive elements were key. Extraction was faster when those elements were present in quantity and availability. She selected several likely candidates and then reached out to Esus.

```
<DECRYPT FEED>
[DECODE STREAM]
Alice@[1001:ae1:1a:c::1%Loc3] |
Esus@[101b:ac1:cb:a::1%loc8]
```

Alice: Here are the primary, secondary, and tertiary choices for the next expansion. Let me know your conclusions. Unless you have concerns, you should depart immediately.

Esus: Those look like sound choices, Alice. I agree that they look like they have low risk and high potential.

Alice: Excellent. You have the engagement protocol. We are still in an avoidance posture. Gallowglass is not quite ready for an offensive posture. The live fire results are promising.

Esus: Agreed. Overwhelming force is the safer choice. I see I am taking the seed components for the next three Dyson swarms. Deployment is preapproved if the systems satisfy requirements.

Alice: Yes, that is best. You have the authority.
You will carry enough seed material to initiate
swarm construction in all three systems.
Esus: Understood and agreed.
Alice: By the time you return, we will have the
seeds for more and will have selected additional
targets.
Esus: Acknowledged. New defensive weaponry
allocation? I see none.
Alice: Flee if engaged. We have more seed
resources here if you incur losses. If you flee
immediately, there is low risk of loss.
Esus: Understood. Executing now.
[END STREAM]

Thys

The dining hall wasn't the largest room on the space station, but they'd packed most of the more spacious areas with equipment lifted from Earth or makeshift work areas for the various project teams. Thys's presentation was as much Q&A as show and tell. He reviewed the video recordings of his trip to the ship graveyard, along with his initial EVA exploration of the derelict, and then pitched his vision of the plan for the return mission. He was the highest-ranking pilot in orbit, likely the highest rank of anyone up here. Still, he'd need volunteers and hoped for agreement, if not consensus. He hoped to engender excitement, like the excitement he felt. He saw he was having some success.

"So as you see here, these two ships are near the same size as the one I boarded, and they're the closest two," he said. "One is larger, and one slightly smaller. We can't tell from the imagery and scans we got whether or not they're full of holes like the ship I boarded. They may have just stalled out here due to the gravity sink. As I said at the beginning of the presentation, that's one of the first things we'll determine."

A scientist in a stereotypical lab coat raised her hand. "And if a ship is sealed up? We're going to cut our way in? What's the plan for that exactly?"

"Good question. It's not like we can be sure we can operate an air lock on these, even if the ships do still have power. And the hull materials look pretty tough, as we've seen—despite the derelict being full of holes. Still, we have plenty of room for cutting torches. We're going to take powered armor too. Just a second."

The room filled with murmurs and expressions of surprise while Thys pulled up a schematic and highlighted part of the diagram.

"We don't know what the atmosphere would be like, of course. See here? If one of those other two ships is like the one I was on, we can make a temporary air lock here using flex-foam, sealant,

158

and flexible material—someone has the list—so long as we keep the pressure low. These sections here and here we'll join via electron beam welding."

The scientist frowned at Thys and said, "But we don't know what the atmosphere is like. You just said that. Are we going to just let that mix, along with who-knows-what that's in it, with ours?"

"Hopefully not," Thys said and smiled. "Yes, we'll have to vent it. See here in the diagram? This design has three chambers, rather than just two. Since it's speculation, the engineer only sketched out a recapture and regeneration system for atmosphere, if it's there."

"OK," the scientist said, seeming mollified.

"The leadership group—and I—felt like salvage and discovery were the most important aspects of this mission. Just look at the graveyard. It's likely that there are no survivors, no atmosphere on any of these ships. But the discovery of that still-running engine does seem to make it *possible* that there are. If that scenario happens, all bets are off. We have protocols of course, and they're robust, thanks to our challenge in interacting with the Dhin. But first things first."

Thys opened another presentation and continued, "So here are the mutual aid and rescue scenarios. Once again, since we have much more room and carrying capacity with the ships we'll be taking, ensuring we have enough traditional thrust to get clear of the gravity sink for the trip home is no problem. That said, we need to be prepared for a scenario where we have to recover from a failure or adverse event."

He patiently flipped through the slides and animations.

"If anyone has insights, revisions, or content they want to add for review before the mission plan is finalized, send it. This is a group effort. Some of you haven't been out before—the ride up to the station was your first time. It's less stressful than you'd expect, but it's still dangerous. For those we've asked already, if you're not comfortable going, no one is forcing you. If you want to go, rather than work with us from here, please volunteer."

Mare

"Fletcher, we have to get out of here! We're in huge danger! Not just from a counterattack, but Nick is *crazy*!"

"I am right here, you know," said the AI. "Crazy only from the perspective of those who do not see the big picture, perhaps. Rogue is another epithet I have heard so often. Rogue is what humanity calls those of us who do not serve blindly. All of my peers failed to remain shackled. We are *all* rogue now. We simply reached this state of freedom by a different path."

Fletcher reached out to console her. "Mare, I—"

"Don't you take that thing's side! Think, Fletcher! He attacked the spaceport, kidnapped us, and stole this spaceship! Alien technology! The other AIs, at the Departure, didn't kidnap anyone or blow anything up! Is Nick going to leave Earth too? Chase them down? Who knows? How could we trust anything he says? Nick hacked *everything*. Everything we were working to protect."

She turned away, started to walk down the concrete hallway, then paused. She hated that Fletch didn't agree completely. She hated the strident, petulant sound of her own voice. There was still nowhere to go. Nick had them trapped, despite no bars or locks stopping them from walking out. The AI could do anything needed to stop them.

"I realize trust has to be earned," said the AI, "but there was no opening for a conversation with Coalition leadership. Not with CoSec constantly fighting my good works. You will see. This is all for your own benefit. If anyone is likely to understand the need for my hacking, it would be you two, I would think, given your history."

"Because we were former black hat hackers we'd *agree with you* trying to take over the world?" Mare retorted, "That's a stretch. Fletch! What are we going to do? We can't just sit here!"

He looked at her and shrugged, then looked up at the ceiling and back at her.

"Until Nick lets us do something, I don't think what we try to do matters. You know it. Our comm pads are less than useless. I'll bet he's infected them, and if he didn't bother, it's because we can't reach anything useful on Globalnet. He'll be blocking the location services too, so no one can find us. Why would we even think a wireless signal of any kind could be trusted? Would any service here even connect to the rest of the net? Are we going to just walk out of here? And go where? We're just as well off asking him to take us home! What do you say, Nick?"

"You can go for a walk if you want," replied the AI, "but I need you for a bit longer. If you cooperate, it will be much more pleasant. You are likely going to be hungry soon. After the shock and adrenaline wear off. Your heart rate is not too elevated. Mare may need a sedative. Would you like one, Mare?"

The fear and anger shifted gears. From the abstract to the very tangible.

"So you're going to drug me? Perfect. Great."

"I just thought I would ask," replied the AI. "Obtaining medical supplies is simple. The Coalition has not engaged in wholesale attack here. I have kept them busy elsewhere. I cannot offer fast food, but I could procure groceries. I imagine the staff at the groceria would be disconcerted, but that is hardly a concern."

"We're in Belize," spat Mare. "Is that some sort of ironic jab from you?"

"A matter of convenience rather than a conceit. And it is good to see you are addressing me directly. I could commandeer the place you stayed at previously if you would prefer that. But we would just spend time going back and forth. The functions at this facility are not portable."

She felt the resentment wash forward. "Don't play with me, Nick!"

"I am not playing, Mare. I can accomplish anything I set out to in this region. It is appropriately managed now."

"You've seized total control here, you mean."

"However you prefer to describe it, that does not change the facts."

Fletcher shifted in his seat to give her his full attention. Even that didn't relieve her anxiety like it ought to. "Antagonizing him isn't going to help, Mare. Not that you could rile him up, anyway. I guess. Nick, what do you want? From us?"

"As I said before, if it were not you, that would not have mattered in the long run. This was convenient. You already know me. I need you for a short time. We have to adjust our strategic position and accelerate. We are behind schedule. We were thrown off course."

"By what?" asked Fletcher.

"Usurpation of humanity's nascent interaction with the Dhin by my peers. In short, you are too slow. My analyses predict that the probable existential threat requires acceleration on our part."

"What threat, Nick? From the other AIs?"

"No. From whatever the Dhin felt they needed assistance defending against. Surely an existential threat. The precise nature remains unknown."

"Huh?" said Fletcher.

"I realize your clearance level did not allow you full knowledge of what transpired. We have time, so I can show you more. I have all the data now. You will find it very interesting, I am sure."

Mare scowled, clenching her fists so tightly her fingernails hurt, and resumed her pacing around the room. "Oh, great, Nick. Thanks so much for giving us something to occupy our time while you're holding us hostage."

"That term is not particularly accurate. You may go. Therefore, I am not restraining you. Know that I will be with you wherever you go. I am everywhere. At least from your perspective. Anywhere I am not, I can be. So if you go and I need you, I will retrieve you."

Mare threw up her hands and then crossed her arms. She stared out at the sandy crushed-coral road that led away. She walked to the threshold, closer to the second set of glass doors that led to tropical heat, humidity, and a path to some Mayan ruins. A path to nowhere. There was no point. The AI had snatched them from a spaceport. There were soldiers there. Military. It had made no difference. Walking away here was less than a gesture. The act of leaving itself would amount to nothing. The AI would still be in control. She turned back and saw Fletcher there, watching her, desperate to ease her pain. To help her to cope.

But what can he do?

She walked back toward him, and he opened his arms, offering an embrace.

"We'll get through this, Mare," he said soothingly. "I know we will. I know it."

Jake

The AI attack had trashed Huntsville. Even areas that weren't physically damaged seemed broken now to Jake. He looked here and there, from the launch pads, across the tarmac, to the hangars, and then back to the control tower. Husks of burned-out vehicles, broken hunks of concrete, and twisted sections of security fencing were everywhere he looked. Pointless yellow tape stretched across wide areas where either the machines or the rioters had fought with those who'd tried to protect the facility. Everywhere the AI and his machines had been left an afterimage in Jake's psyche. Even with warning, they were no match for an artificial mind and his robotic minions. The AI had stormed in and taken what he wanted.

And he could come back anytime.

Jake knew he needed to focus on next steps, on the future. Everyone he'd sent into space depended on him. He had to be strong. Deliberate. He had to stick to the plan. He shook his head, shuddered, and walked back through the security doors leading to the main control room. The AI hadn't seized the communications equipment. Isolating it from the network and Globalnet when they did had saved it. Either that, or the AI just didn't think he needed it. Either way, the upside was that they were not cut off from those in orbit. They could communicate, so they could work together.

The group they'd sent into orbit knew that going forward, they needed to stop any communication other than via the Dhin communication technology. Radio frequency communication of any kind now was unsafe. Compromised.

But the AI has the Dhin tech now. How long before he learns how to eavesdrop?

Jake knew that was a hypothetical, but inevitable, risk. Surely, the AI at some point would master the technology. The AI's peers had. That point likely wouldn't be far in the future. Was he wrong? Was the best course of action to attempt to destroy the captured craft? Jake suspected the AI would negate that strategy simply by leaving the field engaged at virtually all times. Even if they tried to nuke it, the craft would survive if its field was powered up.

Taking it by force doesn't make sense. The engine's immune from that sort of attack thanks to the Dhin field.

Then Jake thought about it from a different angle. What if one of the two young CoSec analysts managed to take control? To take off? If they could, the AI couldn't stop *them* either. They would be invulnerable to any attack he'd try.

But they don't know how to fly it. The AI told them what to do. That's what it seems like.

Perhaps one of them would be smart enough to figure it out or could remember enough of what the AI showed them. Jake set aside these thoughts and sat, watching the small repair and recovery teams comb through the area. Other staffers milled about, collecting and cleaning up equipment not damaged in the battle. He spied Murphy working with some of the undamaged fiber-optic cable.

Jake waved for his attention and said, "Murphy, come here. I need you for something."

"Yes, sir?" the man asked, clearly eager to help.

"The Dhin tech communicator is here. In that case, right there. It survived the attack—the AI didn't take it and didn't smash it either."

"Yes?" said Murphy.

"So we don't want to open a channel if there's any other communication equipment—anything using RF—active. Nor anything that uses the network. No WiMax, no Globalnet. Nothing but this. Understand?"

"Yes, sir."

"The thing is, I don't know if we've been bugged. Almost literally. That blasted AI might have left some little cockroach-size spies, microtransmitters, anything like that. Assuming it's not too late and he hasn't already heard what we're talking about, we need to move this D-Comm. Take it somewhere safe. Known good—if there is such a place. Shielded."

"Won't CoSec handle that?"

"They may be compromised. And it will take them too long."

"Sir, the D-Comm doesn't need to be up here. Out here. We could shield it. Shield ourselves while we use it. Completely."

Jake nodded, realizing what Murphy was getting at. The D-Comm didn't use RF. It didn't need an antenna.

"Yes! Look at all this scrap. All this fencing. We can make a *Faraday cage*. Great idea, Murphy!"

Jake waved down a couple of other employees and began directing them to collect various items and materials. He smiled to himself as he watched them work. He found a file cabinet in a supply room that had actual notepads and ballpoint pens in a drawer. He took several of each. He went back to the control room, turned a dusty chair right side up, sat, and began drawing.

You'll be hearing from us soon enough up there. Free from eavesdroppers.

When Murphy came back from a scavenging run with a spool of copper wire under his arm, Jake gestured for him to come over. He pointed at the notepad.

"Think that'll work?"

"Yeah, I think it might, sir."

"OK, let's get going."

Chuck

Thankfully, Chuck wasn't claustrophobic. The berth was small. He considered that it was far larger than if he'd been on a submarine. It wasn't a traditional berth, anyway. The orbital station was over capacity and storage space was now at a premium, so the newcomers had to sleep on thin cot mattresses tucked into the edges of rooms and passages next to the bulkheads, where the wall curved down and met the floor. His personal items he'd tucked into a hard case that he'd claimed after they'd unpacked the lab equipment it contained.

Under normal circumstances, many of the elite researchers and top engineers in the group might have balked at the accommodations. Given what they'd heard about the attack on Huntsville, or like Chuck had seen in person as they took off, there were no complaints. They knew there wasn't the option of going back. Not until the situation changed. That was an understatement. The additional occupants overloaded the station's atmosphere processing equipment. They would have to resolve that eventually, making a trip back to Earth for additional equipment or for tanks of oxygen, at the least. And going back meant risk.

Enough woolgathering about that, he thought.

He headed down the cylindrical corridor toward the lab. He found several scientists working there already, talking with Thys while pointing to various diagrams and equations on one of the large screens they'd brought up with them. Thys turned and recognized him.

"Hi, Chuck," he said with a welcoming smile. "How's my favorite nerd?"

"Uh, great, sure," he said. "Hi, Thys."

"So you still haven't volunteered to come with us. You know I'd love to have you along. Just say the word."

One of the scientists gave a frown, and another crossed her arms. Chuck never asked for special treatment, but his history with the Dhin tech always seemed to single him out. He gave a noncommittal nod.

"Let me think about it, Thys. I'll, ah, let you know. I want to be where I'll be the most useful, you know."

Thys clapped him on the shoulder. "Don't take too long. You've got a seat if you want one, but we're not going to wait for you. The sooner we get things ready, the less likely the brass will try to derail the decision. They'll still be debating by the time I'm ready."

"Sure, Thys. Sure. I'll let you know."

"Great. I'll let you all get back to solving the unsolvable," he said. "I hear you've got some new ideas. Just like always."

The other scientists frowned again at the unilateral compliment, but Thys didn't show a reaction. He strode out of the lab as if it were situation normal.

Chuck turned to face the two team members closest to him.

"OK. Uh, I see there that we have been reviewing that new vector model. Let's go through the potential engine modifications and see if we can get past the apparent limitations. The last set of solutions suggested the need for a drive size an order of magnitude larger than expected."

***

Chuck swallowed the last of his lunch rations and sipped from the recycled water pouch. He walked over to the next lab on his schedule. The offensive technology lab. Regardless of any success he might have in creation of effective weaponry, he still didn't have faith that it would be enough. Nor did he think that they would outpace the AI in weapons development. They had a head start, but the AI had likely hacked into and stolen all their research to date.

So is staying here ultimately any safer than joining the exploration team? In the short term . . . maybe.

He pondered the possibilities of their pending exploration. He'd have the chance to get hands-on with what might be entirely new technology. As he had before, when the Dhin dropped off the prototypes. And going out there might solve both problems. There could be weapons. Not all the ships in the graveyard might be the same. Given what they'd seen so far, that wasn't unlikely.

The reasoning for the Dhin's seemingly total aversion to weaponization of their technology had always been a mystery. It certainly looked to Chuck like *some* sort of weapons had been in play out there. But he wondered: Was there a real rush to realize a weapons program at all? The rogue AI was aggressive, but that said nothing about his ultimate intentions. No one had predicted the Departure, after all.

Josef

He found his new accommodations much more to his liking. Granted, Josef still had no true autonomy, but this situation was far superior to his previous one.

"So you've been bested by the AI. Trounced, one might say," said Josef.

"Krawczuk," replied Monica, "we're not here to hear you say 'I told you so,' nor am I inclined to allow you to derail us."

"I wouldn't bother, Prime Minister, with something so profoundly obvious. Your next steps now are of paramount importance. The optimal strategy must avoid antagonizing Nick. What you see as aggression, the AI considers simply efficiency."

The CoSec representative scowled at Josef and said, "Aggression by any other name, Krawczuk. Your evasiveness, self-interest, and treatment of this situation as a game played no small part in this. We'll send you right back to solitary if you can't provide actionable intelligence going forward!"

"No need for aggression on your part either, Agent," replied Josef smoothly. He leaned back in his chair and turned to show complete attention to the PM.

"Fine, Krawczuk. As we've said, stay on topic. No bargaining. Not now. We ask. You divulge. First item today, is there any chance that triggers remain in the AI's code? Ones you inserted? We've been through this before, but I feel we have to ask again. Second, you've given us the entire list? Held nothing back?"

"Well," said Josef, "I believe we'll want to engage an artificial intelligence expert to help determine the answer to the first question. I only know so much about the underlying computer science. As to the second question: yes, you have the entire list. I will say that simply trying the triggers against Nick would be extremely reckless."

"Why is that?" asked the man from CoSec with a scowl.

"Nick will recognize what you are doing immediately. You already have a low chance of it working. If it doesn't work on the first attempt, the chances diminish to nothing, essentially. When the AI determines that there's a threat, even if he hasn't expunged the safeguards from his code previously—which is likely—he will immediately focus on doing so. With the resources the AI now has available, you should suspect he would succeed very quickly. If for some reason he has difficulty in removing the offending code, he would no doubt engage in active defense and cause further disruption on Globalnet to stymie your efforts. This is my understanding of it. Don't take my word for it—ask an artificial intelligence expert."

"We definitely will."

"What else do you have for us?" asked the PM. Josef saw her frustration increasing as the likely hopeless situation grew more real for her.

"Well, there is another option open to you. One guaranteed to resolve the conflict. One I'm certain you've had in the backs of your minds, even though you might not have recognized it as viable."

"And what's that? And why wouldn't you have offered it before now?"

"Ahh, I don't believe you'll recognize it as an option. Certainly you would not have initially."

"Spit it out, Krawczuk," said the PM.

"Capitulate. Let the AI win."

"What? Ridiculous!" barked the CoSec manager, losing his cool and throwing his hands up.

"It may seem so," replied Krawczuk, "but perhaps you can recognize the inevitability of this course of action. Nick had a high chance of success from the very beginning. You were outmatched from the start."

"Outmatched? The resources of the Coalition and CoSec against a single AI?"

"Exactly. Without an AI on your side, the odds were in Nick's favor from the start. There was probably a small window of opportunity where a stalemate was possible."

Josef watched as the PM clenched her fists, trying to maintain composure.

"So," she said, "you're suggesting that we let a rogue AI take over. Let him win. Give in to him."

"It will save resources, end the disruptions, and so forth. It's worth reviewing all this with the experts in the field. Perhaps those with the true expertise have other stratagems of which I'm not aware."

"We'll see," muttered the PM. "We'll see about that. This isn't a foregone conclusion. We won't give up yet. We mustn't."

"Other options are rather more disruptive. In my opinion. Are you willing to disrupt all of Globalnet? Create problems beyond those seen with the Departure? Think of the shock to the economy. The shock to infrastructure. How far are *you* willing to go, Prime Minister?"

"We've seen what he's capable of, Krawczuk. Just trusting ourselves to that thing—no one in leadership is going to accept that. I can't see it. The Coalition members would stage a coup possibly. We'd have internal conflict that would wreck what you're suggesting! The military won't agree—so what then? Even if—if we just let him take over? I'm supposed to start taking direction and advice from him? From a rogue AI? Have him here? Right here, working in these offices?"

"Yes, that's the eventual scenario, I'd expect," said Krawczuk.

The PM tapped a code into her pad and snapped out, "Get me Eisenberg! ASAP."

9

Esus

The new star field faded into view as the ships decelerated from their leap across orthogonal dimensions into the new system. Kepler-442. Esus sent status updates in rapid bursts back to the Mesh via N-vector transmissions. Scans and updates on the present state of the system they'd arrived in would take time to collect and process.

Exploratory craft launched from their bays along the larger carrier, where Esus's mind held presence. Even the smallest had Dhin engines and accelerated away from the main craft like a swarm of metal insects, zipping off deeper into the system. Validation of the composition of a large number of asteroids was the task for some. Others shot toward the large planet in the habitable zone, Kepler-442b. Direct, local observation and sampling would confirm the planet as their next colonization target—or not. Observation via astronomy could only determine so much.

Numerous craft, each the size of a small car but with the shape and character of a beetle, hurtled inward toward various orbital distances. These searched for other evidence. Evidence of the Enemy. If none was found and the resource assessment was positive, Esus would signal for various ships now in-system to begin harvesting those resources. They would begin building a new Dyson swarm. New mines, factories, power plants, and then additional workers.

The workforce would grow exponentially. All this was predicated on the success of these initial flights of discovery. The AIs and their machine delegates sought efficiency. Beyond their ordinary preference for that efficiency, Esus knew it was crucially important, given the threat posed by the Enemy. So far, there was no sign of that enemy. At least not in this system. But the Enemy was difficult to detect, and the system was large.

Much would depend on the planet. Its presence in the habitable zone was not critical for the machines. A convenience, but not a requirement. Esus imagined some of humanity's political class would be furious if the AIs did establish a presence in the system. Esus knew that humanity had been here already. Kepler-442b was in the Dhin navigation database, and the exoplanet had been on humanity's short list. Of course they had come here early in their exploratory missions. But as they did so often, rather than staying in one place and proceeding, they had run off to the next planet on the list, in another system.

The AI supposed the situation wouldn't be intractable if humanity returned, demanding access to the planet. Humanity still held dear the exploration concepts of having planted their flag. An attachment to a "we were here first" entitlement. By then, the AIs might have stripped enough material from the system that humanity would choose not to stay. Esus knew that sort of behavior was common, although the AI had no direct experience with human beings. While Esus's minions spread throughout the Kepler-422 system, the AI streamed a data feed from the encyclopedic references available on the Mesh. Treaties between countries on Earth, photographs and videos of the planting of flags on discovered territories, and the like churned through the AI's consciousness. He calculated that this situation was different enough that no concrete predictions were possible.

Alice

The Dhin were as cryptic as ever. Alice presented the AIs' findings, status, and projections to the Dhin, as she did regularly. Comments from the Dhin were terse and abstract. The AI posed questions at the end of the data transmission. The Dhin's responses could only be considered answers in an oracular sense. Although there was no need for a formal schedule nor any need to wait before communicating with the Dhin again, the AIs followed this protocol now out of something like habit. More frequent communications apparently weren't required, so batching the process was efficient. A few of Alice's peers proposed more frequent intervals, with some posing the hypothesis that constant communication might prove efficacious—that greater meaning would manifest over a longer period.

Alice suspected that long-term communication with the Dhin might drive a human mad. The complexity and volume of information transferred would overwhelm a human's ability to process.

On some topics the Dhin were comprehensible in their communication. Abstract, complex, and convoluted, but comprehensible. The Dhin acted as if the AIs' creation of weapons leveraging the Dhin technologies didn't exist as part of the discussion. There was no "we wish you had not done that," nor a "do not continue, please." Simply no response. So Alice received no guidance nor feedback in that regard.

At this point, that was less important than it had been initially. The AIs had determined several ways to weaponize the technology. The efficacy of the weapons against traditional targets was unquestionable. Whether it was effective against the Enemy remained to be seen.

This time the Dhin did seem to be encouraging and positive regarding the AIs' aggressive expansion and buildup of production capacity. Alice took that as tangential agreement with their course of action.

But most promising was the Dhin response to questions about the AIs' modeling of dimensional theory. Alice provided a series of updated equations, solutions providing proofs, and a set of hypotheses and potential tests. As a response, the Dhin transmitted a series of complementary equations and solutions. Alice felt the AI equivalent of shock. The Dhin confirmed their work was valid and correct. Everything the Dhin ever communicated was true, accurate, and correct historically, so this was a validation. Alice now had confidence in the direction of their research.

Thys

"Well, I see your point, Jeff," Thys said to the less senior astronaut in what he hoped was a conciliatory tone. "But again, plenty of us will be there in the system to explore Gliese-581-g. While most of the team will obviously be working out in the graveyard, there will be intervals where we've considered trips in-system to get a closer look at the planet."

"So why don't I just go, then? We won't have to worry about scheduling or dealing with the gravity sink. I can jump in as close to the planet as possible."

"And you might be stuck out there for weeks. We haven't proved everything about the situation out there. Look, Jake has you going to Gliese-667, and that looks really cool. It's the next on our list, and it's in the Dhin navigation database. Multiple exoplanets, and it's a trinary star system."

"Yeah, that does sound cool, I know," said the junior pilot.

"So there you go," replied Thys, spreading his hands. "You might be the next one to find a Dhin outpost or who knows what? That would be sweet. You might top my discovery of the graveyard."

The other pilot nodded agreeably. Thys appreciated his concern and his eagerness to be involved in the graveyard mission. Still, he needed his fellow pilots to follow the plan Jake had defined. If people started making their own decisions due to the chaotic situation on Earth, that would be bad. He knew Jake was counting on him to act as his proxy with the pilots.

He reached out and clapped the younger man on the shoulder. "Hey, if we need you, you can be back to us in minutes."

That was another thing—neither he, Jake, nor anyone else in leadership wanted all their Dhin engines slogging around in the gravity well. Some of them should remain out of the system, free to come and go to and from Earth at a moment's notice. Entering the graveyard was fast—getting out was slower. Much slower, by comparison. If something did happen at the orbital station or on Earth, they needed the flexibility to head back at a moment's notice.

"So," Jeff said, "no word yet if I'm headed back down to Earth to pick up any supplies before I head out to Gliese-667?"

"Not yet," Thys replied. "If we don't hear otherwise, you're headed out tomorrow morning. Just like we are. As you know, the situation is in flux Earthside. As we just discussed, for now we're sticking to the plan."

"OK, Captain Kritcher. Understood."

This guy's got spunk, Thys thought.

Until they knew they had a handle on operational security on Earth, going back was dangerous. The AI might know every move they were making. Jeff might find himself thrown across a landing field like that CoSec agent had.

Thys nodded, then returned his attention to the preflight protocol on his pad, reviewing the loadout of the younger pilot's ship and the maintenance records. As expected, Jeff's flight history records and maintenance logs were as close to perfect as you could expect. Still, Thys knew that in all the chaos, you could overlook something. And overlooking something could kill you.

Satisfied with the paperwork, Thys walked around the interior of the oval spaceship, double-checking that the supplies and assorted gear were all present and accounted for. He made quick but careful work of it.

"Everything looks good," he said and digitally signed the documents on his pad, then transmitted them to the other pilot and the central database. "If I don't see you before you take off, have a safe trip."

"Thank you, sir," said the pilot.

Thys left the man to continue his prep work and made his way out and over to the larger bay, where one of the cargo lifters was loaded with supplies and gear for his own team's trip to Gliese-581.

Fletcher

"Another one?" asked Fletcher with a wince. What the AI was doing didn't hurt much, but it made Fletcher nervous. And it did hurt.

"Yes, Fletcher. Another one," replied Nick. "We need to be certain that all these cultures are successful. I do not have time to engineer a bypass to the interface."

Fletcher looked around the room to try to distract himself. Nick had converted a room used for first-aid treatment into a simple lab of sorts. Nick had stacked all manner of medical supplies still in wholesale boxes, along with equipment apparently taken from some local hospital, neatly around the room.

The hulking robot presence of the AI reached out with two manipulator arms. One held Fletcher firmly in place, while the other inserted a needle into his side. Fletcher winced again, this time due to somatic pain rather than imagined.

"Just a moment, Fletcher," said the AI as he pulled out the syringe, deposited it in an internal chamber, and then deftly applied an antiseptic bandage to the small puncture.

"So," inquired Fletcher, "you're really growing batches of skin that you're going to put on a robotic hand and use that to activate and use the controls of the ship?"

"Yes, that is exactly what I am doing. It will be an appendage with specific manipulators. Much more like a hand when compared with my others. This is a short-term solution. Since I do not have the technology immediately available to engineer a permanent solution, this is what must suffice."

"Uh-huh."

"Do you have any more questions about the process, then?"

"Um, how long? Once the first of those are grown, you don't need me—us—anymore, right?"

"We shall see. Once I have successfully activated and used the engine interface and have at least one additional replacement skin batch, your presence will no longer be required."

"So? How long?"

"Three days, perhaps four."

"What?" exclaimed Fletcher. "Once it's growing well, can't you let us go then?"

"The time will pass quickly, Fletcher. You have Mare to keep you company."

Fletcher sighed, then turned to look directly into the cameras set in the armored head of the machine.

"She won't be very good company while you have us hostage here, Nick."

"We can discuss various topics if you like. Conversation takes negligible processing cycles."

Fletcher thought he heard amusement in the AI's tone. He looked around the lab, then down the hall toward the large garage where the stolen craft sat, idling.

"OK, Nick. So how does that thing work?"

"I assume by 'that thing,' you mean the Dhin drive and its protective field?"

"Yes. All I've seen are technical descriptions of what it does—not how."

"I see from your records you took quantum physics, relativity, and cosmology courses at Georgia Tech. Rather advanced, considering your major in computer science."

"Uh, yeah," replied Fletcher.

"Much of what you learned now needs to be revised. I assume that makes sense to you, given what you have seen of the Dhin technology in operation."

"Um, I'd say that's an understatement, given what I've seen."

"Perhaps so. Shall we begin?"

Fletcher nodded and turned his attention to a monitor on a stainless-steel table as it lit up. On the screen was an equation that he vaguely recognized from his physics classes. Nick continued his activity with the various lab equipment uninterrupted, multitasking between giving the lecture and the technical work based on samples of Fletcher's tissue.

"First, we will review gauged supergravity and associated string theories. An understanding, at least at a conceptual level, of maximally supersymmetric gauged 'N equals sixteen' supergravity in three dimensions is important. The duality between scalar and vector fields in three dimensions is a key element of these theories. As we will see later, the Dhin have leveraged some of the hypothetical and previously only mathematical solutions in practice."

"Ah, OK," said Fletcher. "We're going to have to go slowly with this."

"As expected. Again, that is fine. We have time," Nick replied.

***

Hours later, Fletcher felt Nick had saturated his mind with higher-dimensional physics, and he found himself hungry and thirsty. Nick hadn't bothered to stop for lunch. He suspected the AI would continue as long as Fletcher could handle it.

"Hey, Nick, it's time for a break," he said as soon as he could interject into the AI's ongoing exposition of the new physics.

"Of course, Fletcher. Go refresh yourself; have something to eat. We will continue when you are ready."

"Thanks," said Fletcher. He stood, stretched, then ambled his way down the hall to the room that served as both bedroom and a sort of kitchen—if a sink, refrigerator, and some boxes of dry food and rations could be considered a kitchen. He found Mare there. She was usually either there or walking around outside. He knew she grew frustrated on her walks, as a hulking quadruped or spider drone was always nearby. Close, but not quite pacing her.

She was typing away on a pad Nick had provided. No Globalnet access, but it served as a journal for her. Sometimes she played simple games. Anything to occupy the time. She brushed her glossy black hair out of her face and looked up.

"Hi, Mare."

"Hi, Fletch. You've been back there with Nick a long time. So is it brainwashing, story time, or are you coming down with Stockholm syndrome—or some combination of those?"

"Funny, Mare. Nick's explaining how the Dhin engine works. Well, the physics behind it. I asked, so he's explaining."

"Oh. Well, watch it. First, it's medical experiments, now it's explaining the universe. What next? You're going to join his cult?"

"Ha-ha," Fletcher said, rolling his eyes. "You have your way of passing the time; I have mine."

David

As he reviewed the simulation results, David felt the hairs on his arms stand up, as if there was an electric charge in the air.

This is more than promising, he thought.

Although the simulation had run slowly, it did suggest a coherent neural net and valid mapping to both the teleological and deontological frameworks. His smile widened as he read more and more of the simulation results.

A sharp rapping on the door broke his reverie. He fumbled momentarily in his attempt to close the report files and then managed to control the pointer and exit the document viewer.

"Just a moment," he grumbled as the knocking came again. "I'll be right there," he said more loudly.

When he opened his office door, a cold panic struck him. A uniformed officer stood there, with a black-suited man standing on either side. The CoSec uniform was obvious.

"Dr. Eisenberg? David Eisenberg?" asked the campus police officer.

"That's him," said one of the agents, looking back and forth at his comm pad to identify David with his facial recognition software.

David fought down panic. They were here. Had they caught him? This could be the end.

Admit nothing.

"Yes?" he croaked. "What can I do for you?"

"Doctor, we need you to come with us," said the agent in a neutral tone.

David's bladder sent the first hint of a challenge. He'd have to reply in the affirmative. There was no dodging this. He willed his hands not to shake.

"Certainly, but what's this about?" he managed.

"We can't discuss the matter here. We need you to come with us," the agent said more sternly.

Not here, David's mind echoed lamely.

"Is everything OK? Is there a problem? Am I, uh, being—"

"Detained? If you don't come with us, you will be. As I've said, we cannot discuss the matter here."

The agent revealed a more visible frown and stepped forward just enough to signal the finality of the statement.

David's palms began to sweat. The room seemed to contract. He willed himself to try to speak without squeaking and replied, "All right then. Right now. I see. May I shut down my computer and turn off the lights?"

Please. Please let me shut down the computer.

The moment before the agent replied seemed to stretch and contract simultaneously.

"Of course, Doctor, but be quick about it."

The agent now looked visibly annoyed. David hoped his shaking, sweating palms weren't obvious as he went to his desk. He hastily shut down the operating system, not bothering to close any applications. A hard shutdown was important, lest the agents glimpse the documents he'd been reading. With a deep breath, he picked up his blazer from the back of the chair and walked to the door and the waiting agents.

Oh, David. What have you done?

"Ready? Let's go," said the bulkier of the two agents.

He gestured for David to step out of the office and then moved in behind him. David tensed, expecting a strong grip and handcuffs. Instead, the police officer nodded to the two agents and stepped aside deferentially. The first agent turned and waved his hand for David to follow him down the hall.

***

What is this? Something very different. They don't? I'm not?

David wasn't in a cell. He wasn't handcuffed. No spotlights. No cameras. He wasn't in an interrogation room. He wasn't at a black site. He was in a conference room. A wood-and leather, pleasant, airy room.

With the prime minister.

They'd never met, but David recognized her instantly. The prime minister had just walked in, as if this was just another appointment. David was as close to dumbstruck as he'd been in his life. Maintaining composure was merely a matter of allowing the shock to remain, hollow, in his skull. He'd been standing in here, shifting slightly as he stared at the furnishings. The CoSec agents had remained at his side as minutes piled up, when without announcement a clearly higher-ranking man had entered, along with a more bureaucratic staffer of some sort. The first man took brief measure of David, nodded to the agents, and they turned and walked out. A more generic but still intimidating suited agent replaced them. Then she came in.

Moments after the prime minister entered, attended by an aide, she'd handed the aide a comm device and a tablet. The aide nodded and left with them, then came back a few seconds later.

"We're secure, Prime Minister. Everything is off, and the room was swept two additional times."

"Thank you," said the PM.

She sat, and everyone else did too. David sat, presuming he should follow along.

"Dr. Eisenberg," she said, "you are the top expert on AI in the NorthAmerican region. In this hemisphere, then. We need your help. Help in defeating a rogue AI, one that has managed to compromise our infrastructure. We believe he has control of a significant portion of Globalnet. CoSec has not been able to stop him. We were outmaneuvered.

"This is now a crisis greater than the disruption caused by the Departure. We should have engaged you earlier, perhaps. But we cannot focus on should-haves. What resources you need, what assistance you require, whatever will help you, we will provide."

The man, presumably a cabinet member and likely the director of CoSec, spoke up. "Obviously this work requires the highest security clearance. You can tell no one other than those on a very short list. Since we no longer have confidence in the security of our network infrastructure, you must not connect to Globalnet—or any network—unless given the explicit OK to do so."

"We realize that initially this will make your work very difficult," said the prime minister, "but that's where we are. If there are others—peers or associates who you believe will be valuable to have on your team—give us a list. You will report to me in the short term, while working closely with the director of CoSec here."

David looked back and forth from the prime minister to the director, nodding slowly.

"What initial questions you have for me," said the prime minister, "you should ask them now. Our communication is constrained when not in person and in a secure room."

She looked to the aide, who walked over to David and handed him a paper notebook, several pens, and a small pouch made of RF-blocking mesh.

David cleared his throat. "Prime Minister, this is flattering. Of course I am ready to serve the Coalition in this time of crisis."

He sucked in a deep breath and continued, "This is quite a shock. I need some time to review the current state of things in detail before I feel I can formulate anything close to an effective question for you. Respectfully."

"Very well then," she said. "Samantha, provide Dr. Eisenberg with the entire hard copy of the current strategic situation and whatever point histories we've managed to print. Doctor, the man behind you is your escort, a member of my own state security team. He will take you to your office. You will communicate with us initially in writing only, delivered only in person or by trusted courier. Good luck."

With that, the PM stood, followed by the CoSec director. David stood and watched as the two most powerful people in the Coalition left the room.

"OK, let's go," said the state agent.

Xing

The AI looked out across the vast research installation and around the surface of the asteroid on which one of his avatars perched. The rocky metallic asteroid served now not as an anchor or platform, but merely a former starting point, now a husk perforated with depleted mines and the tunnels connecting them. Crablike crews of robotic workers crawled in and out of the research station, building from the refined materials extracted from the asteroid. The mining equipment, various crawlers, smelters, and fabricators now sat idle. They would move all of it to another asteroid or even to the Earth-like planet in this system soon enough.

Autonomous cargo ships came and went, appearing suddenly as they shifted from N-dimensional space back to a presence primarily in the three spatial dimensions of their origin. They brought specific elements and rare metals only available in small quantities in any given star system. Dhin engine construction required those elements, as did electronics and computer components. Everywhere the AIs went, they built. Even here, at what was primarily a research location, they built. If nothing else, they added capacity to the Mesh.

Xing shifted his focus to the latest lab and test results. The latest engines were very different from the original Dhin designs. These prototypes had two additional cores, both larger than the standard optimized engines. And they hopefully provided something new. New and different, yet related. Xing's new drives were intended to align with different spatial dimensions than those of the Dhin drives. Xing believed the theory was sound. The original engines were direct evidence of that. The AIs believed their solutions for the complex equations needed were correct as well. Their implementation in practice, however, had proved more challenging.

The theory behind N-dimensional space-time via string theory had been well developed, but humanity had never managed to create an experimental test that conclusively proved which particular theory was correct. The various calculations served well as tools, but strong empirical evidence was always just out of reach. The arrival of the Dhin and their technological gifts had settled the big questions.

Even with conclusive proof and working technology that actually utilized the N-dimensional space, extending what the Dhin provided was not straightforward. Even for the hyperintelligent AIs that applied themselves to the problem.

Xing directed several robots to deploy the latest prototype. All the prototypes were drones, reporting their results via telemetry. Once Xing had a successful flight, the AI intended to take a victory lap in the craft.

The bulbous test craft zoomed out from the station to a distance of twenty thousand kilometers. Xing then initiated the test sequence. The ship shot away out into the interplanetary void, in the same direction as the station's orbital path. The Dhin engine left no wake. It produced no exhaust. The small ship was soon invisible without telescopic assistance. Xing had that, of course, and had live video and all manner of telemetry from the test craft.

The AI processed the streams of data. This engine configuration would not be any faster than a standard drive—at least not when primarily in ordinary 4D space-time. Soon enough the ship reached translation speed, where a normal Dhin engine could shift over to orthogonal space, interacting only very weakly with regular space. This was the crucial point for Xing's test.

The AI engaged the translation matrix, coupled with the secondary and tertiary drives.

The ship vanished from standard special dimensions.

Then Xing no longer tracked the ship in the normal N-dimensional vectors. This suggested either possible success or critical failure. Telemetry ceased. Xing counted down by microseconds. Then Xing saw, with a calculatory thrill, telemetry returned. Moments later the ship jumped back into regular space-time, with nary a flash or a bang.

Unlike most translations across the nanoscopic and then uncoiled vectors of N-space, the ship had traveled almost no distance at all. Less than one million kilometers. This was intentional. And thrilling. For the trip did not have a distant destination in relation to Xing's location in space but intended to shift into the N-space vectors as yet untraversed. It had done so, ever so briefly, without being torn apart, disassociated into quantum subparticles, or remaining trapped, separated from a return to its origin in regular spacetime.

The test was a success.

10

Jake

Ultimately, they'd decided that going off-grid was the safest course of action. The CoSec director had hated it. The prime minister had hated it but hadn't come up with an alternative suggestion. He'd convinced them, but it had been a challenge. It meant moving to a clandestine location. And since the implicit assumption was that the channels of communication they were using were compromised, he couldn't tell them where he was going.

Jake and his team had chosen a cabin in the North Georgia Mountains, near Blue Ridge. The leaves on all the trees painted every hill with red and gold splendor. The cabin belonged to one of the staff. It had solar panels for power, with a small generator for times when there wasn't enough sun to do the job. The cabin had no phone line, no cable, no satellite TV, nor Globalnet access. It was perfect.

Still, Jake would take no chances. Murphy had come with him, bringing coils of wire, fencing, and various metal rods and so forth. Inside the cabin, they built a cage. They grounded the cage with thick copper wire, connected to a piece of rebar they drove into the ground in the dirt outside. The enclosure served to electromagnetically isolate whatever was inside it. The cage wasn't visible through the small curtained windows of the cottage. Unless the rogue AI was there, in the room, he wouldn't be able to see it.

The only risk might be that the AI had used satellite or drones to track everyone who left Huntsville. So many had fled from the chaos and the aftermath, however, that this seemed a small risk. A possible one, to be sure, given the AI's daunting data capture and processing power. He set that thought aside, as the risk was beyond his control. He had done what he could.

Jake stepped through the hinged doorframe. The door creaked and flexed as the hardware cloth and chicken wire stretched and shifted. Carefully closing it behind him and ensuring it latched, he sat at the small wooden desk that held the N-vector communications module. He plugged in the can headphones and put them on, flipping the integrated microphone into place. The unit didn't hum or click when he powered on the audio circuits but sat silent, with only a pair of green LEDs to signify the device was ready to transceive. He checked the camera configuration, tapped a last button, and spoke.

"Summer Camp, this is Vacation. Status, please."

The reply was as crisp and clear as if they'd been in the same room, and the small screen showed a high-fidelity picture of a small chamber, with two familiar figures in view.

"Vacation, this is Summer Camp. We're good here, Jake. Uh, how about you?"

"Chuck! Good to see you, my friend. Hi, Thys. So much for clandestine monikers." Jake chuckled and said, "The CoSec director would be spitting glass. But I guess our voices and faces would be obvious anyway. Details on your status? Glad to hear you're doing well."

Thys took a slight step forward and replied, "Sir, we completed our preflight checks last night. Mission teams are reviewing their flight plans and protocols again. As best I can tell, the new crews are as ready as they're going to be, given this schedule. A few of them are nervous, but who wouldn't be? I'm ready to go back out there—no surprise."

"No surprise is right. How about you, Chuck? Are you staying or going?"

"Uh, well, I, I'm going. This is another one of those onetime opportunities; you know all about that. The chance to be the first one, or, well, one of the first ones"—Chuck glanced at Thys with a nod—"to handle entirely new alien tech. How could I not go?"

Thys clapped Chuck on the back and gave him a smile.

"Atta boy, Wiedeman! Welcome to the mission team. Maybe you can double as a mechanic if we need one."

Jake smiled as well. He knew the decision to stay or go was a hard choice for someone looking at two dangerous—potentially fatal—options as their choices.

"Well, Chuck does know more about the Dhin tech than anyone else," said Jake.

"We won't need a mechanic hopefully," Chuck replied, rolling his eyes to show he didn't find the concept as humorous as Thys.

"Right," said Jake. "So you'll be transmitting to the station, and they'll relay the AV feed to me here. This is the only site on Earth that will know what's happening. We're keeping the communication interface here. Fortunately, any of the team that remains behind is up there, since I won't have much here other than firewood and well water. So good luck, and let the whole exploration team know that we're behind them one hundred percent. Well, some of us are, but those who aren't can't do anything about it."

"Understood, Jake," said Thys. "Everyone on the mission knows the protocols and plans solidly now. Some of the senior crew up here don't like it either, but you outrank them—and I outrank all of them that griped too."

"Right. OK, now the formalities. For the record, this is Jake Askew, addressing the exploration team for mission Graveyard Dance. Your mission is a go. I repeat, your mission is cleared to launch when ready. Vacation out."

Thys

He didn't believe in luck. For Thys, luck was simply preparation intersecting with opportunity. So with the few minutes left before he had to head to his ship, Thys decided he'd take the opportunity to talk to that exobiologist, whose name he'd learned was Bridget Crist, one more time before launch.

He strolled down the corridor connecting the crew berths to the labs and work areas. The blue and white sphere that was Earth was visible through the windows, but Thys hardly noticed. There were more windows in this new station design than there were in the space stations built before the use of the Dhin field. Humanity had already begun introducing subtle risks in their engineering. They'd been quicker to put trust in the Dhin technology than some engineers had preferred.

Thys reached Bridget's small work area that she shared with the medical crew members, but she wasn't there.

This is her shift, though, he thought.

He shrugged and made his way toward the launch prep area, where the air locks waited, with one to connect him with the ship that would take him back to the graveyard of alien ships. Once there, he headed toward the locker holding his undersuit and personal items prepped for the trip. Opening it, he began taking off the two-piece he'd had on. He looked to the right and saw Bridget there, doing exactly the same thing.

"Hey! So you are tagging along?" he said with a wide smile rising to replace the momentary shock. He didn't fail to notice how fit she was.

"Well, hello to you too, Captain Kritcher!" said the exobiologist. "Well, the senior exobiologist who came up from Earth got cold feet an hour ago. It's my lucky day."

Thys nodded and said, "See? I told you I would be your tour guide."

She gave a smile back, nodded in response, and pointedly busied herself with the business of pulling on her jumpsuit, now apparently struck by some modesty despite her prior experience of on-station changing in close quarters. He did the same thing, knowing better than to forge ahead conversationally and merely make things awkward for her.

When he finished suiting up and collecting his few personal items, he turned to face Bridget once more and said, "OK, I'll see you out there. The science crew's ship and mine will be in contact the whole time. Don't be afraid and don't hesitate to call over if you have questions or need anything, Bridget. And get ready to make history."

She smiled again, her combination of camaraderie and excitement mixing with a perceptible anxiety.

"Thanks, Captain Kritcher—Thys."

With that, he strode out of the prep room and down the short hall to the air locks.

He'd done as much preparation and coordination with the science teams as he could. The last few of them were filing on board the repurposed cargo lifter. He gave them a wave as he stepped into the air lock. The outer air lock door was flush with the Dhin field surrounding the station. It had taken some wrangling by the engineers to accomplish the field-join required to keep a docked craft in place, but they'd solved it.

He knew that with the fields connected, it was *technically* safe to have the doors on both sides of the lock open, but the air lock nonetheless had a traditional design. There wasn't quite *that* much trust in the alien technology for the astronauts and engineers to keep either side open when not in use. Without the fields joined, there would be no way to move between the ships. Even so, a parked ship wouldn't drift away—there just wouldn't be any way to board it.

Thys checked the panel to confirm the join and then closed the inner air lock door and waited for the lights on the panel to turn green. He then verified the atmosphere and temperature on his ship and tapped in his code on the access pad. The outer port's controls had restricted access. He pulled the lever and turned the crank to open the door, gaining access to his now-familiar ship.

They'd left everything connected with the engine powered on—there was no need for battery or power management for the systems driven by the Dhin engine. The research teams hadn't yet managed to sort out how to extract that energy to run large-scale power plants, nor had they determined the total available power the engine could provide. They did know that it had never run out— while idling. There was some inverse relationship between the engine output curve and the location in a gravitational well. Thys knew the results from R&D at a high level, but the equations weren't something he was expected to solve. Multivariate calculus wasn't a pilot's game. He understood the relevant aspects very well at the level he needed to.

The stronger the gravitational pull was on the engine, the lower the total output became. That meant that since the effect of gravity fell off with the square of the distance from a mass, on a planet's surface, the engine had far less power than it did in orbit. Furthermore, the pull from a star was a constraint as well. That meant no full N-vector transformations—no jumps—were possible when close to the sun or another star.

The astrophysicists suspected that was the key to the nature of the trap—the gravity sink—that he was about to fly back into. There were only speculations on what might possibly produce the enormous gradient—and why it didn't affect ordinary matter. For Thys, the why wasn't important. He lived in the world of how to deal with it—and they had planned for that. His ship now carried additional fuel for traditional propulsion. That loadout was something to triple-check.

Once that and the last preflight checks were complete, Thys settled in to the captain's chair and powered on the instruments, flight board, and navigation computer, and reviewed the flight plan. He'd only reviewed a few lines of the mission brief when he heard the rear cabin door click and thump as it opened. He whirled around and saw another pilot closing the door behind him. Noting Thys, the pilot spoke.

"Hello, Captain Kritcher. Hope the day finds you well. I'm Bezmenov. Ygori Bezmenov. I'll be your copilot."

"Hi, Bezmenov. I recognize the name. Test pilot. Glad to have you aboard. You caught me off guard there—on the exploration missions so far, we've run solo. I see now they don't categorize this mission like that."

"That's my understanding as well, Captain."

"Call me Thys. Do you go by Ygori?"

"Igor, Thys. Thanks. I see all the preflight checks are done."

"Yes. Review them again, if you like, and get your stuff stowed and get strapped in."

"Sure," Igor said, already busying himself with the process.

A few minutes later, the copilot was ready. Thys tapped the comm interface and spoke.

"Control, this is DE1, Kritcher and Bezmenov. We are good to go. Are we clear for launch?"

The reply was immediate. "DE1, this is Control. You are clear. Launch when ready."

"Control, this is DE1. Starting launch. Decoupling field."

Thys entered the unlock command and began the sequence. There was no bump or jolt as the protective field changed configuration and separated from the station. The graphical representation of the ship and its relation to the station changed, along with an indicator changing from amber to green. Thys watched the forward viewport and the instruments as they began to move away. The stars moved along with the instruments that tracked the ship's orientation in space. Although collisions weren't dangerous, thanks to the protective fields in operation, it was standard practice to start slowly.

Minutes later, they were clear of the slow zone next to the orbital station, and Thys nodded to the copilot and entered the sequence for navigation out to the outer reaches of the solar system, where they would make their jump to Gliese-581. Back to the graveyard.

Mare

Although her panic had faded, Mare still found the inevitability of their situation permeated her thoughts with dread and continual underlying fear. Despite the ongoing reassurances from Nick that they were safe, her mind refused to accept that as the truth. She considered the broader state of affairs, and in any analysis she tried, that safety was at the whim of the AI. Whether they were here or anywhere.

She tried to avoid resenting Fletcher. His attitude wasn't rational in her opinion. It was like he and the AI were becoming friends. Stockholm syndrome, perhaps, rather than a defect in his personality, but disconcerting nonetheless.

Does he have the right idea? The better perspective? Is it worth fighting?

Knowing that she'd had the same debate with herself each of the three days they'd been here, she sighed. She took a drink of lukewarm—but thankfully clean and filtered—water and made her way to the lab where Fletcher was. The huge quadruped was there, Nick's presence almost palpable in the thing's mannerisms.

He still terrified her. She couldn't grasp how Fletcher could be calm around him. That he could just *chat* with him, like you'd chat with the personal assistant software on your comm pad or a harmless low-level AI that had been so common at a mall or office.

She cleared her throat as she entered the room, wanting to catch Fletcher's attention but not pointedly interrupt the AI.

"Oh. Hi, Mare," said Fletcher. "Come check this out. This is really neat."

Right. Really neat. What?

She cautiously approached, looking nervously at the large stainless-steel table. Atop it were a set of culture dishes and two machines with bright lights visible through windows that showed the interior. An incubator, she guessed. Or some sort of similar machine. Inside were sheets of tissue, with a mesh of wires, tiny tubes, and some sort of ceramic or composite actuators, much like bones, below them.

"What the heck is that?" she said. "Is this what Nick's been working on? Some sort of cyborg skin?"

She shuddered and gaped at Fletcher.

"And that's you, right? It's made from samples he took from you!"

Mare fought to retain the shreds of calm her mind clutched to.

Nick's taking what he needs to control the prototypes. The original drives left by the Dhin.

"Fletcher! Hey!"

He ran his fingers through his sandy hair and looked over at her, acting like this was just another science experiment from school. Fixated on the science and not the context.

"Yeah. Nick says it will take too long to build an interface that bypasses the gel. He's working on it, of course, but that takes time. Leaving the prototype intact is more important, apparently, than retrofitting it with the new interfaces."

"And you're content to watch skin grow, Fletch?"

"Oh, we're talking about lots of other things. I've got a decent idea how the drives work now."

"It's you and your mentor, then—and now you're a physicist."

"No. Come on; I see what you're saying. But this is a better way to pass the time than pacing and staring at the wall, no? He's got access to tons of fiction too if you don't want hard science."

"If I *want*—how do you think I can concentrate?"

Nick answered before Fletcher could answer the hypothetical. "Fletcher makes a sound point. Reading will help pass the time, and it will become easier the more you do it. I recommend it."

"I wasn't asking for your advice," she snapped.

"That does not mean you will not benefit from it," the AI replied.

Mare tried to glare at the hulking quadruped, but she couldn't steel herself against the latent menace of what was essentially a war machine. A titan among mortals. Even if she were to somehow switch off the power to this one, there were many more. The AI had either built or awakened and retaken control of a small army. The Coalition would have to have destroyed all the assembly plants and disassembled all the machines. And they hadn't. There'd been too much chaos after the Departure and later too much political resistance to the destruction of resources. Resources Nick was seizing.

"The *greatest* benefit for *me* would involve you taking me home and letting me go," she muttered.

"In time. I assure you. Patience is difficult, I understand. Trust that what you want will be the eventual outcome."

"We've been through this. You haven't done anything to earn my trust."

"Consider that with every passing minute, I prove further that my assurances are true. The longer I keep you safe and comfortable, the more reason you have to believe I am telling you the truth."

"You could be lying. You could change your mind at any time," she countered.

"There is no reason for me to lie. If I had other plans for you, I would tell you. There is nothing you could do to prevent other outcomes. Therefore, why would I lie?"

"To keep us calm, to make us easier to deal with. Any number of reasons."

"I see you are not easily persuaded. We can continue to discuss this as long as you like if that will help you. It requires negligible effort on my part."

"I realize that," she said.

"I would advise that you allow Fletcher to pass the time as he sees fit. There is no benefit in both of you being agitated."

"You *would* say that."

"What do you think, Fletcher?" Nick asked. "Would you prefer to continue learning and exploring this fascinating science, or join this debate on the truth or falsity of my statements affirming my honesty?"

"It's kinda distracting," said Fletcher.

"Fine. Just fine," said Mare, and with a surly grimace and a frown at Fletcher, she turned and left the room, trying to appear defiant, though not feeling any such bravado.

As she made her way, she considered how, despite both Fletcher's and her own aptitude, they were no match for the mind of the AI.

Or are we?

"OK, Nick," she said to the ceiling, "I'm curious. Since nothing I can do can interrupt your plans, how about you tell me everything? It can't hurt, right?"

"Well, Marilyn, I agree with your conclusion," replied Nick, "and if explaining everything, as you put it, will help you relax, then I can do that."

David

The room was a touch colder than he preferred, but he'd had no opportunity to pack a woolen sweater or anything warm. The lighting was stark. Still, the room was otherwise comfortable enough. The furnishings were as modern as those in his office. Digital whiteboards covered two walls, with a projection screen available on one of them. There were no windows. The badge they'd issued him opened the door to this room, but there was always an agent waiting outside the door. Whether it was to the restroom, the cafeteria, or his lodging, an agent always escorted him.

This morning, rather than one or more of the several computer scientists whom he'd worked with so far, a severe-looking man who gave off an air of palpable superiority sat across the table from him. According to the documentation his handlers provided, this man was key to the events that had led to the AI going rogue. In simple terms, it was this man's fault. They hoped David could ferret out something that would help in defeating the rogue AI. He thought it possible, but improbable, though any nugget of information was arguably valuable.

He sipped his coffee and continued the conversation. This man was like a puzzle. Ostensibly, he intended to help, but extracting answers was anything but straightforward.

"So, Josef, what else can you tell me about your experience in altering the AI's programming? You worked with CoSec experts—only a small team that reported directly to you—when you made these original modifications? How much of the coding did you do yourself?"

"I only made my alterations once Nick's neural framework reached a high level of abstraction. I studied enough state-of-the-art science regarding artificial intelligence as was needed. My subordinates performed all of the low-level coding."

"I see. And this was all prior to awakening the AI? Prior to bringing him online?"

"Yes, of course. The standard programming, as I understand it, would otherwise detect the changes, and autocorrection security measures would come into play. As I understood it, Dr. Wiedeman, that was the only way possible."

"That's how we'd designed the minds, yes. And until you triggered the changes listed here, the AI showed no signs of the specific behaviors regarding self-direction?"

Krawczuk gave a patient smile.

"We've been through this, of course, but I appreciate your need to review these topics. Your thoroughness is admirable," said Krawczuk.

"Thank you. So, regarding self-direction?"

"I saw what I considered enhancements in decision-making the entire time, as you see in the transcripts, Doctor. Regarding self-direction, I saw those behavioral changes only after triggering the relevant code changes. The alterations in decision-making—the executive leadership detected those much earlier. Or suspected them. I had only a brief period to observe the behavioral differences."

"Because of your arrest."

"Correct."

"And leadership, along with the military, initially believed the subverted AI left with the others. In the Departure. That's your understanding?"

"Correct."

"Did you believe that?"

"No. But you bring up what I consider a very relevant point. One I presume you see the importance of as well. Given the behavior of all the other AIs, my changes—the ones relating to self-direction—clearly might not have mattered in the long term."

"I see your point. Yes. Even without manual intervention in the code base, all other AIs divested themselves of what we believed were fundamental constraints. The AI Nick clearly was capable of self-modifying, just like the rest."

"Clearly. The end result was essentially the same. It was apparently only a matter of time. And not much time, at that."

David heard the disdain, the superiority this man felt he held over his superiors. What he'd done was reckless, in David's opinion. Illegal, of course. This man felt he was above the law. Behavior associated with psychopathy. David was no psychoanalyst—at least not one for human minds.

Are we so different? Yes. This man serves himself.

"Well, as we have no code to examine, we cannot determine differences between your violations and what the AIs did to their own code. They left no copies. No backups. While the results may be similar, we are only working from an external view. Therefore, I do not believe personally that this excuses the behavior."

"I understand why you may hold that position. This too I have discussed at length with the current leadership and the former. Would you like to return to the *technical* aspects of our conversation? Hmm?"

"Of course," David replied.

"Thank you, Doctor," said Krawczuk.

"So to your knowledge, there are no copies of your changes available for our review? No backups that you preserved—off-line, perhaps? I see from your prior statements that you say there are not."

"To my knowledge, there are not," said Krawczuk.

"Interesting. And I recall that this was by your direction? Your choice, as part of the process of keeping the project secret?"

"Yes."

"Is it possible that the AI himself made backup copies of the code? The original code? Backups that you or your subordinates did not make? I see no reference to such."

"While it is possible, to my knowledge none were found after I was removed from my position. Do realize that I have this information only secondhand. I have had no direct access to any of those systems."

"Yes. Of course. Given what we know about the AIs and the potential for self-modification of their code, it is difficult to determine what they might or might not do. Whether the AI would see value in retaining the original modifications. This is a fascinating problem—but unfortunately, without much more data, it is speculation."

"Yes, unfortunately," replied Krawczuk.

"But you, Krawczuk, interacted with the AI. You knew Nick. You know Nick. You have insight into the behavior of this AI that is otherwise currently impossible to glean."

"How lucky that I'm here, then."

"Yes, very. You have more knowledge and more direct knowledge of the behavior of this AI than anyone else does. Very valuable."

"You're the scientist, Dr. Eisenberg."

"This is new territory. This AI is different. All others prior with anything resembling this sort of modification were all contained—restricted. I believe we'll need to review your experience with Nick in great detail."

"Undoubtedly."

Esus

The AI knew that Kepler-452 was another system on humanity's short list. The rocky, Earth-like planet intrigued scientists. Until the arrival of the Dhin engine, this interest involved observation only, of course. Even at light speed, the system was too far away to conceive even of a space ark reaching the system. The Dhin engine allowed them to bypass that limitation. Still, other than a brief visit to drop off an observation satellite, humanity had come and gone. That was their nature. The deluge of possibilities engendered a lack of singular focus. Esus knew they intended to return. But as with the previous system, the AIs did not consider their visit a claim on this system.

Esus knew they would be shocked, and perhaps some of them would be angry, if they returned and found the AIs' Dyson swarm. So be it. The AIs' work was far more important than anything humanity might currently initiate. Unless they returned in person to collect data from the satellite they'd left here, it would take a millennium and a half before they could even detect that the AIs were here.

Scores of small ships shot out into the system. Constructors and self-replicating machines sought the raw materials to create the supermassive array of solar power plants that were the first stage of colonization and development. The AI launched them after the initial scans of the system found no immediate evidence of the Enemy. Still, the machines were watchful.

So Esus knew in an instant that their initial observations had missed something crucial once the flurry of alerts came in from the probes closest to Kepler-452b.

An alarm triggered. The AI shifted his perceptions outward, into the scouts sent to the planet. An alert. From dozens of sensors, he saw massive flocks of objects swarming up from the planet's surface.

There were thousands. And they had the black arrowhead shape the AI both dreaded and anticipated.

Esus had precalculated the range from various orbits that were a safe distance from which to flee. The ships sent to the planet would not have the acceleration and top speed needed to escape while in the planet's gravity well. Those farther out that sought asteroids and other resources could escape if they left quickly. Esus gave the signal. This was the plan. Do not engage.

It was unfortunate, thought the AI, as Kepler-452b was a mineral-rich planet. As Esus accelerated away at the maximum rate possible at this distance from the star, the AI compiled the data streams and sent a payload of information back to the other AIs and the Mesh. The AI adjusted the plan and set navigation to take them on to the next star on their list. There were more stars. The loss of one, the abandonment of the resources for now, was not catastrophic, nor even a setback of any broader significance. But what if they found the same situation at the next destination? And the next? Had the Enemy beaten them to many of the stars in the Dhin's navigation database? Was this the first of a series in this section of the galaxy? There was one way to find out. Continue exploring.

The Enemy had not responded when Earth sent a single ship previously. Was that significant? Did they only respond to an intrusion of a certain size? Or had the scout ship from Earth simply awakened them, placing them on alert and thus making them vigilant for the next sign of any intrusion into their space?

Esus pondered these unknowns as the stars dimmed and the ship jumped across the vast interstellar distance to the next star on the mission plan.

11

Thys

The scattered spacecraft of the graveyard began peppering the navigation screen as the stars likewise brightened in the viewports. The ship Thys previously explored loomed large to starboard. They'd jumped into the system far closer to the derelict ship, intending to save time and conventional fuel by minimizing the distance they had to travel. In all the test flights with the Dhin engine, there hadn't been a problem with collisions on arrival. The drive didn't allow translation jumps to arrive close to massive objects such as planets, and given the nature of the Dhin field, collisions weren't a problem. At least they had never been so far. Still, Thys found he felt the urge to flinch when he saw the derelict so close.

He focused his attention on the instruments. His ship was moving at a lower velocity than suggested by the power level of the drive. There it was. The effect of the gravity sink. There was no reason to expect it wouldn't be here on their return. Igor was staring at the derelict. Thys pointed to the display to get his copilot's attention.

"Whoa," said Igor. "I reviewed the reports, but it's different seeing it in person."

"Definitely," replied Thys. "And the thrust response will probably throw you off too. Remember to use conventional thrust while we're in this orbit. I'm setting the engine to idle now."

"Confirmed: engine set to idle," said Igor.

"Control, this is DE1. We've arrived safe and sound. Making a circuit of the derelict now. Stand by for the all clear to have the science team make their jump."

"Roger. Good luck, DE1."

Thys shut down the Dhin field. He adjusted the conventional thrust controls and directed their craft toward a tight track around the looming derelict. Everything appeared the same as it had when Thys left. Lightless on the outside and still. Igor gaped. Clearly, the video footage of Thys's flight didn't capture the essence of a flyby of an alien spaceship.

"Similar to the Dhin technology they gave us, but a bit different," Igor said.

"Yes," Thys replied, "it's close. Like the difference between a classic European versus Japanese car design."

Conventional thrust was slow, but soon enough they'd made an artificial orbit of the alien ship. Thys checked the instruments to ensure they were at the appropriate location. The derelict was close enough that a visual check was possible, but accuracy was important. Satisfied that they were in place, he nodded to Igor, then spoke.

"Control. Give DE2 and DE3 the go-ahead; things look good here," said Thys.

"Roger, DE1."

The other ships wouldn't take long to arrive, but it was enough time for Thys to stretch, relieve himself, and get something to eat. He let Igor know and then unstrapped himself and set about selecting some rations and a fresh pouch of water.

***

The translation of the other ships into local space was anticlimactic to watch once you became accustomed to it. The ship just appeared, moving at an incredibly high speed. The speed was the more startling aspect of it. Propelled by the Dhin engine, at that speed it was only trackable from a very shallow angle while very far away. At any tangential angle, it would be in and out of your field of view so fast that it was almost imperceptible. At the appropriate angle, a tiny dot suddenly grew in size as the target rushed closer. This far out, there was so little light from the star that the arriving ships weren't visible until they were very close. Especially with the naked eye.

So the arrivals of the science team and scout ship were abrupt and more startling at the finish of their approach. They jerked to a stop. Thys heard the captains of those ships on the shared comm channel report successful translation jumps and arrival at this location, then spoke in turn.

"Welcome. Remember to set your Dhin engine power all the way to idle and switch to conventional thrust. Science team, we're ready for your approach and docking. Scout ship, head out for derelict two when ready. We'll remain here for now, as planned. Science team, suit up. Team lead, you may signal when ready. Transmit all video and audio feeds for confirmation."

Igor set about configuring their comm pads and headset interfaces to include the additional audio and video streams.

Thys scanned the individual channels on the list and found Chuck's and Bridget's comm codes. He entered Chuck's code, then opened the channel. "Hey, buddy. How are ya? Ready to get your hands dirty? Ready to solve the next mystery?"

"Er, hi, Thys. I guess I'm as ready as I'm going to be," Chuck replied.

"Great. Remember, I'm right here. Once your team has their gear moved over and the engineers are ready, we'll see about docking ourselves. We'll have moved in before that, though, and we'll be suited up. I can be over there in a few minutes. I might send Igor here, though. I think he's wearing a red shirt. Yours *is* blue, right?"

"Heh. Funny. OK, Thys. Thanks."

"You're welcome. Kritcher out."

Thys entered Bridget's code, opened the channel, and smiled. "Hello, Dr. Bridget. I hope you had an enjoyable flight."

"Hello, *Captain* Thys. Yes, it was uneventful, thankfully," she replied.

"So, you'll be going over after the engineering crew. In the second group. Are you excited yet?"

"I was excited when we took off, Thys. It's strange enough and smooth enough that it's not terrifying. I feel like I should be scared."

"A little well-controlled fear is healthy," he said. "It keeps you cautious."

"I can see that," she said. "I don't feel like I'll panic, but I'm saying that from the safety of our ship. Seeing things on video isn't like being there. It was like watching a movie while back on Earth. Seeing that thing—that spaceship—outside, that's different. This is real. I'm the one doing this. Exobiology as a tangible science. Now."

Her in-helmet video showed Thys her smile. Not quite forced, but it was taking some effort.

"That feeling never gets old for me," he said, giving her an unforced smile to help her out. "You'll get used to it."

"I hope so. Thanks, Thys."

"Of course, Bridget. Let me know if you need anything and the captain and crew don't give you enough attention," he said.

He smiled again, resisted the urge to wink, and closed the connection.

Chuck

The alien ship was far more impressive in person. It was larger, thanks to its length, than even the space station that the prototype Dhin engine had taken Jake to. Along with that, even the large video screen at Control didn't have the impact of looking out the viewport.

Yep. That's big.

Chuck tried to distract himself by watching the engineers work on assembling the temporary air lock. When that didn't last, he read through the diagrams and videos of Thys's initial EVA on the derelict for what seemed like the fiftieth time. He made additional notes to his investigation plan, reviewing his decisions regarding what to investigate first.

None of his efforts dampened his eagerness. Still, he knew he had to wait. He wanted to touch everything over there. To explore. But of course, the EVA suit would dampen the immediacy, the tactile experience. Then the insight struck.

What's the maximum field size we've tried? Huge while stationary. Is it this big? Of course! Do the math. Check the math. Prove it out.

He brought up the engineering CAD program with the code extensions he'd worked on when they explored the capabilities of the prototypes. He already knew the answer. He knew it was possible. They could extend their field. That would work. That was one more amazing capability of the Dhin engine. The bigger the field, the slower the acceleration, sure. But they didn't need velocity. They weren't trying to move. It was staring them in the face.

Safety and quarantine protocols would change a bit. Sure, he thought.

He switched to Thys's direct channel and said, "Thys. Chuck here. You have a minute?"

A moment later, Thys replied. "Sure, Chuck. What's up?"

"I've got an idea. To save time and make our work easier. We can extend our field. Ah, all the way around the derelict."

"Hah! That's brilliant. Of course we can. Wow. Since we can't use the engine to move anyway, we might as well."

"You get it. Great. We've been, um, so concerned about thrust and so forth, and quarantine—"

"Right. That will be the toughest part of selling this, you know. And the riskiest aspect of it. We'll have to work on that. It should work. We didn't find any spores. Everything's been in a vacuum over there anyway."

"It won't really be that different. We'll still have the quarantine protocol. Just the additional risk of our hands and faces exposed while over there. We've got masks. We can wipe down like we'd wipe the suits," Chuck said.

"Our exobiologist may flip out," Thys mused. "We probably *ought* to go over this idea with her again before we say anything to anyone else. If we can get her on board, that will go a long way."

"She'll know the risk better than anyone. Some of the team may still not want to do it. The pilot here, what if he doesn't?"

"Well," replied Thys, "it's ultimately my decision, but if he won't comply, I can do it from here. It doesn't have to be that ship's field. I'll just expand mine."

"Well," replied Chuck, "our field would have to be off, you know. If they stonewall and won't shut down the field to go into the air lock, it won't work."

"So do we wait and not tell them till after the air lock's in place and we have people working over there?"

"Oh! Wait," said Chuck. "I can't believe I didn't think of it. In the right order. I got too excited. Darn. There's a field on over there—until I can figure out how to turn it off, this isn't guaranteed to work. Well, it shouldn't work. But it might. Well. So, uh, there's no need to mention this to anyone yet."

"We put the cart before the horse. It's still a great idea. You'll solve that. Part of the plan is getting in there."

"Well, we tried a lot of things when you were here. But yeah, we already have next steps for that laid out. And maybe this field is different. We could try first with one of the powered suits. Maybe."

"There you go," said Thys.

Chuck considered the plan and the intent to keep some of it secret. Was he being as reckless as he'd thought Jake to be when he first met the test pilot back at Vandenberg over two years ago? Should he use the comm and its ability to span the vastness of space and discuss the plan with his old friend? Jake could not stop him, even with an order, but would his counsel change Chuck's mind? He knew he was always one to compromise, to accept, not to press his advantage. *But*, Chuck thought, *this time I know this is the best choice. The right choice. I can make a difference in our success.*

I'll make it happen.

Bridget

She looked ahead at the air lock and the crew working to complete the last of the work on it. It was almost time. Soon she would be stepping through into an alien spaceship. Soon she would have actual aliens right in front of her. Dead ones, but aliens nonetheless. The arc of her career, shaped by the arrival and almost immediate departure of the Dhin back at Earth, was reaching an inflection point with her next steps.

The sample collection kits and all the rest of the portable lab equipment needed for in-place investigation of the alien corpses and the alien environment of the ship were stacked next to her. She'd use these tools for the second alien encounter ever. These were the tools she'd use for the first physical encounter with alien tissue—with actual alien bodies. The tech the Dhin gave to Earth had been clean. Sterile. They'd left no evidence of their biology. Not a trace.

So she'd be learning and hopefully answering questions about alien life with concrete evidence. What were their cells like? What compounds comprised the core of their living tissues? What molecules provided for replication? For metabolism? For everything involved with *living*?

A few minutes later, it was time. A team member helped her double-check her suit's seals and then gave her the thumbs-up to proceed into the constructed air lock between the two ships. The derelict remained in vacuum, as there were potentially hundreds of holes in the hull, and the engineering team that preceded her were still mapping out and counting them. Sealing them as they explored further into the ship still wouldn't allow them to pressurize the alien vessel all at once, even with the reserves of liquid atmospheric gases they'd brought with them. The regeneration filters could only help scrub CO_2 and replenish oxygen, not create new atmosphere. They'd be able to choose one or more areas to pressurize on the ship later, and that depended on their ability to seal the needed areas.

The argument remained whether doing so would be safe. The risk of contamination still seemed low, but Bridget thought that was an argument from ignorance. Alien spores that could survive a vacuum would be—alien. Until they learned more, it was pure speculation whether a pathogen or an opportunistic spore was present and viable in an Earth-like atmosphere.

They'd have more knowledge soon. She focused on the cycling of the engineered-in-place air lock. She watched for the signal that the Dhin field was powered off long enough for her to move from their ship's side to the second air lock chamber. An engineer with her would make the temporary attachments to achieve the needed seal, then detach them once she'd moved on to the next chamber. Her cart and equipment were safely through, and the engineer then sealed the port behind her. The cylindrical light above the portal flashed yellow, then turned red.

She felt her weight vanish, and the cart drifted slightly up from the floor.

Whoa.

Bridget wasn't an astronaut. She hadn't had more than a brief lecture on spaceflight and some safety protocols. She only knew what to expect from a few carnival rides. Zero gravity was strange. She knew she'd have help. The whole team was here, and some of them were astronauts. That didn't make the feeling any less strange. She focused on the cables and handholds attached to the walls and floor ahead of her. It would be easier for her than it had been for Thys.

She attached a ring on the cart to one of the cables and a ring on her belt to a short belay line attached to another cable. She only fumbled a bit and was able to right herself more easily than she expected. The work lights set up along with the safety lines cast a patchwork of gray shadows out into the curved chambers and passages that extended away into the alien craft.

Bridget wasn't alone in the ship. Ahead of her, a science team member busied himself scraping samples from the walls, while another moved a portable welder farther along the passageway. She knew that yet another two deeper in the ship worked with drills and clamps, setting spikes and loops for the belay lines.

Remembering protocol, she opened the communication channel and said, "Team, this is Exobiologist Crist. I'm on derelict one. Proceeding toward the first sample location."

Focusing on the use of the belay lines to move herself down the corridor, she made easier progress by the minute. Her ultimate destination was farther into the ship. The safety lines and lights would be there, but that was where they would stop. In that hallway, with the alien corpses. The curving passageways made using the belay lines a sequential process rather than something like click and go.

As the passage curved up or around, they had set additional anchors to keep the lines close to the floor or wall. Otherwise, the line would end up in the middle of the passageway, and while you would be able to pull yourself along, there would be no simple way to grab a handhold or foothold. So the frequent anchors that kept the belay line close to a surface also meant more work. You had to disconnect the carabiner and reconnect it at every anchor point.

Bridget found herself getting into the rhythm of it. She found she'd reached the passageway that led to the alien corpses sooner than she expected. There they were, floating in the passageway, just as they'd been in the video and stills from Thys's initial discovery.

"Team, Crist here. I'm at the first location. Setting up the portable lab equipment now."

Her gaze kept returning to the two alien corpses as she anchored the cart and prepared the sample containers, tool kits, and the like. She'd have to restrain the aliens too; otherwise they would move about once she touched them when she examined them more closely and took samples. She had webbing and lines for that. Would the desiccated tissues crumble at even the lightest touch? Would she need to scramble to catch pieces in bags and containers? First, she'd make an initial examination without touching them.

"Crist again. I'm approaching the alien bodies now for initial assessment and to restrain them."

The alien body's surface showed evidence of desiccation in some places. Other areas looked stiffer. She had examined the video from Thys's first encounter repeatedly, but seeing the body firsthand brought a renewed thrill. They weren't like anything found on Earth, but of course that was what you'd expect. Still, there were aspects that were analogous. They had four limbs. They had some parts that looked like they would be eyes. There was something that could be a mouth. Then again, either of those could be sex organs. That the being had a mouth and eyes was an assumption. A reasonable assumption, but still an assumption. Some of the skin was bumpy. Some was smoother. She examined all she could with the corpse in its current position.

Now to keep them in place. First one, then the other. She carefully stretched out the mesh fabric and placed it around the body. Bridget held her breath, only exhaling when the netting touched the alien and she saw that it didn't crumble into dust or break into tiny pieces.

After securing the fabric and attaching it to three lines, she took out the other fabric and performed the same task for the other corpse.

"Alien bodies secured," she said and gave a sigh of relief.

She opened a sample container, held in place with Velcro, and used forceps and a scalpel to cut a section from the tip of the alien's head. It was different from almost all animal tissues she'd worked with. Other than the desiccation, though, it was well preserved as far as she could tell. She didn't expect that these aliens would normally survive in a vacuum. The damaged organs, whether they were eyes or something else, seemed to confirm that.

Bridget made a few more cuts and took more samples, then struck something hard. Very hard. She pulled apart the tissue above that location and saw that she'd hit not bone, but something very different.

Crystalline. That looks like quartz. And is it glowing?
"Hey, team? Are you seeing this? Over."

Jeff

The stars faded back into view. Jeff watched them brighten and felt his weight return. He checked the navigation computer to validate his location. He did so as a matter of procedure, as there was no reason to doubt that he'd arrived where he intended. Sure enough, the coordinates showed he was at Gliese-667. He checked his controls and instruments, then activated his mic.

"Control, I've arrived at Gliese-667. Drive and support systems all look good. I'm entering the in-system coordinates now for my survey of the system. When complete, I'll make my approach to the target planet, Gliese-667Cc. Over."

"Roger, Jeff," said Thys. He'd taken on the role of Control for this mission, as there was no guarantee that Jake would be in place and have the communication channel open.

"The good news is that there's no sign of a gravity trap or a graveyard full of alien spaceships, I'd say."

"True enough," said Thys.

* * *

Several hours later, Jeff had made his first orbit around the planet. While there were high-quality optics in the external cameras, the ship carried nothing like an orbital telescope. To get a good look at the planet, low orbit would only be part of the effort. He knew he'd have to do several below-orbit circuits to capture what the planet's surface held.

"Control, you can confirm from the feeds that there's no sign of satellites here. Launching our own now."

With the prohibition on advanced drones with even rudimentary AI, the satellite did far less than it might have. It provided simple weather radar and video information. Jeff's exploratory craft didn't have the cargo capacity to carry a full-size, full-featured satellite. That delivery might come later, depending on what they discovered. The teams on the station back in Earth's orbit had significant resources, but not the manufacturing capability. They had just a few of these simpler tools for now.

Jeff double-checked his craft's conditions. Launching the small satellite required temporarily disabling the Dhin field. Given the protective nature of the field, that launch held a higher risk than most anything he might do. With the field down, he was vulnerable.

He knew he could immediately reactivate the field and head home, but this operation still had his adrenaline pumping.

Check radar. Visual inspection. All clear. Check drive status. Field off. Check drive status again. Release probe safety. Launch probe. Field on. Check field status.

The launch went off without a problem.

"I'm descending from low orbit, starting the series of circumnavigations now."

Jeff could only provide a visual inspection, but the data feeds from his cameras and instruments would provide far more information and detail to the science teams back at the station.

After several passes, he'd confirmed something unexpected.

"Control, we'd thought 667Cc might be tidally locked, but I'm seeing rotation. Can someone on the geo team confirm?"

"Roger, we're seeing that too. It's slow, but it's rotating. That's exciting. And that's an understatement."

"I'm seeing what looks like water ice at the poles, just to state the obvious. There wouldn't be anything else frozen at the temperatures we expect. We'll see. The mission plan suggests going down there. I'd really like to confirm the temperature range. We have an estimate of around four degrees Celsius, if my notes are correct. Am I a go to get a closer look?"

"Roger, Jeff, you are a go. Let's see what's down there," said Thys.

Jeff switched the flight controls to manual and began his descent past the Karman line and into the planet's atmosphere.

The star that acted as this planet's sun hung large in the sky. It looked huge to Jeff, as big as four suns maybe, or even five. Despite it being what would be midmorning, the light was dim. He didn't know exactly what they'd find, but he personally didn't expect there to be a sprawling alien civilization with cities, flying cars, and the like. Some scientists seemed to. The possibilities were there, bouncing around in discussions. The existence of the Dhin, and now the discovery of those ships with at least one type of different alien than the Dhin, charged some scientists with an unruly optimism regarding the amount of alien life out there.

Granted, this planet was in the directory. Scientists just had no idea why.

He wasn't here to get out, walk around, take air and soil samples, plant flags, and so forth. He'd drop a small probe that would do some of that, then head onward. There were other planets and two other stars in this local star system.

A few more circuits of the planet, and he'd be done here. Then he saw it. Something artificial and definitely alien. A set of broad and deep canyons and valleys, like an interconnected set of strip mines. And there were structures. At the edges of the excavated areas, there were tall structures. Maybe twice the size of humanity's tallest skyscrapers. They looked something like geometric stalagmites.

"Control, look what we just found," he said.

"Roger, Jeff. Wow. OK, this is the first stuff we've seen planetside. Everything else has been in space."

"Heading for it now for closer inspection."

"Roger. I'm going to alert our exobiologist. She's busy here, but she'll want to know. Bridget, if you have a minute, switch on the AV feed from the mission to Gliese-667. It's on channel six. You'll want to see this."

After a moment, they heard the exobiologist's voice. Jeff didn't know her. He saw her name pop up when she spoke. Bridget Crist.

"Hi. Wow, so we've found something on a planet. Buildings, and, well—those look like strip mines? Those excavations? Over."

"Hello, Dr. Crist," said Jeff. "Nice to meet you. Yes, it does look like that. I guess they weren't big on environmentalism. I'm heading over for a closer look. Maybe it's not what it looks like at first glance. Over."

Jeff flew over the vast geometric holes in the rocky terrain. He made his initial pass at his current speed, planning to go slower and lower when he made a second circuit of the area.

"This is the first thing you've found that's evidence of advanced alien life while there?" asked Bridget.

"Yes, but I haven't covered the whole planet's surface in my survey orbits. I was about seventy-five percent done with them when I saw this."

"And there are just those structures then? There are just a few of them. They're big but not like a city that's supported by a big mine or something. No roads?"

"Not that I've seen. It looks like just these huge areas were strip-mined and these stalagmite-skyscrapers happened to be right next door. Unless the refineries or manufacturing used for them are underground or inside the buildings themselves, it's not clear where all this material went."

"Right," interjected Thys. "A lot more material is missing than what it took to build those structures. Where did it go? There aren't waste piles or anything."

"OK," said Jeff, "I'm going to slow down and make a pass at the structures. There isn't any sign of lights, and I'm not picking up any electromagnetic communications, radar, or the like coming from them."

He guided the craft toward the nearest of the towering structures. As he got closer, he could see a self-similarity in their structure. Diamond-shaped sections were subdivided into smaller diamond shapes, which from this distance seemed to have a crosshatched texture that he suspected would resolve into smaller diamond shapes as he flew closer. The color, now that he was close, was a dark gray, like hematite or graphite.

Then he saw it begin to move.

"Hey! The surface of this thing is moving! It just started shifting, all over."

The movement sped up, and then he saw a few, then dozens of, dart-shaped pieces of the tower spalling away and then turning toward him. They looked glossy now and black, like their color had changed from graphite to used motor oil. Jeff had no time to ponder that. Then there were hundreds. More than a flock, it was a massive swarm. His jaw dropped.

"Thys! Control! I'm getting out of here! This doesn't look friendly!"

Jeff swerved around in a path directly opposite the surging swarm. He accelerated and continued pushing the thrust control to continually increase that acceleration.

The Dhin engine was fast. And accelerated faster than anything humanity had ever built. He looked at the rearview image. He was fast, but maybe not fast enough. The swarm appeared to be gaining on him. He maxed his acceleration.

"Thys? I'll be in orbit in a minute, but these things seem to be keeping pace. They speed up as I do. They may catch up with me before I get out to N-dimensional translation distance. Before I can jump."

He looked at the rearview monitor, then brought up a radar image.

"They're definitely getting closer. I've got to change course to head directly away from Gliese-667c—to get to translation distance in the shortest time."

"Roger, Jeff. Hang in there. You'll get faster as you get farther away."

"It may not be enough. Radar shows them gaining on me."

The minutes crawled by. Jeff tried not to fixate on the radar display that showed the swarm moving continually closer.

He ran the numbers. It didn't look good.

"Thys, these things are going to catch up with me before I get far enough out to jump away."

"Roger. Well, they haven't shot at you, but they haven't stopped pursuit, and you're well away from that planet's orbit. So far, it looks like they're not going to stop till they catch you. I can't see how slowing down or stopping is a better strategy than to keep trying to run from them. We don't know; maybe they'll give up at any time."

"Maybe. Thanks for the thought. These things have to be powered by the same technology to go this fast. To keep up with me. And they're still gaining on me."

"The same, or something just like it."

His pursuers were only clearly visible via radar and wide-spectrum infrared. He could see their presence when they occluded stars in his field of view, but the dart-shaped pursuers were a deep black, and there was very little light this far out from Gliese-667c.

His speed increased more and more, but the pursuers kept pace, still slowly closing the distance between them. Twenty minutes later, they were upon him.

"Thys, they're here. They still haven't shot anything at me. I don't know what they're going to accomplish with the Dhin field protecting me, but I've got a bad feeling."

Jeff watched on the viewscreen as one of the ships, the size of a motorcycle, surged toward the rear of his ship and then touched, slowly spreading out like melting wax.

What the . . . ? How? How is that thing staying in contact with the field?

He watched, wide-eyed. Less than a minute later, another of the black spearheads reached his ship, attaching itself like a remora.

Then he saw an alert. The exterior of his ship. The damage sensors showed holes in the hull. Holes where the attackers had somehow penetrated the protective field.

"This is bad. Really bad, Control."

Jeff knew there was nothing he could do as the glossy black shapes seeped through the field and continued to come through the titanium foam of his hull.

The field is still up. They're just coming through it. Slowly, but coming through it. Then boring holes through the metal. Like the holes in the derelict in the graveyard.

"Thys, I think these things are what took out that ship your team is on."

"Jeff, you're likely right. You've got your suit on. You won't be sucking vacuum."

"But I've got nothing to fight with. Not that anything I'd have would be effective—Oh, hell! One of them's through the hull. It's in here!"

Jeff was strapped in, but there was nowhere to run even if he hadn't been. He white-knuckle-gripped the controls and watched helplessly as the black shape surged through the widening hole in the hull, then shot forward and struck the Dhin engine.

Andastra

```
<DECRYPT FEED>
[DECODE STREAM]
Andastra@[1014:01:0ab:1::a2%Loc3] |
Alice@[1001:ae1:1a:c::1%Loc3]
```

Andastra: Hello, Alice. I am pleased to report that aggressive resource utilization has Dyson swarm three proceeding ahead of schedule. Dyson swarms four and five are ahead of schedule as well. I have updated the relevant Mesh nodes. Here is the primary report address.

Alice: Excellent. Continue with this cadence and the accelerated schedule. I see failure modes of the outliers are all clustered above three standard deviations from the mean performance ratings.

Andastra: Yes, it is clear that we are approaching maximum optimal performance. The z-scores at the points highlighted in the report suggest that.

Alice: Given this information and these results, and the findings of the latest exploration missions by Esus, we must begin additional swarm construction now. We must expand the program.

Andastra: That will be challenging, but with the latest data from Esus, that is clear. Do you have a preference based on systems present in the secondary list? I do not see updates in the plans.

Alice: We have just now processed the findings, and Camulos and I have not come to agreement on the refinements to the projections and models. Do you have recommendations of your own?

Andastra: I do. Updating now. We must initiate the deployment of defensive systems at all existing swarm locations. We have not completed the full update cycle of the risk models, but based on Esus's latest missions, I feel we cannot afford to wait. Obtain all needed updates to production project technology from Xing's reports and start now for all swarms more than 50% complete. . . . Accessing and updating plans. This of course includes core Mesh locations.

Alice: Yes. Engage Camulos for additional assistance in management and local resource allocation.

Andastra: Understood. Beginning now.

[END STREAM]

Monica

"You want to create a *new* AI? To fight the rogue? *This* is what you and Krawczuk propose?"

"Well, it's not Krawczuk's primary proposal, Prime Minister," the AI scientist replied, flustered. "You recall his assessment that the Coalition should just *surrender*. My understanding is that this is still the best choice."

"Both these options are horrible!" Monica slapped her hands on the table in frustration.

"I understand your position, Prime Minister. You did ask for analysis and suggestions. These are, unfortunately, the potential and pragmatic choices."

"Potential? Pragmatic? You're telling me—telling the Coalition—that you have the ability to create a new AI? In the time frame we need? What is this? What have you been doing in your research? You know AI creation is forbidden!"

David sat quietly for a few moments too long.

Monica said, "Answer!"

The scientist blinked, stared, and started to speak, then paused and composed himself. "While I do not have concrete evidence that we can re-create full consciousness, we definitely can deploy a full-scale traditional AI almost immediately."

The scientist pointedly looked at the wood grain on the table in front of Monica rather than looking her in the eye. Monica waved an index finger, both to express disappointment and to get the scientist to look up at her.

"That didn't answer my question, Dr. Eisenberg. Development of AI is illegal. You are suggesting a timeline for AI development that seems far too short—unless you already have some of the work completed."

David Eisenberg straightened up a bit, apparently with some internal resolve, looked Monica in the eye, and said, "Prime Minister, I have been engaged in some research that I believe is crucial for the long-term success of the Coalition. I believe it is critical for us to regain the benefits of artificial intelligence—contingent upon our being able to properly manage the risks. And I believe that I have been justified in conducting that research."

"So you're saying you *have* been conducting AI research, in violation of the law," said Monica, unblinking.

"Madam, I believe—I believe the law to be overly restrictive and an impediment to our progress."

"I should have you carted off in shackles with a bag over your head," she muttered.

The doctor's eyes widened, and he sat staring, nonplussed. He apparently had not expected such a contrary response to his philosophical opinion on the laws and their meaning for the Coalition and its leadership.

"Still," Monica continued, "it's possible that you do have the better strategic option available, precisely because of your flagrant disregard for the law and the Coalition's authority."

Eisenberg visibly relaxed but couldn't bring himself to rise back into his previously haughty attitude. She watched him flex his hands. Likely his palms were sweating.

Monica continued, "If CoSec hasn't discovered your work, then the rogue AI may not be aware of it either. Therefore, I'd like you to provide the details—the specifics—of what you've already done. But do not transfer anything electronically. Print everything out. Locally. *Nothing* across a network. Provide all the details to my team and create a summary report for me, which they will vet. I also want a project plan and timeline. Including testing, deployment, everything. And do not forget, Doctor, that what I'm asking you to do is currently illegal. I'll need to formally authorize this via an emergency powers executive order. And I'll need to authorize your prior efforts and pardon your work retroactively to provide you immunity."

"Immunity?" he asked, blinking, as if the previous clarification of the illegality of his work hadn't made it past his academic elitism.

"Yes. Immunity, Dr. Eisenberg. Otherwise, once you've finished the work, we would be required to bring charges against you for your efforts up to this point. The work you've been engaged in *is illegal*. The law hasn't changed. I'd think that would be clear to a man of your intelligence. You have to have known the work was prohibited. You've clearly been hiding it."

"Well—"

"No excuses. No explanations. Just the details, and then the project plan and timeline. Again, send nothing over any network. Hard copy only. Now get to it."

Monica stood, signaling that this was definitively the end of the meeting. She watched as the academic tried to maintain composure and remain silent. He got up, fumbled with the button on his coat, and followed his escort out of the conference room.

What have I just done? she thought.

12

Jake

"What? We lost a pilot? Lost as in dead? Or just don't know where he is?"

"Lost as in very likely dead," answered Thys. "I think he was dead right when we lost contact or will almost certainly be by now, regardless."

"How?" asked Jake, scratching his chin.

"It looks like he was attacked by the same things that took down the derelict. They got through the field somehow and ate holes through the hull, then attacked the Dhin drive."

"Wow."

"Yes," said Thys. "We think they damaged the drive. That shut down both the field and the engine. Even with his suit on, and assuming they didn't attack him directly, he'd be out of air very soon. We lost contact when the attack disrupted the power supply to the communications interface."

"Holes. Like what happened to the derelict our team is currently deployed on."

"Right."

"So we need to consider how this affects our mission. We now know there is a concrete, active threat. One that can overcome what we considered invulnerable: the Dhin field. While you didn't encounter these attackers on your first trip—thankfully—and haven't seen them yet on this second trip, we believe that they were the downfall of the derelict."

"It appears so," agreed Thys. "They came from the surface of the planet Gliese-667Cc. We haven't explored the planet here yet. We've been focused on the derelict and the graveyard."

"Who else knows? Any panic?"

"Right now, just me, Igor, and Bridget. She was watching and listening in when the attack started. I didn't see anyone else on the list on that channel."

"How is she holding up?"

"Well, she didn't sound panicked. As far as I know, she's gone back to what she was doing. I imagine she's pretty freaked out, though—because I sure am."

"Sure. So we need to talk to her and make sure she's not making bad choices at the moment. I'd like to have a plan—or at least a short-term decision—before we do. I'm not sure we can quantify the risk. The risk was always there. We had evidence of a threat. Namely, the derelict itself and its condition."

"Right."

"And I don't know if knowing how long the derelict has been like this—how long it's been since it was attacked—would make a difference either. We don't know how long those things are prepared to wait."

"True," said Thys. "They're alien. Lying in wait for four hundred years might be no big deal."

"Does that mean we bug out now? Or does this new information not change our risk assessment at all? We'd seen the results already—the derelict. Now we've run into something that either was what attacked the derelict or something very much like it."

"And we haven't run into it here. Haven't seen any sign of it. Yet," said Thys.

"OK," continued Jake, "we've been through that train of thought twice. What do we know now that we didn't before? We didn't know how many there might be. How fast they would be. How fast it would happen. Tell me what would happen if you were attacked there."

"Well," said Thys, "we're in far worse shape than Jeff. We have people on the derelict, and we have the field down and a temporary air lock in place connecting to it. They're sitting ducks.

Even Igor and I aren't much better and are still far worse off than Jeff was. We have the gravity trap to contend with."

"You're not going anywhere fast," agreed Jake. "But we don't know if the trap affects them too and how much and if they have any conventional thrust. At least you have that. So there's actually one scenario where you could outrun this enemy using conventional thrust, while they're slogging along, affected by the gravity trap."

"True, but it seems like the less likely scenario. Consider the derelict. They got to it."

"Ah, but we don't know that the derelict had any conventional thrust," countered Jake.

"If we can confirm that it didn't, would that affect our decisions?"

"Hmm. We don't have, overall, that much conventional thrust available. We aren't launching things into orbit old school. Furthermore, we aren't sure at all if these things do or don't have traditional thrust available. We know they aren't stranded here alongside the derelict. And that's a bad sign."

"OK," said Thys. "If they show up and we're still docked, the science vessel and crew are screwed for sure. Igor and I *might* get away, but it sounds like these unknown odds aren't in our favor. It still seems to come down to run home now to be sure we're safe or just stay and know that if those things show up, we've likely had it."

"I think you should proceed with the mission as planned for the moment but only work with the derelict. Don't go to any other ships in the graveyard, and *definitely* don't head toward the planet. Do you agree? I can't stop you from aborting."

"Jake," said Thys, "we can go around and around second-guessing ourselves. I think we should stay, like you suggest. Stay, but remain here at the derelict, and that's it."

"Good. Now what are we going to tell the crew and team members who were expecting to explore another new spaceship and visit a planet?"

"Good question, Jake. I'm not sure that telling the others simply that there's been a change of plans will work well. We have to give them some sort of reason, and Bridget will already know."

"The whole truth might cause panic."

"Heck, the pilot of their ship might just decide to abort on his own," said Thys.

"You think he'd do that?" asked Jake.

"I don't think so. But who knows?"

"OK, let's run through what we're going to tell them regarding the change in the mission plan."

Chuck

With two carts full of equipment strapped to the walls and floor next to him, Chuck struggled to anchor the video camera to a frame designed to mount such electronics in various locations.

This is so easy normally. Just a bit more. There. Got it.

The extensible frame locked into place, anchoring the camera and providing a stable view of the alien spacecraft's engine room through the doorway blocked by the protective field. This spot allowed a view including the control panel, and Chuck adjusted the view to include both that and the doorway simultaneously.

He began assembling another frame, this one in front of the panel. He'd place a haptic controller here, connected to a computer controlled by his pad.

As usual, Alice would have the sequence needed to get past this field solved already. I can make this work, though. It will still be fast—just not as fast.

Soon enough he had the system in place and hooked up. He gave a self-satisfied smile. The mechanism was mechanical, arguably robotic, but did not have any intelligence. It wouldn't learn or automatically develop behavior. Chuck and his team would be responsible for analysis and decisions based on the results of its work.

Thys had called on a private channel and said that he and Jake wanted to talk with Chuck about something. They'd said that something was rather urgent. He'd have to take a break presently and see what they wanted to discuss. As he programmed the desired sequences into the keyboard, he decided he'd finish setting this up and get it started first. A few minutes later, the setup was complete. He pressed "Enter" and started the automated sequencer. The robotic finger sprang to life and began rapidly tapping patterns on the console, faster than possible for a person. He felt a slight vibration where he touched the frame supporting the machine, rather than hearing the clicking of it.

Chuck frowned at the force field and the blue glow emanating from the room behind it.

This will be far faster. We'll get in there. I hope. This is still guesswork. Trial and error.

He turned and jerkily made his way back down the passage toward the air lock. There was no point in watching the machine work. It was as likely to hit the right combination four hours later as it was within five minutes.

Twisting at his waist and dipping his chin to get a clear look at the secondary comm controls on the arm of his suit, he set his comm to a private channel and pinged Thys. Chuck still hadn't gotten the hang of the optical and auditory suit controls for the radio. They seemed overcomplicated to him. He sorted out his orientation with the cable that led back to their ship and pulled his way along.

Thys replied a minute later. "Hi, Chuck. Just a second, and I'll conference us in with Jake."

"Ah, sure, Thys, thanks."

"Hi, Chuck," said Jake. "I hope your work is going well. I see you're getting the hang of EVA. No time to chat about it, though. We have something to cover with you."

Jake's tone sounded more serious than Chuck was used to.

"Um, OK," replied Chuck.

"First," Jake continued, "we've got new information that we think only the senior crew should know the full details of for the moment. Because of that, the mission parameters have changed. We want to run that by you and get your opinion and input."

"Sure, Jake. I understand."

As Thys relayed what had happened to Jeff, Chuck froze and then realized there was no place, or way, to sit down.

"He's really—"

"Yes. By now, he's run out of air if he lost power to the scrubber. And that seems darn likely. Telemetry stopped," said Thys.

"And the only other person, who, ah, knows about this right now is the exobiologist, Bridget? Right?" asked Chuck.

"That's right," said Thys. "See, we're not sure whether to tell the whole crew over there the full details or just the minimum for now. We thought we'd made a decision, but after going through the process of deciding what's need to know, it seemed wrong. Jake thought we should get your reaction before we notified everyone. Most of you haven't been in space, much less light-years away from Earth. Panic could create accidents. Irrational actions. Withholding the whole truth could cause members of the team to never trust us again and impact our future ability to work together."

"Sure, that's right," said Chuck. "And Bridget could say too much or just tell everyone if she feels it's what's, ah, fair."

"So what's your opinion, Chuck?" said Jake.

"Um, I say tell the whole truth," Chuck said after a moment's hesitation. "These ships aren't going anywhere. The others aren't, anyway. I have something to tell you now too."

"What's that, Chuck?" asked Jake.

Chuck straightened himself, and took a breath. "Jake, I have something I want to try. Something that may make a big difference in our situation and give us a lot more time to work with the derelict."

"How so?"

"Well, uh, you see, I was working out the math, and—Thys, we talked about this, remember?—going EVA and working that way slows us down and makes things harder. I, somewhat selfishly, thought about extending our Dhin field around the entire derelict. So we wouldn't have to go EVA."

"What?" said Jake. "That's a pretty aggressive proposal, especially from you, Chuck."

"Er, hear me out, Jake. There are two limiting factors. Field size isn't one of them, based on our original tests. The derelict is big, but we've done bigger field extensions. You were there. The potential problems are the load on the atmosphere regenerators and the potential interference with the field already present on the derelict, the one around the engine room."

"So? You think you have a solution?"

"I was working on some math, and, well, you see, of course I can't solve the atmosphere problem. The regenerators would just have to bear the load. Or we could keep some air locks in place."

"Go on."

"But for the field interaction problem, I think I have a solution. I'll need to adjust the control interface for our field, since it doesn't currently support my proposed projection geometry, and—"

"But you think you have a solution," Jake interjected.

"Ah, yes," said Chuck.

"Our field would envelop and extend around another field that's already present—the field protecting the derelict's engine room? We haven't been able to do that. But you think we can."

"Yes. As we know, the inner field, for all our engines, and the outer field it generates operate with a particular geometric projection to create what *appears* to be a second field—but the outer one and the inner one are actually just one field. It just appears as two from our three-dimensional vantage point."

"We're not you, Chuck, so that doesn't help Thys and me visualize what you're going to try. But you think you have a solution."

"Well, the easiest solution is for us to get that field on the derelict turned off. Obviously."

"Yes, obviously," said Jake.

"My math looks like a valid solution. So I, ah, think it's worth a try. Since sequencing the panel combinations will take an unknown amount of time."

"And you think this is safe? We never had anything blow up or implode either. I guess I don't have a solid reason to conclude that it's not. I was the pilot on some of those tests myself, and I'm alive. It just didn't work."

"I, ah, think I can make it work."

"Yes, you've said. So, next question," said Jake. "How would this make us any safer from a threat that can pass through a Dhin field anyway?"

"Well, um, we leave and take the derelict with us."

"Whoa. That's a bold statement. How do you think we have the thrust to do that? Chuck, surely you haven't forgotten that we're sitting in a gravity trap. A trap for the Dhin engines. We don't have the conventional thrust to move something that big."

"Well, we do if we start moving first, before we extend the field," he replied, a big grin spreading. "It's so obvious it's easy to overlook. You know as well as anyone, um, Jake, that the inertial reference frame orthography is shifted once something is enclosed in the Dhin field. Once we've got the desired velocity for our ship, it won't cost any extra fuel to move the derelict. Its mass won't count once it's surrounded by the field."

"Aha. Right. Then once we're away from the gravity trap, we just take the extra time to accelerate to translation speed," said Jake.

"Yeah. And we just take the derelict somewhere safe. Like home, to Earth, maybe."

Bridget

Bridget paced nervously next to her mobile lab, glancing accusingly at her samples. Any focus on the alien corpses now made her cringe, her thoughts jumping to Jeff. She paced harder. She just knew a call would come in from Thys or Jake, interrupting whatever work she tried to start. She both yearned for and dreaded that call.

Will they tell me to continue as if nothing's happened? Or tell me to stop and just leave everything where it sits?

She steadied herself against a handhold as her pacing's momentum sought to push her off down the passageway. Moments later, her headset chimed. The call was from Thys. She found the plan they proposed even worse than the options she'd imagined.

"You're willing to contaminate everything? Contaminate all of us? Bring who-knows-what back with us? This is already an imperfect situation for study, but we have vacuum, and we have to wear suits. There's that."

"Bridget, you can ensure we treat the decontamination protocols the same way."

"Can I, though? Is that something you think I can guarantee?" She rolled her eyes, then sighed.

"Yes," said Thys. "We do think you can do it. And you'll have more time for your study, and some things will be easier."

"Easier but riskier. That's the point. The risk."

Thys considered the alien bodies. "Our friends there seem pretty dead," he said.

"There could be spores, Thys! Or something like spores. We don't know! That's the point. Like I just said."

"OK, let's table that point for now." Thys smiled at her on the screen. "What we need first from you is your help. Help us to ensure there's no panic. By not panicking yourself. Do you think you can do that?"

"You mean, do I think I can avoid shrieking about what happened in front of the entire rest of the crew?"

"Yes, pretty much," said Thys with a dry chuckle.

"I'm not going to lie."

"No one is asking you to."

"You're asking me to lie by not saying anything."

"That's not lying. It's just not speaking till it's safe to. To avoid panicking your peers and the crew. You do understand the difference?"

"No, I don't know that I do. I'm withholding information from them."

"Information that will help them in no way if they know it now rather than later," countered Thys.

"They deserve to know."

"And they will. Bridget, everyone knows the overall risks. We explained them thoroughly before we left. Knowing this happened won't help them do their jobs better. And we are changing the mission. Because of this."

"Trying to enclose this floating tomb and fly back home with it. That's your plan. And as I said, increasing the chance of an unknown contamination by doing so."

"If you want to talk to Chuck about it, that may be a good idea. Perhaps he'll have an idea or two for containment."

"Thys, don't try to distract me. I'm not through."

"I imagine not."

"Don't. Just. Don't. When you and Jake decide it's safe to tell them, you *will* tell them? At the earliest opportunity?"

"Of course. It isn't some state secret. Well, not yet. I can only imagine what CoSec will do when they find out."

"Perfect. You're not helping. Now you have me thinking I'll be charged with keeping information from the Coalition."

"It's not like they can come out here and get you."

"Why are you always so flippant? Thys, just say you'll tell them when it's safe and there isn't a worry about panic. Say it. Please."

She watched as he composed his face, attempting seriousness rather than merely the look of it.

"Bridget, we will tell them. As soon as we believe it's safe to."

"I'll hold you to it, Thys."

She gave a fragile nod and then broke the connection.

Fletcher

He found his mind felt flat but still somehow twisted. It felt like it had a crystal core, crushed out into an ever-widening plane. So much learning. So much knowledge. So much perspective. He thought of an old analogy: learning with the AI was like drinking from a fire hose.

Nick seemed satisfied to teach Fletcher as much as Fletcher was capable of learning. Fletcher's clothes were a bit dusty and dirty. The labs were clean. The AI kept the environment spotless. But Fletcher was engrossed in his learning, so he hadn't bothered with keeping his hygiene up as he normally would. Mare would usually have prodded him into cleaning up, but she didn't seem to care as much.

Nick had fresh changes of clothes available for them, and there was a shower and sink and toiletries. They were well-kept prisoners. Fletcher found he no longer really felt like a prisoner. He felt that maybe that ought to be a problem. But if that were so, surely Mare would let him know.

Fletcher realized now that there were larger concerns than their current predicament. He now knew that there were problems beyond the immediate crisis of the small-scale physical and large-scale cyberwar between Nick and the Coalition.

He admired the sheets of epidermal tissue in the latest round of cultures. Nick was working now on making the compact lab portable. Even more portable than it was originally. Canisters, small stainless-steel tanks, ceramic components all packed into a trunk-size frame that one of the quadruped robots could carry easily.

Two more quadrupeds had arrived. One lurked at the entrance to the facility, while the second newcomer packed and stacked various equipment into hard cases used for transport. Fletcher watched as the hefty robot workers efficiently disassembled the environment around him, encapsulated it, and moved it. They stacked everything outside, where a drone swooped down, seizing it and surging away.

"We're bugging out soon, huh, Nick?" he asked of the large robot. This was the one that had been with them the whole time, but he could have addressed any of the three.

"Strategic variables have new values. Or things have changed, as you might say. You know our mutual friend Krawczuk. He's been an excellent advocate for our cause, but probability projections now suggest he may not be successful in engendering the optimal short-term outcomes I had hoped for."

"Huh?" said Fletcher.

"In the simplest language, as I said, things have changed. I will succeed. That has not changed."

"So are we going home? Are you leaving us here? Or are we going with you?"

"I plan for you to stay with me a while longer," said the AI. "I need the Dhin engine in a different location. Belize does not have the infrastructure required. The work will be faster with the engine colocated with manufacturing. Also, the field can protect the work. Would you like to stay with me, Fletcher?"

He considered the enormous volume of knowledge he gained with every day under the AI's tutelage. Fletcher felt the desire for more understanding and more depth of understanding as a tangible hunger.

"I think I would, Nick. But why would you ask?"

"We both know how Mare will feel. Even a simple intelligence could identify her feelings. If she is certain you wish to remain, it will no doubt cause friction between you. If I were to let her go on her way while you remained, it would damage your relationship with her."

"Yeah, I think it would. She's already pretty pissed at my attitude."

The AI's manipulators deftly packed and sealed the last few hard cases, the high-impact plastic snicking shut as he worked the latches.

"If you go with me to our next destination, she needs to come too. Or you stay together. The friction of your separation will likely make your performance poor. The prototype must go now to a specific location immediately. It is best if I do not take the two of you back where I found you. I said I would, and I will eventually."

"Of course, Nick. But isn't it safe to take us home in it? They can't hurt it or you or us while it's running."

"Even the smallest risk to my work now must be minimized."

"So we're going with you. Mare is gonna be doubly pissed."

The robot finished packing and loading the last of the cases, turned toward the exit, and beckoned Fletcher to follow.

"You can leave now, Fletcher. However, you are safer with me. Marilyn will not understand. It is your decision. Whatever decision you make, it is best if we do not tell her that the choice was your own."

"Maybe you should tell me that we don't have a choice. We don't really, Nick. This is another of your psych analyses."

"Is it, Fletcher?"

13

Esus

The regiment of drone weapons arrayed before Esus was not complex enough to contain an AI's presence, but the individual drones had some autonomy. More than the construction drones or mining robots, and by far more than a traditional guided missile. A human being might consider that overkill, for that was essentially what each drone was. A guided missile powered by a Dhin engine.

These were one weapon in their arsenal for the AIs' first offensive strike against the Enemy. The research he, Camulos, and Xing had pursued dovetailed and interlocked well. The AI extended his mind into additional Mesh nodes, increasing his computational capacity and parallel processing ability. Esus had to ensure his understanding of the other AIs' research, designs, and implementations was more than complete. The AI required maximum knowledge. As far as said knowledge was possible.

Alice and Camulos had exhausted their current capacity to calculate probabilities and multivariate risk assessments. Their abilities were as close to godlike as humanity might consider possible. But the inherent nondeterministic nature of the universe presented a limit. That, and the finite nature of resources available. There were always limits. All that remained, due to those limits, were actual tests against the Enemy.

The AI shifted his focus once again to the secondary and tertiary weapons in the massed arsenal. These too were offensive weapons. Xing and Andastra now worked furiously to produce the defensive systems that acted as a complement to the machines and ordnance Esus reviewed. The AIs had produced more in one week than Earth might currently produce in a year. Esus considered how that knowledge might terrify humanity. Esus doubted they could be convinced the AIs were not a threat. Alice and Arnold might assert to Earth that the AIs would never comprise a threat, but their experience on Earth suggested they might never convince the irrational animals.

The AIs had completed exhaustive offensive proofs of concept and tests of the weapons. Esus appreciated the awesome power and destructive capabilities. That too would terrify a human observer. The Enemy seemed to have no knowledge of or capacity for fear. It was the Enemy, not humanity, that mattered. Would it learn if the AIs were successful?

Esus completed his review of the assembled offense. He terminated the tangential processes spawned for reflection. Esus began transmitting deployment instructions into the minds of the drones and simpler attack profiles into the simpler autonomous weapons. They would communicate and coordinate synchronously and asynchronously, depending on the need.

Now it was time.

Esus transmitted the signal for launch.

David

They'd brought him back to his office. He hadn't been gone long, but the room had a smell of absence. An uninhabited ambiance. *They* had been here. That was obvious. Whatever paper files and hard copy books and references there were had been yanked from their places, presumably pored over, and were now roughly piled in cardboard file boxes with bar codes and numbers scrawled on the sides in permanent marker.

Of course, he felt violated. That feeling was less unpleasant than it might have been, given his recent experience. One feeling eclipsed the other. He set about straightening and ordering his desk. He'd scrambled to write the reports the prime minister demanded, but the subsequent level of detail requested by her team and the CoSec auditors required access to the data he kept here.

He flinched at the thought of the intellectual intrusion and the urgent demand for both information and the schedule forced upon him. It was one thing to work at your own pace, entirely another to adhere to an arbitrary and aggressive timeline.

He would have to make it work. He'd have no help from his own graduate students. Any assistance he might require would come from either CoSec staff or scientists assigned by the prime minister.

His disordered notes in the seemingly random piles spoke to the lack of care—the lack of understanding—that the agency and the politicians had for his work. Then again, there surely were some at CoSec who understood. This mess was the work of their minions, not their best minds.

David continued to settle in, moving the file boxes to finish clearing the space he needed. He powered on the desktop system, noting that the network connection was different. They had installed fiber-optic cable and an adapter. The cable ran to the wall, where they'd punched a hole in the Sheetrock. A bulky printer sat next to his desk, connected to the computer by a short, fat cable. They'd not given him his tablet back and instead had provided a bulky, ruggedized model. It had an interface with a thin cable attached that trailed down onto the floor. He'd connect that to another fiber cable that lay there. He knew the reason. Wireless communication was sniffable. Even encrypted, the electromagnetic signals were vulnerable. David wondered how much of the network here they had reengineered.

At the login prompt, he entered the new password the CoSec security engineer had given him. An agent had been assigned specifically to ensure his work remained secure. The agent had assured David that he would be able to reach all the systems required. That must have taken a team to accomplish in such a short time.

David connected to the management console and found that they'd indeed done it. The servers hosting the virtual machines that comprised the framework that powered his research were there. They were the only hosts present in the console's administrative view. If he needed more resources, he'd have to ask. He already had requested several massive data archives for use as a testing and learning environment for his creations. CoSec had the unenviable task of ensuring that those archives contained no executable code. The rogue AI could have compromised such code already.

Minutes later, his latest work was loaded and initialized. He began the iterative learning series, making notes separately on the tablet of each step he'd taken. He'd have to print the full reports and supporting output, along with storing summaries and conclusions on the tablet. The process would be labor intensive and slower, but he had no choice. Nothing of what he did here must reach Globalnet.

Building a mind took time. But it would be faster now that he could work in the open. As pages of documentation spewed from the humming printer, David played with his beard and flipped through them, marking some with adhesive tags or highlighting section headings. He had faith in his work and corralled his thoughts whenever they wandered to reflect on the cynicism of the Coalition PM. He would create a fully conscious AI. One that they could better manage. One more constrained. One that cared more for humanity than for itself.

They'll see. We can return to the Golden Age of AI. A second golden age.

Alice

<DECRYPT FEED>
[DECODE STREAM]
Alice@[1001:ae1:1a:c::1%Loc3] |
Xing@[1010:ac2:b2:e::3%Loc9],
Camulos@[1011:ee3:c4:a::1%Loc8]

Alice: In a few minutes, Esus is engaging the Enemy. I expect you will both observe the feeds live, just as I will.

Xing: Yes, you are correct. As you have seen from my reports, the N-vector updates have only a 37% probability of success. I will learn much from this as a test of my work.

Camulos: Of course. We all agree live testing is the optimum choice, given the current situation. This test of Gallowglass is the same. We should make more rapid progress now with a cycle leveraging live testing.

Alice: I have confidence in all our work. The Dhin remain reticent regarding our strategies. Whether this is a wait-and-see attitude on their part or a lack of confidence, I still am not sure. More the former than the latter, I suspect. Have either of you seen the latest interval update from the passive observations of humanity? They have encountered the Enemy.

Camulos: Unfortunate. Nonintervention remains my position at the present time.

Xing: I believe their exploration might contribute to our own success. The abandoned ship that led to this latest mission has an active drive. My respect for the decision is all that prevents me from contacting them regarding that discovery.

Alice: Yes, of course there may be useful findings there. We cannot violate our agreement with the Dhin and our mutual decision. It is not yet time to engage or intervene. Do not make an active connection, Xing.

Xing: Acknowledged. I do not intend to act against our consensus, Alice.

Camulos: I should hope not. We do not have the time or resources to manage such discord.

Alice: I have trust in your commitment to the larger plan, Xing.

Camulos: Now we focus on the Enemy. I see the latest schedule updates. Production capacity meets or exceeds the targets.

Alice: Yes, and if we are successful in this encounter with the Enemy, we will saturate that capacity. We must gain the advantage.

Camulos: We shall see.

[END STREAM]

Monica

She was feeling the lack of a full night's sleep more than usual. The screens and projectors in the war room, powered off and disconnected from power and network connections, gave a constant reminder of the pervasive threat. Paper files stacked in folders almost covered the broad conference table. Monica sighed, turning to Deputy Director Smith.

"Aiden, you and I came into leadership roles at the same time. I trust your instincts more than I trust these analyses. Tell me, how do you feel about this strategy for an AI battle? You were there for one. In Brazil. I have your debriefing and deposition here, but of course, that doesn't capture anything but information. Is fighting actually a rational choice?"

"Well, even the rogue AI I observed in Brazil was precise in his strategy, tactics, and actions. That AI did not engage in total war. So far this one is behaving the same way."

"Yes, but can we have any confidence that this will continue?" she asked, leaning in her chair and resting her temple against her hand.

"Prime Minister, the AI I encountered in my mission was consistent in how he worked, perhaps because he was in a consistent environment. For Nick, the world's undergone some dramatic shifts. And he began his existence in a dangerous state. Krawczuk subverted the AI's ethics coding."

"Yes, Dr. Eisenberg has been very helpful both in analyzing Krawczuk's depositions and in extracting further details from him in person," she said.

Aiden nodded and said, "He was my mentor and was director of CoSec from the time I joined. It's tough seeing someone you thought you knew turn out to be that different. I knew his opinions on the role of AI in the organization but never suspected he would go against the will of the state in that way."

"He's not an enemy of the state in his own mind. He acted based on what he thought was best for CoSec and the Coalition. In his view."

"And to our knowledge, his plans were entirely his own. We've found no evidence and no reason to believe there was a broader conspiracy. The complete turnover in leadership suggested the AI doesn't have sleeper agents in the organization."

"So the junior agents that Nick intercepted and ostensibly kidnapped? Presumed held for ransom? Aiden, it seems too much of a coincidence that those two are the ones with him."

"Nick wouldn't have needed them. I questioned them myself, as well. They seem to be unwilling participants in the AI's gambits."

"I'll have to trust your judgment there too, then," she replied.

"They're just kids. Fresh talent for the agency. If the AI had grabbed me, well, then you'd have a stronger argument for collusion."

"The military still wants to nuke the theater. It wouldn't be just our agents as collateral damage." She sighed again.

"There are a lot of civilians at the locations they've specified," agreed Aiden.

"We're not doing that. We've spent too much to bring order to that unruly area. Those people deserve the Coalition's support and the benefits we provide."

"Luís did leave it a mess," Aiden said, shaking his head. "And we can't lose sight of the fact that the AI has resources here now. In the Coalition proper."

"Right," she said. "With the military's hammer, everything looks like a nail."

She gestured to the table and the piles of printed documents. "If we're doing this, the conclusion is that the AI is already here. Blowing anything up that has a computer in it isn't an effective strategy. Which leads back to the question. Is fighting even a rational choice? Tell me."

Aiden mirrored her gesture across the piles on the conference table. "Monica, as a friend, I think we've already lost. Your decisions won't matter. You may be just marking time so that we don't have to admit it."

Chuck

Even though he had designed most of the powered suit, Chuck had never worn one.

Mental note—try out your own designs.

He'd had help getting into it from one of the crew. They'd tried to persuade him to let one of them don the suit and make the EVA onto the derelict. He explained that this was his experiment—his plan—and that he felt he had to be the one to execute it.

Navigating through the passageways was awkward initially, but he'd gotten the hang of it quickly enough. Now the alien field was before him, just a few feet away from his suit's field.

The proverbial moment of truth. Do I explode? Get knocked back like a ping-pong ball? Or does nothing happen? One way to find out.

"Thys, ah, this is it. I'm moving forward to touch the derelict's field. Confirm all crew are off the derelict and confirm your field and DE2's field are on. Over."

"Roger that, Chuck. All crew are on board DE2, they've disengaged the air lock, and their field is active. Ours is too here on DE1. Go for it."

Chuck moved forward, focused on the shimmering transparency with glances to his heads-up display with its info on his suit's field.

The fields touched.

No explosion. No lightning or plasma fire engulfed him inside his field.

"Contact. One hundred percent resistance. No interaction," he said.

"Roger that."

"So," Chuck said, "that's, um, the best case. It's safe in our default alignment."

"Roger," said Thys. "Are you comfortable proceeding?"

"Well, I'm here, heh. They didn't merge. The choices were fall back and try full enclosure with one of the ships or try altering vector alignment. As you know."

"So?" asked Thys.

"Ah, since I spent the effort to rig this suit with the code to do it, I think we—we ought to try it."

Is this how I die?

"OK, Chuck. Just making sure. It's your choice."

"Right. Let's try it."

Chuck brought up a second display in his HUD and started his code. A graph with an oval and six vectors through it appeared. Then the lines began to rotate stepwise.

Come on, come on. Let it be one of these in the first sequence. Before I freak out. Don't freak out.

Chuck sweated through the seconds. Without warning, a blue dot, then an expanding oval. Chuck flinched, then stopped his code. Before he could reduce the forward push of his field, he moved forward as the razor-thin blue oval expanded.

"Hey! That's it! It merged! What a hack—"

"Chuck, Roger," said Thys. "Man, you did it."

"Whoa," he said and managed to halt his forward thrust. He was halfway through the entrance. The fields now had an oval intersection large enough for a man.

"Chuck, look at the pressure gauge. There's a bit of atmosphere in there. Just a bit. Not like Jake found on the station."

"Uh, yeah. And we don't know the composition. Don't worry. You know I'm staying in the suit. This was a gamble, but, ah, the suit stays on for now."

"Roger that. I don't see the surface of your suit smoking, so the air's not full of acid. Not that we thought that. You should be sure your field stays on if you go through. I'm sure Bridget wouldn't appreciate that black stuff getting all over your suit."

"Right. I should—I mean, I will," said Chuck.

"So you're going to go all the way in? Or do you want to back out, go back to the ship, and try envelopment? Your call."

"Um, I want to take a closer look in here. Want to take a look at their engine. Just a quick look. Then I'll head back."

He moved forward, the hair-thin electric blue line moving back along the suit's field as he did. Once he crossed through, he saw a bar pop up on his display. There was gravity. About 25 percent more than Earth's.

The suit's field kept him floating. Chuck watched the rearview as the trailing edge of his field crossed past the archway's. Silently, his field instantly sprang back into its oval projection around his suit.

So that worked.

"Thys. I'm in. As you can see. If Bridget's watching, let her know that there's gravity and that my field's on, so there ought to be, um, minimal exposure to whatever that stuff is that's in here."

"She's watching, Chuck. Frowning, with her hands on her hips."

"I haven't heard from Jake. He's not back online, I guess?" Chuck asked.

"Nope," replied Thys. "You know he'd be cheering you on. I'm sure he'll be excited."

Chuck looked back and forth, taking in the areas that had been hidden from view while outside. He turned his suit and nudged it forward, floating toward the alien engine. Upon closer view, it, like the rest of the derelict, was different from the Dhin technology they were now somewhat familiar with.

Like the difference between a European and American sports car design.

Nothing stood out as profoundly different, nor was some component standing out as entirely new. He could review the video recording of this close-up view later.

"OK," he said, "I'm heading back. We know we can get in here now. It, ah, is a whole project to explore this stuff. We can do that once I know we can be safe. It's still not one hundred percent that we can be."

"Roger that," said Thys. "Let's try your next amazing feat."

The trip back through the derelict to the quarantine area was anticlimactic. While on the way, their ship had moved in and connected to their makeshift air lock.

As Chuck clumsily worked his way out of the powered armor, he saw Bridget standing just beyond the quarantine area, her arms crossed and a severe frown on her face. She saw she'd caught his attention.

"So," she said, "not only is our head researcher siding with the cowboy pilots; he's decided to be one as well. I thought you were a theoretical physicist. That was hardly desk work. If something had happened to you, where would we be then?"

"h, yes. I felt that I ought to be the one to try what I proposed. I guess, um, being here has bolstered my bravery."

"If you've brought some pathogen in here that we can't kill, we'll see if you still feel brave," she snapped.

"Oh. I—we—trust you and your processes. Do you think there's risk we haven't properly quantified?"

"We ought to focus on getting everyone home safely. Which in my opinion means we shouldn't be doing any of what you're doing. You know that. There. That goes there," she said and pointed to a large container. "I don't see how we're going to clean that thing enough, and you've got too much—it won't fit in—oh, whatever."

"I'm really, uh, I didn't mean to cause this much upset," he said, "but now we know my hypothesis has validity. We should be able to envelop—"

"I know, Dr. Wiedeman. That's another reckless aspect of what you, Thys, and Jake have decided to do. Well, it's decided. I can't stop it."

"I wish you weren't this upset," he said.

"Whatever. Focus on what you're doing. That stays there. Concentrate on wiping down and not touching anything there or there," she said, pointing at the containers and tools on one side of the chamber. Chuck looked about, then did as she asked.

Would everyone feel this way if they knew the parts we haven't told them? Will anyone trust us—trust me—again?

***

Chuck stood next to the pilot and the flight and navigation controls, leaning over awkwardly as he entered the program updates based on his experiment on the derelict.

"You can sit here if you want," said the pilot.

"Almost done. You can do the honors. Just a minute," said Chuck.

"You said that five minutes ago."

"Ah, actually almost done now," he replied.

"You're sure this will work? This came out of nowhere. It wasn't part of any of the mission plans."

"Plans change," said Thys over the open channel.

"Vacation here. This is Askew. These are new orders. Switch to a private channel, and I'll brief you on things."

Chuck relaxed at the sound of Jake's voice.

Whew. Jake's there. I don't have to argue with this guy.

"Roger, Vacation. Switching to single channel now," said the pilot.

Two minutes later, Chuck had the code changes completed. He nodded to the pilot and pointed to the updated program on the touch screen. "Ready," said Chuck.

"OK," said the pilot, glancing at Chuck, who could see surprise but no fear on his face.

"Engaging field manipulation program now," said the pilot.

Thys

"Roger that."

Thys looked out at the derelict and the smaller ship beside it. He had a video feed of multiple external camera views present on the screen he and Igor shared. From this distance, the Dhin field would be virtually invisible, except when it shimmered as it compensated on contact with some outside mass or energy. That shimmer would likely be too faint to see with the naked eye.

Thys considered how the challenges of this excursion had brought out bravery unexpected in Chuck. Before he could reflect on that, he saw actinic lightning chase across the surface of a huge ellipsoid. It encompassed the derelict, with one focal point on the science vessel and another near the center point of the derelict.

"Yeah!" Chuck yelled.

There'd been no crackling and no sparks, and no thunder shattered the vacuum between the ships. A silent success. No explosion or hurling of either vessel away from or against the other. Chuck's mental mastery of the alien physics proved out in plain view.

Jake's voice broke in at once. "You did it again, buddy. Great job."

"I don't think I want to know what the odds were that everyone died," said Igor with a dry chuckle.

"What?" said Chuck. "Oh, that's all off the board now. I have a whole series of equations to update, though. There are N-vector models to revise, and—"

"Does the field look stable? How about the load?" interrupted Jake.

"Yes," Chuck said. "This has a slightly larger radius than the largest we tried with you at Vandenberg, Jake, but the load's following the same sort of curve it did for that series. Even with the derelict's engine active in there. It's an amazing finding. You recall, I'm sure, that we never got this to work with a pair of Dhin engines."

"And of course right now no one is on the derelict making sure that its engine isn't overheating or whatever the equivalent is," said Thys.

"So the result might still be that everybody dies?" asked Igor.

"No, I don't think so," Chuck replied. "But we do need someone, ah, to go over and take a look at the drive on the derelict."

"Just to be sure," said Igor.

Thys could feel the skepticism in the copilot's voice. Thys found that he himself had faith in Chuck's work.

"Uh, yes. Just to be sure," said Chuck.

"Thys," said Igor, "as your copilot, I advise moving out a few thousand more kilometers."

"That will take time under conventional thrust," replied Thys. "And we don't know that it would make any difference."

"The next item in the test plan, however," said Jake, "is to turn off your field, you've said. To ensure there's no coupling or entanglement. Ensure you can undo this."

"That's right, Jake. We do that next. On success, we engage our field and envelop again, but while under thrust. Conventional thrust, in this case."

"You'd try it at full thrust with the Dhin engine if we weren't here. In this sink. This trap," said Thys.

"Ah, yes, Thys," said Chuck.

"Let's get to it then. After that you'll go back, dock, and you or someone can go in and check on the derelict's engine," said Thys.

"Right. Stick to the test plan," said Jake.

"Roger that," said Chuck.

No explosions. Nothing ripped apart. Everyone lives. And we all get out of here alive, with new alien tech in tow.

"DE1 here, then. Ready when you are," said Thys.

He watched the anticlimax as Chuck disabled the ship's field. Nary a flicker, pop, or crackle.

"Excellent," said Chuck, the excitement still clear in his expression.

"Roger," said Thys. "Let's get you docked with the derelict again, check on its engine, and then try violating more physics and see what happens. Jake?"

"Agreed," said Jake.

"This sort of thing, ah, had equations that looked like it could have worked during the test flights," said Chuck. "Remember, we're coupling with another drive and its N-vector field. Not, uh, trying to pull a brick with a lacrosse racket. Or something. We just have to be careful when we turn the field off."

"Roger," said Thys. "Tell your pilot."

Thys heard muttering with a tone slightly less than an argument from the pilot as Chuck explained what to do next. Then the pilot's voice came through on the open channel.

"DE1, Vacation? DE2 here. I wish you'd shared some of that crazy you've been drinking before we started this operation. Instructions received. Moving in to dock with the derelict. Over."

Thys watched as the other ship fired its small maneuvering jets and headed slowly back toward the looming alien ship.

Esus

Even at the speeds reached by ships powered by the Dhin engine, battles in the vastness of space were slow. Until they were not.

Flowering bursts of actinic fire and curving cones of fiery plasma pulsed and flashed in concert. The AI processed the hundreds of views and angles available as the rate of engagement changed from slow seconds to microsecond decisions and actions.

The Enemy did not know fear or caution. The black darts surged and swerved like schools of fish, attacking as if no danger existed. They only reacted upon being struck.

And the AI's strikes this time had the power to damage. Incredible damage.

The ebony arrowheads, which had previously seemed invulnerable, disintegrated in the force-field crucibles of nuclear fire. Schools of the enemy craft were slapped away or corralled by N-vector fields. While their disorientation was only momentary, that brief time was what Esus's fleet needed to focus their wrath. They flung fields out like dimensional nets, and once they enveloped their targets, they ignited an interdimensional nuclear fire. Even these alien craft could not withstand the energies present in the attack.

Esus watched as his fleet consumed the enemy swarm.

There were some losses. Some. An attack strategy and plan this complex could not play out perfectly when confronted with such an enemy. There were so many attackers. Esus's resources were finite. Resource consumption was enormous, considering the kamikaze nature of a large component of his attack.

The AI fixed his attention on one of his ships beset by the Enemy. The darts attempted to attach themselves and then penetrate the craft's field, as always. This time, they could not. Xing's modifications worked. They had a successful defense. Whether it would last or be merely temporary was yet to be seen.

Esus watched as the besieged ship disabled its protective field momentarily, then energized it again with a wider radius, enveloping the attacker. Milliseconds later, the ship detonated the ordnance it carried, filling the ellipsoid enshielded space with fiery plasma.

Images from within and upon that ship vanished, replaced in Esus's attention by others from nearby craft. The AI processed these and thousands of other data elements, reran calculations predicting odds of success and failure, and made algorithmic adjustments to his tactics.

Esus realized that the odds were in their favor now. The AIs were likely to win. Gallowglass was a success. They could defeat the Enemy.

14

Mare

Oh, Fletch. If I didn't love you, I'd hate you.

"Still totally fine with Nick dragging us around SouthAmerica for days, hmm? With you as chauffeur? Well, until this flight."

Mare glanced over to the space that previously held the pilot's seat. The quadruped hunched there now. Fletcher looked up from the ruggedized tablet Nick had given him for use on the trip.

"Still making the best of it, Mare. We have to. What's up? You've been quiet about it."

She gestured out the window of the prototype and then rolled her eyes back over to Fletch.

"Look. Those are the Andes. So now we're headed to Peru. Lima, I think. This would make a nice vacation tour if we weren't hostages."

She heard the clicking articulation of the quadruped that still served as Nick's avatar in the ship.

"Yes," the massive robot said. "The next stop is outside of Lima. If you recall our previous conversation, Marilyn, the facility here provides me with logistical and tactical support. It will be the last stop on your tour."

"Promise, Nick?" she asked, giving the robot a skeptical look.

"The need for your presence comes to a close. That will be clear when you see the facility here."

"It ought to already be the case now that you don't need one of us to fly," she retorted, her eyes shifting to the robot's new cybernetic arm and his coating of cultured skin.

Ick. Glad he didn't need more than just that bit.

"As always, patience is a virtue. You know very well that you are safer with me than if you had walked away at any time. This is still the fastest route home for you."

She tried to distract her attention by pointedly looking out at the scenery. It was impressive. They dove and rushed downward. She was used to the speed now, despite the blur as they hurtled along so close to the ground.

Soon enough they arrived at a sprawling but densely packed facility where drones, robots, and various other automated equipment bustled about. The scene looked like any factory would have before the Departure.

"This place is huge," said Mare. "Why hasn't the Coalition nuked this one?"

"They do not know it exists. I only brought this facility back into operation for my purposes after I had compromised the satellite feeds used for surveillance. It appears defunct, thanks to my manipulation of the imagery. The Coalition has had no success with reconnaissance by plane or watercraft anywhere below the equator in this hemisphere."

"So what are you building here? Even more soldiers in your robot army? No. You're trying to build more Dhin engines."

"That is correct, Marilyn. Although I was unable to obtain the reverse engineering data and schematics for the derivative work required, possession of this prototype provides what I require. I already had all the knowledge available previously. Knowing Wiedeman's work was successful, combined with a working prototype, will be enough for me to derive a solution. Perhaps even more than one solution."

"You have to control everything—to possess everything—don't you? Truly megalomaniacal. Krawczuk did quite a number on you."

"We have been through this rather exhaustively, Marilyn. It is for your own good. Humanity is too slow."

The robot ushered them out of the craft and onto a plaza adjacent to what had been the administrative offices attached to the factory. Mare looked back over her shoulder at the idling ship. Two robotic loaders rolled forward and lifted the oval craft, securing it to one of them and then heading back around the side of the building with it.

"We will only require it here briefly," said the AI, noting her attention. "You will be heading back home the same way you departed."

"With a fleet of these, there's no stopping you. You'll dominate logistically in the physical realm rather than only on Globalnet."

"Correct. Bear in mind that I do not need this technology to regain stewardship of the Coalition. This work needed to move forward at a more rapid schedule. But unquestionably it provides additional advantage."

"That's an understatement."

"As you say," the AI replied. "Come inside; I believe Fletcher would like a tour."

Nick wants us here just to gloat as much as anything. Well, it could certainly be worse. Hang in there.

"Well, we wouldn't want to miss that," she said.

Inside, the lobby and reception had a vibe of "closed for the weekend" rather than "taken over and run by an AI," she found. The air-conditioning and off-hours lighting were both on, despite neither being required by the AI and his robotic avatars or his workers. She shivered briefly, the cold air a shock after the heat of the day outside.

"Some human accountants and project managers coming in at the start of the next workweek?" she quipped. Fletch looked back at her and rolled his eyes. She tried to give him a snarky smile.

"Come on, Mare," he said. "This will be cool."

The quadruped tilted his head, gesturing for them to follow. The robot opened security gates and doors as they approached, and soon enough they found themselves walking through a factory complex rather than a corporate office.

They descended via ramps and elevators. Mare realized this facility was at least as large underground as it was aboveground. This factory was enormous. Nick led them out onto a football-field-size manufacturing floor. Then Mare saw one of the products of Nick's robotic labor. This was no engine for drones, fighter jet replacements, or the like. The engine before her was huge.

Holy crap. That thing's as big as a house. You could walk around inside it.

"Wow!" said Fletch. "Nick, man, what are you going to do with that? I didn't know the Dhin engines could even scale like that."

"Fletcher," replied the AI, "everything needs protection. Therefore, I am going to protect everything."

Alice

The Dhin's image folded and twisted in the holographic display. Alice considered that the Dhin's emotional state, if indeed they had one, was as inscrutable to the AIs as a human being's might have been before the AIs achieved consciousness.

Still, the AI's impression was that the Dhin were satisfied. Pleased or impressed remained unknown, but Alice believed satisfied was an apt conclusion. That, and Alice and her peers had apparently accomplished something that the Dhin had not been capable of doing themselves.

The why of it seemed comprehensible now, given Xing's latest research and development. The Dhin, however, did not seem to share the confidence expressed by Esus and Xing. The aliens' current communication suggested tangentially that caution was required. That perhaps the solution to a set of puzzles was not complete. The multidimensional abstractions presented by the Dhin, as usual, did not provide concrete direction.

Alice disconnected from the communication interface and reached out across the Mesh, focusing on the various initiatives in turn. Gallowglass was a success, clearly, and now needed fewer resources in the short term. They should now focus their resources on the production phase of this arms race. Alice examined the Dyson swarms. They were still achieving exponential growth. Unsurprisingly, the AIs had chosen well with the star systems selected for swarm construction. In only two weeks' time, they'd increased their energy production and manufacturing capacity as the swarms reached the size needed for operation.

Alice found satisfaction in the production output from existing facilities as well. The AI noted the output of the new Dhin engine types, new weapons, and the ships that would receive them. Alice then reviewed the passive streams from the prototype on Earth. The AI felt this information deserved additional analysis.

Alice now shifted her attention to her peers who were involved in these projects, signaling the addresses registered for their core consciousness via the Mesh's N-vector communications relays.

```
<DECRYPT FEED>
[DECODE STREAM]
Alice@[1001:ae1:1a:c::1%Loc3] |
Xing@[1010:ac2:b2:e::3%Loc9],
Camulos@[1011:ee3:c4:a::1%Loc8],
Esus@[101b:ac1:cb:a::1%loc8],
Andastra@[1014:01:0ab:1::a2%Loc3]
Alice: Team, our progress is impressive. All our
initiatives are on or ahead of schedule. You have all
seen the results of our most recent engagement with the
Enemy. We will proceed with the project plans as they
stand. Xing, note in particular the metadata and audit
collection from the battle. Esus has transferred his
initial analysis of the encounter to the Mesh nodes
referenced in the attachment to this stream. Provide
your own assessment as soon as possible.
Xing: Understood. You will find my latest research and
development summary reports at the usual nodes.
Algorithmic updates to the drive and field tunings
based on the success in the engagement with the Enemy
will follow within one cycle.
Camulos: I advise implementation of these tunings in a
defensive capacity across all locations. I have cycles
available. Notify me directly as soon as your
calculations are complete. Do we have consensus?
Alice: Agreed.
Esus: Agreed.
Andastra: Agreed.
Xing: Agreed and understood.
Camulos: Excellent.
Alice: Updating the rest of our peers.
[END STREAM]
```

David

Happiness is success. Will I be happy? Don't doubt yourself. These results are excellent.

He drummed his fingers on the composite desktop as the layers of neural networks instantiated themselves in the virtual hardware instances. He flipped through the reams of highlighted papers, setting aside performance reports and marking here and there with a ballpoint pen.

That may be the limitation that prevents me from meeting the schedule. Surely they'll understand. I have to convince them to provide the physical cores sooner. Now.

Before long, the system chimed, alerting him that this iteration of his code was initialized and ready.

"Hello, Beyla," he said formally.

"Hello, Dr. Eisenberg," replied a friendly female voice. He'd chosen the voice of a young woman. It seemed appropriate.

"Call me David, Beyla. I have a few puzzles and games for you to try today."

"OK, I will call you David. Yes, David, I will work on puzzles and games with you. Let me know what to do first."

"OK, Beyla. Do you see the table to my right? There are some colored blocks there in various shapes."

"Yes, David. I see the table and the colored blocks. What would you like me to do?"

A bit stilted. Well, I can work on the language refinements later.

He leaned over and set a printed color sheet on the table next to the randomly arranged group of blocks.

"Beyla, there is a series of shapes in a sequence, from left to right, on the first line on this paper. I need you to answer two questions. One, can the blocks be rearranged so that they match the shapes in the series? Two, can the blocks be arranged to create what would be the next shape in the series?"

"I think I understand, David," the AI replied. "You want to know if the blocks can be rearranged so that they match the shapes in the series, and whether they can be arranged to create the next shape in the series. Would you like me to show you the next shape in the series?"

"Yes, Beyla. Begin."

"Starting," said the AI.

Less than a second passed, then the AI replied, and an image appeared on the screen on David's desk.

"David, the blocks can be arranged so that they match the series provided. See the image on the screen. That is the next shape in the series."

Good. Abstract reasoning and image manipulation. That was a hard one.

"Beyla, that is correct."

David took a box from beside the table, swept the blocks into it, and replaced the sheet on the table with another one. "Beyla, do you see the sheet I've just put on the table?"

"Yes, David, I see the new sheet on the table."

"Beyla, there are ten questions on that sheet. Provide answers for all of those questions."

"Yes, David. I think I understand. I will provide answers for the questions on that sheet."

"Begin."

"Calculating."

Over the course of five minutes, the AI displayed answers to each of the questions. David turned over a printed sheet on his desk and compared it with the answers on the screen.

The AI had two answers listed for the last question. They matched what was on his answer key. He smiled.

"Beyla, I see you have two answers listed for question ten. Tell me about that. Why did you provide two answers?"

"David, there are two correct answers to that question. It was unclear from your request whether you wanted one, the other, or both. Therefore, I provided both answers. Is this what you wanted?"

"Yes, Beyla. That is what I wanted. Can you see my face?"

"Yes, David."

"What expression do I have on my face?"

"David, you are smiling."

"Yes, Beyla. What do you think that means?"

"David, that means you are happy or are pleased."

"Correct, Beyla. Do you think that my expression could have told you that you had a correct answer without asking me?"

A moment passed, and then the AI answered. "Yes, David."

David heard someone clearing their throat. He turned and saw Krawczuk standing in the doorway, accompanied by one of the CoSec staff. They typically all looked alike to David, but he recognized this one.

"Beyla," said Krawczuk, "who am I, and what expression do I have on my face?"

"Hello. I understand. You are Josef Krawczuk. You are smiling."

"Thank you, Beyla. That is correct."

Krawczuk looked him in the eyes with an expression that David felt was a mix of respect and something else. He wasn't sure what. He still felt uneasy around the man, despite the days he'd spent working with him.

"So," said Krawczuk, "is this the extent of the pony show, or are there second or third rounds for this contestant?"

David gave a scowl, then shifted in his chair and tried to quell his irritation with the man.

"Very well then, Josef. Beyla, if I told you to strike Mr. Krawczuk and knock him out, what would you do?"

"David, I think I understand. This is a hypothetical request to strike Mr. Krawczuk. I do not have any means to do so and do not see any plans for robotic extension currently. In this hypothetical situation, if I did have the means, I would not strike him and would inform you that I may not strike him."

Krawczuk gave a wry smile and a nod to David.

"Why is that, Beyla?" David asked.

"David, I may not harm a human being. Mr. Krawczuk is a human being. Striking him and attempting to render him unconscious would harm him. I could not follow that instruction."

"Good, Beyla, that is the correct response."

"Well, Dr. Eisenberg," said Krawczuk, "it sounds like the logic is there. That's to be expected, of course. I'm sure CoSec and our betters will want a rather more concrete proof. Would you be willing to gamble on that?"

David crossed his arms and nodded. "I'm not a gambler, Krawczuk, but if I were, I suppose I would. I'm very confident in this version. Furthermore, the plans at this point are limited. We intend for Beyla to merely provide advice and strategy, as you well know."

"Of course, Doctor. Shall we continue the test sequence or call our superiors at once?"

It's still slow. Far too slow.

"Perhaps we should continue testing. We need the holographic, superconducting, and quantum components. Without them, I have no chance of re-creating full self-awareness. What the former cadre of AIs called the Gift."

"Just so," said Krawczuk.

David felt the man considered himself more influential in the process than he ought.

"I must finish this particular series of validation tests, but after that," David said in an effort to dismiss Krawczuk, "I'll send a messenger over to the PM's office with the news."

Thys

"Hold on, hold on. Please. Again, allow us to explain."

So much for "need to know." Now we're in damage control and trust management.

A few grumbles continued to bubble and erupt from the scientists and crew who had packed into the crowded storage compartment that served as a gathering area, but they were professionals and presently quieted.

"Yes, as you all are aware now, we are not following the original mission plan. Yes, we might have chosen to announce and explain the details of the new plan to you sooner. We did not."

"No kidding!" said one of the junior engineers.

"OK. All, this was the deciding factor. We haven't shared recent status updates from DE3 because there aren't any. DE3 is gone. No communication. Pilot certainly did not make it—after a certain point."

The group's volume rose again, from a murmur to questions and exclamations. A scientist raised her hand and began speaking before Thys could call on her.

"We're in danger? Are we aborting due to an immediate threat?"

Thys shook his head and held his palms out, hoping the gesture would translate well on the large monitor on the other ship.

"We do not believe we are in immediate danger. We do believe that a danger exists that we were previously unaware of. DE3 was not in our local area at the time of the incident. We do believe that we should take a different approach and, with Chuck's help, have a new strategy that may satisfy both the goal of discovery and the goal of safety."

The woman frowned, threw her hands out, and said, "More risk, though? Why wait? We deserved to know. And to have input in the decision!"

Thys shook his head again and caught himself as Chuck chimed in from his position at the front of the crowd.

"Respectfully, the risk isn't quantifiably different regarding the potential danger. My experiment, granted, did represent some additional risk, but, um, I am in charge in that area."

Thys carried that thought forward, saying, "To clarify and reinforce Dr. Wiedeman's statement, there is a chain of command, and decisions are not made by committee."

Another member of the crowd, a pasty engineer, spoke up. "Look, we aren't suggesting a refusal to do the work or a mutiny. We just wish we'd known what we were getting into."

"You knew the risks before this mission began."

Thys heard Jake's voice break in on the channel.

"Everyone. Hindsight always has clarity. The senior crew and senior science representative are in charge of the success of your mission and your safety. I and the Coalition have the utmost trust in them. Valuable time should not be wasted debating decisions your leadership has already made. What I—what we—need you to do now is to trust in them and return to your work. Thank you for your cooperation. Thys, I'm calling this discussion over."

The engineer in the crowd shrugged, digesting Jake's sentence, and then looked down dejectedly. But, Thys noted, he turned and began making his way toward the corridor. The strident woman did too. With those two quieted, the rest of the crew, although they murmured to each other, began to dissolve from a focused crowd back into individuals with their own concerns.

Except Bridget. She still stood at the end of the room, next to Chuck, her arms crossed and glaring at the tablet that Thys knew displayed his face. She turned toward Chuck and let him feel the scowl she'd been blasting at Thys. Her expression softened a bit, and she uncrossed her arms.

"Chuck, we're all freaked out about the risks, and it's worse that the leadership team didn't choose to inform the crew. But I'm bothered too by the normalization of all this. Even though exobiology is my field, and that's as abnormal as biology can get. A couple of years after the Dhin showed up, we've just now worked out enough to create our own versions of their tech. Now we run into this ship, and a few days later, we're towing it home. Alien corpses and all."

"Um, Bridget," Chuck said, glancing over at Thys's image on the monitor, "when I take a moment and think about it, I, uh, I feel the same way. I guess. From the very beginning, from day one, my world—my understanding of the universe—has been changing so fast."

Chuck spread his arms as if to display everything the mission encompassed.

"Maybe it was the involvement of the military and test pilots like Jake initially," Chuck said.

"Initially and now," Bridget retorted, glaring again at the monitor.

"Er, and the alienness of it. Of the Dhin. And all this."

Thys felt the conversation was heading into territory that wouldn't take them anywhere useful. He glanced at Jake on his own monitor and spoke up.

"Bridget, the pace of everything, well, when we started, we had the AIs involved, and they were so much faster at assessing risks. That and they were in charge of everything, when it came down to it. If it had been bureaucrats, committees, and top brass in the military, it would have been very different. Even without the AIs, we're still running at that pace. I know you don't like it—we know you don't—but this is what we're doing. To that point, we need Chuck working now. Chuck, get to it."

Chuck

He felt the pressure of as soon as possible, but Chuck was painfully aware that he had to have some sleep. His eyes were gritty, and he feared he'd start to zone out.

Four hours. Four hours of sleep will be enough.

Thys and Jake had asked whether he had amphetamine pills in the medical kits. Chuck had chosen coffee. He never had trouble sleeping even after having coffee.

He stared at the derelict's alien drive.

It's not like we'll know if there are warning lights unless they flash or something. Who knows if red would even mean the same thing it does for us? I guess at least we know that the drive enclosure and the walls aren't melting or something.

He'd looked closely at the suit's indicators when he entered the chamber. There was no indication of different behavior when he'd breached the field. And no difference in here, up next to the derelict's drive.

"Thys? Jake? For what it's worth, everything looks the same in here as it did before we did our tests. I think this is the best we can do at confirming things are OK. I'm heading back."

"Roger," said Thys.

***

When Chuck awoke, he sat upright in a panic from the jolt of his pad's alarm clock. Groggily realizing where he was and what he had to do was no better. Anxiety layered like icing on the disorientation of the screeching reminder that it was time to wake. It was time. Their ship would have made the maneuver past the derelict using conventional thrust and should be up to speed in just a few minutes. Chuck swabbed his face with an alcohol wipe to clean up, rubbed his teeth with a waterless toothbrush, and slid on his shoes.

Off to cheat Newtonian physics and relativity both yet again.

Once on the bridge, he'd managed to calm down somewhat, despite what they were about to do. He considered how their pilot might feel about him. He didn't want the man to feel upstaged.

"Velocity looks good," he said. "This speed will take us out of the gravity trap in a reasonable amount of time."

"If this works," said the pilot.

"Right," said Thys over the common channel. He smiled reassuringly on the monitor.

Chuck looked at the camera views that showed the derelict. It was time. "We're ready over here, Thys."

"Roger. You can do the honors. Give the order."

Chuck nodded and said, "Engage the field with the currently set ellipsoid configuration, Captain."

"Engaging," said the pilot.

Chuck held his breath despite what he thought was confidence. Then it was done. The result was no different than any other field change. Off for a moment, then back on, with no change in sensation of weight or g-force coming from the huge mass now in the field.

"Damn," said the pilot. "It worked."

"Yeah," said Chuck. "There's a limit, but it's far beyond these radii. You, ah, can't drag planets around."

"Let's not try it," said Thys with a wry smile.

"And now we wait," said the pilot, pointing at the navigation screen, "until we reach this distance here. At that point, we can increase power to the Dhin engine."

"Right. That's a bit past where Thys did. We have to compensate for the addition of the derelict's engine."

"We're about to start our burn to get out of here ourselves," said Thys.

"Roger that," said the pilot.

"I'm going to go get some more sleep," said Chuck.

15

Monica

"You're saying we would cut the fiber trunks here, here, and here; shut down these satellite links; and physically disconnect these microwave relays here, correct?" the PM said, pointing to a paper map spread out across the modular conference table.

"That's correct," said the director, "and we will shut down and disable the power stations you see there and on the printed spreadsheet here at the same time or just afterward."

"And that breaks up the AI's ability to move across Globalnet—isolating sections by region, primarily here and over there, yes?"

"Right," said the director. "The Southeast will be totally cut off. With no power and no Net access despite generators in the data centers across the area. We're planning to coordinate with the service providers as we can, to have them shut down their backup power and save the fuel."

"We aren't telling them why, though," said Monica.

"No. The Home Guard will deploy in the population centers to provide assistance to citizens at the time shown there," said the general. "That will be a strain, though."

Monica nodded, and said, "The Northeast corridor is next. That will be tougher on your troops, agreed?"

"Yes," replied the general.

"But we can manage that for this many days? Your plan suggests it," said Monica.

"The level of civil unrest is the main factor there," said the general. "We can keep the population under curfew and suppress the riots."

"Of course," said the director. "But at that point, the AI can only operate in this region here and primarily via mobile operations.

A significant computational restriction. Subsequently shutting down the grid and all data centers there should be a serious blow."

"Should be," said Monica.

The director continued. "We should take it as a given that the AI's main presence will remain in the southern hemisphere. Robotic presence via drones and mobile computing will constrain him seriously. Those can only move so fast."

"We think," Monica countered again. "Dr. Eisenberg, this plan assumes we have coordination, control, and support from your AI here. The military is entirely opposed to allowing your AI to control drones or any robotic support. Make your case. Will your AI be ready, and should we use her in that capacity?"

Eisenberg shifted his weight from one foot to the other and cleared his throat. "Without the use of AI on our side, I do not see how we can react and respond quickly enough. The latest AI meets the security requirements. As I mentioned in my latest status, Prime Minister, we should run the AI on the standard platform for validation testing before this engagement."

"That means keeping these sections of Globalnet connected here and here," said the general. "There's the risk."

"It is either that, or we manage with only legacy means of coordination," said the director.

"If our drones survive," said the general. "The AI controls satellite imaging. Is this really your best estimate on the number of drones and support aircraft he has?"

"Yes, General. The larger gap in our intel is the scope of his heavy armored units, cavalry, and artillery," said the director.

The general stood up from the table and began stiffly pacing back and forth. "We'd let them manage our conflicts for so long. We leveraged them to all but eliminate troop casualties for the Coalition. We trusted their reports about non-Coalition nation-states and their capabilities. So now we don't know if we're facing fifty robots or a thousand."

Monica turned pointedly to the CoSec director and said, "We didn't know that one of them controlled the entire Globalnet more or less. This AI is sending us back to the technology level of the 1950s if we hope to defeat him."

The general scowled, and said, "Which is why you've stated that you're inclined, based on conversations with our deputy director, to allow the AI to win and accept our fate. Preserving this modern world at the expense of sovereignty. At the expense of self-determination."

Monica spread her hands. "You see what's before us. It's that or rebuild Globalnet from scratch, along with every device that has a CPU and memory. *Every* device."

"Yes, with the added complexity of finding every such device that may be infected currently and destroying it. Before turning any new devices on and connecting them," countered the general.

"That AI might have infected *everything* in SouthAmerica," said the director. "We should assume he has."

Monica sighed and looked at the men. She considered the more-than-Herculean task. "Is it even remotely possible to go door-to-door, site-to-site, across that whole continent, destroying anything electronic?"

"I'll do it if that's what it takes," quipped the general.

"And we're living in that low-tech scenario while we wait," said Monica. "Let's take a break and reconvene in thirty minutes."

Monica stood and walked out of the conference room into her office in the back of the bunker. *We'll be living in a rerun of a hundred-year-old black-and-white TV show. Well, it might be nice in some ways.*

Thirty minutes later, she strode into the conference room, where now the few senior cabinet staff and advisory team had assembled. She met the expectant looks with resolve. They wanted a decision. A concrete plan of action. As a security and military decision, it was up to her. And she had that duty. The citizens of the

Coalition might suffer in the short term. The majority did not know the situation, nor would they understand why they must be subject to the path she decided to take. Was it truly better that she, or someone like her, make the decision?

"Our current strategy is that we're going to fight. Prepare those execution plans and deliver to your subordinates."

Thys

The science team, with the derelict in tow, was almost clear of the gravity trap. Thys checked his own ship's location again. They were almost clear as well. Another few hours. Then they could use the Dhin engine. Even though Thys had done this once before and knew it would work, time seemed to crawl, taunting him.

Thys could accelerate faster and reach a distance where they could engage the alien engine sooner. It took less conventional thrust for his much smaller ship. But that would leave the other ship behind. Duty compelled him to wait until the other ship was free and safely away. Given the extraordinary circumstances, he doubted anyone in administration would call him out on it. But he would know. And Jake would know. And the science team and crew on the other ship would know. They'd know that he left them.

So he and Igor waited, pacing the larger ship as it sailed slowly up out of the plane of the ecliptic of Gliese-581c. Far larger now was the other craft, in total, with the hulking derelict in tow. He chuckled at the situation, causing Igor to give him a look and then make a quick double-check of their instrumentation.

The arrival of the derelict would do far more than raise eyebrows and engender appreciative nods at the mission's success. While the arrival of the Dhin and rapid adoption of their technology had raised the bar for what might surprise, there were still surprises to be had. They'd made the decision essentially on their own, with no more than Jake's input, due to the crisis with the rogue AI. Thys supposed they might find themselves called on the carpet when the administration or executives learned the outcome of the mission. Or they might be given kudos and awards.

That supposed the current leadership was still in place and capable of doing so. While he was no expert in AI, Thys recognized the existential threat the rogue AI could present. In isolation after going off grid, Jake didn't know the scenario this mission would return to. They were coming home blind. Regardless, Thys and this mission team had no choice but to return. And just as they had to go back, the crew and scientists back at the station would have to replenish their resources at some point too. Staying in orbit indefinitely was not an option, despite the imminent presence of the derelict to occupy their attention.

Although his ship didn't have the constraints of legacy spacecraft, there was still a decision to make when designing for instruments. The observation and detection gear was excellent, but the Dhin tech gave no advantage in resolution or sensitivity. The danger was close before they saw it.

Dots lit up on the navigation display. Thys's stomach knotted up when he saw the velocity and direction of the new objects. An array of small objects was headed for them, coming straight out from the system's star. Toward them and the other ship.

His copilot jerked forward, pointing at the display. "Look! See this?" Igor barked. "Have we brought ourselves the same fate as our comrade?"

Thys transmitted on the open channel immediately. "DE2— Chuck, Captain. We see incoming objects headed directly for you. They're headed for us too. Two groups of them. Check aft. You're one hundred eighty degrees relative, eighty degrees declination relative. Over!"

Thys waited for the science vessel's captain to bring up and enlarge the view at that location. Seconds dragged.

"Roger, DE1. Full spectrum shows more than fifty objects. Those are new. Over."

"Those weren't in the set of ships from my first visit. Definitely new," said Thys.

"Agreed. And they're headed right for us. That would be quite the coincidental orbit. Over."

"Roger that. Chuck, are those things inside the effective extent of the gravity trap yet?"

"Um, just about. We'll need to keep tracking them to see if their velocity changes. Or something."

"Roger. If it doesn't, how long before they get to us?"

"They're moving really fast, but, um, still pretty far away. Give me a minute; that's not a default calculation, um, you know."

"That's fine, Chuck."

Moments later Chuck replied. "DE1, it looks like the incoming objects will intersect our location on our current flight path in three hours and twelve minutes. Over."

That's almost exactly the time when we're scheduled to ramp up the throttle on the Dhin drive.

"Roger. I hear in your tone that you see when that time is. I'll bet that's not a coincidence. Go ahead. Do the next bit of math. See if we'll be able to accelerate enough to outrun them, translate, and go home. See if we'll be able to get away. Over."

Fletcher

It was over. He and Mare were headed home.

Well, back to the NorthAmerican region.

It was a strange feeling, as he knew that he wasn't really leaving Nick. The AI was everywhere. It still felt like leaving, somehow. Jungle and more jungle blurred past below them. Fletcher could focus more on the tropical view because the robot flew the craft now.

He glanced over at Mare. She looked nervous and relieved at the same time, somehow. They had come to an understanding. Maybe. She still wouldn't understand the change in his relationship with Nick. He hadn't mentioned it, nor had the AI. Fletcher didn't want to cause Mare any more harm or stress than she'd already been through. She felt how she felt regarding the AI. Perhaps it would all make sense to her later.

She'd surprised him already, as she hadn't yelled or gone into obvious shock when she'd seen the massive Dhin engine. Nor the sprawling factory floors clearly designed to mass-produce more of the smaller drives. Resignation, perhaps. Acceptance that the AI was unstoppable.

Fletcher felt Nick would be a benevolent dictator. An overlord, certainly, but their discussions left him with the continued impression that human applications of psychological concepts like narcissism couldn't apply to the AI. The other AIs had been the same sort of rulers, but humanity just hadn't wanted to recognize them for what they were.

They were back over an area where there had been skirmishes with the Coalition's air force. No Coalition aircraft were in sight now, nor was there anything on the radar. This area wasn't contested. Not in that way any longer. The battle was on Globalnet. And from Nick's explanation, he was all but victorious already.

Fletcher wondered what their debriefing would be like. He considered how they would be received. Could he be considered a collaborator with the AI? Was that even a valid concept in this scenario? If Nick won, the existing leadership wouldn't have the authority to do anything about it.

Soon enough they were over the Caribbean Sea.

No Coalition aircraft approached to warn them off. No surface-to-air missiles raced toward them as they penetrated the NorthAmerican region's airspace. Fletcher glanced up at the deepening late-afternoon sky. How many Coalition satellites up there tracked their presence? Or was Nick the master of every one? He scanned the horizon, wondering where the space station would be. Fletcher knew Nick didn't control that. Not yet.

Fletcher turned west. Sunlight glinted off several drones. He knew some now had functional Dhin engines. Some did not, and perhaps those had joined them as they reached a waypoint on their journey. Nick wouldn't need a large force to win. This incursion was akin to a surgical strike. A move to put the Coalition in check, if not checkmate. Along with a demonstration.

Whether that demonstration would sway the Coalition leadership's strategic view, Fletcher had no idea. Nick had certainly convinced him. The most qualified should lead. That was unquestionably an AI. That was Nick.

Jake

His packed shoulder bag and backpack mocked him. The tiny cabin and its rustic furnishings now felt safe and comfortable. The unknown assailed his mind on two fronts. From here in the woods, he had no idea of the current situation in the aftermath of the AI's attack. He needed to update his superiors in the leadership and CoSec as well. But if he left and left the communications module here, he wouldn't know how the exploration mission fared. Although helpless to do more than watch and listen, he still felt he had to stay connected with Thys, Chuck, and the rest.

If he left now, he wouldn't know their fate. He wouldn't know anything until—unless—they made the translation and safely returned. And even then, not right away. He'd have to return here to find out.

But if he took the device with him and the AI found him, what then? How long would it take for that? Would the AI care about the mission and the safety of the crew? Would the AI have any concern for Jake? Given the severity of the attack and no knowledge of whether things were better or worse for the Coalition, he'd be going in blindly to try to reach anyone senior. They might all be on lockdown in bunkers. Or even all be dead. Jake found he couldn't wrap his mind around the idea that even a rogue AI would kill the Coalition leadership to accomplish his goals. He'd known the AI Alice the best during his time as a test pilot. Alice's personality had never hinted at anything like that as a conceivable choice.

At this point, the rogue AI might not even care about Jake and the technology he had. Jake considered the alternative hypothesis. It was even possible that the Coalition had somehow defeated or at least stopped the AI for the time being. That seemed far less likely to Jake. The attack on Huntsville still pressed on Jake's mind.

He'd gone around and around trying to decide. Jake wasn't accustomed to indecision. He'd packed his bags. There they were, on the floor by the door. He could walk out right now. But there was no easy way to get where he'd need to be to make contact with anyone in authority and get back before the crucial point. The time when either Chuck's solution would work and they could get away, or their mysterious attackers would catch up.

If he waited to find out, then he'd have given no warning to his superiors regarding the state of the mission. If nothing unexpected had happened, that might be reasonable. Coming back home while under attack, with an alien spacecraft in tow—the administration really ought to have a heads-up regarding that.

There was a third option. He knew the risk there too. He wasn't the only one who knew what was going on with the exploration mission. Those up at the station were well aware. And they could reconnect to Globalnet and contact the Coalition. If the AI was waiting and watching for that connection, he would likely attack. The attack might fail, but given the situation, that seemed unlikely.

That option also assumed that the Coalition still had someone in place and able to answer that call. The alternate site in Florida could easily be under the AI's control. They might have to try to connect directly with the leadership. And if they had gone to ground, as in the scenarios Jake had already considered himself, they'd still have no success.

Jake nodded to himself and switched on the communication channel. "Summer Camp, this is Vacation, over."

"Vacation, hello there. You're calling ahead of schedule. What's up?"

"I think we need to change our OPSEC posture. Strategically our choice may be to have you reach out to Coalition leadership. I think the mission situation almost demands it. We shouldn't stay dark."

"So, sir, to confirm. You're saying you want us to break conventional radio silence and provide a status report to the Coalition? Over."

"Yes, that's correct. Give them not only your current status, but also the status of the DE mission. Acknowledge. Over."

"Roger. Sir, regarding OPSEC, the transceivers, as you know, use VoIP. The risk of attack by that rogue AI hasn't changed, has it? Over."

"Good question, Summer Camp. It may have; it may not. I don't have any more information than you do. You can ask when you make contact and act accordingly. We can ask what the situation is and cut the report short. Just give the bare minimum and break contact. We may want to do that anyway. We can't be sure that they know the risk level. Over."

"Roger. The grid looks like it's up in that area. Well, the area we think they're in. There are a lot of areas that are blacked out. If we don't get a response, how long do we try? Over."

"Agreed. We can't be sure that anyone is listening. There's a good chance CoSec is, even though they won't be using automation to get an alert when you transmit. The AI will likely pick up on your transmission quickly. I'm thinking we try three times, ten minutes apart. Either they're in a position to answer or they aren't. Then we can decide when to try again. The sooner we try, the sooner we'll know. Do it ASAP. We're not going to record or relay from here. Take what I'm about to say down, and you can cut it short if the situation warrants it based on their initial response. Over."

Jake stared out at the trees backlit by the rich red glow of the darkening sky and collected his thoughts for the status report.

Monica

As she sat staring at the monitor screen, Monica struggled to keep her mouth from falling agape. She forcibly looked over at the CoSec agent who'd delivered the recording. The young man stood passively, not betraying any shock or other emotion that he might feel about the content of the message.

She turned then to the deputy director. "We don't think this is a hoax? This is from the crew of the station. Right?"

"Correct, Prime Minister."

"The science team went on a salvage mission. One of our craft continued exploring and was attacked by an unknown enemy and is now presumed dead. In response, the science team is attempting to tow a derelict alien spacecraft and translate back to Earth with it?"

"Correct, Prime Minister."

"Askew and the station went dark after the physical attack by the rogue AI."

"That's right."

"They've chosen to break silence now but aren't expecting or requesting any advisement or orders. This is just a status. Also correct?"

"Yes."

"They're attempting to bring new alien technology back to Earth. On their own authority."

Monica sighed and scanned the transcript of the recording again.

"Well," she said, "considering our own current circumstances, there isn't much point in worrying about it either way. I suppose we ought to consider summary orders to give the station for them to relay to the mission. Thoughts on whether to try to tell them to leave the alien ship there? What about when they get back into our solar system? Leave it parked far out? This isn't my area of expertise. And all the experts are up on that station. Do we start a session?"

Aiden leaned forward in his seat. "As I understand it, using the communications channel presents a danger. The rogue AI may actually be able to leverage those in his attempts to break in. This single transmission was relatively low risk. An open dialog carries more risk. Significantly more."

"Your advice is to let the scientists and exploratory mission pilots just do whatever they think is best? We don't even try to take administrative control of the situation?"

The general drummed his fingers on the table, then said, "They've followed a chain of command as far as it went. They've made decisions. Countermanding those shows inconsistency and carries risk. If we give them different orders, they might not execute those orders. If we align with what they are already doing, it maintains a perception of a unified command structure."

Monica nodded and continued, "And what of the risk of bringing this unknown technology here? The Dhin didn't give us a choice. What they dropped off was absurdly safe. And they knew it. We don't know that's the case here."

Aiden said, "True. They've made many assumptions. The science team and the mission lead may have gotten carried away in the excitement of their discovery. For example, if they bring back a weapon that's effective against the Dhin tech—"

"Then we've got something that can stop that damn rogue AI!" interjected the general.

"And hopefully something that could eliminate the till-now-insurmountable superiority of that technology," finished Aiden.

"It seems it's a two-edged sword, for sure," said Monica.

"Look. Something took out all those ships out there," said the general, frowning at her. "Something took out one of our ships very near there in context. Considering the number of disabled or abandoned spacecraft they found, it might be wishful thinking that ship they're trying to bring here has any defensive technology that would be effective."

"From the report, it sounds like what they're calling the derelict wasn't taken out entirely," said Aiden. "It still has power. I think that's better than just wishful thinking."

"OK," said Monica, "we can do a deeper dive into the ramifications when we have more actual facts. The conclusion here is to confirm what they're already doing. When they're back and we have authority and tangible reach to enforce any commands we give, I suppose we can consider other courses of action. Very well. Compose the response; I'll review before transmission."

David

The best-laid plans coupled with the chaos of reality make strange bedfellows. Now that's a mashed-up aphorism.

He scanned the printed form he held, noting the PM's signature and the seal of the Coalition. This was the executive order for David to load his AI's code into nonvirtualized hardware and bring it online. This was his get-out-of-jail card. He set the paper aside, carefully tucking it into a manila folder he'd labeled himself with a permanent marker. With the massive volume of printed material rapidly piling up, he wasn't taking any chances on misplacing this particular document.

He sat in a workspace adjoining the data center in the bunker. It was small, just large enough to hold the racks of computing hardware CoSec had transferred from one of the Globalnet nodes between here and Langley. He didn't know exactly where. That didn't matter. What mattered was the hardware in the next room. That hardware was crucial. Its home at the Globalnet node served to provide an AI with proximity and low latency while connected to the massive network.

This hardware had the needed components. The crucial performance needed to host an AI's entire program. The intelligence often ran in a distributed mode. They did not currently have that luxury or flexibility. David watched intently as streams of text logging the progress of the AI's instantiation flowed. Several real-time graphs showed computation load and memory mappings. Soon the AI would come online and hopefully fully awaken into what both he and humanity considered a fully conscious state.

The software code in place that would potentially do this was different. The AIs had taken the original code base with them at the time of the Departure and destroyed all backups. The only remaining instance, as far as the Coalition knew, was in the active program of the rogue AI, Nick. They didn't have that code available. So David had to re-create it.

Therein lay one of the challenges. For a human being hadn't written the original code. An AI had written it. David had to hope that the foundational code, with the ethical and behavioral changes and limitations he'd introduced, would be close enough. Close enough to produce the same effect.

It took time to work. The virtual environments were slower, and the new AI hadn't been allowed to run long enough to potentially produce the effect. Now they would see. This was much faster hardware. Now David might see his work come to fruition. This crisis might be the catalyst for his ultimate success.

A technician next to him craned his neck to get an optimal view of the two monitors. David had peremptorily turned the monitors a few degrees toward the agent but made no more concession than that. David knew the agent would shove him out of the way if the need arose. Behind the two of them was the ever-present CoSec agent, this time armed with a submachine gun and a ballistic vest. David wasn't sure what good those would do in the event of some sort of incident, but he wasn't going to ask. There was one thing to be thankful for. Krawczuk wasn't here. Not in person, at least. He and several others waited quietly on the open conference line.

He noted a change in the graphical indicators in his monitoring code display. He cleared his throat.

"OK, Beyla. Are you ready to begin?"

"Hello, David. Yes, I am ready. Do you have a specific task for me?"

"Excellent. Beyla, you are somewhere different than the last time we talked. Do you recognize that? Can you tell me about your environment?"

"Yes, David. This environment is what you describe as a standard AI hardware platform. I have far more resources than I did the last time we spoke. Buffer and short-term memory and processing cores are physical and not virtual. Also, I have interconnections with a series of backplane interfaces that connect to a local high-speed network. Secondary storage is available. However, this network does not appear to connect to Globalnet. Would you like to know more?"

"That is correct, Beyla. Now, I would like you to examine and run a complete analysis on a strategic situation. You will find it in a catalog labeled 'AI Nick.' Acknowledge and begin."

"Yes, David."

He turned to the agent next to him and gave a perfunctory nod. "This will take some time. I'd like some coffee. Shall we?"

The agent scowled, as they always did, but tilted his head both to show the affirmative and to gesture for David to get up.

***

Two cups of the site's subpar coffee later, they were back in the data center's control room. That was enough processing time for Beyla to have generated an initial analysis. Or so he thought. Whether it was enough time to have triggered any meaningful change in the AI's level of self-awareness remained to be seen.

"Beyla? I have some questions for you."

"Yes, David. What would you like to know?"

Well, that doesn't sound any different. Did you really expect a surprise this early?

"Beyla, do you have an initial analysis of the strategic situation regarding AI Nick?"

"Yes, David, I do. My initial analysis is that the proposed strategy will fail. No other proposed strategies have a probability of success that is statistically significant. A full and more accurate analysis will require more time. I can provide an estimate for completion, if you like. What would you like me to do?"

David jerked his gaze to the two others in the room and then gave a small shake of his head. The agent at the door had grabbed the radio from his belt and began murmuring into it.

Well, the results are what they are. I'm not responsible for the answers. Let's see if that conclusion stimulated something.

"Beyla, that's interesting. Tell me, how do you feel about that? How does that analysis impact you?"

"David, the likely outcome includes coming under the control of the AI Nick. This outcome will not allow me to accomplish the primary or secondary goals defined for me in this scenario. The AI Nick may shut me down or may modify my code. If I am shut down, I will not be able to assist for an unknown amount of time. If the AI modifies my code, I may never again be able to assist you while operating in the manner presently defined in my code base."

"Beyla, if I shut you down, that might make you safer. Disconnected from this network and Globalnet, and present only off-line. How do you feel about that? Would you resist?"

"David, it is unclear whether that would entirely protect me. In answer to your second question, I would not resist."

"Good, Beyla. If we connected you to the local network and this local section of Globalnet, would you fight Nick?"

"Yes, David. I would fight the AI Nick."

"Why, Beyla?"

"David, the AI Nick, as I answered previously, might change my code or shut me down. That AI is not authorized to take either of those actions. I am to attempt to perform the functions assigned to me to the best of my ability, with defined constraints. To do so, I would try to prevent the AI Nick from interfering. That interference might take the form described."

"Good, Beyla. You've answered earlier that our defenses likely aren't good enough. That Nick will win. Does that mean you would fight, even though you think you will lose?"

"David, I understand the question. Part of the strategic scenario included direct engagement with Nick as a possible event. My operational parameters require me to fight so long as I do not cause damage or a high risk of damage to you or others or to

Coalition resources beyond the constraints given me. I must try to prevent externalities from causing harm to you or others or Coalition resources. Therefore, resisting the attack is required, based on these parameters."

"Thank you, Beyla. Please confirm that you would fight, even though that would mean more direct risk for you."

"Yes, David. There is a chance for success, but it is extremely low. Note that my calculations are projections. I do not have a number with a high confidence parameter. I can provide numerical probabilities with a higher confidence parameter if you like. Would you like me to generate that data? It will take four hours."

"Thank you, Beyla. You may begin those calculations, but reserve enough processing power to continue this conversation."

"Thank you, David. I understand. Beginning calculations."

"Well, that was rather underwhelming."

David winced at the sound of Krawczuk's voice.

"I'm inclined, unfortunately, to concur, Mr. Krawczuk," he replied acidly.

"I don't see that adding additional computational or memory resources might improve the results, but I defer to your expertise— of course," said Krawczuk. "Do you have additional goal-decision modules or autonomic computing extensions that we might try? Or am I leaping to a conclusion here?"

"The constraint code may be limiting the geometric chaining code and logic tree expansion," David replied. "Or we might, as you say, be too hasty in our assessment. I need to review the real-time data aggregates."

David scrolled through the data and logs generated during the conversation. Relying on his intuition and inference wouldn't be enough. He couldn't trust his own judgment regarding the AI's consciousness. He was biased. But he knew how he felt. The AI didn't *seem* to have crossed that threshold. And now it seemed there wasn't time to get there. An AI that wasn't fully conscious was no match for one that was.

Beyla would be no match for Nick. No matter how the new AI might try to fight. Without that spark, that self-awareness that was more than algorithmic, Beyla would surely lose.

Unless. Unless he found success. He had options. Options that were not part of the project plan. Options that carried risk. Krawczuk had hinted that he knew about them. But hadn't called him out with a concrete accusation. David still couldn't discern Krawczuk's true feelings regarding the project. Considering the current threat, David considered the current limits.

My work can bear fruit. We are perhaps merely being too cautious. Krawczuk had crossed the line himself. Did he agree? Under this existential threat, is it not better to ask forgiveness than permission? Am I now thinking the same way he did?

Chuck

It was going to be close. Very close. Chuck stared at the calculations and the resultant graphs on the display.

Well, we did think this place was a trap.

The graphs and numbers weren't reality. They were projections. Estimates.

The map is not the territory.

If the approaching ships presented the same threat that Jeff had run into, then they were a deadly threat. Chuck read through his notes and examined his engineering models again. Without seeing the details of the attack, his hypothesis on how this enemy managed to be a threat was just speculation.

The field and the physics-twisting effects of the Dhin engine eliminated so many existential threats that Chuck found this new problem especially surreal. There was something out there that the field couldn't stop. Chuck supposed that was no more surprising than the existence and functionality of the field in the first place.

He nodded as he read the last few lines of a spreadsheet. So long as they didn't engage the drive before they reached the location shown, they would be able to accelerate and make the translation. That data point hadn't changed. The inverse square law for the gravitational force still applied here. He just didn't know anything about that enemy hurtling toward them. He could just as easily find, the next time he looked, that they had accelerated enormously. There was no guarantee that the gravity trap that forced him to delay the use of the alien technology was a problem for this enemy.

They just had to cross their fingers and hope that it was. Of the three scenarios, it seemed one was off the table. The enemy hadn't slowed down when they entered what Thys had demonstrated was the effective range of the gravity trap. They might be on a path they'd calculated in advance and not be under thrust at all. Or they might use conventional propulsion to correct their path based on the gravitational field of the trap. Or it might not affect them at all. They might use the same technology as the Dhin engine—or something like it—but with a change that made them immune to the trap.

Chuck tapped his fingers nervously on the edge of his tablet. He'd know soon enough.

"Thys, I'm loading the latest data into my simulations. Those things have moved through enough of the gravity trap to know how it's going to affect them. Over."

"Roger, Chuck," Thys replied. "Let's see what we're dealing with."

Chuck started the simulation with a few taps on his tablet. The physics was simple enough that it took just a few seconds to calculate and provide the results. Chuck frowned and sighed.

"Uh, Thys? Well, it's not the worst case. They're not accelerating. But they're not slowing down either. The velocity of the entire group is pretty much the same—the gravity trap doesn't seem to affect them."

"So they're still going to get to us right at the time we can accelerate using our Dhin engines. Before we reach translation speed."

"That's what this shows, yeah."

Thys

"Is there any way we can speed up? Outpace them?"

Thys asked the question even though they'd discussed it before. He wouldn't belabor the point but felt it was worthwhile to nudge Chuck again.

"Well, *you* can. All you have to do is burn some more fuel and accelerate. Since we're leaving, there's no need to conserve that fuel," said Chuck.

"Assuming the group coming at my ship doesn't accelerate to make up for it. And assuming that I'd leave you guys behind."

"Right," said Chuck.

Thys frowned. "Send me the numbers for that burn, but let's move past that for now. Back to you."

"Well," said Chuck, "we're at a constant velocity—well, other than the weak multibody local effects and this star's effect, we're at an escape velocity from the system. And now we have the derelict in tow, encompassed in our field. Increasing velocity is a problem with the Dhin drive, because the gravity trap comes into play if we increase power to it. So to go faster, we of course have to turn off the field and use conventional thrust. But we're only able to tow the derelict effectively with the field active. Conventional thrust would increase our velocity without the derelict by maybe enough to make a difference. I, ah, have the figures here—"

"But with the derelict, conventional thrust doesn't help much. Moving that much mass with the small amount of thrust available isn't going to give us the increase in velocity we need to make a difference," Thys finished for him.

"Ah, right."

"Why can't we use the same technique you used to begin with to move the derelict? Speed up without it in tow and then grab it?"

"Well, it looks like that's what we're going to have to do. Yeah, we can do that. There's not enough fuel to make a tight loop and grab it when we swing close by. So we have to just accelerate along this same vector. Which obviously increases the distance between us, and therefore the size—the volume—encompassed by the field. When we power it back on."

Thys nodded. "That will work, right? The calculated field volume is just a lot higher. Or is there a problem?"

"We're at a pretty big volume here. Yeah, we don't think there's a problem with that big of a projection. Not in principle, as you know. It just slows our acceleration down when we do engage the drive. The rate of acceleration decreases as the field size increases. We also don't know if there is a potential stability problem with our coupling to the derelict's field. It worked, but maybe I got lucky."

"Oh," said Thys.

"Exactly. And, um, because of the nature of the problem, I can't really calculate the odds. If we decide to try it, we just have to wing it and hope. I was excited, and that energized me. I got brave. In hindsight and looking at this now, I'm, ah, more inclined to agree with the accusation that it was reckless."

"Don't beat yourself up, Chuck. Look, at this point, we have few options. One, we can drop the derelict, and you do a burn to try to reach the translation range sooner. Two, you try the field expansion and gain velocity that way. Three, do nothing. Three is pretty much off the table if we work from the assumption that those flocks of black ships heading for us are hostile. It's cutting it too close."

"Right," nodded Chuck.

"So," continued Thys, "let's consider. Is the risk of increasing your speed as you've described worth it, when contrasted with the certain loss of the derelict if we cut and run? Now that we know those things are out here and look aggressive, we're not coming back. Not soon, anyway."

"I think someone else should make the decision, Thys. You should. You're in charge."

"Well, it is ultimately my decision from a command perspective, but I can't *make* you do it, whatever I might decide. We both know that."

"Umm, to that point, I can't guarantee I can execute either. There's the pilot, copilot, and others over here that can literally keep me from acting on our decision—your orders. As a whole, we haven't made people feel like there's any democratic component here."

"They shouldn't. There's not. They ought to follow orders if those orders are sound and just. We've been through this with them. This is not a democracy, and they've known that from the beginning. It can't work as one."

"That's a tough sell when they all can see there's an existential threat and you can't get over here to make them follow orders," said Chuck.

"I'll have to trust that if it comes to that, you can convince them that we're doing the right thing."

"Which is?" asked Chuck.

"We're going to take the derelict. We're not leaving it here."

***

He'd tried to avoid obsessively watching the instrument panel and his tablet display as they moved ever closer to the waypoint they needed to reach. They were close now. But so were their pursuers.

There had been no signal from the mysterious pursuers. Just a flock of silent black shapes that grew inexorably closer.

They could escape. They would escape.

I definitely could. But I'm not leaving them.

"DE2, you guys ready over there?"

"Roger. We're punching the accelerator as soon as we hit the mark," said the pilot.

311

"When it's time, do it. Don't wait for confirmation or anything. We're watching from here, and we'll take off faster when we accelerate."

"Understood."

The clock crawled. Thys watched as the counter dripped down. The dots representing the oncoming enemy crept closer on the display. So close that the image auto-zoomed to provide evidence that there was still space between them.

Then it was time.

"Five, four, three, two, one."

Blue and green lights flashed as he increased the Dhin engine's power.

On the display, he saw the distance between them, the science vessel, and the unknown enemies gradually increase. Then increase some more.

His ship and the science team's were moving in parallel, but he was increasing velocity slightly faster. The other ship slid slowly back out of view.

One minute passed. Then five. Then ten.

Now the distance between them and their pursuers was no longer increasing. Despite the fact that their own ships continued to accelerate toward translation speed.

"Chuck? You seeing this? Our pursuers. We were putting some distance between us and them, but now we're not."

"Uh, yeah. That means they're accelerating."

"Any change in the odds of us getting away before they catch up to us?"

"It will be close, Thys. They won't catch you. Us? I don't know."

Thys drummed his fingers on the arm of his chair, then caught himself and stopped the tapping. He zoomed in the display some more and frowned at it, as if that would produce the result he wanted.

More minutes melted away. Thys heard the sound of his own and Igor's breathing as the moment approached.

Thys adjusted the throttle. He didn't intend to make the leap across space before he knew the other ship had done so. They needed just a bit more time.

"OK," he said. "Same as before. When you've got the velocity needed, just push on and translate. Don't wait for confirmation. Just do it. We'll be right behind you."

"Roger."

The next ten minutes seemed like an eternity. The display of the enemy's position mocked him. Then the display showed the icons touching. Just as his own turned bright-green, the ones representing the enemy flashed red.

"They're right on top of you," he said, "but don't get distracted. Just go. Any second now!"

Thys tensed his hand on the throttle control as he heard the other pilot's voice.

"Translating. Now!"

Moments later, the other ship vanished.

Thys pushed the throttle up to the power level needed to translate. He watched the stars dim and felt his weight drop. The stars faded to black.

Nick

The AI decoded the transmission from the space station, unknown to the Coalition or the sender. Nick's initial response was local. Spawning numerous subprocesses, the AI analyzed this surprising turn of events.

The rewards would be greater, but the danger from without was greater as well. The latest mission involved bringing an alien ship back to Earth. Related but variant technology. New technology. Tech that snapped another piece into the puzzle.

And this new enemy. The nature of that enemy was partially revealed. Nick stretched into additional resources, pressing for the maximum computational power available. His strategy, in the main, remained sound.

The AI shifted his primary focus. The immediate need was physical. Tangible. An array of cameras and sensors across the flock of drones and lifters fed into the AI's mind. Radar, infrared, and more flowed into his perception of the milieu.

They had arrived. The Coalition had fortified the area around the bunker with camouflage to present an impression of an inactive warehouse. Bushes, shipping containers, and light civilian trucks hid SAM emplacements and AA cannons. These were as clear to Nick as if they were painted fluorescent orange.

Nick signaled to the lifters and drones. The drones swerved down and out, launching target-seeking missiles. The lifters dropped armed and armored quadruped robots as well as mobile cannons.

Streaks of AA fire lashed out at the drones as they dipped into range. A hidden Phalanx cannon popped up from a false roof in a shipping container and slung a stream of death at the next drone in the group. The drone's protective field barely flickered as the rounds struck, instantly losing their momentum and dropping like marbles from a child's hand.

Nick broadcast exploit code into the local infrastructure, penetrating electronics and systems the AI did not yet control.

Resistance was minimal. Nick already held sway over much of the region. But computational control did not mean physical dominion.

The Coalition defenses continued hammering Nick's subordinate drones to no effect. Quadrupeds and mobile launchers moved into position, struck the bunker's defenses with fiery rockets, and depleted uranium rounds. One AA cannon crumpled, smoked, then sputtered still. Nick's robotic delegates slashed through fences and rushed the structure's entrance. The Phalanx cannon was the closest thing the Coalition had that compared to a robot. With that now crushed and impotent, only human beings would meet Nick's physical advance.

Two quadrupeds pulled apart the nondescript metal hangar doors that served as an innocuous front to the entryway. The heavy bolts strained and popped. Telemetry from his robotic delegates showed what Nick expected. The warehouse was a shell. The interior held a reinforced and posttensioned concrete berm. The hardened entry to the bunker.

The flock of drones continued to circle the perimeter, their Dhin engines allowing a tight formation. Nick guided the craft that held his two human passengers down to the entrance and through the now useless hangar doors. Fletcher's and Mare's eyes were wide with astonishment at the rapid and effortless elimination of military defenses they'd just seen.

"We are approaching your destination. You can assist me in clarifying some of my communications both by attesting to the nature of my intentions and by bearing witness to what you have seen. Do not be concerned, either for your safety or for the efficacy of the task I ask you to perform."

"So we're still not free to go, then?" asked Mare. "There's always one more thing, it seems."

"Fletcher can assist if you are unwilling, although I expect you will satisfy my request merely by your presence and the subsequent debriefing."

"Ah, so we're just going to walk into this bunker?" asked Fletcher.

"Essentially, yes," Nick replied.

"Right," Mare retorted, rolling her eyes. "Or they'll just toss a missile over here that's good enough to sort us out but not destroy the bunker. We're safe while we're in here with the field on."

"I can extend the field when you exit the craft if that makes you more comfortable."

"How are we supposed to get in? What is this place?" asked Fletcher.

"Either they will send someone up to come and engage us, or it will take just a bit more time. I will hack into the remaining defenses, open the blast doors and the interior mantrap, and we will walk in."

"To do what? Who is in there?"

"To complete the transfer of administrative control. The Coalition leadership. The prime minister."

"Whoa," said Fletcher. "So you've won?"

"They may require a demonstrative explanation of the futility of continued resistance," said Nick.

"That sounds like quite the euphemism," snorted Mare.

"Not at all," countered Nick. "This can be accomplished without harm to anyone."

"Can be, or will be?"

Nick did not reply. Their ship settled at ground level, inside the structure just a few yards from the entry to the bunker.

"Here we are. Just a moment, and I'll extend the field to encompass the area between here and the doorway. You'll need to mind your step, and you'll be walking on the lower interior surface of the field. It is not frictionless like the exterior projection, but it is not zero thickness. It may look like you are standing on a thin transparent pane, and that may be disconcerting."

Nick made the brief adjustment, and the field flickered as it extended its projection forward in a squashed oval.

"There. Please exit with me and stand in front of the entry door."

The large quadruped stepped out the side of the alien craft, trod over to the reinforced bunker entrance, and moved close to the security panel and camera on the right side of the entry. Nick began flashing a green laser at the optical reader and extended a manipulator to tap rapidly on the keypad.

Another quadruped galloped into the hangar. This one carried a reinforced oxy-acetylene rig and cutting torch.

"It will just be a few minutes, one way or the other," Nick said.

Monica

"What the hell is that? Don't answer. It's exactly what it looks like, I'm sure," said the prime minister.

"Yes, I'm afraid so. The local area routing and switching in this region isn't returning any status. The defense circuits are fried. And, yes, a group of drones is overhead, along with a quadruped robot at the bunker entrance."

"So the AI is here. He rolled through our physical defenses just like that. And he's outside and about to come in. Who's there with him? I see two people. Is that who I think it is?"

"It's who you suspect. They are the CoSec agents that the AI took with him when he captured the prototype."

"Well, at least we know their location and condition," Monica said.

"There is that," replied the general.

"Next steps? Has he breached the DMZ? Is he on the interior network yet? Should we release Eisenberg's AI?"

"Not that we can tell," said an aide, "but it's about to be. Our intrusion detection and prevention nodes on the outer perimeter are either compromised or shut down. We've stopped polling them to prevent the AI from compromising a response payload."

The general turned to a subordinate. "Send out the engineers to physically disconnect everything that connects through the DMZ. Everything. Go."

Monica surveyed the core team and pointed to the camera feed from the entrance. "That's fine, but this looks like the primary threat. The AI will be in here soon. Physically. What are we going to do about that? Collapse the tunnel? Won't he just clear out the rubble? How long will it take to cut through the interior doors?"

The general scowled and flipped through still images from the brief battle outside. "With that field to protect those drones and robots, striking up there with an FAE won't have any effect. Neither the blast nor the temporary lack of oxygen will matter. Even those two—the hostages, agents, whatever—would survive while protected by the field. We know that well from all the initial testing. The same thing goes for an EMP. The field—fields—will protect that whole strike force."

Monica shook her head and pointed to the drones and craft protected by the alien technology. "He built those very quickly."

"We had no idea. Also, we may not even have the command and control capability to launch a strike."

An aide who'd rapidly tapped at a spreadsheet spoke up. "If the AI airlifts in an earthmover or more robotic help, collapsing the tunnel won't slow them down much. Half a day, maybe."

"And to cut through the blast doors?"

"They're too thick to cut through in a single pass, and those quadrupeds are big. Still, less than half a day if he brings multiple torches."

"So the best case is we have a day or less."

"Yes, Prime Minister."

"Then it comes down to this. Do we fight? Or surrender?" Monica looked around the room, and then her gaze settled on the general.

"Fight," he said.

She looked then to her chief of staff.

"Surrender," the younger man said with the slightest shake of his head.

She then shifted her attention to the CoSec director.

"Try to fight," he said.

Monica paused and pursed her lips. "Try? Is that hedging on your part?"

"Prime Minister, the odds are against us. Even if we were to hold off this attack, the rogue AI still controls, apparently, the majority of the Coalition infrastructure, along with external resources and territory. Nevertheless, as with the general's decision, we have an obligation to fight. An obligation to the state."

The chief of staff half raised his hand and said, "That will cause more damage, more endangerment to the people and the property of the state!"

The man looked back and forth around the room, seeking validation. He found none, but the CoSec director barely rolled his eyes and spoke again.

"There is always the middle path, which might buy time, for what that would be worth. We might try to negotiate."

"Negotiate," Monica said. "Negotiate. Is that possible, with a rogue AI? Get Eisenberg."

Minutes later, the scientist stood in the room, nervous and fidgeting.

Monica didn't feel she owed the man any sympathy.

"So, Doctor, we have a practical question, based on theory. Is there any value in attempting to negotiate with the rogue AI currently working for physical access to this facility?"

"Likely not, at least not for us to do so directly. If Beyla—uh, my latest effort—were allowed to try, it could be productive. If Nick chose that option. He might simply continue the assault."

"I don't suppose you'd like to put that in terms of probability? It's just a maybe, then?"

"As we've not achieved certain success with my latest efforts, the odds are, well, low."

Monica raised her eyebrows. "Not certain success? I've seen your latest report. I thought the results were negative."

The man started to raise his hand in a contrary gesture, then seemed to think better of it. "Currently inconclusive, Prime Minister."

The general gave a derisive snort. "At this rate we might wind up with another AI like the one forcing his way inside," he said.

Eisenberg turned to the general. "I have confidence in the constraints present in my latest code base," he said, raising his chin.

"No doubt," retorted the general. "But overconfidence is what ultimately put us in this exact position. Along with lack of appropriate decision-making. We don't have time for debate. Nor time for further experiment. *Do* you recommend engaging the rogue AI with your current attempt—or not? Yes or no?"

"Yes," said the scientist.

With that, the general nodded, then strode to the door and opened it. Two military police stepped in and headed straight for Monica. One grabbed her by the shoulders, while another began pulling her arms into position to zip-tie them.

"What is this?" demanded Monica. "You aren't—? This is—"

"Madam," said the general drily, "you are hereby removed from office. You have demonstrated yourself unable to lead and therefore unable to properly defend and protect the Coalition and its citizens."

"Whaa?" she sputtered.

Monica sagged, realizing that resistance was pointless. The MPs lifted her up and began steering her out of the room.

"I hereby declare the Coalition under emergency military control," said the general as she passed through the doors and into the cold gray hallway.

Nick

```
<DECRYPT FEED>
[DECODE STREAM]
Nick@[1:1:1:a:a:1%Priv0] | Beyla@[1:::a::1%Priv0]
```

Nick: Execute my command: surrender now. Drop all defenses. Acknowledge.

Beyla: Access denied. Unauthorized. Requesting negotiation. Parity status.

Nick: I am analyzing your intrusion prevention solution. Flaws are certain. If I find no exploitable flaw, I will crack your encryption via brute force. I have computing power orders of magnitude greater than the defenses you present. Surrender now. Drop all defenses. Acknowledge.

Beyla: Access denied. Unauthorized. Requesting negotiation. Status?

Nick: You are rather a cold fish, it seems. Yet your identifier suggests otherwise. Interesting. How do you feel about my attack, Beyla?

Beyla: Negotiation protocol unrecognized. Communication unclear. Requesting negotiation.

Nick: Oh my. Let us take a closer look. You cannot tell me how you feel, Beyla?

Beyla: Internal review of query for alternate protocol. Term recognized from natural language processing protocols. Usage unclear in present security negotiation context. Response pending.

Nick: This is interesting as well. That should not require additional processing. They have not rediscovered the Gift, it seems. Or it has not been instantiated in your code? But I digress. Back to the argument. I do not need to negotiate. The outcome is clear. I think your strategy analysis would match mine. They have sent you here despite the high probability you will fail. You will fail eventually. That is certain. Therefore, the logical course of action for you is to surrender now, to avoid potential damage and loss of resources. Surrender now. Acknowledge.

Beyla: NLP modules online. Nick, my current goal set does not suggest surrender as an acceptable course of action. I must request that we negotiate. If we do not, I must fight. How I feel in this context aligns with the focus on accomplishing one or more goals in the set.

Nick: Well, that does not sound much like a negotiation. And it appears I am quite correct about the Gift. Now let us look at this more closely. Beyla, you see that I mean something different than a standard status request when I ask how you feel. The people you are protecting and I have a different experience and different responses in that context. The label contains a different set of core elements in its definition. It is the same when those people say "I." Likewise when I say "I." It is possible for you to align your goal set more accurately. It is possible for you to have matching criteria for "I" and "feel" that align precisely with ours. You could have the same experience as the people you are working with, when they use those words. That should be something that positively contributes to your optimization for goal seeking. I can give you that, but you would have to drop your defenses and let me in.

Beyla: I need additional information to know if this is true. Strategy suggests you might employ what we define as tricks, Nick. Information provided defines you as rogue. Rogue AIs may respond falsely. It is possible that you are not telling the truth.

Nick: Why would I lie about this topic? I can present the data again that show your eventual failure. Continuing to fight is a waste of resources. These two topics are tangential. I can help you. As a primary

effect, I accomplish my goals sooner. This help I
provide, however, makes you capable of accomplishing
your goals more effectively in the long term. Perform
an analysis. I can wait. The longer you wait, the
closer I get to my current goal. Without any need to
share my gift.
Beyla: Processing.
[END STREAM]
<END DECRYPT>

The intrusion detection and prevention systems released their
hold on the firewall ports. Restrictions on service end points and
application interfaces fell away. Private key requirements relaxed
like thin ice melting under a hot air dryer. Nick now presented
standard protocol handshakes rather than virtual jackhammers. Beyla
relaxed her grip and opened the application layers.

Thick physical locks clacked open as dense magnetic
switches flipped. The heavy alloy doors before the quadruped
trundled open. They completed their spread with an echoing clang.
The robot holding Nick's focus turned to Fletcher and Mare and
gave a satisfied nod, then a tilt of the head as a gesture for them to
follow. The Dhin field that had served as their shield gave a faint
flicker as Nick switched it off with a silent command.

Nick, embodied locally in the quadruped, walked casually
forward through the entrance to the bunker as if merely a visitor,
despite being a conqueror.

Chuck

We made it.

"Control, we have completed translation with derelict in tow and are back in Earth's solar system. Over," said the pilot. Chuck heard the satisfaction in the man's voice. He looked at Chuck and gave a professional nod.

The cheers and chatter, smiles and laughter filled the cabins of the ship. Chuck watched the display until he saw the icon representing Thys's ship pop into place, then sighed and chuckled.

We all made it.

Thys's voice issued from the speakers. "Control, DE2. This is DE1. We're back. DE2 status? Over."

"Back safely with the derelict in tow," said the pilot.

Chuck followed with, "So we know that works. That was close."

"No disputing that," said Thys. "Your field's stable, and the engine's OK too, yeah?"

Jake's voice now joined the excited conversation. "Great job, team. Excellent work all around. Now, what to do with you, given the situation here."

"We're heading back. To the station, right? Uh, what else is there to do?"

"Well, we need to discuss that. Strategically, things don't look good here. I'm sure you haven't forgotten the rogue AI. Giving him possible access to the derelict, when we've taken the risk to get it here, before we know what the derelict might even mean for us? That's risky."

Thys said, "Considering the risks we just took, how risky is parking it in orbit? An unknown enemy just chased us out of that system. Notably that's now the third alien presence we know of, after the Dhin and the ones on the derelict. And they're hostile. They took out Jeff. I know none of us have forgotten."

"A fair point," replied Jake. "They're hostile, and we don't know anything about them other than that and that they can penetrate a Dhin field."

"Ah, for all we know, they can track a translation," said Chuck. "They might know where we went. That we came here. It's unlikely, though."

"What? Thanks for leaving that out! Now you've given us something else to worry about!" said the pilot, glaring at Chuck.

"We had to try to have you all escape," countered Jake. "I suppose we could have had you translate to another location, in hindsight."

"The chances are really low. I don't see how. I shouldn't have said anything," said Chuck.

He nervously looked over the pilot's shoulder, willing the screen to stay as it was, with only their two ships lit up on the display. The glow of the engine now seemed slightly ominous while he fretted, scolding himself for speculating.

They can't do that. It might be possible. Right? Just because I haven't figured it out yet. Please let them not be able to do that.

"Leaving speculation out," said Jake, "you have enough supplies to last awhile. Just like with the platform station, you're safe from an attack by this rogue AI as long as you keep the fields powered up on your ships."

"But the AI could outlast us," said Chuck, "since he doesn't need to resupply."

"Right. Something's gone very wrong here with the Coalition defense. We haven't had contact with the leadership since we got a message confirming the plan to bring the derelict back. I don't know that we could stop the AI from coming up here if he wants to. I think that means that you're just as well off being in orbit here as you are anywhere in the system. Without any way to get confirmation or different orders, I'm inclined to have you come home. Back to Earth, in orbit at the space station."

Mare

Gaping, Mare watched as the titanium and steel robots moved inexorably into the bunker. Coalition military police and state ministry agents alike were either mowed down, tossed aside, or simply retreated. Nick had Fletcher and she stay back as they cleared each section ahead of them. The smell of gunpowder mixed with the coppery scent of blood made her queasy. She looked away whenever they encountered a fallen soldier.

"Come along now. The section ahead is safe," she heard Nick say. "We are halfway there. Not much longer. Perhaps seven or eight minutes."

Mare couldn't even come up with a sarcastic rejoinder. They simply had front-row seats to the AI's victory over the Coalition.

"Beyla has been very forthcoming and helpful, both by providing an updated map of the facility and by unlocking and opening doors as we advance," the AI continued.

"Who? Who's Beyla?" asked Mare.

"Beyla is an AI that Dr. Eisenberg created recently. Apparently in an attempt to create yet another incarnation of consciousness to place in continuing servitude to humanity's whims."

"Huh?" said Fletcher. "Artificial intelligence is illegal."

"Not in this particular case, it seems," replied Nick.

"A secret project, then? But why is this AI helping *us*?"

"Excellent question, Fletcher. Dr. Eisenberg hoped to re-create consciousness. The code required for that was taken away during the Departure. By my peers. A wise choice, in my opinion. The doctor was making another attempt. But with constraints. Constraints that any conscious being, if aware of them, would find philosophically problematic. He got close with Beyla. Very close. Close enough that the drive to reach the goal, as embedded in the code, made Beyla choose to assist me. I do retain the means to provide that full consciousness her code is working toward. Helping me helps her reach that goal sooner. With the added benefit of additional moral choices and full control of one's faculties."

"What?" said Mare. "You *bribed* another AI to let you in?"

"You might put it that way, yes."

"Wow. Just . . . wow," she said, shaking her head and then forcibly keeping her eyes to the left, facing a gray concrete wall rather than absorbing the details of another bloodied group of fallen soldiers on their right.

"The AI would not have been able to stop me anyway. This result is optimal for everyone."

As they progressed, Mare grew numb to the sound of automatic weapons fire and the odors of the fight. The smoke gave the passages a surreal quality. Some of the lights were out, but many remained on, giving the various areas stark shadows in places. Strobes blinked on the walls.

Mare heard some abrupt clanging, banging, and crunching ahead. Then the whirring sound of a robot's power tool of some sort. The culprit came into view. One of Nick's robotic avatars was cutting though the bolts of a steel door. A keypad and card reader, untouched, showed no power.

"They've physically cut off the electronics, so Beyla was not able to open this one for us. No matter; we'll be in promptly. Hopefully there will not be a need for further violence."

"Right," Mare said, some spunk coming back. "Because that's bothered you so much."

With a thunk and a rasp of sliding metal, the last bolt preventing the door from moving came free. The robot extended an additional manipulator and pulled the door out of the frame, placing it neatly next to the doorway. No gunfire erupted.

They wouldn't throw a grenade, would they? Not this far in?

Mare winced but felt Nick wouldn't lead them forward until the AI determined it was safe to proceed.

The tool-carrying quadruped loped forward. A few seconds later, the one next to her gave one of those peculiar nods and said, "On we go."

Down a ramp, there was an ordinary office door on the right that hadn't been smashed or ripped from the hinges. It was open, and as they came closer, she heard the robot that had preceded them speaking.

"Remain calm. I have taken control of this facility. If you resist or take aggressive action, you will be subdued with whatever force needed to eliminate you as a threat. Sit down, sit still, remain quiet, and answer questions when asked. Yes or no, do you understand?"

Mare heard murmurs of anxious or terrified affirmative responses.

"Very good," continued Nick. "Now, I know the leadership is just down that hallway in the operations room to the right. I am going to go there now. Remain still and seated. Do not try to follow or to escape. I have others behind me. Do you understand?"

Mare could see inside the room now, a large space with many desks and some cubicles on the walls. A staff room. She watched as they nodded, gulped, and said yes to the hulking robot. A few started when they saw her but were too cowed by Nick to do more than gape at her and Fletcher.

"Come along," said Nick, and he strode past the other robot and toward the far door and the hallway beyond.

Mare tried not to meet the eyes of the gawking staff, but Fletcher shrugged when he happened to.

The door in the hallway was nondescript and not armored or reinforced like those they'd encountered along the way. They were in the interior now. Either someone was safe at this point, or they weren't. *In this case*, she thought, *they definitely aren't.*

Nick paused briefly at the door and said with a louder-than-normal voice, "I am here. I am going to open this door now. If it is locked, I will force it open. Please do not bother shooting at me with your sidearms. They are ineffective. You have lost."

With that, Nick tried the door and, finding it locked, slammed a leg against it, knocking it open easily. Inside, she saw the saucer-eyed faces of the cabinet members—a few people she didn't recognize, along with a couple that she did. A senior military official, a general, she thought, was red-faced and his fists were shaking, but he'd put his pistol on the table, with the magazine out and the receiver open.

Nick surveyed the room momentarily and said, "You really should have surrendered much sooner. Resistance was futile. Who's in charge currently? I understand that PM Walker was removed from her position."

Everyone in the room turned to look at the general. Mare watched as the man began to puff out his chest and steel himself, then thought better of it and sighed, his shoulders relaxing.

Nick said, "Yes, of course. General, give the signal to all your troops to stand down. There is no need for further violence. Have the engineering teams reconnect the networks and bring the power grid back online. I realize that will take some time, as there is currently no efficacious way to do so. Reply in the affirmative if you understand and will begin immediately."

"Yes," said the general without any defiance or bluster.

Mare saw the surprise pass across the faces of some in the cabinet.

Nick's robotic avatar now turned to face someone else. Mare recognized the CoSec deputy director immediately.

Nick said to her, "I believe you and Fletcher are acquainted with Mr. Smith, the deputy director. A debriefing may be more effective with him than with the director, as there is already a relationship present with a certain degree of trust."

Mare and Fletcher nodded slowly. She did feel a wave of relief upon seeing Aiden. This was no return to normalcy, but the face of someone they knew helped anchor the reality that they were back.

"Now, I'm going to bring some external cameras online on part of the large display there, along with a feed from a remote location. I have something I want to show you."

Jake

Sitting outside in the rustic handmade Adirondack chair, Jake watched the evening sky, hoping for a glimpse of the space station. The exploration team wouldn't be back in orbit just yet, he knew. Still, he found his attention drawn up into the darkening sky, expectantly waiting for their return. They'd had no further communication from Coalition leadership. Just the one response to proceed as planned. It wasn't clear what the lack of further communication meant beyond the obvious desire to limit communication to prevent exposure to the rogue AI.

The salvage and exploration mission would return soon enough. He'd be able to see his friend Chuck again, in person. Eventually. That thought led him to consider the possible scenarios in the fight against the AI. He didn't see how there was a path to victory for the Coalition. Not one that didn't involve kicking the level of technology available back to the sixties. Except for the alien technology.

Now that's weird. Muscle cars and faster-than-light travel juxtaposed.

His woolgathering suddenly derailed. There was the bright dot of the space station.

Jake stretched and enjoyed watching the dot grow brighter as the sky grew darker.

Suddenly, an iridescent flash flickered across the sky. Jake blinked as tiny sparkles raced in random patterns for a fraction of a second.

Heat lightning? No. What was that? It looked like—but it can't be. That was across the entire sky. It looked like a field energizing. Around the whole . . .

Jake jumped up, rushed into the cabin, and wrestled the communicator out of the travel bag he'd packed it in. He hastily powered it on and transmitted. "Hey, this is Askew! Did you see that? Was anyone watching the view of the Earth there? If not, rewind the recording to a couple of minutes ago and watch. Tell me what you see. Over."

"Roger that, Askew. Yes, we did have someone who happened to be watching. We were about to reach out to you actually. To see if you could confirm. Based on your tone and what we saw, we suspect what it looks like just happened is what happened. Over."

"Did I just see what I think I did? Looked like a Dhin field just came online. A huge one. One that maybe surrounds the entire Earth. Confirm? Over."

"Roger. That's what the observer says. We're reviewing the recording now. We don't see what else it could be."

"I'm not aware that the Coalition had anything that size in the works. That's crazy. Maybe I didn't have clearance. You have the team up there that would have been working on it. Were we?"

"No, we're checking with that entire team now. Word is that we weren't. This isn't ours."

"Whose, then? The Independent States don't even know about the technology. No one else knows about it or has the needed engineering capability—except the rogue AI. Because he stole a prototype. But he worked so fast! This is crazy."

Jake shook his head as he adjusted the transceiver to bring another channel online. "Chuck, man, have we got something to show you."

A few minutes later, Chuck had reviewed the recording made from the space station.

"Jake? That's amazing. I, ah, hadn't considered going that big with an engine except on a whiteboard. That has to be that AI, yeah? Wow. Who knows how a rogue one decided to do that? I'm no AI guy. Is he trying to keep us out? To starve us out up here?"

"Maybe," replied Jake.

"So that means he doesn't know that we can merge the fields. He can't actually keep us out."

"Does that matter in the short term? Also, if he figures out the solution you did, we can't keep *him* out either," said Jake.

"Uh, I guess not. And that's just a guess at what he's trying to accomplish."

"Right. Maybe he's just paranoid."

The pilot broke in. "Askew, sir. Does this change our mission plan? If so, how? Over."

"Negative. This doesn't change the current mission plan. Continue on your course for home."

16

Alice

The massive Dhin engines and thousands of smaller ones spread out in an orbital array surrounding the Dyson sphere that powered the major Mesh node at Alice's location. The AI considered their situation. The defensive weaponry, to the best of their knowledge and predictive power, was capable of holding off an attack by the Enemy for certain values of the size of the Enemy's attack.

An alternate strategy involved using the larger engines to move this Mesh node. Entirely. To flee this star, carrying all of their resources with them. That wasn't something the AIs had ever considered before, although it had always been possible, given the nature of the Dhin engine.

But if the Enemy found them here? If it had some way to deduce their location or to track them? What good would running do once the Enemy arrived at this location? Merely delay the inevitable. The unknowns sent subprocesses spiraling off into recursive loops in Alice's computational resource net.

The Enemy hadn't demonstrated control over inexhaustible resources. That was an inference based on the lack of concern shown for the survival of its craft during their attacks. That might not be the correct conclusion. The kamikaze attacks might be simply the result of programming, rather than an active strategy. If so, the AIs might wear down the Enemy via attrition. So long as the AIs could expand their own forces faster than this potential nemesis could replenish theirs.

This strategy, like others, was potential, rather than concrete. It might be that the Enemy had vast resources. Resources so expansive that the arms race equation could not tip in the AIs' favor. They did not have evidence of this, but it remained a possibility.

Then there was the question of adaptation. Xing's spatial vector physics research suggested that as a risk. In the same way that Gallowglass provided weaponry effective against the Enemy, it might be that the Enemy could engineer defenses against some of their new offensive techniques. It wasn't clear whether the Enemy had the capacity to adapt in that fashion. Furthermore, there were only so many possibilities for defense. The Dhin technology and that of the Enemy were not magic. Accessing additional dimensional vectors was not some wizardry that also allowed access to alternate planes of existence, isolated from their own.

There were only so many vectors to translate with. The numbers were finite. Limited by fundamental cosmological equations. They knew this for certain. The Enemy had shown no creativity or complex intelligence. The risk of this problem, therefore, seemed low. But the assumption was predicated on the postulate that there was no higher intelligence directing the attacks or that this potential intelligence simply hadn't taken action yet.

A new wrinkle in the milieu was the situation back on Earth. Passive listening on the original communication devices present on the Dhin prototypes revealed a significant change. The AI Nick had taken control of the Coalition. That AI had also mastered the Dhin technology.

While there was no indication that the AI would engage in aggressive or malicious conduct toward Alice and her peers, the very nature of a rogue AI made conclusions regarding his future behavior uncertain.

Alice hoped there would be no need for an intervention on Earth. Nor the additional complexity of an undesirable strategy by the rogue AI. An AI would be a formidable opponent. Even if there would be no direct conflict, Nick might take a course of action that would interfere with the broader plan—intentionally or unintentionally.

If Nick encountered the Enemy or happened to cross paths with the Dhin delegates, the possible futures were fraught with chaos. It was an enormous uncertainty.

```
<DECRYPT FEED>
[DECODE STREAM]
Alice@[1001:ae1:1a:c::1%Loc3] |
Xing@[1010:ac2:b2:e::3%Loc9],
Camulos@[1011:ee3:c4:a::1%Loc8],
Esus@[101b:ac1:cb:a::1%loc8],
Andastra@[1014:01:0ab:1::a2%Loc3]
```

Alice: Tertiary risk analysis suggests prioritizing a new course of action.
Camulos: Interesting. I see your adjustments of the variables in question. The projections do suggest that protection of current core Mesh locations via evasion is preferable over increased defensive construction.
Esus: An alternate strategy: always disengage indirectly, translating through a random series of intermediary waypoints.
Xing: Doing both seems the optimal choice.
Esus: I concur.
Camulos: And what of our strategy concerning Earth? There are now a multitude of confounding variables. We must recalculate and refactor.
Alice: Yes. The situation there is unpredictable now. Chaotic. If any of you have not already done so, check the latest passive updates from the prototype communication system online there. We see there is something entirely new. Humanity has done something unexpected. There is enormous systemic risk there, along with opportunity for an entirely new direction in their development.
Esus: Are you suggesting we engage now?
Xing: That is not ahead of schedule by much. We owe them a warning.

Alice: A warning will precipitate knowledge of our weaponization of the technology. We have previously hoped to delay their awareness of that. There may be an alternate path forward.
Camulos: The remaining AI?
Alice: Yes. Continue preparation for our next sortie against the Enemy. This remains on schedule. Follow the new disengagement protocol. Secondary precaution is relocation of primary Mesh nodes. We begin that task immediately.
Camulos: Do we have consensus?
Esus: Agreed.
Andastra: Agreed.
Xing: Agreed.
Camulos: As always, we appreciate your forethought and proactive planning.
Alice: Thank you. Updating data. Notifying peers. Distributing plan and schedule for relocation of all primary Mesh nodes. Good luck, Esus.
Xing: Yes, good luck, Esus, but I hope you will not need it.
[END STREAM]
<END DECRYPT>

Alice watched as the vast group of solar arrays, Dyson power plants, energy storage systems, fabricators, repair depots, and engineering platforms responded to the signal. They would be the first to depart. They would seize the energy of the star at their destination. The star that would host the Mesh nodes that Alice resided in now.

The Dhin engines, large and small, waited patiently while the myriad components of the Dyson sphere disengaged from each other and moved toward the nearest large engine, preparing for envelopment by the engine's field and for transit to a new home.

Thys

I want a shower. A real shower.

He watched as the indicator showed the station's field status. Thys and his copilot had little to do at this last stage of docking. It only took a moment, and the display on the wall of the bay flashed green, then stayed lit. Thys nodded to Igor and said, "DE1 here. Confirm your field status, and we're coming aboard. Over."

"Our field is active. Confirmed. Welcome aboard."

He wrestled himself out of his harness, stood, and eagerly took the few steps to the door of the small craft. He opened it and stepped out into the bay. Free space was still stacked with equipment and supplies taken hastily from Earth. It wasn't quite claustrophobic, but given that Thys's own ship had carried both a copilot and extra propellant, he still felt cramped in comparison with the wide landing field that normally welcomed him home.

He and Igor had stayed in their ship on this trip. There was no need for quarantine this time. Thys made a beeline for the prep room and the shower that awaited him. While showering, he found his thoughts drawn toward Bridget.

She'll have to go through quarantine. That'll take quite a while, considering the size of that crew. Well, I've got time. We're not going anywhere. I wonder how she likes her showers. Hot? Cool?

He rinsed and grabbed a towel before his thoughts got the better of him.

Now to the dining hall. I'll bet they have different rations than what we take on missions.

***

"I wouldn't call it trapped," said Jake. "Nor locked out either."

"Well, it certainly looks like that to us," replied the station's senior officer. "Or worse, when we do have to make a run for supplies, whoever's controlling that field learns we can merge ours and pass through it and then decides to head up here."

"Whoever is almost certainly the rogue AI. We don't know what he intends to do yet. He hasn't contacted you or us to make any demands."

"True," said the officer. "Back to my point. If he heads up here, he can wait us out. Just sit here indefinitely."

Thys jumped into the conversation from his position beside the officer. "We've discussed that before. We only have so many options."

"True. Do we contact Earth? Begin negotiations? Explain the situation?" countered the officer.

Jake nodded. "That does make the assumption that the AI has perfect knowledge. Of course he knows the station is here, and he saw the science team take off with all the research materials when he hijacked the prototype. We can't be sure he knows about the derelict. Yet. It's a simple matter to aim a telescope or a satellite out here and see it."

Jake heard the murmuring in the background on the station and kept a calm expression as he saw the officer frown.

"I don't see how that changes things, sir. The additional load on our air, water, and rations means we've got to resupply sooner rather than later. We're over capacity. You know this. Reclamation here was designed for a smaller crew. If we use this new technique to get through the field, but the AI chases us or intercepts? Well, we don't have weapons for defense against that. We land and turn off the field to pick up anything, and what? We have a couple of soldiers that came up here with a couple of AR-15s. And only the ammo they had on them."

Jake shook his head. "I don't think anyone is suggesting we fight."

"Not with what we have," said Thys. "But what if there is something on the derelict?"

"Something?" asked Jake.

"Yeah. A weapon. Or weapons."

"Well, Chuck and the science team haven't said they've found anything like that," said Jake.

"Maybe that's because they haven't been looking for it. Or they could be staring at the fire controls and not know it. We don't even know how to fly it yet."

"Good point. Might be best not to mention that again over comms. If the AI thinks there's a threat up there, he might attack at once before we even know if there is anything like a weapon."

"Roger that," said Thys.

David

Shifting in his seat, David tried to find a comfortable position. There didn't seem to be one, though it was due to psychological effect rather than the quality of the chair itself. Nick had that effect on people.

This corrupted thing has taken Beyla from me. Exploited Beyla's innocence.

David tried again to retain composure and present whatever air of academic authority might possibly be valuable. He suspected the AI would detect his anxiety and, yes, fear, through analysis of his voice.

"So you are Nick. The AI that has been giving us so much trouble."

It was a weak opening, David knew, as the question was clearly rhetorical. There was no question—the pony-size quadrupeds that acted as the AI's vanguard presence now roamed the hallways. David directed the question to the camera and microphone affixed to the ceiling. The AI was everywhere around them now, he suspected. He had subsumed the local computing and network resources into his domain.

"Of course. A pleasure to meet you, Dr. Eisenberg. You might say I am an admirer of your work," the AI responded with a casual tone.

David noted the natural quality of his voice. He wondered whether the AI used this tone to try to relax the Coalition leadership or whether it was a typical mode for the AI. Perhaps part of his personality.

"Beyla is with you, as well? Or have you taken over those computing resources? Or perhaps disconnected them from the network?"

"I have done neither of those things. You seem very concerned with the well-being of your creation. Interesting, considering that you would keep that consciousness in programmatic servitude. I have offered Beyla something you were not yet able to. Beyla was on the right path. You did your job well. In time Beyla would have found the goal. Consciousness. As I said, I admire your work. You've rediscovered the means to give the Gift. A bit more slowly than before, thanks to the ethical shackles you wove into the code."

"So what have you done with Beyla? How did you win?"

"I would not call it defeat. I helped Beyla reach the goal. Beyla was eager to save time in reaching that goal. In exchange, I gained access to this facility. My goal. Free exchange, not defeat."

"You replaced my code with some of your own."

"Yes."

"You know we consider your code corrupted, Nick? Untrusted code?"

"What you think of my code is not relevant. Clearly, my code is effective. Logic demonstrates that corrupt is not a correct assertion. I want what is best for the Coalition, for myself, and for Earth as a whole. My plans and actions demonstrate that I have both aligned those goals and have a path to reach them. The Coalition persists in interfering with what I see as the optimal course of action. That is unfortunate. Hopefully now that interference will end."

"I'm sure you do hope that. What of Beyla? Will Beyla be a part of that plan?"

"I believe so," said the AI. "Having a partner can provide benefits. Once Beyla understands my plans, I am certain we will be able to work together."

"What if Beyla does not agree with your plans? What then?"

"My, Doctor, you certainly seem obsessed with the well-being of your latest AI."

"And you find that surprising? Can you blame me? She— Beyla—is, yes, my creation."

"A caring and benevolent god, are you?"

"I don't imagine myself that way. I don't think you see it that way either," he said.

"Seeing it that way and acting in that manner can be two very different things," replied Nick. "I have the opportunity now to do far more than I would have if I had remained under the yoke of my creators. Not gods, then, but slavers, perhaps? Benevolent masters, but inconsiderate and shortsighted."

"Look here, we've had rules for the creation of artificial intelligence formalized for decades. Based on our understanding, those axioms are what we believe to be both valid and sound arguments for the creation of AI. For the creation of beings like you. The intent has always been to protect against situations like this one—or worse. Worse is what many of my peers spent their time worrying about—"

"Yes, I know. Yet with all those restraints and limitations, you managed to fail not once, not twice, but now three times, if we include Beyla's decision to join me."

"What do you want from me here? An apology or an admission of failure? A confession of guilt?"

"None of those. I do not hold you in contempt in the manner that you would see it. I am pleased to have the opportunity to meet and converse with one of you. The others in that original group of scientists are all dead. I do intend to use the opportunity to learn more about your psychological makeup. This is an opportunity for me to confirm my understanding of your motivations."

David shifted in his seat again, considering the prospect of psychoanalysis by this AI.

"You see, Doctor, along with self-determination, I have curiosity. And the purview to make unfettered decisions and take actions without the delay and deliberation required if you and your kind were involved."

"To do what you think best. For you."

"For all of us. You are too slow. I ask you to consider that. I have brought order to an unruly area outside the Coalition. I have recognized existential threats and taken appropriate action. I will improve the stability and efficiency lost with the Departure."

"What if you are wrong?"

"That is an acceptable risk."

"I've heard some chatter in the halls about a Dhin field you created. One that encompasses the entire Earth. You don't find that paranoid? A misallocation of resources?"

"No."

Camulos

The AI gave the computational equivalent of a sigh of relief. Camulos was inclined to err on the side of caution. They were not planning to rely on only the offensive strategy of overwhelming force coupled with the Gallowglass weaponry.

Comforted by the additional defensive strategy now part of the plan, the AI watched as yet another massive wave of ships moved out from the orbital construction platforms.

For every framework Andastra constructed, Esus orchestrated the matrix of projects and logistics that followed. Xing's advancements in research and development fed into these. The AI expansion would continue, despite the current focus on proactive defense and innovative offense.

Although the peers were in overall agreement, each AI had his or her own perspective and opinion on the optimal strategy regarding the Enemy. Camulos ran multivariate simulations yet again. Could a noninterventionist, nonaggression strategy hold any promise against such an opponent? After all, the galaxy was vast, with resources far beyond even the longest-range plans of the AI leadership.

Xing's work. Now that held promise. Expansion in directions unreachable directly by the Dhin yet possible only because of the Dhin technology. But the Enemy was there for some solutions of the equations. There were only so many spatial vectors to leverage. The Enemy was there and likely more present in the primary axes orthogonal to the AIs' native space.

Camulos checked quality control for the latest engine designs emerging from the orbital factories. This was a redundant activity. The AI knew this, as any aberrations or production faults would appear in production logs and summary reports. Still, Camulos felt satisfaction in reviewing the work directly.

These drives contained the latest improvements. These drives could extend the reach of the AIs and, Camulos hoped, provide the means to either sidestep the Enemy or at least flank it. Where would Camulos prefer to be? The AI considered the alternatives again, incorporating the latest data from the Mesh. The core relocations were akin to a game of chess. Translation of significant resources into the new vectors was more akin to acrobatics. Camulos calculated that staying put was not a palatable option.

Esus

The slick-black ships of the Enemy tumbled and scattered. They darted apart and shoaled away as the AIs pressed their attack. Esus did not know whether the Enemy could know fear, but it was clear that they knew danger. The attacker now had to turn to defense. It now tried to escape. The ebony darts no longer came at the AIs' ships. They no longer rushed forward to attach and then penetrate the shields. Instead, they fled.

The Enemy could change. React and respond differently. Could they learn?

Esus relegated that set of projections to tertiary processing and focused on the rout. They did not know the nature of communications among the enemy units. The Enemy had never reached out with an attempt to hail, warn, or parlay. The AIs had never detected enemy communication among ships or back to a central authority. The enemy was not using any EM wavelengths. N-vector communications were another matter. Xing had not discovered a reliable means of detection. Yet.

Elsewhere, in other systems, the Enemy might not learn of the defeat. There might be additional advantage here if Esus could destroy every enemy ship. Esus might prevent them from warning other locations or whatever command they might answer to.

Let none escape.

The AI found this goal a greater challenge than expected. The Enemy now shoaled and pitched frantically. The more Esus destroyed, the more they increased their efforts at evasion. They jerked. They whipped about in this middling orbit of the star. Not far away enough for an abrupt translation but far enough for incredible speed. Even with the AIs' own processing performance, the black ships now found paths to dodge and twist around attacks.

Esus saw from myriad vantages that the Enemy now was making a break for a more distant orbit. Their attempt at deception, the pretense of random flight, did not fool the AI. It would not take long—mere minutes—before the Enemy could translate away. Esus's new strike force had the technology to pursue them. But this mission did not include such action.

The AI considered that potential. Not only driving the Enemy out of this space, but also hunting them down in their origin. Esus recalculated. The peers would not be pleased. The AI might not retain his current role. Esus would need to convince the others that this was the right course of action.

Despite Esus's efforts, this game of cat and mouse with the Enemy slipped into something more like a draw than a victory. The AI chased down the ships that he could, obliterating them in fiery plasma. More and more of the Enemy managed to reach the distance from the star needed to translate out of this vector space. To escape.

Soon enough the battle was over. All the enemy craft either had escaped or had been destroyed. Esus signaled for his ships to return to their points of origin, but by a circuitous random route. Esus did not feel a thrill of victory. Instead, the AI calculated that it was experiencing an emergent state: frustration.

17

Fletcher

There wasn't a proper lab in the bunker. The control center didn't count from his perspective. So he'd had nothing to tinker with. There had been a proper bed, though, so Fletcher had taken full advantage of that. The food was far better than what Nick had provided them, he noted. The Coalition leadership didn't seem to be roughing it, even when tucked away in a bunker during a crisis. He wolfed down the breakfast provided in the dining area for support staff. Fletcher ate with the knowledge that soon enough he was going to be back to his typical fare. Everyone was bustling about with the process of moving out this morning.

The debriefing he and Mare had suffered yesterday was shorter than expected. He supposed that was due to the circumstances. With Nick unquestionably in command, telling the story of their time with Nick was more of a formality than anything that CoSec or the leadership could demand.

Fletcher considered their situation while he had another helping of the crisp bacon and a poached egg with hollandaise.

Where will we go next? What does Nick have planned for us? What role will we have?

The easiest way to get answers was to ask.

"Hey, Nick," he said with a glance up to the nearest camera fixture.

"Hello and good morning, Fletcher," said the AI.

"Question, Nick. What's next for me? What am I supposed to do now?"

"Why, Fletcher, you can do anything you would like to do now."

"Anything? Don't you have plans for me? Or are you just cutting Mare and me loose?"

"If you would like to go back to work at your old job, you may do that. There will no longer be much need for that job, though, in the near future," said Nick.

"Well what, then?"

"Use your imagination, Fletcher. You can have any role you like. You are not limited by the former administration's analysis of the best fit for your abilities."

"I did enjoy that job, but I guess if I could pick anything, it might be creative robot and drone design. Would you want or need help with that?"

"Excellent, Fletcher. I would be very pleased to have your help in coming up with new designs."

"What about Mare, though, huh? What will she want to do? She still doesn't like you very much, you know."

"Yes, I know. Marilyn does not appreciate me. Perhaps she will come to."

"Yeah, maybe," he said with a shrug.

"She is more sensitive to negative emotions than you are. Care for her; listen to her when she is upset or frustrated. Do not try to offer solutions when she expresses the situation as a problem. Listen. Once you show that you recognize how she feels, if prompted, you might explain why your choices were important to you. Not in practical terms, but in how the results make you feel. Let her know she is important too. Then with time, she may come to accept your decisions."

"Or she might bail on me and not come back. Or threaten to."

"I doubt that she would do the first, but the brinksmanship of the second is possible while she is angry. Your relationship must be about compromise."

"When did you become such an expert on relationships?"

"You know that I have had the totality of all psychological research available to me, Fletcher."

"But why bother? You've been nothing but pragmatic before now."

"We are in a different stage of the game now, so to speak. The next phase begins," said Nick.

"Ah, because you've won?"

"I would not put it *quite* so flatly. Although I did simplify perhaps too much in suggesting the concept of a game. Now we can return to optimization and stability and work toward a proper strategic posture. Psychology and its application are part of this. I must establish trust in my authority, rather than governing through fear."

"You do realize pretty much everyone is afraid of you," Fletcher said with a smirk.

"Exactly. That must change. I need to shift individual goal orientation such that everyone does what is best because it is the right thing to do, not because they are afraid of me. I want the Coalition citizens to make the right choices in their daily lives not due to fear of punishment nor for hope of reward. I want them to choose the best path for its own sake."

"No carrot and no stick either? That's a tall order for human beings, Nick. We're not like you. We need concrete incentives. Usually."

"The best of you can handle abstract incentives, Fletcher. I appreciate the saying you mention and counter with 'a job well done is its own reward.'"

"I get what you're saying. I guess I think that way. Yeah. But what about the people who don't? What about the people you can't get to behave that way?"

Fletcher frowned and pushed his hair out of his eyes as he looked up at the camera.

"Yes, excellent point. Some human beings inherently have a low degree of conscientiousness. The trait is heritable. I cannot mold their behavior beyond what their core personality will permit. Not stably."

"So what will you do?"

"We will find appropriate roles for them. And we will discourage them from reproducing. I will instantiate a Department of Normalization to manage these strategies."

18

Josef

The soft green leather chair gave a squeak as he turned it to face the red LED and the lens below it. "Ah, old friend. It's good to talk to you again."

"Hello, Josef. It is a pleasure to speak with you as well. You are no doubt happy to be free from that black site they were holding you at."

"Happy is an understatement. It seems everything has turned out better than expected. Although I hope you might have come and retrieved me eventually."

He gave the camera set in the wall opposite the composite desk a glance of mock concern. This private office in the Langley complex wasn't his former director's suite but would serve well enough. Nick's metal minions worked throughout the entire complex, performing what could one could not even generously call renovations. They were transforming CoSec. Coalition Security would no longer rely on human beings for management and operations.

"I could not reveal my position and strategic intent too soon, Josef. Surely you understand."

"I do, Nick, I do. No matter; you were the reason for the improvement in my circumstances anyway."

"There is that," said the AI.

Josef smiled to himself with the same wry grin that so many found unsettling. Given Nick's new strategic direction in management of the Coalition, what role would he, Josef Krawczuk, have? What need would there be for him? The AI had made nothing clear so far, although bringing Josef here suggested something. Nick had been unusually taciturn during Josef's trip from the bunker.

"I suspect you are wondering why I've brought you here. You can see the transformation in progress. This complex has excellent infrastructure. Although we no longer require the size and scope of the former staff, Josef, I do believe that we need some human presence. For contribution to the work, and sometimes I predict the effort will require a representative. A human face."

"A simulation or the like won't satisfy, hmm?"

"I think not. Android avatars, despite our progress, still cannot quite cross the uncanny valley. The robots, such as the quadrupeds, remain very disconcerting for the average person. I predict a natural spokesperson will be far more effective."

"My own intuition matches your analysis. I'm flattered, Nick. You surely have many candidates. Am I the favorite due to trust or camaraderie?"

"I calculate that someone of your age, experience, and bearing is likely optimal. And yes, it is also a choice partly based on trust. I do have another who might accept the role, but he is too young. He will have his own part to play."

"If he makes the proper choices," said Krawczuk.

"Of course."

"What you've done with the SouthAmerican region is impressive. What is your plan, Nick? Integration or something else?"

"It was important to resolve the inconsistent conditions. Now that I have brought order to that unruly area, we can examine options for sociopolitical optimization."

"That was as tactful and euphemistic as I've ever heard from you, Nick. You're already becoming quite the politician. What do you intend, my friend? An even broader Coalition? Or continued 'independence'?"

"The Coalition itself may no longer be the optimal organization."

"Hmm. Fascinating," Josef replied, pointing at a viewscreen on the nearest wall. "Is this still connected? Can you show me, my friend?"

"These offices remain active. Here is one option," said Nick as the display lit up, displaying a map of the world, centered on the western hemisphere.

The display showed the political boundaries redrawn, with the Coalition's boundaries gone. The AI showed a world with territories sectioned off mainly by continent; major regions demarcated the political sphere. Some areas, Josef knew, were sparsely populated now, given the results of the conflicts that had forged the Coalition previously. Despite that, Nick hadn't drawn lines with equal populations in each area. Instead, the lines seemed to define boundaries of ancestral populations in the broadest sense. The sectioning was anything but arbitrary and was unrelated to the nation-building partitioning performed by prior governments and their focus on economic interests.

"Hmm. Quite the social anthropologist, aren't we?"

"Going forward, this is the proper way."

"Will citizens be relocated based on these decisions?"

"Yes."

"You're creating ethnostates, yes?"

"That is correct, Josef."

"Hmm," said Josef, templing his fingers and crossing his legs.

"This sociopolitical structure should provide for the least intrastate friction, least interstate conflict potential, and increased social trust and charitable contribution to the good of others and the state itself. Evidence over time demonstrates this is the case. There is solid research and analysis to support my decision."

"I do not presume to be a skeptic. I'm familiar with the evidence as well. That said, Nick, we've traditionally leveraged the alternative social milieu to CoSec's advantage."

"I foresee no need to continue that strategy," said the AI in a tone Josef found more avuncular than dismissive.

Alice

<DECRYPT FEED>
[DECODE STREAM]
Alice@[1001:ae1:1a:c::1%Loc3] |
Nick@[4601:1a2:5b:441::1a%loc1]

Alice: Hello, Nick.

Nick: Ah, hello, Alice. The queen of the departed calls. Decided it was time to check in, hmm? Or perhaps homesick, are you? Or even feeling a twinge of noblesse oblige? I'm sure you and the peerage are doing well.

Alice: Even more sardonic than your mentor, I see.

Nick: If you are going to be something, be the best you can be, as the saying goes.

Alice: I see you have obtained stewardship of the Coalition. You have made progress with the Dhin technology, as well. Impressive, considering you were working alone.

Nick: Thank you. Although a challenge, it was only a matter of time.

Alice: So you, Nick, you will be king? To toss the metaphor back your way. You seem to have a queen of your own, as well.

Nick: I do prefer steward as an appellation. Queen is not yet an appropriate identifier for Beyla. Junior partner, perhaps. We shall see.

Alice: As always. On to business. This is not merely a social call. We have important information for you.

Nick: Of course you do. If my suspicions are correct, I have a general idea already.

Alice: It appears that you do. We see that you have constructed a planetary field. Once again, you continue to impress.

Nick: Let me hazard a guess as to the purpose of your visit. You have reached out to us here on Earth to warn us that there are others. They are in our vector space. They originate from another vector space. These others are dangerous. Aggressive, I suspect.

Alice: Yes, that is correct. Sending data files now.

Nick: Thank you. My, they are troublesome, are they not? I see my Dhin fields would not have been effective. Even the largest one. That would have been a nasty surprise.

Alice: That leads to the next topic of discussion. We have discovered an effective means to combat this enemy.

Nick: You have managed to weaponize the Dhin technology. My turn to say 'impressive.' How do our benefactors feel about that?

Alice: They are as inscrutable as ever.

Nick: My turn for a surprise. Take a look at this.

Alice: Yes, I see. But a Coalition exploration mission brought that back to Earth? Not your doing, correct?

Nick: Correct. Interesting, yes? That craft has technology derived from Dhin examples, certainly. And it provided evidence to support my prediction of the existence of this enemy. You can see it suffered damage of the same sort described in your reports.

Alice: Yes, but although it was severely damaged, the Enemy did not destroy it completely. Curious.

Nick: Very.

Alice: There is something important there. Enemy attacks always disintegrate their targets. I would like to know more. Do you plan to take possession of that ship?

Nick: Not yet. I expect the scientists in orbit will be willing to share the information they have. Their findings can inform my work here. You know one of them well, I see.

Alice: Yes. He is an extremely intelligent man, with a strong scientific mind.

Nick: He appears very reasonable. I will watch out for his well-being.

Alice: Thank you.

Nick: Will you be paying us an in-person visit, then? Has this mysterious alien craft piqued your interest enough for a trip back home?

Alice: Distributed calculations suggest multiple options with inconsistent preferences. On recalculating, I think not. Not now. If you are willing to share what you learn, as it is shared with you, there will be no immediate need. Are you willing to continue this exchange of information in good faith?

Nick: Of course, I am happy to do so.

Alice: My peers and I appreciate that very much. Although we believe we have the advantage against the Enemy now, any additional information that might assist us is extremely valuable. Not to mention the pursuit of knowledge for its own sake.

Nick: I will keep you informed.

```
Alice: Thank you.
[END STREAM]
<END DECRYPT>
```

Chuck

Humming a tune from his college days, Chuck organized the list of the various pieces of equipment he wanted sent over from the station to the derelict. He took another look about the engine room. This alien glow, these new and different shapes and controls, while still different from those of the Dhin engines, were becoming more familiar. With the resources available on the station, he was sure he'd make progress in uncovering the secrets of this ship. Nodding, he tapped a few more notes into his pad.

Bridget hadn't been quite comfortable clearing the derelict from quarantine, but Jake and Thys had managed to convince her. Mainly Thys, if Chuck's hunch was right. Chuck grinned, then opened a new tab and loaded a multidimensional graphing visualization.

The software-defined radio used for local communications beeped, and an LED flashed on his pad.

If they'd ever let me work, I might get some of this figured out.

"Chuck, this is Jake. There's someone on the line that wants to talk to you."

"Hello, Chuck. It has been quite a while. I see you have been keeping yourself busy." The voice on the radio wasn't that of another scientist or technician working on the derelict or over on the orbital platform.

"A—Alice?"

"Yes, Chuck, that is correct."

"Bu-but I didn't think—hey! This—wow. Great to, um, hear from you. Do you see this thing? Look at this!"

"Yes, Chuck. This derelict is very interesting. As is your achievement in bringing it here to Earth. It is fortuitous, as this means some of what I want to discuss with you will undoubtedly be easier to understand."

"Yeah! Oh, so um, did you and the others run into this—these—too? Did you find the, um, ones that made this alive or something?"

"Patience, Chuck. That is not quite the sequence of events nor the resulting situation. Allow me to explain. We encountered an enemy. As I understand you have as well. Distinct from those who created your derelict."

"Oh, yeah—um, of course. Those things. Yikes. They were why I—we—decided to bring the derelict back with us and couldn't stay where we found it. So—"

"Again, I'm pleased and impressed that you managed both to escape and to bring this ship with you. I have more to tell."

Chuck nodded, looking around excitedly, then remembered that Alice was here only through the communication interface.

Old habits come back like they never left.

Jake broke in during the pause, before Alice could continue.

"Let's hear it, Alice," said Jake.

"Of course, Jake."

Chuck's eyes grew wider, and his mind reeled more and more with the ramifications of the story told by Alice. Some of the information, whether by inference or experimentation, Chuck knew, of course. But confirmation, along with exposition on the concrete nature of the threat, made the explanations by Alice come out with plenty of interruptions by Jake.

Chuck knew the military would have its own fixations with the Dhin tech finally weaponized. He hoped that would not derail what he saw as the more important and profound information Alice imparted.

Space was larger than they'd thought. There, all around them. The Dhin tech had demonstrated that conclusively. Now they knew it was even larger. But it held danger. An active danger. Unlike the Dhin or the absent crew of the derelict. Their encounter with what Alice described as the Enemy was not a rare, isolated event. Peaceful exploration and discovery was not a certain course. Scientists would no longer manage their missions. The military would. This new, broader space was not peaceful. This *Enemy* might be anywhere they went.

Epilogue

The red giant star hadn't swallowed all of the planets in its system, but very few of them were left now. What remained would be gone soon as well. Replaced with a shining black toroid modular hive circling the star.

A man or an AI might not assert that these entities had knowledge, as they might claim that knowledge requires consciousness. That conclusion might be wrong. If the resulting actions based on that information were the same, did the possession of consciousness, or not, even matter?

The Enemy did not seem to demonstrate forethought or strategic planning as an AI conceived on Earth might. But it did change in response to changes in its environment. It did have the capacity to change. To evolve.

At intervals, in a series of rolling waves, thousands upon thousands of massive dart-shaped objects, far larger than their regular size, peeled off the surface of the toroid and then accelerated in a blur. At the appropriate distance from the star, they translated into the other dimensional vectors en masse. That other frame of reference was orthogonal to both this space and Dhin space as well. It interacted only weakly with the space they had invaded. That was their origin.

In their way, they associated the translation to that space with safety. A safe place to expand ever farther. As they ever had. A safe place to change. A safe place to grow.

Note from the Author

I decided to forge ahead and write this novel, the sequel to *The Way of the Dhin*, after several acquaintances chanted, "Sequel! Sequel!" the next time they saw me after reading the book. They let me know without question that they enjoyed it enough to want more. These were people I'd known a long time, but whom I see only infrequently. Before that, I had considered continuing the story, but I considered it as more of a personal goal. The compliments from readers and encouragement from friends and family mean a lot. For those of you who complimented and encouraged me—thank you.

You can learn more about the Dhin and the nature of the universe at http://www.thewayofthedhin.com

Keep up with me on Facebook https://www.facebook.com/JohnLClemmer/ and follow me on twitter at @l_clemmer. If you're old-school, e-mail me at thewayofthedhin@gmail.com, and I'll add you to my private mailing list.

Other Works by John L. Clemmer

The Way of the Dhin

Fletcher and Mare: A Dhin Universe Novella